THE PRIEST'S ASSASSIN

DANTE'S ASCENSION BOOK 2

TRAIBON FAMILY SAGA

THE PRIEST'S ASSASSIN

DANTE'S ASCENSION BOOK 2

AWARD-WINNING AUTHOR
V.C. WILLIS

Priest, Prēst, or Prestere

Pronunciation */prēst/*

1. An ordained minister of a church having the authority to perform certain rites and administer certain sacraments.

2. a person who performs religious ceremonies and duties.

3. Ancient Greek and Latin for "elder (of two)", "old", "venerable"

Table of Contents

Map of Grandemere
Perines
Glensdale
Farm
Sullen Lake
Willow Waters
Tavern Way
Frigid Waves
Hidden Swells
Thirsty Crossing
The Church
Captiva City
Red Waves
Amethyst Harbor

CHAPTER 1

Red Wine in the War Room

The ring of eyes around the war table all stared silently, waiting for me to say something about what incited them to throw angry words at one another. *This isn't my place to be sitting here, but...* Even a matter as trivial as who would be escorting Princess Sonja Regius and Royal Knight Valiente Animamea back to Captiva City seemed to bring the worst out in those who sat across this wooden plane. Winter had started to show signs of fading, the muddy ground peeking through snowy fields and icicles melting away to puddles on the streets. Scanning the room, I refused to give up my stoic silence. My thoughts still circled back to all that had unfolded—starting with Falco.

What I wouldn't give to have my mask on right now to hide my expression. In the end, all I care about is making sure I go where John goes. He seems set on heading back to Captiva City. After our encounter with the Fanged Lady, only the library in the Cathedral's catacombs might still hold some answers for what vile magic cre-ated the wretched thing. To think it was Falco's mother's soul inside the blade all this time... But I want to know why. For what purpose did the Vendecci family have with a weapon like that? How did they do it? Does this mean magic really exists in the world? And at what cost?

"Crowned Blood Prince Traibon." My royal title shook me from my thoughts, bringing me back to the mutterings before me. "We'd appreciate your opinion on this matter." Royal Guard and King's Regent Ruth Burns never asked for a thing. This was a demand, her way of calling me to do my royal duty even after abandoning it long ago. "We're waiting for at least some opinion from Your Majesty, whether it be agreeing or disagreeing. Say something, cousin."

Leaning back in my chair, I drummed my fingers on the table, taking stock of them all, including the shouted words I had paid no heed to moments before. Like my father had done, I scanned them, bouncing from face to face, earning arched brows in anticipation of my lips parting. Ruth scoffed at my rebellion. She had seen this move and knew all too well I aimed to take my time.

What does she expect me to say? I may be the Blood Prince, but is it really so easy for me to claim this chair as if I didn't renounce my title over a decade ago? And being a bloodeater this late puts me at a disadvantage...

Having a bloodeater's senses had changed my understanding of how my father was so clever in the past. The way their scents floated in the air, the shifts in their heartbeats and breaths, and even the movements their bodies: it told me volumes of their emotional and physical states. My silence had been more than a refusal to take on my role as the Crown Blood Prince of The House, but a realization I was in over my head as a bloodeater. *I can't tell if I'm nauseated or excited.* The added strength had been manageable. I knew my body and how to limit myself or when to push myself physically; *the old farmer taught that much to me.* As for my senses—no. My cravings had been unnerving me more every day.

I feel thirsty, yet no cup of wine nor water can satisfy me. And when it sets my throat on fire, my only thought is... John locked gazes with me and tilted his head as if sensing the foul thoughts. *I shouldn't think of his smell and flavor every time I think about food. Will there be a day I won't be able to resist this?* I went back to searching the other's faces for answers to my own internal struggles when at last I met the heated gaze of Royal Knight Valiente.

"Are you just going to ogle us to death?" drawled Valiente, running a hand through his loose locks of dark, wavy hair. "Lives are at stake, and it seems you don't care—"

"It seems you have the matter all worked out." I shrugged in annoyance, snorting John's scent from my nose. "Let me recap all that I've heard. May I?"

They all glanced to one another, murmuring, and nodded for me to continue as they settled into their seats. Calming heartbeats in my ears signaled they were ready to listen. Leaning forward, I inhaled deeply, taking in everything their bodies betrayed, and did what I had seen my father do a million times at this very table. *To think I would finally get to be the one to unravel the war room on my own accord.* This is what it meant to be a Blood Prince, and what it meant to challenge a Traibon by coming into *our* war room and watch as we dominate all who dare to enter.

They began to shuffle, even physically sweat. A smirk crested my face as a memory echoed from a time my father settled an argument between two farmers over a pig. He knew the pig didn't belong to either of them. And now, I understood how he'd figured it out so precisely.

"Ruth, you intend to be the second knight in Princess Sonja's sentry." I gestured to each of them as I named them in my retelling, and recognition lit up their faces as I continued around the room. "And Father John here wants to travel with you as a farmer and not as a priest. Then—" Narrowing my eyes, my smirk dropped, and their hearts fluttered, and breaths stilled. "—I'm expected to ride all the way to Captiva City as the Crown Blood Prince of The Court." Silence fell over them as they all digested how I consolidated an hour-long squabble in mere seconds. "You sound like a bunch of children playing pretend going on vacation to grandmere's house across the flower field. Your plan is as disheveled as your attempts to work together."

They winced, and before anyone could counter, I pushed forward with the details they had missed. *They wanted my words, whether agreeing or disagreeing, and they shall have them.*

"Ruth can't go." Huffing, I cut her words off before she could begin her rebuttal. "My fa—the King has already dubbed you his official voice and escort. You are Regent, not me, and he did not make that choice lightly."

Ruth blinked. "I suppose you're right."

"You," I pointed to John, then to Sonja, "and you will leave here in the same manner you arrived: as a priest and the mother superior of The Church. Word has travelled over the cold months; they'll be looking for a royal regime coming south from Glensdale since they are looking for a prince and princess. Instead, you should be clergymen travelling in warmer weather back to the cathedral for study or to report to the archbishop."

"That's good." Valiente nodded. "But that leaves the matter of you."

"What of me?" I raised an eyebrow. "I'm simply a bodyguard for the Father of Glensdale."

Ruth asked, exasperated, "You aren't really going to continue to act like an assassin still, Dante?"

"I haven't stopped being that." My words slammed into them, bodies tensing all around.

John folded his brow, and the frown on his lips told me more than enough. He hated the fact I refused to give up on this promise to be his sword and shield until the day he drew his last breath. No matter how much he pressed to change my mind over it, that final moment against Falco had made it clear. Only I would ever be capable of protecting what I cherish most in this world. They were all angry, frustrated because they knew my words had truth to them.

Be smart when you start travelling with him. Carry on like low-class citizens, and you'll skirt under the eyes of those who hunt you. Snorting, the old farmer's words snuck into my mind. Cold winter nights spent discussing tactics and prying how he had survived with Viceroy Falco's men out hunting him all this time had intrigued me on more than one occasion. *No one wants to attack a shit-slinging stableman, but you can go as far as offering to do the work and earn a free night. If you're with a group, your roles have to make sense and seem in order. You don't see priests travelling with royalty, and no one travels with mercenaries unless they've got the money or are collecting a bounty.*

"If you look like clergymen with bodyguards moving south, no one will question it. Many places offer free rooms and food for members of The Church, which will keep us from exposing too much coin. The only issue is we do need at least one more fighter. Safety in numbers and a fifth should put us at an advantage. We have defense, but I can't be the only offense we have if we cross Falco's mercenaries or worse, Fallen Arbor." Drumming my fingers, I struggled over the options. "We could use a guardsman, or maybe we can see about an assassin from the guild."

"I can fight too," John offered and winced when I sent him a heated glare.

"That defeats the idea of being covert." Valiente pushed back on John's offer before I could speak. "Clergymen aren't supposed to do much else than protect other clergymen. It just means in this setup, Sonja's defense is the two of us, meanwhile Dante has a point. He's right: we need another offense fighter, or better yet, a scout or ranger of sorts."

"Reports suggest there are mercenaries travelling between villages more so than normal." Ruth had said this earlier in the discussion, but her words hit firmer now that she couldn't come with us. "They are looking for you, Princess Sonja. Possibly even John and Dante, depending on if Falco thought they would try to leave, and he aimed to kill them before that could happen. He may be dead, but the contracts he made are still in place and possibly paid for. We have no way of knowing exactly how many or where your party might run into them."

"Is there anyone who can fight to your caliber, Ruth?" Valiente shifted in his seat, searching for answers as he smiled wider, meeting her gaze.

Don't tell me... Valiente's heart fluttered, and I smelled Ruth's scent coming from his direction. Frowning, I turned to Ruth and there she smiled. Once again, I smelled Valiente's scent from her direction. *That only happens when...* A subtle shift in their bodies made me tilt my head in disbelief, both of their hearts racing despite the stoic exteriors grinning across the table. *Arousal. These are two people aroused by one another's presence. They aren't challenging one another; that's what they want the table to think. Those two? It wasn't just private sparring lessons? I see we've been busy sharing beds with one another over the winter months.* Narrowing my eyes, I took in a deep gulp of red wine, hoping to numb the senses that had discovered their sexual soiree against my will.

"No, besides who sits at this table, no one has beaten me in a sparring match." She sank in her chair, rubbing her forehead. "By the blood, all the ones who would be good fits are still cleaning up on the frontlines. The treaty may be signed, but it seems Princess Sonja's father refuses to acknowledge this until his daughter is returned to him."

"I'm so sorry." Sonja lifted her chin high. "When I get you back—"

The doors opened wide, cutting her words short. They all rose to their feet in alarm. My blood ran cold seeing my father march in, weak and thin, but still with the never-waning powerful ambience dominating the room in an instant. His glare met mine, and there was a sense of pride to see me in *his chair*. Behind him was a cloaked figure, small and petite wearing the emblems and a mask of the Assassin's Guild.

"Please sit, and know Princess Sonja, none of this is your fault. In the end, our children are suffering on behalf of the greedy old men who came before them, myself included." King Traibon's voice filled the room like thunder. "I've been looking for a solution to your problem."

"Our problem?" Ruth furrowed her brow, refusing to sit with the others as the King approached her.

A chuckle rolled from him as he clapped a heavy hand on her shoulder. "Don't tell me you didn't realize they needed a scout of some kind for this journey? I bet you were thinking you could go. Admirable, but you have promised me to take on the role as my Regent until I'm well again."

Ruth's face flushed. "Your son had just pointed that out to us. Forgive me for my eagerness to aid my dearest cousin after just discovering he's still alive."

"Forgiven. At least one of you can pick apart a plan." He motioned to her chair, and she allowed him to sit. "Let's talk about how we can strengthen your strategy. As I was saying, I have brought you Red Wine."

"Forgive me, King Traibon," started John, "but drinking in a moment such as this—"

I cut John's words short. "Welcome to the war room, Grand Master Assassin Red Wine."

Back on my feet once more, I bowed my respects, and the cloaked woman mirrored the motion.

"Thank you, my Blood Prince." Her voice was deep and immense for her stature, worthy of royalty with the way she articulated each word and her words infallible. "I have come to offer my services. When your father informed me of your plight, it seemed best for me to accompany you."

Princess Sonja copied my gesture, standing and bowing to the assassin. "I am honored to meet you, Master Assassin. Not many of my caste in The Tower can say we've seen your presence and lived to tell anyone."

Red Wine nodded, her mask giving away nothing of her reaction. "Wise words, Princess. I'm thrilled and thoroughly impressed by your own actions. Not many in the world would be so selfless to put one's life in danger to bring peace to Grandmere's people."

Princess Sonja's eyes widened. "Kind words from someone who has probably seen more bloodshed than the years I have lived in this world."

"I like her." She turned to King Traibon who nodded in agreement. "May I speak freely?"

"By all means." I gestured and sat. "You are every bit of an important voice as the others at this table."

"Excellent." Her mask was nothing more than a snow-white emotionless face with a single red tear down the left cheek.

At first glance, most would mistake the tear as blood dripping down the smooth porcelain with the richness of the color and stroke of the paint. Her hood covered most of her head and was part of a black leather cloak covering her shoulders and the top of her long red coat. Her white blouse peeked through a black overbust corset that buckled high on her neck. Black trousers tucked into a tight-laced set of knee-high leather boots. Trinkets and medals showed she had served in the war a number of times in several roles.

She's a decorated veteran. That day on the battlefield... could it have been her that saved me?

Maroon eyes locked with mine. We were picking one another apart. Not one inch of skin showed through her clothes which complemented her curvy figure. Sleeves gave way to her leather gauntlets, but her appearance hadn't been what caught me off guard. Her scent came to me as if familiar yet new, and it unnerved me in ways I couldn't describe. The prodding eyes from under the mask told me she too had some sense of recognition, though we had never met.

"I will be your scout." She broke our gaze and cleared her throat. "But don't think I'm simply joining you as a scout. The Assassin's Guild has lost contact with a vital resource in Captiva City, and I'm going there to investigate. Also, we're not too keen to be sending one of our own out so... green." She gestured to me, and I scoffed. "You can fight, you can even take a hit like no other I know from the stories I've heard, but my Blood Prince—"

"Dante. Call me Dante," I corrected, stiffening in my chair.

"Dante," she echoed flatly. "But it is my responsibility as your Master Assassin to train you in our ways, teach you the secrets, and more importantly, show you how to disappear when the time arises."

"Traibons have a knack for that by nature," grumbled King Traibon under his breath. "So much so all my sons have managed to elude me."

There was a round of snickering around the table before I interjected, "So, that settles it then. I get to play assassin a little longer, John continues his journey as a priest, Princess Sonja will get to go home, and Valiente won't..." I rose my glass of red wine to the knight in question, "...have to keep stealing kisses from my lovely cousin Ruth."

"Dante!" Ruth flustered, grabbing her goblet and tossing it across the room.

Laughing, I finished mine. "We set out tomorrow. Try to rest, dear cousin."

"You're one to talk," she hissed over King Traibon's laughter.

Walking over to my father, I offered a hand to shake with the assassin. Red Wine obliged, and I yanked her forward. A blade pressed against my neck, my face close enough to smell her, to see the strands of brown hair and some of the braid coiled in the hood. She tried to break free from my grip, and I tightened it.

"What's the meaning of this?" she spoke in a hushed manner.

"How many knots?" I wanted to know. *I needed to know. This smell...*

"It is of no concern to you." She broke free, and the blade was gone as if a mere coin trick. "I advised you not to get so brazen with me, little prince."

I gave her a knowing glare before leaving the war room. My father had paused, his heated glare stinging against my back. He didn't move, and he didn't intervene. Instead, he watched with such deep curiosity that it made my skin crawl.

She smells like a Traibon, but that isn't my sister, nor direct kin. So, who the hell is she?

CHAPTER 2

Sword versus Shield

Gathering books from my desk, I paused, lost in my racing thoughts. Shaking my head, I looked to the tomes in my hands, trying to ground myself once more. One book had pages ripped from it, the edges feathery against my fingertips. *If we even made it to the Cathedral by some miracle, exactly how many more tomes were in the same state? Is this worth our lives? Worth John's life to find even a clue on matters long forgotten?* Someone had taken the pages that were titled "Types of Soul Weapons and Their Properties" as hinted by the table of contents in its front matter. The author was unknown, and the age of the books damn-near archaic, though the vocabulary made me suspect they may very well have been daemonis or someone from the Old Continent.

KNOCK-KNOCK-KNOCK

Frowning, I abandoned the stack. I could sense it was John, and my mood soured further, inhaling to hold my breath and steady my nerves. *I don't feel like I can trust myself around him after that night...*

"I don't want company. Go away," I shouted over my shoulder, twisting to lean on the desk.

"Not even with me?" John's voice sent a shiver through me, the door closing, and he slid the lock. "Usually if you don't want to be disturbed, a lock does a mighty fine job of it."

His words coaxed me to turn and face him. "And what has brought my beloved priest to my bed chambers so late?"

John's blue eyes looked to the ceiling, nodding as he spoke, "I think I can come up with more than one excuse why I'd be here tonight."

This ache in my chest, the way my heart races at the sound of your voice—how can I refuse you? At last, I caved and smirked. "I should know better by now to ask such a dangerous question of you."

"You should." John closed the gap between us, reaching behind me to retrieve a book. "No luck figuring out the author, I take it?"

"To think such a thing as a *Soul Weapon* exists in more than one type," I confessed, putting the distance back between us as I made it to my wardrobe. "Did they teach you about fighting magic in the priesthood?"

"That's just it." John separated the collection and stacked the books he had stolen from the catacombs in their own tower. "They teach us to defend ourselves, how to handle someone suffering from the Madness, what makes human and daemonis the same and different, yet not a word of magic. Then, there's the library in the catacombs they forbid us to step inside without the archbishop's approval or devoting ourselves in its servitude for five or more years. What lies under the Cathedral seems completely different from the game of politics unfolding above it all. I'd say that place has some hint of magic or at least has some clues as to its existence."

"Is that so?" I pondered, rubbing my jaw.

"In fact, there are weapons in cases, books written before the church was built hidden on the wrong shelves, and yes, many of them talk of the old ways or in the old tongue. Magic—these speak of it as if something found in the Old Continent far past the Hidden Swells or the Frozen Queen's Tundra beyond the

Perines Mountain range. According to the text, those who followed the Grandmother who founded this land sought to live life without magic. I find that hard to believe. Unfortunately, much like these books," John flipped open yet another book with the ragged edges where pages once laid, "many have pages burnt or ripped from them. I figured the two of us could divide and conquer in hopes of finding enough hints to piece together what the Fanged Lady and the Madness truly had in common."

"Right." Scanning the dusty items in the wardrobe, I reached for my leather satchel. "You had to serve the library and catacombs for three years in order to gain access to those books. How do you intend getting back in there? Will you have to join for another three years?" I snorted.

"It's supposed to be five years." I spun to lock eyes with him, my heart skipping a beat.

John, you didn't abandon the church or your duties so easily? "But you were there for ten years, seven in training, and three..." Anger rose in me. "What did you do?"

He laughed. "I may have bought myself a break to come back home to... sort out my grandfather's death and burial. That became possible when Bishop Marquis took an unsavory interest in me and decided to back my establishing the church in Glensdale. So, if you've been pondering if I knew he was up to no good prior to my return, my love, I was. Though, Brother Montgomery had made it very clear I would need to finish my time there with him and insisted I return by next summer. Can't blame the old man. No one ever volunteers to do the extended years in the old crypt anymore. He was desperate for someone who could do some heavy lifting."

Closing my eyes, I shook my head. The old farmer whispered, *Don't let John's innocence cloud you. Sometimes I think he does it on purpose since the boy is as clever as a fox when it comes to getting his way or taking what he wants.* A smile grew on my face, *oh how right you were, old man.*

"Look, I just couldn't bear another day wondering if you were still there waiting on me."

Here it is, the very conversation I had spent a year trying to avoid since his return last spring.

"So, I came home. Not for the sake of the farm, but for you specifically, Dante."

"And I was still there." I flustered through a pile of abandoned clothes, none of which fit my physique anymore since I had last touched or gazed upon them. "Shit, I'll need to see if the tailor can work through the night. I didn't think…"

"Dante," John fussed, "I came back so I could bring you with me."

"And what would you have done if I came back here before then? Would you have known to seek me out as the Blood Prince?"

John laughed. "Prince, maybe not, but as royalty to the house and non-bloodeater I had pieced together rather well. If you think leaving the farm would have freed you from my determination to be with you, you're sadly mistaken."

Another echo from the past haunted me, and a shiver shook my shoulders. *And I mean he'd go above and beyond to get what he wants if it means crushing a hornet's nests in both fists and walking through a river in a blizzard. That boy is stubborn, I tell you.* I snorted at the memory.

Biting my lip, I couldn't look at him nor express that I had thought to seek him out in Captiva City like a love-stricken fool on more than one occasion. Instead, I went to the only chest drawer that had clothes that fit me and picked out the most mundane among them. Curses and slurs filled my mind. Everything princely I tossed carelessly to the ground. I had indulged, laying with my lover, and drinking my wine without worry over the winter months.

How careless… how foolish I have been to allow myself to dream so freely.

"Dante." His voice was sterner now.

Again, I dared not meet his gaze. He'd already expressed his frustrations when I stopped allowing him to share my bed with me a few weeks ago. I had bit him, fed on him out of the pure joy of the act, and it had rattled me. *Falco.* My time with the Viceroy had flooded me, and I feared becoming the lust-filled bloodeater my ex-lover had been for me. *This wasn't what I wanted: this need to feed on the very thing I promised to protect.*

"Dante, look at me," demanded John.

It was strange, talking with my father and comparing the difference between me and the other bloodeaters. For them, including the King himself, any blood would do. They craved it all the same. As for me, I gagged at the thought of taking in any blood from anyone but John. It seemed that perhaps my transition was not as much of the Fanged Lady's doing, but something more archaic and forgotten. *Ashton was like that, but he never told anyone how he did it,* and my father didn't say another word of him. My curse had only strengthened while everyone had weakened and started to lose their appetite for drinking from the flesh.

How could I let my guard down so easily? It's never so simple.

John's hand gripped my shoulder, twisting me to face him. His lips locked with mine. The force of the gesture knocked me into the chest, bottles toppling in a great clatter. Deepening the kiss, John's hand snaked under my shirt, the heat of it gliding over my torso. I moaned, the sweet taste of blood filling my senses as the wound on his tongue opened. *Hungry,* I pulled him into me. His shirt thin, my hands caressed the rolling hills of his back muscles. My fingers followed the divot of his spine downward until I could force my way inside the back of his pants and squeeze his ass. I could feel how hard he had become, how much he wanted to make love to me.

I can't do this... Ending the kiss, I searched his eyes. "I hate how easily you break me."

"If you're going to ignore me, you shouldn't leave your door unlocked for me so often." He grinned, starting to kiss my neck.

Chills rippled over my skin as his beard prickled at my neck. "John, are you trying to tell me we won't be able to return for two years?"

He suckled at my neck, hands sliding down the center of my torso. *John heard me; he didn't want to answer. Granted, was I not doing the same a moment ago?* Meanwhile, my body betrayed me as it reacted to his advances. Inhaling swiftly as his fingers began to unbutton my pants, I braced my hands behind me on the chest. I wasn't going to stop him; I didn't want to stop him.

"Shouldn't we tell someone?" I offered, leaning back to deny him my neck.

"I did. I told you, just now."

"John." I scoffed, but it soon shifted to a moan as the heat of his fingers found what they had sought. "Truly infuriating."

"You are." He sank to his knees. "But I love that about you."

"I can't say the same." The stroking of his hand made every muscle in my body taut. "But I meant shouldn't we tell my father? Or Ruth?"

"Don't worry, I left a note, but I did discuss this with Valiente," he muttered, his breath washing over my cock.

"Valiente," I echoed flatly, the unyielding jealousy biting at me. "Why bother talking to him about it?"

John looked up, his blue eyes striking as he knelt before me. "Because it makes you jealous hearing that name leave my lips."

The heat in my cheeks made me look away. "Is that so obvious?"

Lips slid down my cock, and I grunted, the wave of pleasure hauntingly beautiful. He slid back and forth slowly as if tasting everything my body offered. The velveteen tongue caressed the underbelly of my hardened shaft, tipping me closer to the edge. It seemed the absence of play had killed my ability to hold up against my own desire. My hips rocked, wanting to ride deeper down his throat. John gripped the back of my shirt, knuckles digging into my muscles. He pulled me closer, deeper, and I released.

Panting, I closed my eyes in defeat. "You can't be doing this when we leave here."

Wiping his chin, he didn't look at me, just whispered, "I know."

"Two years is a long time." My heart raced as I watched him sit on my bed. "A long time to put back the broken vows."

"I know," he repeated. "Now fuck me, Dante. Break me once more before we need to pick up the pieces and began this game all over again."

Laughing, I let my pants fall to the floor and pulled my shirt off. "One more time..."

And I will be back to being the stoic shield watching my beloved sword fight his way through life once more. Perhaps fate only gave us this fleeting moment to be as one, but it feels like an eternity of pain is all that will follow.

CHAPTER 3

Basque, Colonel, Jasmine, Elegance, and Biscuit

Basque snorted, his feet dancing and making all the guards nervous. Every muscle in the black stallion twitched with anticipation. He knew he had work to do and was excited to spend time with his masters once more. The leatherworkers tailored a saddle and bridle set for him after it was clear he would do far more saddle riding than wagon pulling as the horse of a prince. The silver flourishes on the black-dyed leather made him look worthy of a warhorse, minus the fact he couldn't sit still. The other horses watched him with ears back in disapproval. Steam rolled from his nostrils, the air still cold enough to entertain clumps of snow and ice on the cobblestones this early in the morning.

Seeing no packs on Basque, I frowned at the stableman struggling to hold his lead.

"Where are my saddlebags?" I demanded.

"I'm sorry, my Blood Prince. He wouldn't let anyone near him. After he broke my assistant's ribs, I dare not risk life or limb." The man bowed deeply, his voice and body shaking as he addressed me. "I offered a draft horse, but they said to just bring

17

the bags. In fact, they insisted you'd take care of the matter personally. I'm so sorry to have failed at such—"

I rose my hand to silence him. *The damn horse acts like a monster. The entire town fears him, or worse, has been kicked or bitten by him. He's spoiled...* Looking to Basque, my glare made him stand still and at attention. The attendants all around spoke in hushed murmurs, some in awe while others chuckled at the idea of it.

"I see we're still terrorizing Glensdale in my absence, Basque. No, I apologize. Will your apprentice be alright?"

"Y-yes, just a broken rib is all. They paid for his doctor," he sounded astonished over the idea. "I just...I don't have any more helping hands at my stable. He'll recover in about a month they say. I can make do by myself, but if I come to harm..."

"You did good." I patted the man's shoulder, making his shaking cease. "Now, step aside. I'll handle this."

Reaching down, I scooped up the bags. They were empty, but Basque didn't refuse me when I slapped the leather over his back, buckling it into the saddle. Everyone whispered in admiration how well the monstrous horse behaved for me, but no one paid heed to what I offered the brute before starting. *What they don't know is how I bribe this asshole with a pocket full of peppermints every time.* Basque knew if he let me have my way, he'd be rewarded handsomely.

Absolutely a spoiled creature. Won't do a damn thing until I offer him sweets unless John asks it of him. Granted, I can't help but think if someone tried to pry into the saddlebags, they would be seeing stars or buried six feet down. I like those odds.

Glancing over at the other horses, it seemed we would be riding with a few I had broken in personally. John would be riding my old mare, Jasmine, a docile grey dappled Walker. Valiente had been gifted one of Ruth's older warhorses. We called the old chestnut Colonel, and he'd seen a battle or two, probably killed a few men and had his share of scars to show for his services. He wasn't as large as Basque, but a close second. As for Princess Sonja, she would be riding a retired stallion named Elegance, another Walker from the Royal stables who was a dappled grey color. All the other bags were well-packed, the horses freshly shoed and groomed per standard royal, or even high nobleman, standards.

They did what they had been trained to do. I hate thinking all this hard work was for nothing, but I'm sure my father will make it up to them. We can't have run-of-the-mill clergymen riding on horses fit for a prince. It's so blatant with the emblems and tassels in the colors of The House. We can't hide who we are like this, even the braiding in the manes and tails is a dead giveaway.

"I'll need all their braids undone," my bark made all within earshot flinch. "Royal emblems and tassels removed. We can't let the enemy or The Tower's guards think we are royalty or even of higher class than the knights and priests we are traveling as." My voice roared, sending the stablemen into action. "I know this isn't per regulation, but it's necessary. I apologize for the added work." Tugging on the saddlebags, they were in place, and I could move on to the next step. "Any gear above your own means needs to be removed, even if it means trading with the staff here. They shouldn't be of finer cloth, no emblems, and best if looked as if used once or twice." I scoffed at the blankets and bedrolls, all of which had The House's royal seal on them. "We need to look like clergymen returning to Captiva City, not royalty from The House going south for vacation. Grab the maids and butlers and have them help."

Without question, they all jumped. *I don't think I've ever given orders of this caliber to the staff. They really do respect me as Crown Prince, even after abandoning them for so long.*

The house staff poured out from the manor with unmarked supplies. I waved off the apologies. They had done everything to protocol. No one had told them our circumstances, nor did we want them to be fully aware of the dangers in case a spy remained among us. Guards pulled up their horses and swapped out bedrolls, blankets, even steel cups and plates. Nothing new remained as I insisted, and they kept the finer made items for themselves as payment for acting quickly. Food was pulled out and repacked in a commoner's way, certain items removed like pastries and similar sweets. These were luxuries. In the end, the only items remaining were bread, jerky, and a few jars of minced meat.

"They're going to starve on just that," fussed the head mistress of the house, Mrs. Ivette. She had braved leaving the manor to see what all the fuss was about. "This is too far, Prince Dante. You may have played farmer, but you don't have to keep living that way."

I smirked, packing the last of my needs in my own saddlebags. No one had dared to assist me when Basque nipped at the maid who had walked too close. "I'm hurt to think you don't think I'm clever enough to hunt game, Mrs. Ivette. How do you think I lived out there for so long?"

"You might be hurt, but I've never seen you harm a living thing that hadn't earned it." Her heated glare matched her hands on her hips. *I remember how this frightened me when I was caught sneaking pastries.* "You should take more. Winter hasn't gone away just yet."

"You should have seen him kill those chickens that first year, madam." John had marched pass her. "He didn't seem the least bit sorry about it, even at supper time when he ate them with the dumplings."

The grand entrance as always, John.

I spun to meet his smirk, and nostalgia took my breath away. His golden braid properly tight bounced against the black jacket. Even his beard had been trimmed. He tugged at the white collar, unhappy to be back in his role as a priest once again. Behind him, Mother Superior Sonja was no small feat, a pure vision of glory and grace. The outfit didn't take away from her curvy body nor the bright green in her eyes. She was pretty as a Tuxedo Finch backed by the polished-armored Knight Valiente. The headpiece served as an excellent means of hiding her braid, obscuring it completely. Valiente winked at me as I locked gazes, his face freshly pruned and braid falling tight behind him in a black rope.

That's what took them all so long. They were dressing the part.

20

"Going for the rugged look, are we?" John smirked, greeting Basque who nuzzled him. "Did you even bother to do anything with your hair?"

"You sound disappointed, John." Reaching inside my coat's inner pocket, I retrieved my mask and placed it on. "Is this better?"

John narrowed his eyes. "Is that what game you're playing at?"

"That, and you get to ride my old mare." I pulled myself onto Basque's saddle.

"I don't know how to ride," he reminded.

"Today you learn." Patting Basque's neck, I reached forward so he could steal a peppermint. "The mare knows what to do anyhow, so you just have to sit there and look pretty as a nun."

John scowled. "If I fall off, you'll be the one to pay for it."

"I advise keeping your feet in the stirrups and a grip on the saddle horn at the very least." I chortled, pleased with myself.

Turning Basque around, I watched as the stablemen assisted John onto the old mare. She stood still as a wall, and despite the sour-faced rider, she seemed not to mind the weight on her back. Knight Valiente and Princess Sonja rode up beside me, their natural poise making it clear they weren't strangers to riding in the least. They watched as John squirmed and shifted, grunting to find some position of comfort on top of his saddle.

"He's never ridden before, has he?" marveled Valiente.

"Not without me sharing a saddle with him." I puffed out my cheeks.

"You shared a saddle with him?" Sonja guffawed. "But isn't that what you do for children? Isn't it awkward for two grown men to...?"

The sharp glares from Valiente and me was enough to bring her mute.

"I see." She politely covered her mouth, a weak attempt to hide her smile.

"Besides, Basque is going to be doubling as our pack mule." Basque sidled under me as if thrilled at the news. "And if we must make a run for it, he can't exactly bolt or fight like the others. He and I will be offense. John will have to learn to ride on our way south."

The clacking of an approaching horse caught our attention. A dark bay in a breed I had never seen came around the far corner with Red Wine in its saddle. The horse was small, athletic with thin legs, but the movements were smooth and surefooted even on the icy ground. Red Wine's hood seemed unphased by the canter, the cloak bouncing behind her as they approached. She led the horse to circle us, the mask doing nothing to deter the fact she was inspecting everything from their attire to the way the horses had been saddled. At last, she brought the mare next to me, her horse as tall as Basque's shoulders.

"Must you ride something the size of a wagon?" she hissed at me from under her mask.

It seems I've already frustrated my master this morning. Something tells me this will be one of many times...

I chuckled. "He'd kill a man for a peppermint from my pocket, so I'd say that luxury alone is worth riding him. We call him Basque, not wagon. And her name?"

The dark bay horse danced in place, her neck long and curved. "Biscuit."

Basque nipped at her and the mare, forcing both to make space. "He's as aggressive as his rider, I see. Good work unknotting the braids on the horses and swapping gear. I thought I would have to insist, but you seem to have done this on your own. Thank you."

"Please don't underestimate me, Master Assassin." I scoffed. "My father is a master tactician, and my former mentor was very much the same. I would dishonor them both if I didn't put some thought into my actions."

"Is that so? We are to stop at Madame Plasket's Apothecary for a few more supplies and weapons. I'd advise you and the priest to abandon..." she paused, looking at the claymore with silver and blue decorations. "Your weapon of choice is a claymore?"

"It's what the Lord Knight Thompson trained me to wield, but good luck getting that rapier from John. It's a family heirloom."

I tilted my head. "I suppose it's not exactly an assassin's first choice. If you think I should abandon it—"

"I was mistaken. They looked like royalty, but those aren't the markings of a current... house." She stumbled on her words. "Let us be on our way."

What a peculiar emotional response. Did she know Lord Knight Paul? Or did she know someone else who used the claymore? Could his scar be from her?

C H A P T E R 4

Training on the Road

The birchwood trees seemed like silent striped sentinels. Solid, they ignored my stares as I searched for some signs of what had happened over winter. Passing the path we would have taken back home to the farm, I could see John's eyes linger on it. *He's as bad as I am. Some part of him just wants us both to go back to being there, being together despite all that unfolded.*

Red Wine had taken point in the front; meanwhile, Basque and I loitered in the back. It seemed fitting since I could see up ahead and far behind thanks to his height. Sadly, I had to be wary of low-hanging limbs and the occasional icicle. The tiny horse Red Wine rode intrigued me, its trotting almost worthy of a tip-toed ballerina. Nothing like it had ever come through our stables, but the horse had energy and speed, making it as restless as Basque at times. It didn't need much from its rider to know when to turn, speed up, or slow down.

She's been riding that mare for a few years for that level of intuition between them. The old mare I put John on is like that, but this is worthy of training on par with Colonel.

Red Wine would race ahead a few times, disappearing completely from view as she faded into the trees that made up Glensdale Grove. It was the forest region that the farm called home wedged between the Willow Waters river system to the west and Sullen Lake in the east. *For once, I'm glad I memorized all those maps during my youth.* We would have taken a boat to our first stop, a township called Tavern Way, but the large chunks of ice floating in the lake hadn't dissipated completely. Besides, we would still have to travel most of the way on land to reach Captiva City anyhow.

We'll have to make it through the guards and battlefields even. I know clergymen's passage are sanctioned by all sides, but will they let Red Wine and me continue to play bodyguards? Granted, Princess Sonja and Lord Knight Valiente may be our ticket through that dilemma.

The sound of galloping brought them to a halt as they waited to see who was racing around the bend. The familiar dark bay and Red Wine came into view, and she slowed down on her approach. The horse snorted, happy to have released some energy, and Basque shifted under me as if wanting his turn next. We started again, a steady pace that would get us to Tavern Way by nightfall and not seem like we were on the run or over-exhaust the horses if we needed to escape sudden danger. She mumbled something to Valiente, and he took point as she cantered to the back and spun her horse to keep pace with Basque.

"Are you really set on using the claymore as your main weapon?" Her eyes were fierce under her mask. "It completely defeats the concept of being an assassin, you know?"

"I spent a decade training with one, and I'm far better with it than any broadsword or rapier," I confessed. "Is it that big of a problem for you?"

"It's not that..." she paused, and it piqued my interest. "It's a two-handed weapon, and an assassin relies on using both hands freely. It seems you are hellbent on being the least stealthy assassin in history." She held her breath a moment before releasing it, as if battling with her own decision in the matter. "I suppose you'll have to learn when to use it and when to abandon it. We are in warring times, and it does have the value of intimidation."

To me, the claymore is a one-handed weapon. I know old man, don't tell anyone, but this might be that one time I should. Besides, if an assassin could leave that scar on your neck, something tells me I would have been dead already. I can't shake she's the one who marked you, so she should know this...

"What if I told you I can wield it one-handed?" I offered.

She glared at me, the mask seeming to frown at me for even putting the words into the air. "Prove it. I don't believe you." Straightening her back, she seemed angry at the idea. "I only know two men in this world who could do it. You buried one six feet under the cherry tree a few years ago, and the other is still missing."

I flinched. "Exactly how much does the assassin's guild know about me and the old farmer? Hell, about what's going on and who seems formidable?"

"Does it really matter? It's not that we were spying on you in the shadows." She snorted. "We are just really good at gathering information. Granted, the one source that's eluded us is *Arbre Tombé.*"

"Then this means no one knows my secret." I nodded to myself.

"What secret?" she guffawed. "You're an open book, Dante. It's almost embarrassing at times."

Ouch. I pulled the claymore off and held it with my left hand. The muscles in my arm stung. I hadn't been practicing and I could feel it. *This is what Lord Knight Paul meant. If I don't swing it every day, my muscles lose the ability to properly handle its weight. Shit.* She watched as I moved it as freely as a rapier before putting it back in its holster. The whole time Basque seemed unmoved by the metal's weight, and I had kept my balance on the saddle. Red Wine looked me over again, her eyes pausing on the claymore's hilt for a minute.

"Did you take that from him or was it a gift?" she demanded.

"A gift," I scoffed. "Not like I'd live that long with the old man and kill him for it later?"

She looked away in thought before declaring, "Fine. I'll allow it."

Huffing, I pushed back, "As if I was going to concede."

"Oh really?" She halted her horse. "Let's trade weapons and spar a moment. If you think so little of my knowledge, let me show you exactly what it means to be a Master Assassin. The path is clear up ahead, anyhow." Whistling, Red Wine managed to get everyone's attention. "Keep going. We'll catch up after a sparring lesson."

Sparring with a Master Assassin feels like facing the old farmer for the first time all over again. I'm going to regret this. I know it.

John lowered his brow. "Here in the middle of the road?"

I climbed off Basque. "Apparently so."

"Can I watch?" John offered.

"No." Red Wine and I both huffed in unison before shooting a glance at one another.

John threw up his hands, the mare he rode following Sonja's Walker without any direction from him. Once they had disappeared, Red Wine unsaddled and approached. In one hand, she offered a dagger, in the other, a rapier. I paused, and at last defaulted to the dagger. *Unlike most, I could take a hit or two to get close enough to strike. Besides, even with two hands, she wouldn't be able to lift and swing the claymore with much speed.* She placed the rapier in its halter on the horse.

Turning back, she motioned for the claymore. Under that mask of hers, I imagined a toothy grin. *I've made a deal with a devil.* Pulling the claymore from the saddle, I unsheathed it. I drove the blade into the ground before her, far away from the horses so not to startle or harm them in our sparring match. She readied her stance, widening it to be more surefooted in the mud. Both hands gripped the claymore's hilt, and the glare from her eyes told me volumes about how easily she slipped into a battle mindset.

If I didn't know better, she's used one before. And from those medals yesterday, she's been on more battlefields than I even know about.

"You swing first," I insisted.

"Are you sure?" She tilted her head, making me feel uneasy.

This is a bad idea, but I refuse to back down. I want to know more about her. This might give away more about her past.

I nodded for her to start, and she didn't waste time. She spun, instead of attempting to strike directly. Her aim seemed to be focused on using her momentum to handle the hefty weapon. It left her back and sides wide open. I bolted forward to strike hard and fast. My blade reached her and met with a pinging of metal.

"Caught you." She had deflected with a dagger.

Confusion barely crested my mind as the flat side of the blade smacked me and knocked me to the ground. I stared up in disbelief. One hand held the claymore as if it were every bit as light as the other holding a dagger.

"Come on, big guy. Don't tell me one slap of the flat side is all it takes." She stood, waiting for me to scramble to my feet.

Who is this person?

Back on my feet, I came at her. Taking a strike from her dagger across my forearm, I locked blades with the claymore, managing to shove it upward. Our eyes locked, my right hand twisting to aim the blade down on her. A foot slammed into my chest, knocking me to the ground again.

"Not bad. Wasn't expecting you to hold it there and strike." Red Wine stumbled back, tightening her grip on the weapons. "Again."

I stood once more. "You're every bit as strong as I am, but so tiny. It's embarrassing."

She laughed. "It just makes it easier to throw my enemies off mentally."

Everything I had assumed about the petite assassin was now invalid. "You've done this before I take it." Inhaling deeply, I tried to slow my breathing and heartbeat. "I can't lie—feeling a tad intimidated. Let me try this again. Calmer."

Boy, you can't judge your enemy before you fight them. The old farmer came back to mind, nagging at me for my mistake. *You can hunt a hundred bucks, but it only takes one to turn and come at you to make you realize they can fight back and kill you just the same.*

Well, this is no buck, old man. Flustered, I began circling Red Wine, and she followed, calm and at the ready. *What I do know is she's a Master Assassin. That had to be earned by skill. Another thing is she's not wearing all her veteran medals from yesterday. She's fought in battles more than once and has built up experience and reflexes I can't even imagine. I can say she's also a bloodeater; her reflexes and scent tell me that much. Ah, but I also use the claymore with one hand, so...*

Launching myself at her, she readied her stance, claymore and dagger poised and pointed in my direction. I swapped hands with the dagger, and she shifted to match, so she could lock it with the claymore. *Yeah, I would have done the same. I got her.* She swung the massive blade. *And you'd assume the attacker would block with the dagger, but...* I dropped down, using the mud to slide into her legs and knock her off balance.

"Caught you," I echoed her words back at her.

I aimed to roll on top of her and pin her with the dagger against her throat. Much to my surprise, she was quick to abandon the weapons, freeing her to be more agile. By the time I rolled into a crouch and found her missing, I had a tiny blade at my throat. Mud dripped off us both.

"Nice try," she growled. "Crafty, but not used to an enemy who's willing to sacrifice weapons, I see. As I said, you'll need to learn to do that with the claymore if you want to live a day longer."

"I'm sorry. Can you blame me for being cocky about being able to wield it one-handed?" I panted, the blade retreating as she began slapping mud from where she had rolled to her feet. "And I thought you said only two people can wield it one handed. Or was that intended to be a lie to deceive me?"

"It wasn't a lie. I said *only two men,*" she corrected. "And I suppose I can confidently say two men still can." She picked up the claymore and offered it to me. "Keep that dagger. It helps to counter, but only switch the bigger weapon to your right hand when you're desperate. You have a lot of power behind that left arm, and if you clock them in the gut or jaw, you can throw the fight in your favor."

"How did you figure out I was left-handed?" Mud caked everything. Icy and slimy, I sighed in regret. *And we still have at least two or more days of riding on horseback...*

"That wasn't hard. You favor that hand when handling the reins and when using a smaller weapon. Try to shift those behaviors or even them out at the least." She used her cloak to wipe mud from her gauntlets and hands. "Though it seems you've had deeper training than I had expected. Would you like me to teach you more about using that claymore as a bloodeater?"

"I'd be a fool to say no, but may I ask who taught you to use it like that?" *Perhaps this will give me some inkling as to who the hell you are.*

"My father," she answered without hesitation.

She's definitely not Lillian. My sister favored the bow more than anything, but something tells me Red Wine can match even the best marksman if need be. Plus, my father thinks little of the claymore and calls it a pissing contest for size.

"And for the record, yes, Lord Knight Paul's scar was my doing. Granted, he surprised me with it. I nursed him back, trained the farm boy further before I left, though he learned much of it on his own. Humans have limitations that you and I don't have." Her words sent a chill across me.

"Why would you..." I slid the claymore into the halter and pulled myself back onto Basque. "What benefit was it to save him and train him?"

"I secretly hoped he would face Viceroy Falco one more time and end him. He had the best chance of it, should the need arise. That is, until he became too old. I sometimes forget how fleeting a human's lifespan can be." She pulled herself onto the dainty horse. "Let's catch up before they make it to Tavern Way. I didn't take the time to scout the town, so we may not be completely out of danger's way."

Basque thudded up beside the tiny mare. "How old are you?"

"That's rude of you, Dante." She pouted. "Besides, I lost count. I'm younger than your father, and older than you."

Seeing I would get no straight answer, I changed subjects to the more pressing matter at hand. "Do we know who they are looking for?"

"You," she replied. "The reports are showing that out of all they were able to question, it seems they were under the orders of killing you if you left Glensdale or returning you alive to Falco for a bigger bounty. It seems the Viceroy couldn't get over his taste for you, Dante."

A visible shudder shook my shoulders. "I was made very aware of that when we crossed paths my first day back."

"I'm sorry I wasn't around to stop it. I had matters to attend to in Winter's Perch," she sounded sincere about the statement.

"Not your responsibility," I remarked.

She rode ahead as if her mask couldn't cover the expression she made under it.

"Wait." Basque picked up speed, closing the gap between us. "Isn't Winter's Perch in the Perines mountains? Who would want to go there?"

"That's a story for another day." She slapped her legs, and the horse took off.

Who in the hell are you, Red Wine? More importantly, who exactly was your father? Falco? No... couldn't be. Did one of his mistresses manage to give birth?

CHAPTER 5

Tavern Way Inn

The sun had set, and cold nipped at our backsides as we entered Tavern Way. It seemed our presence spooked the townsfolk as we made our way down the main stretch toward the inn and stables. Shutters slammed shut, and shops flipped their signs and locked their doors. We all shuffled in our saddles, looking to one another with unease. The reaction was highly abnormal for a band of clergymen travelling through, a common enough occurrence since this was the eastern main trading hub. *They've been expecting us.* The sounds of laughter started to fill the air as the Tavern Way Inn came into view with doors open and golden light cast across the snowy intersection. *And they seem too drunk to care.*

"I'll stay with the horses," offered Valiente. "At least I have a better chance of surviving an arrow to the back."

"He's got a point." Red Wine chuckled. "And I'm going to scout the town out." She unmounted and waited for me to do the same before slapping my shoulder. "I'll leave the tavern arrangements to you, my apprentice. You can do that much, yes?"

"Thanks for the vote of confidence, Master." I shot a look at John and Sonja. "I suppose we might be sharing a room as busy as this place is. Maybe split it up between two rooms: Mother Superior and the knight to one room and us in the other?"

"I've made arrangements for my own room. Worry about you four." Red Wine trotted off back the way they came.

She's seeing if anyone followed us, I imagine. Didn't even think about it. Was that why she really wanted to spar? See if someone would jump out at the arguing stragglers or come out of the woods to follow them over the bridge?

Turning to John, I asked, "You've stayed here before, right? Any idea how to persuade the inn keeper?"

John shrugged. "I didn't even stop here on my way home—I kept walking and slept in the woods when I came home."

"Of course you did, farm boy." I nudged him as I walked past and through the door.

"We did the same, but by then we..." Sonja's words were cut short by John as he pushed her to walk between us. "Well, I mean, it's not too horrible of a walk in good weather."

"Don't worry, Mother Superior." John cleared his throat, looking at the quieting patrons. "I'm sure we'll find a room for at least you and your knight. We can take to the stables if we need to."

People were scattered throughout the modest establishment, seated at tables or the bar. The bustling variety of men and women seemed to be there for a drink or food, enjoying one another's company for now and later. Their chuckling had dwindled, and now they whispered among themselves as we pressed farther inside beyond the roaring hearth. All eyes were on the assassin leading a pair of clergymen to the far end of the horseshoe-shaped bar top. The bartender wiped his hands dry, motioning the patrons to get back to their laughter and mind their own business. He had four-knots in his short braid, making it clear he owned this plot and business.

Good, I'd rather deal with the owners. It's easier to work deals. "I need a room for my clients." I motioned to Father John and Mother Superior Sonja. "If possible, two rooms."

The man with dark rings under his eyes sucked on his cheek, looking over the clergymen before snarking, "And what kind of clergy travel with an assassin?"

"One's who paid enough to contract one for protection from Viceroy Falco." *Who cares if they know that much? Everyone knows he's hired headhunters for clergymen and even stablemen over the decades. Nothing surprising on that note.* "Do I need to go fetch her Captiva City sanctioned knight for service here or no?" Anger rose in my voice as I slammed the bar top with my palm, the clap loud as thunder. The whole place jerked and fell silent once more. "How much for a room? Do you even have any available?"

"W-we have a-a few." He pulled open a book, flipping through it as he plucked the quill from the ink bottle. "I can't give you both a room for free. Sorry, Father." He gave John an empathetic look, acknowledging the hierarchy between them. "Fifty gold for the other room."

John reached for his coin bag, but I gripped his wrist. "Are you kidding me?" I let the anger seep back into my voice. "I bought a horse in the capital for that much, one that could pull the walls down if it wanted to."

"We're desperate." He shrugged, swallowing.

"Then you must be giving the mead out for free with this many here." I motioned to the room which burst into laughter. *So, they're just locals with that reaction.* "Look, I don't see anyone manning the stable out there. I'll get it swept and cleaned and tend to all the stock there including our four. All I need is a room in trade." I softened my tone, "And we'll pay for all our meals and drinks. Or do you tend to hunt someone down to help us with our tack at fifty a night and reshoe all four horses while they're at it?"

"His boy came down sick," offered the woman serving a drink to a patron. "He'd be a fool not to take you up on that offer since it's been three nights since the last cleaning. Jacques here isn't known for getting his hands dirty or tending stock. He's got too many knots tying him up, sir."

Another round of chuckling made the man shove the quill back into the ink bottle. "Woman, I don't know why I even keep you around here!" He turned back to the shelves of liquors and wines. "I'm going to keep this one off the books as a favor, assassin. Don't think I don't know what that fucking mask on your face means."

"Shush! You know you ain't cleaning up after this lot every night." Her words incited another round of laughter from the locals, the bar owner's face reddening.

"The stables better be spotless when you leave. Two rooms, and you pay for your food and drink." He pointed at the clergyman. "This man is worth his weight in gold if he's risking his life and reputation at inns for you." He slammed the book closed, grumbling as he put it away. "I might seek him out next time I travel. What name do you go by?"

"Bloody Half-pint." Red Wine came marching through the door, motioning for a pint from the woman. "He's my apprentice, Jacques. Now you have two favorite assassins you know by name!"

"Not you again." Jacques scoffed. "Please tell me you plan on leaving in the morning with this Half-pint of yours."

"Aw, Jacques, I thought we settled this last time I came." She chuckled, slipping her mask off. A scar ripped across her lips, disrupting the cupids bow, and her maroon stare was striking. Freckles painted her cheeks and nose, and dark eye makeup made her seem like an enchantress while strands of brown hair clung to the sweat on her face. "Didn't I save your ass twice now?"

"I'm still not convinced you didn't set me up, Red," he mocked, shoving two keys to me. "Here. Just be sure to take her with *you* in the morning."

"Don't worry. She goes where I go." Sniggering, I turned to John and Sonja, giving them each a key. "Let's go deliver the news to Valiente, and I'll start tending to the horses. Looks like I get to sling shit for a little longer."

"Do you have a bath?" John asked, pulling two gold coins from his pocket.

The woman offered out her hand. "I'll get it going, but it's gonna take me a while, Father. We don't keep the water heated, so it's always poured fresh."

"I prefer it that way." John winked at her. "Here's another coin then for a mead while I wait here next to Miss Red Wine."

"Why don't you sit and have a drink with us, Dante? On me?" Red Wine had spun on her stool, leaning on the bar with her legs crossed and raised her mug high.

"Can't. I have to go to my second job." I narrowed my eyes at her. "But after that, maybe you can share the story behind that badge of honor." I motioned to my lip to imply her scar.

"Ah, that old thing." She gave a fanged grin. "I suppose I can share that story with you when you finish tossing the trash out. Try not to get too dirty."

Cursing my luck, I was back out into the freezing night air. Valiente had started gathering a few items from his saddlebags when he greeted me. He nodded, and I began collecting reins in silence, shoving my mask into one of Basque's saddlebags as I worked down the row. Valiente finished grabbing the essentials and disappeared inside as I led the horses to the stable beside the tavern. I froze. The stable was a complete abandoned mess. Tying the horses by the water trough, I kicked loose the ice trying to settle back across the surface.

Well, she did say it's been a few days, but this place needs entire rafters replaced.

It took a few minutes to locate all the tools, and I was thankful they weren't in the same shit-covered state as the stalls. Basque snorted and stomped. I halted, still half bent over two stalls from where I started at the entrance. He only did that when someone approached, a way of warning them not to come close. Another loud thud on the mud and Basque whinnied. A shuffling of hooves made it clear he was ready to bow-up on someone and had rattled the other horses. Cussing came to my ears, and I stepped out of the stall, leaning on the pitchfork. Two men cloaked in all black wearing tricorns were backstepping as Basque put himself between them and the other horses.

I really think he will kill a man for a peppermint. Perhaps these are just thieves? Glad to see the big guy is going to play protector, though Colonel seems annoyed.

I watched in silence as the men were too distracted by the giant horse to pay heed to their surroundings. They reached again for the old mare's saddlebags and were nearly clipped by Basque's front hoof. Again, the man jumped back, shoving his friend to give it his try. Basque locked eyes with me, nodding his head and curling his lips.

Yeah, yeah, I know. You want me to do something about it. Steam rolled out of him like he was some kind of demon, but I knew he was fussing at my lack of action. Clearing my throat, the men turned to face me. Each of the intruders pulled out a dagger and rapier. *Take out the trash, huh?*

"I wouldn't aim to steal from any of those horses. That one has taken out guardsmen and broken down city gates simply for being in his way. He's just being polite with you before snapping that reign and trampling you at this point."

They looked to one another, then back at me. "You're the one travelling with the clergymen."

"I am." I narrowed my eyes at the hilt of the claymore still on Basque. *Good thing Red Wine gave me that dagger earlier.* "You got business with them?"

"Not quite." He rolled a shoulder and settled his stance, both their faces obscured by black masks across their nose and mouth. "We've been hired to take out the assassin travelling with them."

I nodded. "I think everyone in town is a little annoyed by her. If you're looking for her, she's in the tavern, but I wouldn't fuck with her unless you know how to fight like your life depended on it because it will."

"Not her. *You,*" clarified the other, pointing at me with his dagger. "You're the one we need to bring back alive to *Arbre Tombé.* That prince posing as a bodyguard assassin."

"Shut your trap," hissed the other.

I paled. *Fallen Arbor. If they are looking for me...* "And what would they want with an apprentice who tends to the stalls? Do you really think a prince of bloodeaters would be out here shoveling shit for a living?" *Take the bluff. Please, take the—*

"Who cares..." a voice hissed from behind me.

I dropped the pitchfork and did a wide sweep with the dagger. The third attacker was dressed very differently. *Is he a member of Arbre Tombé?* He seemed graceful, his attire fitting of a businessman or high nobleman complete with a cane and bowler hat. Even his moustache was styled small and tight, but more notable was the fact... *He's braidless?* With a twist of the cane knob, it broke apart to reveal a hidden rapier. *And armed with some hidden weaponry. Shit.* A slice in his coat revealed how close he'd managed to get to me without me knowing. It was too shallow for skin.

This shithole has muted my sense of smell! I would be a dead man between that and the distractions his underlings caused. Should have stayed hidden a moment longer in the stall, really take a minute to assess the situation. Next time, I'll know better. I knew we were being hunted but not by the likes of Arbre Tombé. I know, old man, I made the same mistake twice today: underestimating my enemy. Dammit.

The two men behind me launched into a direct attack, drawing my attention back to them. A jab of a rapier came first. I sidestepped and aimed to slash at his side. He ducked under my initial sweep; his partner's dagger dug deep into my torso. Gritting my teeth, I managed to grab his wrist and wrench it, so he would abandon the lodged weapon. I pulled it out, blood splattering against the hay laden floor. I was now armed with two daggers; *this should give me better odds against three foes.* Blocking the next rapier jab, I managed to slice the cheek of the assaulter. He retreated. The two fussed on who would try next.

Spinning back to the bowler hat, I saw he had come rushing in sooner than expected. "You'll be ours next, child of Traibon."

I rolled my torso down the blade, spinning myself like I would if I had been swinging the claymore. He ducked the first strike, and the jab from my second dagger dug in his shoulder. He grunted, taking the blow, and not flinching. By this point, I had rolled to his arm and my first dagger ran across his wrist and fingers. *Too busy taking the first strike like a man to see I was aiming to maim your hand, jackass.* It was too dull, unlike the one from Red Wine. The rapier dropped.

"Keep him busy," spat the bowler hat.

A shout and thudding of boots from behind told me volumes. I ducked. One of the assaulters toppled over me, their dagger missing its strike. I flung him up and over. Twisting back to their partner, I leapt forward, not missing my next target. Both daggers dug deep into the man's chest; he gurgled, blood spilling from his lips. With a sickening suctioning sound, the blades pulled free. I locked eyes with the *Arbre Tombé* man holding his bleeding hand. He had managed to tie a hay string around his arm to slow the bleeding from his wrist. *Resourceful and smart. I expected nothing less from the ones Ashton disappeared chasing.*

"Dammit, can't you imbeciles stand your ground!" he shouted, trying to heat a small blade in the stable hearth.

My view was obstructed by the other henchman with manure across his face. "This operation's gone to shit, Landon."

I shrugged. "Should have at least let me finish mucking the stalls."

"Fuck you, Prince Traibon!" The henchman had grabbed up another rapier and came at me with a flurry of strikes.

Backsliding, I could feel one nick my cheek. The heat of blood trickled down my face, and I clenched my jaw. Flipping the daggers around, I went on the defense, deflecting where I could. He managed to back me out of the stalls, gaining enough distance between me and his leader, Landon. *Whatever he paid you, I hope it was worth your life.* I managed to hook one with Red Wine's hilt, and with a twist, broke the blade. He tossed the broken piece at me, and I took the hit to the face, refusing to take my eyes off him. The henchman roared in frustration, swinging wider. The blade skirted the edge of my coat as I leapt back. I readied my daggers, flipping them back to an offensive position.

The man hopped back; he steadied his feet. He launched forward in proper study for a rapier. I braced myself. *I'll take the hit, so I can cut him down. John's already going to know...* Tightening my grip, I inhaled deeply to take the blade. A large hoof came into view, connecting with the man's head. Eyes wide, I watched the skull-crushing hit launch the man. Blinking, I turned to see Basque snorting steam and bobbing his head. Colonel curled his lips as if grinning over their small victory.

"T-thanks, Basque. I'll owe you a ton of sweets for that." Catching a moment to breathe, I refocused. "Landon."

I ran for the stable, but Landon was gone. A horrific smell lingered in the air and I covered my nose. Landon had managed to burn his wound close before vanishing. Looking all around the blood-painted floor, I searched for clues as to which way he had gone. *There's no tracks. Did he just vanish, even with that injury?* My muscles burned with the tension I held, and after several minutes, I placed the dagger back in my belt. Marching over to the water trough outside, I assessed the damage. My face had started to bruise and swell, blood drying from the cut on my cheek. Reaching down to my stinging side, I felt the wound was slow to close.

Healing has become painfully slow like when John—No, I refuse. It's out of the question to drink from him, but once he sees this... Shit.

<h1>Chapter 6</h1>

The Priest's Bodyguard

I scooped up the icy water, desperate to wash the blood off my face, hands, and shirt. Basque began nuzzling me, searching for his peppermints. *You really did kill a man for peppermints. Monster.* Pulling a handful from my pocket, I tossed them to the ground in a panic. *John can't see me like this.* Searching my torso, I yanked my shirt up to see the red badge still bleeding, the flesh sliced open like a stuck pig. *Fucking dagger hit the same mark as when John…* Choking on my thoughts, I shoved the shirt down, anger building as flashes of our fight with Falco lingered in my mind. The starburst-shaped scar from The Fanged Lady remained white against the tanned skin of my torso and back. It served as a constant reminder of what we did in desperation in the heat of the moment.

First, I need to do something with the bodies. I can figure out my wounds later.

Flustered, I gripped the wheelbarrow from the stall I had been cleaning. With a heave, I lugged the first dead man into it, the body still freakishly warm and not yet rigid. It wouldn't be long before they'd stiffen, and by the midday sun, start to decompose and gather vultures and scavengers. Wheeling outside, I found the crumpled remains of the second. A pool of blood surrounded him, his skull caved in like a crushed melon. Grimacing, I tossed the corpse into the barrel with his buddy and rolled to the woods. A path had been worn leading away from the stables, and as I pushed farther down the pathway, I could smell the dung heap.

At least it's far enough for the wolves to dig them out and drag them off.

By the time I finished mucking the remaining stalls and settling the horses in, the bodies were completely covered. There were no signs of Landon besides the top knuckle of a finger. I stepped on it after abandoning the wheelbarrow on my way to stoke the fire in the stable hearth. From the smell of his blood, he seemed human, which meant he couldn't fully recover from his injuries. A missing finger and ragged slash across the wrist would prove useful for identifying Landon in the future. *I didn't get a good look at his face, but the voice—I'd know that voice.* Throwing a few logs into the hearth, I sat down to catch my breath. Feral dogs licked the blood off the cobblestones outside the stables while I stared aimless at the flames, recalling everything that had unfolded.

This is my life now. I kill to protect my life and his. Granted, it's not like I went looking to kill them. They came looking for me. For Prince Traibon, to be exact. Here we were thinking we were going up against mercenaries looking for the princess, but if Viceroy Falco was in alliance with Arbre Tombé, *this could prove dangerous for everyone involved. Didn't Ashton disappear chasing them down? In fact, why would Ashton get involved after renouncing his crown? Feels like there's far more to their interest in me than...*

"Dante, I came to see if you needed a hand?" John's voice lingered at the stable entrance, and I bit my tongue to force silence. "Wow, this stable is... falling apart."

I shifted, making sure my back faced him, trying not to reveal my bruised face and my still-bleeding torso. *If I can buy a little more time to heal.* "It was so shit covered, I couldn't bring the horses in and had to take out the ones who were here. Trying to make sure the hearth is good and warm before coming back in. Stay close to Red Wine until I'm done. It's not safe out here, Father John." *Dammit, I sounded too scripted.*

Basque shuffled in his stall, and John scuffed his boot against the ground. "It seems you did your share of bleeding as well. It's hard not to miss the dogs fighting over that pool of blood out front. Exactly whose puddle is out here anyhow?"

Forgot about that... Looking to the rafters, I couldn't shake the defeated sensation weighing down on me and confessed, "Three men jumped me."

"Three?" John sighed, coming closer to sit next to me in front of the hearth. "Falco's men?"

"Not sure." I swallowed, hoping those blue eyes hadn't looked me in the face. Catching his glare and the twitch in his cheek, I added, "But they did say they were with *Arbre Tombé* and looking for a Prince Traibon."

John held out his hands to warm them. "Why would they be looking for you?" he asked, wrinkling his face.

"I haven't the slightest idea unless they are still looking for my brother." I shook my head, not sure what to think of the situation even after pondering on it for so long. "I managed to kill two, but the third man, he was strange. No braid, dressed like a nobleman, hell of a fighter though we didn't fight long."

"Where'd he go?" John flipped my hood down, glaring at the bruise and cut on my face. "Did you see where he went?"

"No idea. I cut him good. He's going to have a scar on his wrist and a mangled finger. Managed to chop the top off one digit." He moved toward my face, and I leaned out of his reach. "It'll be gone by morning."

"Well, I'd prefer next time you don't use your face as a damn shield." There was the tinge of anger in his voice I had expected sooner as he tugged the hood back up. "Where else did you get hit? You're not a practice dummy, yet you seem hellbent on treating your body as one."

He reached to pull back the bottom half of my coat, and I gripped his wrist in alarm. "I'm fine. It'll heal."

John searched my face and smirked. "In that case, I need my bodyguard to escort me to the bath. It seems enemies are afoot."

"You seem to have made it out here on your own just fine," I drawled, tossing another log into the hearth.

"I had Red Wine watch me from the door." He loomed over me, crossing his arms. "In fact, she's the one who told me it would be a good time to check on you. Something tells me she was fully aware of our guests waiting out here to approach you."

"This doesn't shock me in the least." With a huff, I stood. It took everything not to wince as my torso stung, and the wound opened again. "She offered for me to have a drink before *taking out the trash.*"

"Come on. At least you can wash off the blood and mud." He stood, crossing his arms in a way that suggested he wouldn't take a single step until I moved first.

Caving to his pressure, I left the stables with John close behind me. Red Wine was sipping her mead and hissed seeing the bruise on my face. Her eyes dropped, catching the red stain before I could cover it better with my coat. A smile crested her lips, and she spun back to enjoy her drink. John approached the tavern maid, and she handed him a key. I glared at Red Wine's back, wondering if I should mention what unfolded. Inhaling deeply, the soreness in my chest was a reminder—she *too* was a bloodeater. *I'm sorer from that kick than where she smacked me with the claymore. She knew before me that we were being followed. I'm sure of it.*

Turning to follow John, the barmaid cleared her throat to call our attention back to her. "Only one at a time. You paid for one bather, not two."

"But he's my bodyguard," declared John, pointing at my face. "He's already been mugged outside your tavern! You think I'm going to get naked without him there in the room to protect me? Forget it. Who do you have to protect me while I bathe?"

Red Wine snorted her mead out her nose. My face flushed, and I covered it with a hand, praying that I looked more annoyed than embarrassed. *Too far, John. Too far.*

44

The tavern woman waved us off. "I ain't dying for you, Father. Might as well be that brute you already paid to risk life and limb fer ya."

There was a wave of laughter from the patrons as we walked past the staircase and down the hallway. At the far end, one door had been painted white with the word *bathhouse* scrawled across it. John unlocked the door and stepped inside, the steam rolling out into the hall. I turned, arms crossed to start my guard duty. John gripped the back of my coat, scruffing me like a kitten and jerked me inside. The door slammed, and he slid the lock into place.

The room was tiny with most of the space filled by a large metal drum full of water. Under it, a crude furnace had nothing left but hot coals glowing red in the wake of the slamming door. A single chair sat next to the tub and shelves burst with jumbled items on the walls. If we weren't mindful, we would knock elbows trying to undress at the same time in the small open space near the tub. John rummaged through the containers, whistling as he went before settling on two. He held them up to the lantern, one with rose petals and another herbal blend. The whistling stopped, and he opted for the juniper-based medley, the smell making me cough when he opened the jar and dumped it into the water.

"John, I can stand outside," I insisted as he began to remove his jacket. "There's not enough room in here."

"Nonsense. Strip down and let me see that stab wound," he demanded, cutting me down with his stare.

He pulled the chair up against the tub, motioning for me to sit with his brow raised high. Against my better judgment, I relented and took off my coat. A hiss escaped me as I pulled my shirt out of the healing wound. By the time I tossed them on the shelf, I began to bleed once more. Taking a closer look, the opening was struggling to close as normal. *Poison? Maybe that herb from before to counter the healing process?*

"Sit," demanded John.

His back was to me. I didn't have the energy to argue with him. He rolled up his sleeves, unbuttoned his collar some, and reached for some clean cloths. I snorted. *Would have thought he would strip down naked by now, but he's hellbent on playing nurse tonight.* John leaned over the tub, and I watched as he stirred the water and began dipping a cloth into it. I stepped forward, sliding into the chair, straddling it. The silence between us was mesmerizing as I watched the herbs and steam spin.

My chest ached. *I was looking forward to private little moments like this, but under better circumstances.*

Wringing out the cloth, John turned to me and frowned. "How am I to clean this one?" He knelt beside me, his fingers making the muscles in my abdomen jump.

"You can reach it just fine. I'm tired, to be honest." I nuzzled my arms, closing my eyes as he began to wash away the blood. Something about the simplicity of the act was comforting. At first, he was tender, and as he began the process of cleaning it, I did my best not to react to the stinging sensation it brought to life. My frustration peaked at last. "Clean it. Don't dig it out to be bigger."

"The blade was coated with something," he muttered, bringing the lantern closer and dipping the cloth again. Cracking open an eye, he seemed upset on every level. His face was serious, lips tight with concern. "It left an oily residue so I can see where to scrub, but some of it is deep and is going to take me being aggressive. It seems to be the reason it hasn't healed in places." Again, the cloth stung as it scraped and dipped into the opening. This time I couldn't keep myself from hissing. "Sorry," he breathed.

I grimaced. "Brings back memories, though I recall I was the one doing the scrubbing."

John scoffed. "Paybacks are hell." We both managed a smirk as he stood, dipping the cloth once more. "I pray it's not always going to be like this."

The words hit me, knocking my breath away to leave my soul aching.

"Lean back. Let me have a look at this bruise on your chest." I searched his face, but his eyes were locked on Red Wine's footprint.

He dipped the cloth. The sound of water dripped back into the bath as he once again wrung it out. I slid the chair back, giving him space between the tub and back of the chair. He squatted to be eye level to the red and purple mark across my left pec. Golden strands of hair shifted, falling to block his eyes from me. The heat of the cloth pressed firm against the injury.

My eyes fell to his lips, my heart fluttering. *When you get like this...* John was so close, his breath sent a shiver through me as the scent of him filled my lungs. *When you're so close and all I smell and feel...* He looked up, parting his lips to express concern. *I can't stop myself...*

The chair toppled over on its side as my lips pressed against his. John's back thumped against the tub. The cloth hit the ground between us as his hands pulled me into him, deepening the kiss. Blood filled the span, and I gripped the side of the tub. Hunger rattled me and I suckled, swallowing. I pulled away, my heart racing as his flavor lingered on my tongue. John's eyes dropped to the wound and scar. He tilted his wide, flicking his eyebrows.

"I guess that does speed it along."

Licking the blood from my lips, I slid a hand over the closed wound. "It helps to have it cleaned."

"Well, if you don't mind, I still want to take a bath." The sparkle in his eyes told me that everything had fallen in line according to his plan. "You joining?"

Licking a fang, I picked up the chair, swinging a leg over it to straddle it once more. "We'll take turns."

John frowned. "You're impossible at times."

I smiled, running a hand through my hair, feeling rejuvenated to a mind-numbing amount. "And I love you, too."

Inhaling deeply, I held my breath. I was backed against the door, though still only two armlengths from the tub with John undressing between. The golden braid of hair nested between his shoulder blades as he unbuttoned his shirt. I exhaled as the shirt dropped to the floor. The white-scarred cross seemed like ancient magic etched across his skin. Not one flourish had failed to leave its mark. Despite the trouble it had given him, it healed smooth and bright. He had only seen similar brandings on the duke's horses. His complexion was paler than mine, but the skin was sun-kissed as if his years working the farm were stained into his flesh.

I bit my lip. He shot me a look over the shoulder as he began unbuckling his pants. *Always wanting my eyes on him and nowhere else.* He let them drop and wasted no time climbing in. The muscle in his legs flexed, his arms bracing him tense enough for me to admire the lines of his forearms. Groaning, John's body disappeared into the tub. Steam rolled up from where he sank. Juniper and herbs disrupted the pleasure I took smelling his scent, seeing and sensing his arousal. Every muscle in me fought the urge to join him, to throw the chair to the ground once more and abandon the walls I was trying so hard to rebuild. *We might be fine to lose ourselves here in this shithole of a tavern, but if we can't pull back now...stuck in the catacomb library together for two years might prove impossible. What is he thinking?*

Chapter 7

Desires and Speculations

Leaning back, my head pressed against the door as I covered my face. Everything ached with the rising tide of desire building at my core. Cuts and bruises had faded in the wake of our kiss, a power only he could give me, and it always pushed me to my limits, emotionally and physically. *Why did he let me do that?* The heat of his lips still lingered on my own. *I shouldn't but...* I kicked my boots off, unbuckling my pants. *This might be our last chance to... fuck.* An exasperated sigh escaped me. I rose to my feet, leaving my pants stretched across the floor.

Leaning on the side of the tub, I admired the view. John's eyes were closed. Narrowing mine, I knew his heart had picked up speed, and I smirked. He was waiting for me, his excitement growing as he heard the rustling and light slap of bare feet on the stone floor approach. A mixture of frustration and flattery rolled through me. *Maybe Red Wine was right. I'm an open book if you can pull me along so easily, my love.*

"You should really let the patient rest," I announced.

He cracked open an eye and shrugged. "I haven't done a thing but tend to your wounds. Glad your face doesn't look like shit anymore."

The juniper stung at my nostrils as I stirred it with my fingers. "Why the juniper over the rose or even lavender? It smells horrendous."

"You're not the only one that took a beating today." He leaned forward, drawing in his legs to make room for me to join opposite of him. "I'm not use to riding a horse, and my thighs and lower back are killing me. Juniper is supposed to help, or so Madame Plasket has advised on more than one occasion."

I laughed, leaning back against the tub's inner wall before sinking down to my shoulders. "Jasmine is old, so she's not as smooth as she once was."

"Granted, I'm glad not to be riding Basque for this long as wide as he is." John sat up, splashing water on his face.

"Speaking of Basque," I started, waiting to lock eyes with him, "he killed a man for peppermints tonight."

"Of course, he would," snarked John. "The damn monster would take on an entire brigade for a single sugar cube." A chuckle escaped him, the smile on his face making my heart flutter. "But he wants the sweets only from you, it seems. So as long as he can't be bribed, we're safe."

I splashed water in his face in reply, laughing. "Such dark thoughts."

"Says the assassin to the priest," he scoffed.

Inhaling, I frowned at my reflection on the water's surface with my maroon eyes like dark splotches of blood in the ripples. "We need to figure out what my nickname will be. Please, no more Danseur. You can't call me Dante or Prince or *my love*."

"I know," he spoke with a deep sadness in his voice. "Can't I just call you Bloody Half-pint?"

Shaking my head, I refused to allow him to deflect the matter with humor any longer. "I don't think my reputation as the priest's assassin is going to get us very far once we're in Captiva City."

"You find a name then. Something endearing. Something that would help us draw out Fallen Arbor." It was a curious offer he made as he looked away.

"So, you really want that to be our aim? What do you have against them?" I furrowed my brow glaring at him, my heart racing for fear of where he was taking this. "It's not like they have anything to do with the Madness or Falco."

"I think they have more involved in Grandmere than we realize." He sucked on his cheek a moment and finally met my gaze. "Think about it. After everything we've discussed in the war room during the winter, don't tell me you weren't already thinking there's obviously a clear connection between it all: civil war, soul weapons, Falco, Fallen Arbor, and even the Madness."

Rubbing my tongue on a fang for a minute, I exhaled and gave him a disapproving expression. "Of course, I'm seeing a connection. You do realize Fallen Arbor is the reason Ashton went missing. If my brother, a Champion Supreme who never knew the taste of defeat, went missing chasing after them… exactly how is a runaway prince and his priest lover supposed to overtake them?"

John looked up in thought, replying, "Well, we're resourceful and not exactly good at being Lone Wolves like your brother."

"Sometimes I wonder who needs to be doing the most praying between us, Father," I blurted in disdain.

"I hate when you call me that," confessed John.

"Oh?" I couldn't hide my smirk at the thought. "And what do you prefer me to call you?"

He matched my smug expression. "I can't lie. Last night when you breathed *my priest* was quite arousing for me."

My smile dropped. *I deserved that one.*

"Speechless, are we?" He came closer, and I refused to move or react. "I believe you uttered that phrase a few times, my love. And it's usually the moment you bend me over and f—"

I kissed him. The scent of John's arousal overpowered me and the lustful memories muted the juniper in his presence. I wanted him in all the wrong ways. Water sloshed as I backed him against the other side. My grip wrapped around his hard cock as he deepened the kiss, moaning. His palm slid down the middle of my torso. John's touch against my hardened shaft sent a shiver through me. I began kissing on his neck, and when a fang nicked him, I froze. *Shit! What was I about to do? Is it so easy for me to forget myself and…?*

"I can't do this. Not like last time," I muttered into him, my heart pounding in my ears as fear conquered my excitement. "I don't want to be like *him.*"

"Dante," he gruffed, stroking me as he began kissing my own neck. "You do realize if I wanted you to stop, I would have said so. Are you really still upset over that one time you fed on me and made passionate love to me?" He laughed, but it faded, and he pushed me back to look me in the eyes. "You're not Falco."

"What if I didn't stop in…" I swallowed, the hunger and itch in the canines begging me to repeat that act once more. "What if I can't stop?"

"If you think…" John grabbed my shoulders and shoved me hard against the other side of the tub. Water slapped against the floor. "I'm not strong enough to push you away, you're wrong."

I dropped my gaze, my glowing eyes like flames in the reflection. "Shit, do they always do that?"

"When you're angry and when you make love to me," he admitted. "It's even better to see when you have your mask on. Scares the shit out of people. It's great."

"John," I scolded his unwelcome compliment. "I just…we just can't do this until we're some place more private."

His thigh slipped between mine as he leaned in. "Isn't this private enough?"

"We shouldn't." I pushed back.

He pinned me harder between him and the tub until his lips and beard tickled at my ear. "Bend over."

A shudder rolled over me at his provocative command. "And what makes you think I'll do that for you?"

"I'm not asking," his voice rumbled with raw desire. "I want you to kneel and yell my name until I'm satisfied."

"Stand up," I replied.

"Bend over," he countered, and I laughed.

"Your effort has me hot and bothered, but if I let you have me, I want to make sure you're ready," I offered. "Now stand and lean on the other side."

He sloshed away eyes narrowed at me. After a short pause, he stood. Water snaked across his body in the warm glow of the lantern. I throbbed with want, but I saw what he offered in this. He'd never taken me in this way, nor any man or woman. *There's always a first time, and I suppose I can't lie to myself. I've been secretly wanting to do this with someone who loved me the way I love him.* I wasted no time to run my tongue down his cock. He inhaled quick, closing his eyes to take in all that my mouth offered. *If this is his first time, it's best he's hard as a rock. Otherwise, he might get too discouraged.*

I took him deep inside my mouth, pushing him to the back of my throat, sucking and pushing and pulling him between my lips until he hardened. I pulled away, but he gripped my hair, shoving himself to the back of my throat again. And I let him. His hips rocked, enjoying the moment. *I will gladly submit to him if it'll keep the hunger at bay.* At last, he allowed me to move away. Reaching behind him, I grabbed the bottle of oil we had both eyed since we entered the room. Rising to my feet, water dripping filled the silence. We locked eyes as I poured the oil onto his cock, and I stroked him to ensure he would indeed be stiff enough. *It's been a while even for me to be on the receiving end, but I've been fantasizing about him switching roles.*

"Take your time." I searched his face, trying to gauge the thoughts lurking behind those blue eyes and stoic expression. "You can be aggressive. I don't mind."

"Good." He was quicker than I had anticipated, hands gripping my shoulders once more.

Water slapped across the side of the tub and poured over from the shift of our bodies. I caught the side of the tub with my hands as he bent me over, fast and hard. The burning coals hissed, and steam rose as the water burned back into the air. He pushed inside and I grunted. *Too eager but...* At my core, I fought back memories of Falco, but they were soon far from my mind.

John pressed hard against me as his hands caressed my body. He surveyed me, assessing how I reacted, how he wanted to take me before continuing. I tried to push myself up, to sit up, and he shoved me back down. His body leaned on top of me, and I was quickly reminded he was every bit as big as I was physically.

"I want this to serve as a reminder to you." His words were erotic and dark as they lingered in my ears. "I'm not Falco. And I'm not afraid of you."

"John, you can't be—" *Since when could you be so aggr—*

His hand tugged at my braid, wrapping it once around for good measure. My back arched, and he slipped deeper and throbbed. His other hand glided down over my shoulder blade, over my ribs and hip until he gripped my cock. *He's going to try and break me.* A smile came to my face, his movements mimicking how I took him that first time. Slowly, he pulled back until he left me, lingering there teasingly before he pushed tauntingly slowly back inside. We moaned as he throbbed, hard and slick with oil. He tried rocking his hips and stroking me, but the broken canter was driving me crazy.

"Dammit..." John panted in frustration.

I cupped my hand over his, helping him stroke. I rocked into him, and he released my braid and braced his hand in the small of my back. He was gaining speed, watching himself thrust in and out. I studied the concentration on his face until the water rippled too much to keep the image. *He's got it now; he's enjoying it, and I can let myself relax.* Shifting, I was able to arch more, improving how he stroked with me. My hand tightened over his, not allowing him to retreat. *So close now.* The heat of his other hand made me throb as it slid up across my chest, and he gripped my shoulder to steady himself. Nearing my peak, I started to moan.

"Harder," I breathed, feeling how he lingered on the edge of his own release.

He started moaning. "I'm going... Dante, I'm..."

"So close..." I muttered, letting his hand free as I bent over to where I had started, leaning against the tub. "Don't stop."

He retreated to gripping my hips, thrusting hard against me. We were both moaning as he peaked, my arm bracing the weight of our efforts against the tub's edge. Seeing the cloth on the ledge, I grabbed it up in a rush. I released into it as he pushed hard against me, his cock throbbing in his own orgasm. He folded over on top of me hugging his arms around me. He grinded slow against me, riding out his orgasm a little longer.

"That was," he marveled, "different."

I laughed, tossing the cloth to the floor, and patting his arms. "Let go. I need to clean up before they suspect we are doing more than just talking in here."

Rushing, I was the first to finish cleaning myself and climbed out. I cussed under my breath, realizing my gear was still mud covered. I spent the whole time playing diplomat for sheer joy instead of cleaning it. Grabbing up another cloth, I dipped the pail into the water. John gave me a baffled expression. When I lifted the filthy pants, he nodded, unravelling his braid to wash his golden hair. I scrubbed furiously, starting with the pants, then the shirt and coat. Throwing another log on the tub fire, I brought it back to life as John climbed out. The pants were dry enough for me to slip them on as knocking erupted at the door.

Inhaling deeply, I cracked the door and filled it with the bulk of my shirtless body, knowing John still stood naked just behind me. "What do you want?" I barked.

"Ashton?" Red Wine's maroon eyes were wide. "Fuck. I'm drunk. Scar is in the wrong spot. Wrong side, but..."

I blinked. "What did you just say?"

"Never mind me, uh, the bar wench, she thinks you're in here riding the priest so..." Her eyes narrowed, bouncing from the right pec to the starburst scar in my abdomen. "That's from the Fanged Lady too, isn't it?"

I gripped her, pulling her through and shoving her on the chair as I slammed the door shut. "Who the hell are you?"

"Whoa, sore subject." She threw up her hands, her demeanor loose and careless. "I knew you reminded me of him, and I may have had one too many between that and Frank being a dick in

Winter's Perch." The Master Assassin's red cheeks were nothing as she leaned over to whistle as John trying to put his pants on, bumping into me from behind. "You were riding the priest!" Chortling, she met my gaze and her smile dropped. "Oh, you should go back with me. If they saw you..."

"Is she drunk?" John buckled his pants and pulled on his shirt. "Is the fucking Master Assassin our lives depend on fucking shit-faced? Really?"

"Hey, not many folks get stabbed by that bitch," she slurred, her hood falling. "Ashton was hit once by Falco, in the chest there." She pressed her fingers into me, shoving me back before I could reach for her braid. "No peeking. You'll eventually earn the right to see how many knots I have, little Traibon."

"Wait, you knew Ashton personally?" John slipped on his jacket, placing jars and the oil back in its rightful place.

She grimaced. "I'm the reason he went after Fallen Arbor. He's the reason I need to find my informant in Captiva City. Apparently, they can't find Ashton either, and the last person who knew anything was Frank. They were the last to see him alive, but Frank wouldn't talk to me. Said leave it be and chased me out of Winter's Perch."

"Then let's get their attention," my voice took on a dangerous ambience. "I'll play the part of Ashton."

Red Wine burst into laughter. "You can't even wield the claymore or fight at the same capacity as him. You think he'd be thrown in the mud that many times or even let those assholes draw blood?" Her laughter stopped, and her breath caught. "You'd have to be crazy to want to become the target of all his enemies. You wouldn't last a week unless you could hold your own like he could."

"You're my mentor. Teach me to be him."

She guffawed. "I never won a match against him! There's no one that can compare to him in fighting prowess."

"And you're the only one I know who's ever fought him," I growled, unnerved that the scarred-lip woman before me had been so close to my brother. "Please. If we are to give ourselves a chance at Fallen Arbor slipping up or even getting Ashton to come out of hiding—"

A haunting expression filled her face. "You're right." She touched the scar on her face and seemed to sober. "Fallen Arbor is dangerous. They are using every dirty tactic and using dark, terrible magic. Regardless, if you two are really going to be so brazen..." We looked to one another and nodded. "Fools. Such fucking fools. You're going to get me killed, so promise me one thing: you let Frank and Ashton know *Raphaëlle Le Denys* never stopped loving them." She stood, shoving me back. "Let's be straight. You may look like him, but you'll never reach the greatness he is and always has been. Get your clothes on and meet me in the woods behind the tavern. Your training starts now; there will be no rest. I'll teach you everything *he* taught me about the claymore."

I need them to think I am Ashton, that the man behind the mask matches the name that once reigned over entire armies as Champion Supreme.

CHAPTER 8

The Mask of Ashton

The silence between us unsettled my nerves. Moments ago, she was leaning on the doorframe and slurring. Now she marched in a way that reminded me of a soldier getting into the proper mental state to enter the battlefield. Somewhere in the cold dark, a barn owl hooted an ill omen. The old farmer's voice whispered, *you hear that?* Goosebumps pimpled my skin as the sour memory rolled forward. *Silence followed by nothing but the owl's call is an ill omen.* I had laughed it off, not realizing the very next day the old man would die on me. *Take heed, Prince. They stand for wisdom, but you don't get wise because life's sweet as a rose in bloom. No, the wise are those who have seen death, and worse, caused it with their own two hands.* For the first time in a long while, the claymore seemed heavy, the sense of a great burden added to it once more. *And now this secures I will be causing my own share of deaths, does it not?* My past haunted me, always rolling back after I fooled myself to think that I'd made peace. Instead, it forewarned that it was my future I should fear the most.

Red Wine stopped and spun to face me. I froze, waiting for her instructions.

"You do realize I haven't ever been this upset in front of anyone for decades." Her eyes picked me apart, her lips in a deep scowl making the scar ugly.

"I'm sorry," I whispered.

"You really never got to meet him?" She crossed her arms, baffled by the thought.

"He went missing before I was born," I confessed.

She brought her hand to her lips in deep thought. "I can't afford to take my time with you then. You will be training, and any time you do something not on par with Ashton..." Her maroon eyes glowed. "...I will not let it go without punishment."

"Understood." I pulled the claymore free, letting the point thunk into the ground. "So, let's get to training."

"Take your offense starting stance," she demanded.

Obediently, I shifted my body, holding the hilt in both hands, left hand on the bottom half. I held the blade between us, the tip pointed at her as if awaiting her incoming attack. She palmed her face. Silence lingered as she muttered in an inaudible language, clearly disgruntled. My heart sank as she began talking to herself, pacing back and forth. *She's trying to talk herself out of this... what language is that? The Old Tongue? Or something else?*

"What's wrong?" I braved, holding my stance.

"You. You're all wrong. This is all just wrong," she spat, angry and frustrated before even starting. "You're going to get killed, or I'm going to get killed pulling this off."

"If I can't change by sunup, I'll abandon the idea." It was a dangerous gamble, but it made her hand drop, and she met my gaze. *She knows I mean it. Or she plans on forcing me to fail with that much on the table.*

"Fine. I highly doubt you'll change my mind," she disparaged.

She came over and began kicking my feet and legs. I shifted to the side, a wider stance and leaning more weight on my back leg. Swapping my hands, she raised my elbows and pushed my arms back. Stepping back, she circled once before getting more aggressive. Grabbing the sides of my face, she moved my head, tilting my face up instead of my normal downward glare. Shoving down on my shoulders, she made me squat deeper, legs aching to hold the weight of the blade and my back burning as muscles stretched in new ways. *This is going to make riding Basque painful tomorrow.* Circling back to the other side, she nudged my elbow again and scoffed. A shove on my chest made me grunt under the shift in weight and duress rattling my entire body.

"You feel that?" she spoke flatly. "That's his starting stance, and he would hold it for hours. Hurts like shit. I know from personal experience. Hated this part."

I swallowed. "Now what? What's the next swing and pose?"

"This is the first lesson. You don't break this stance until the sunrise." Her tone was dark as she paced around me and pushed my face back into position when I tried to look her way.

Without warning, she punched me in the gut. The wind left me, my legs shaking. Wheezing, I was desperate to bring the air back through the stinging fire that made up my lungs. Gritting my fangs, I gripped the claymore tighter, trying my best to reset in the way she had put me in until I could feel the burn of the pose come back to life. *Remember that sensation. This is the right pose. She wouldn't lead me astray. To her, it's impossible to master anything that she knows is of his design and will.*

"Good," she breathed.

She circled and slammed her heel into my lower back, right into my kidney. A cry escaped me, and my footing shifted. I scrambled to reset, and she slammed down on my arm with the point of her elbow. I glared at her she walked faster now, another heel crashing into my thigh as I managed to get my footing back into place. A cold sweat began, but I persevered through the pain. Another fist in the ribs. I sucked in air and focused on getting my elbows back to where—a punch to my spine sent me over my limit. Another cry of pain and I fell forward against my will, my legs numb and nerves on fire.

Crossing her arms, she frowned. "Ashton never fell once. If he didn't dodge it, he took it in like a stone wall."

Anger boiled at my core. Scrambling to my feet, I kicked off my boots and tossed my shirt and jacket to the side. My entire being was aflame with adrenaline and rage. Jerking the claymore up, I cracked my neck and rolled a shoulder. *I can do this. They made him sound like a monster, then I too will become just that. After all, I need to protect John at all costs.* Taking a deep breath, I squatted into the newly learned offensive pose. My eyes were on Red Wine as I did so, the pain from her hits trying their damnest to hide the way I needed my body to feel to master it. *She's making sure I can't tell how to hold the pose!* I could see her eyes dance around my pose, checking the placement of my feet, the hands and elbow height.

"Chin up." She started her approach and I tensed. "You need to give the enemy the sensation they are below you, not above."

She kneed my ribs, and something cracked. Wind left me and I clenched my jaw. *Fuck, she broke a rib. She can't be serious.* A boot to a thigh, a punch to the jaw, jabs to the gut, and heels to the back. The sadistic dance continued, and no longer could my eyes focus on the birchwood trees surrounding us. She circled time and time again. I dropped to a knee, losing balance. She responded with a boot to my face, and I rose back into position without complaint. *Everything hurts.* I knew only pain, and there was no sign of sunlight in the black sky overhead. Steam rolled from my lips and nostrils. Each pant rattle shook my lungs until it ceased in a sharp stabbing sensation if I dared inhale too deeply. Blood dripped thick off my chin, my lip busted and cheek swollen. Sweat painted my skin as bruises and abrasions ran streams of scarlet down my body. A lifetime of torture seemed to pass between us. My mind went blank, all thoughts proven impossible.

I lost count of the number of hits, the number of cracks as she broke me in ways I didn't think possible. At one point, I coughed, and blood rose to my lips and dribbled down my chin in a gush. The world grew dark, my vision failing in the building agony. My sense of smell was destroyed after taking a punch to the face. A crack and blood trickled from my nose and over my lips. Another hard hit and my shoulder popped. The claymore dropped to the ground. Visceral, I roared, popping it back in as I crushed it into the pommel. Without even a thought, I went back to the position. All I knew was anger in my new world of torment. Another punch and my brow split, and my eyesight went dark at last.

The next wave of hits seemed nothing but a bad dream. My pain hit a peak so high, it couldn't be added to nor surpassed. I was dry heaving, throbbing and ill from pain and adrenaline mangling and I wanted... *Blood.* A single thought is all I had. All I could smell, taste, want... *Blood.* A strange calm came over me, the hit and jabs making me aware of where she circled. It was like a rhythm being beaten into a drum and all I could think was... *Blood.* Her leather gauntlets hit harder now, scrapping and ripping my skin. Rivulets tickled down my torso. It seemed odd as I recognized it: *my blood.*

Through it, I could smell beyond my own for the first time, and my heart raced with another wave of adrenaline. I could smell *her blood* under the boots and gauntlets. She was taking a beating, my body like a boulder, and I tried to search for her through the darkness. *Salt.* The sky had faded to a dark blue, lavender rising in the east. I glanced back to where her fist thudded hard against my torso. Something cracked. *Not mine.* She clenched her jaw, tears running down her face. *Salty blood.* Her mask had tears of blood painted on its face much like her own as she continued beating and kicking me with the despair written on her face. The non-stop assault had her panting, but she had not wavered. At some point, I had stopped falling to my knees or dropping the claymore. *Something inside me... broke.*

An orange ray of sunlight broke through the trees. The telltale sound of a blade unsheathing brought me to react so fast, I hadn't registered what it was I had done. My body held the pose, the claymore not dipping in the slightest as I crushed her wrist in my right hand. Another squeeze and it popped and cracked under the pressure. The dagger fell, and she paled, locking eyes. I felt like a confused monster, nothing like I had experienced with the Madness. *This is different. Something ancient and pure. A need for survival at any cost by way of fighting.* She tried to pull her wrist back. I squeezed tighter, and it cracked again. A wail escaped her, and she pounded against me.

"It's not fair!" The words took a while to push past the fog that had settled within my mind. *Her blood. She's family? To me?* "How could you do it!"

My thoughts scattered, I blinked in confusion. "I did what you asked of me."

"I know..." she sobbed. "And curse you..."

I let go and she fell to the ground. Ignoring the pain of my broken body, I stood over her. At first, chin down but I shifted, my chin high as I leered down at her. Her braid lay in the open, *17 knots.* The rolls of knots started from the top of her forehead and made a mohawk down, but that was to trick an untrained eye. Before me was a broken-hearted queen.

"Who are you?" I wiped the blood from my face.

She was taking her gauntlets off, calming herself. "That's a story for another time."

"What will it take to get that answer?" I squatted, coughing, and spat blood to the ground. "Dammit..."

She refused to look me in the eye. "Find Frank and bring them back into the fray. We can't win against Fallen Arbor without them."

"When we're done in Captiva City, we will head to Winter's Perch."

Locking gazes with me, she marveled, "I didn't think you were paying attention."

"I'm a quick study." My eyes fell to the crushed, broken wrist, and my heart fluttered. "Can you even heal that without..."

"Forget about me." She gave a nervous laugh. "Your priest has been watching us all night."

Blood. That craving was... Trying to question what I had brought upon myself chasing after my brother's shadow, I looked to where every part of me had been gravitating toward. John leaned against a tree with arms crossed. At some point, he had retrieved my things and folded them at his feet. Birds were beginning to sing and fly across the sky as the heat of the morning sun melted icicles that rained down on us.

"Do we have a deal?" John's voice was aimed at Red Wine.

"He will need to heal before we go," she warned. "He will need to heal often every night we camp; can you endure feeding a monster, priest?"

"Are you going to teach him to be Ashton or not?" *There it was. The stubborn need to hear the exact words from the person that it matters most from.* "Answer me."

"Yes," she hissed, pushing a bone into place in her wrist. "But it's going to take its toll on me, you, and especially him. It's going to compromise my ability to protect you all."

"I'll do what is needed then." He grabbed up my things and marched up to me, scoffing. "You're both a mess. I just pray Fallen Arbor will get as rattled when he reminds them of Ashton."

Scowling, she warned, "No one should be able to draw blood easily on him if he can master his style. Use that sense of survival in every fight. He fought like an animal, Dante. I endured the training and failed many times over what you did in a mere few hours. I can only train you so far because I never mastered his style. No one could master or duplicate it."

Their words didn't matter. I gripped the front of John's coat and pulled him to me. Kissing him deeply, I drew the blood I thought endlessly about during the barrage of suffering. *My blood.* My body ran hot as he pushed hard against my own lips before breaking it. *Only mine.*

"I'm sorry," he muttered. "This is all I can do..."

"Me too..." I whispered, kissing him deeply, hungry for blood, hungry for him, hungry to feel complete again.

This isn't what I wanted our love to be, but it'll have to get us through this if I'm to find a way to protect him. We both know the price, and we both are willing to pay it...

CHAPTER 9

Assassin Trade Secrets

Not another word was exchanged between the three of us for some time. I had gone to the stables, prepping the horses, and walked them to the front of the inn. Never had I been so desperate to wear my mask as I did in this moment. My wounds gone, John's blood still haunting my tongue, the agony in Red Wine's eyes told me volumes of her own personal sacrifices. We were doing something so dangerous, it seemed we had given our very souls over to an unknown darkness.

I can't let it bother me. Shifting in Basque's saddle, I couldn't shake the tension my muscles felt. *I've taken a beating, but last night... It's left my body strung tight. I feel as if I must relearn to use my own arms and legs.* Another wiggle and I changed my posture completely, at last feeling as if my body would allow me to sit still.

"That's better," Red Wine commended me, and I sighed. "I imagine your body is restless, but that stance is designed to not let you fall, and it will change how you carry your body. You sit in the saddle like he does now."

"I feel like a visitor to my own flesh," I protested.

"You did insist becoming him," she disputed.

Her words bit at me, and I wanted to know more. "How thirsty was Ashton as a bloodeater?"

Biscuit stopped, halting due to her body language.

Swallowing, I spun Basque and asked again, "He was a bloodeater, wasn't he?" *Why is my gut twisting? But I need to know. Do I even want to know...?*

"That's just it." Her eyes were fierce under the mask, and she spoke with certainty. "I never once saw him feed."

"I don't understand..."

"Frank once told me he had only fed on one person... and after they passed..." She stumbled on her words. "But that was long before I was even born, so I can't say. All I do know is he grew weaker by the day because of that... and..." She touched her mask, her voice barely audible.

"Don't blame yourself." My words caused her to jerk her hand away, and I moved Basque forward again, leaving the conversation there. *I've caused her enough pain as it is.*

"W-wait." Her horse danced on its hooves and caught up. "What right do you have to forgive me on his behalf?" she spat.

I stiffened. "That wasn't what I meant." Basque halted, and she spun Biscuit around. I spoke with authority, "He could have easily made the choice to abandon you. Let fate take its course. You can't be mad at a choice someone else made, even if it cost them their life."

Basque tried to go around, but she backed Biscuit in the way. "You sound so much like him in this moment..." I flinched at her words. "It makes me nauseous."

With that, Red Wine turned and trotted to catch up to the front of the group. *Why do I feel some pride in putting her in the corner enough to confess that?*

Valiente had taken point as they strolled down the road. They had passed some loggers and a few travelers on foot, but nothing out of the ordinary for the region. Red Wine had stayed silent for hours. In the middle, John and Sonja spoke of The Church and her stay in Glensdale. During winter, she had assisted John with the church while I had been forced to be briefed on royal matters and anything that could be of use for bargaining peace with King Regius. *Remember, you're now the Crown Blood Prince of The House, Dante.* Goosebumps rolled over me at the memory of my father's warning. *But should you ever decide you must take up this birthright, I want you to be well-versed in what I have done to prepare our nation for your reign.*

A curious smell drifted on the wind, and I began searching the woods to my right. Scanning the trees, I looked for the only thing I could describe as a jasmine-laden individual. We had travelled for a while, the smell following and changing distance on occasion as if gauging the idea of approach. When a few travelers showed up on the bend, it disappeared completely, but soon after reappeared. At last, I rode up to Red Wine, who seemed unphased by my approach.

"I smell jasmine," I announced. "But it's the wrong season."

"Yes, you're absolutely right, Ashton," she drawled. "Keep as you are."

"What does that mean?" I ignored the condescending attitude.

"It's an informant, but I am waiting for a more natural opening for us to meet." She shifted in her saddle. "This is something we've done for a long time that's worked in our favor as bloodeaters. Granted, our guild has roots in flowers and herbs being founded by apothecaries, but I am glad to hear you have a nose for it."

"Is it always jasmine in winter?"

"It'll either be something that shouldn't be blooming in the season or all wrong for the location," she offered in short.

"Is there ever a smell that means something other than someone is delivering a message?"

She stiffened in her saddle. "Yes, but I've only experienced that once."

I waited for the answer, but none ever came. "Well, what is it?"

Looking to him, she brought her horse to a stop. "Honeysuckle."

"Honeysuckle?" I furrowed my brow. "What kind of flower is that?"

"A wonderous smell from a special garden in Prevera. Only place I have ever seen it, though they say it's from a completely different continent." She snorted before finally saying, "You smell that flower, you run for your life because Fallen Arbor is upon you. Trust me—you will know it and never forget it."

The sun had rose to late noon and Valiente paused, turning to the group. "Take a break? Eat something?"

We all nodded, but Red Wine nudged me, and we left them and the horses behind. I followed her through the trees. The road faded from view before we hit a small clearing. We had only stood there for a minute before a familiar mask appeared and kneeled before us. *Ale from the time with Madame Plasket in the guild lair.*

"Master, the bridge isn't safe. Fallen Arbor has been spotted there," warned Ale.

"We can handle their henchmen," retorted Red Wine.

"It's Landon," countered Ale.

The silence and shift in Red Wine made my gut twist. *Was it Landon of the Fallen Arbor that put the scar there? Or has something to do with Ashton going missing? Shit, I didn't even tell her he was there at the stables that night.*

"And they say he's been injured," he offered.

"That man? Injured?" Red Wine snorted, and at last, pressed on, "What kind of injury?"

"His right hand and arm we suspect. He's been keeping it gloved since he reappeared at the bridge camp," he reported.

"And where did he go in that span of time?"

"We lost him, but he went north before we lost him. Mead said there were two more with him when she last had their tracks." He spoke in an apologetic manner as if this was unacceptable to even be reporting to her.

"It can't be helped. Landon is smart and quick-witted."

"The right hand—it should be missing a finger and a scar on the wrist," I offered, and the two assassins spun to look at me. "Henchman in tripoint hats, all black. Landon wears a bowler hat and a rapier masked as a cane, yes?"

68

Red Wine gripped the front of my shirt and coat, growling as she spoke, "How do you know this? Have you been working with Landon this whole time?"

Inhaling deeply, I could sense the fear in her shaking hands pressing against me. "He's the one who jumped me in the stables."

She released me and began pacing. "I take it all back."

"Take what back?" I asked, baffled at the reaction.

"Ashton would've taken the same beating if Landon was leading the team that jumped you." She sounded thoroughly impressed as she continued with her assessment. "You should have been captured, and I would have been none the wiser. Exactly how did you manage to land an attack on him?"

Swallowing, I crossed my arms. "A move Lord Knight Paul taught me. I was pinned, but the henchman was scrambling to reset, and he pulled the rapier. I wasn't going to be able to avoid the strike, but I could roll down the blade. Took forever to stitch the slices in my coat, but I aimed for his shoulder, and he took the hit. What he didn't see was it was intended to distract from the other attack to disarm him. Sadly, the henchman had a shit blade, or he'd be missing more fingers or even his hand."

"He can't be serious? A fledgling assassin able to land a strike on Fallen Arbor's main operative?" Ale marveled, rising to his feet in disbelief.

"We might have a chance," muttered Red Wine. "We actually might be able to pull this off then. Thank you, Paul, you are a fucking wonderful human being. You really weren't joking about it all. *Teach me the bloodeater way anyway.* He'd nag me for hours asking that. It did pay off in a way I never imagined..." She spun to Ale, shaking his shoulders. "We're going to rattle the cage. Tell Madame Plasket and King Traibon I'm sorry, but we can't miss this chance. We might find Ashton if this works out... or at least, what happened to him."

"Okay..." Ale looked between us, confused. "And by rattle the cage, you plan on doing what exactly?"

"Spread the word that Ashton is back," she announced, pointing to me. "He'll play the part. He looks like him, and after hearing this and his training last night, we have a chance at turning the tide against Fallen Arbor. We need Landon to question that it wasn't little brother last night, but Ashton himself back for revenge. Really fuck with their heads on this. My informant made it clear they are looking for Ashton just the same as we are, even now. Frank said Fallen Arbor will be forever looking over their shoulders thanks to what they did, but... we can do this."

"R-right," Ale sounded uneasy, his voice shaking. "Do you really think they are going to be convinced he's Ashton?"

"That's our problem," I declared. "Red Wine is responsible for helping me play the part. I can learn to fight and act like him. We are fortunate my father's genes are strong and his sons could pass for twins."

Ale nodded. "So spread the word, which is?"

"Ashton aims to expel Fallen Arbor from Grandmere," announced Red Wine.

"That's a tall order." Ale rubbed the back of his neck, pondering on it. "How about we first start with *Ashton is back* and add the rest like a slow drip to unnerve them and keep them guessing? I don't think declaring full out war this fast is going to give you the time to train our beloved Blood Prince to take on big bro's role."

"He's got a point." With a deep breath, I added, "And this is a complete flip from moments ago when you gave me shit for..."

"Hush," she spat. "Fine, let's start with the first part. Let's see how Landon reacts. In the meantime, we can't cross the bridge. Any word if it's safe to launch a boat from the Sullen Lake mill?"

"It's still too iced up," answered Ale as he took a pocket watch out and flicked it in the sunlight a few times. "But the brackish Willow Waters seems to be clear. I advise taking the long route all the way through the Farmlis Woods and go south to Leifseid to take the road leading to the west entrance into Captiva City. As we know, no Fallen Arbor have been reported there."

"W-wait." I unfolded my arms in alarm, fussing, "But doesn't that take us through the thick of the current battlelines?"

"It does," confessed Ale as a raven landed on his arm. "But it'll work as cover if you are going through with this... unorthodox plan." He stared at Red Wine, and repeated, "*Ashton is back.* And are we doing this as a silent operation, Master?"

She slid her mask off as if this signified how confident the order had become. "We are spreading the word, but you and I will be the only ones aware that it's really Dante. Agreed?"

He pounded his chest and took his mask off. "On my personal identity, I swear by this." He turned and bowed deep with the raven fussing at shifting his balance. "I am honored to know our princes have been such brave individuals. May you fight well and live long, Prince Dante."

The young man rose, and I realized who he was. "The carpenter's son."

He smiled, a sense of pride filling him. "If you were wondering why I wasn't always around to assist my father, you have the answer before you."

Laughing, I jested, "Is half of Glensdale working for the guild these days?"

He winked. "Perhaps we are, Prince. For the sake of protecting Grandmere more so than providing for the Civil War. Most of us would rather not end up as Falco's soldier, but I suppose you freed us all from that fate."

Nodding, I couldn't argue with the thought. "It is why I took the Fanged Lady so long ago."

We waited as Ale replaced his mask, and Red Wine scrawled words on a tiny stripe of paper. It was rolled tightly, tied with care, and off the raven went. Ale disappeared, and the march back to the others was silent. There wasn't much to say. We had put the plan in motion and now on a grand scale. The question was, as the raven flies, *will Landon really believe he faced my brother in the stables?*

John shifted, gnawing on a chunk of bread. "Where did you two disappear to?"

"Training," answered Red Wine, snatching his bread from his hands as she walked past, eating the rest.

"Hopefully not like last night," he rebutted.

"We can't use the bridge," I announced. "Fallen Arbor is waiting there for us. So, we're going to head for Leifseid."

"Shit, that's going to add a week to getting there." Valiente took a swig of his water. "But I'd rather not face them. I have to get her back at all costs, and a few days travel is a safer bet."

"Agreed."

I thought they'd fight me more, but something tells me Valiente might have crossed swords with them at some point.

C H A P T E R 10

As the Raven Flies

By the time we reached the shores of Willow Waters, the sun had set, casting the land in a golden tone before fading to a dark purple. Resorting to traveling by lantern light was dangerous, but we weren't safe on the road now that we drew closer to where Fallen Arbor might be looking for us. *We started off so carefree, but the reality of the dangers has struck a chord with all of us.* Once at the shoreline, we followed it north for a while until we came upon a boat. Red Wine checked inside, flipping the burlap tarp up and seeming happy with her findings. I could only assume this was intentional, even prepped for us by Ale and Mead before they even reached out to us. *Being part of the Guild has been quite the blessing on this journey already. How many more times will we need to rely on them to get where we're going in order to stay safe?*

"We'll camp here for the night." Red Wine spun and began unpacking saddlebags and unbuckling the saddle from Biscuit. "The horses will have to swim across, so we'll have to get a campfire going on the other side and let them dry off and warm back up. It'll be a two-day delay doing it this way, but it should break our trail for anyone tracking us and give me time to train Dante."

"Sounds like you've had to use this tactic a few times." Valiente wasted no time echoing her tasks, goading everyone to do the same. "Should we do the horses in phases?"

"A few times more than I care to confess, but yes. Let's do them one at a time during the day tomorrow in hopes of keeping the smoke and flames small." She started piling her things off to the side, and we dropped our own alongside them.

No one complained as we carried out the chore in silence. The only stare that stung was the one coming from John. He knew what *training* implied, but we had come to this arrangement together, knowing the cost. Valiente set out to prep the camp, and John rushed to help. *He's trying to keep his mind off our burden, but I can't let our emotions get in the way of our goal, can I?* I unsaddled Basque, tossing the heavy saddlebags at John's feet, and we paused. Our eyes locked, and something strange washed over me, a connection as if my heart fluttered with his own for a moment. I turned away, confused. It wasn't abnormal, but there was a new, feral need building that I couldn't put to words or even emotions to identify what I had felt in that fleeting glance.

Dammit it all. Something's shaking loose, deepening my love to something... terrifying. How far will I break myself, and can I really hide it from him? Or could it be he sees it, sees through me like he's been able to do from the very beginning?

Basque started to follow us in the woods, and I turned, commanding, "No, you stay here in camp with John."

The Nivernais seemed insulted, ears flicking back as he snorted.

"Go on." I pointed, and he turned away.

"Ornery, are we?" Red Wine scoffed. "Like his owners."

I huffed, unwilling to add anything else to the conversation. We found a clearing, and I repeated the motion, kicking off boots and pulling off my shirt and coat. Without instruction, I got into the pose and waited. She circled and I stared down at her from where I squatted, waiting for the barrage of attacks. Rubbing her wrist, she seemed to be scrutinizing my pose deeper, more thoughtful now. A tap here and there, she adjusted it ever so gradually. My muscles didn't burn nor ache like they had done the night before, and she registered the confusion building on my face.

"He once told me that after you imprint this first pose, it makes the rest easier," she offered.

"It's a little unnerving to be honest. I haven't felt... myself physically all day," I confessed.

"Can I ask you something?" Her voice softened as she rubbed her wrist again. "Rumor has it you only drink from the priest."

"What of it?" I took a deep breath, the stance bringing a calm despite knowing how it all unfolded last time. *The downside is the Guild is quick to notice every little detail.*

"Well, did you change because of the Fanged Lady or was it your willingness to devote everything to being John's guardian and protector?" She unbuckled her gauntlet, her wrist still discolored. It must be aching in the icy temperatures. "Because I'm about to reveal a secret that only three people know including me, your brother, and of course, Frank."

I furrowed my brow, heart racing as my anxiety rose. "I don't understand. You can only become a bloodeater by using the Fanged Lady," I corrected. "And if you can survive a week of no blood, you can break the spell and become immortal like... wait, Frank the Immortal?"

Red Wine reached down and found a clump of snow and pressed it under her. "Yeah, that Frank. They are a Fanged Lady bloodeater, but Ashton wasn't, and I suspect neither are you. Now, that doesn't mean getting stabbed by her or taking in the curse doesn't have any effect. Ashton disappeared many times after being bitten, and we thought him dead after Viceroy Vendecci thought it cute to stab him in the chest with her. Even Ashton wasn't immune to the Madness, but he could overcome it with time."

My muscles tightened, itching to move, and I ignored it. "Are you saying I became a bloodeater on my own accord?" *I didn't want this, but I can't reveal that. John knows that, and it was John who made me.* "But if that were possible, more of us would exist."

"It's just a theory." She leaned on a tree, icing her wrist. "Ashton once said something. It was about where we came from, the old legends. You know them? Or were those not part of your studies either?"

"I know them," I snorted, the forest growing silent as the temperature dropped further. "The ones that say our ancestors travelled with Grandmere or the Great Grandmother of our people were the ones I favored as a child. After crossing the Hidden Swells, they came to this land and found humans struggling to tame the land. It was here we earned our title of daemonis and daemons, those who serve as guardians. But that didn't last long. We ended up in this Civil War, but even that comes with two versions: how it was written and how Fallen Arbor orchestrated it."

"You're a quick study." She lit the lantern and squatted close to the light, inspecting her wrist again.

"Why haven't you healed?" I kept fighting the urge to drop my chin. "Do you need to feed?"

Shaking her head no in reply, she pulled out a familiar salve, rubbing it on her injury. "I don't heal as fast as others, but that's because I don't feed. Too scared to try to be honest." She half-laughed. "But you—you have the priest. And like Ashton, you will get stronger after each feeding because you've become his sworn guardian. All we can assume is it's an ancient blood pact. I think Ashton went on pure speculation and took a chance of dying for all the right reasons, and that's how he became practically a war god incarnate."

"You leave me with more questions than answers every time we speak about him." Mulling over her words, I circled back. "What do you mean you've never fed?"

"I've never fed," she confessed once more.

"But you're a bloodeater," I offered.

"Of the purest kind, so they say." She shrugged, closing the salve. "I was born by the normal means and between two bloodeaters, but from childhood, I showed the same abilities as my parents. Normally two bloodeaters just have a normal daemonis child who later in life becomes one through the Fanged Lady.

76

Needless to say, the tipping point for the Traibons and Vendeccis was when I would be sold to a competing lord for breeding stock. I was something stronger, which meant to serve as a trump card in the gladiator games."

"So, let me get this timeline straight." I cleared my throat and started again. "You're older or younger than my sister Lillian?"

"Older." A hiss escaped her as she buckled the gauntlet back over her wrist. "And no idea if there were any others like me. I was just born when the Civil War started. Granted, on the Old Continent, there's a race stronger than us. Not sure why Fallen Arbor is so invested in dissecting us to satisfy power they already have."

"No one talks about the Old Continent or even comes back from there alive. Even the ship traders have to meet merchants on islands because the laws are so strict and secretive." I watched as she walked over and placed the lamp at my feet. "Are you saying you know what's happened on the Old Continent?"

"You can say I was there for a short time—against my will. You shouldn't believe everything about how things are. There's a lot more trading and illegal activities unfolding on the seas than what is revealed to commonfolk." Spinning around, she marched back to the tree, and she leaned on it once more. "It seems Fallen Arbor is the tyrant and single ruling body over there besides the Ogre Clan that still stands in their way. Granted, Warlord Sebastian helped Ashton smuggle me out, but Fallen Arbor used civil war and implemented the rigged gladiator system as ways to manipulate the others until they had full control. It was after that when we made it back to Grandmere and discovered The Court had been driven back. That's when Ashton went for a head hunt for Fallen Arbor. I believe that's the battle where your sister went missing, no?"

"Wait, so Fallen Arbor does have plans to—"

A whistling hit my ears, and I dropped the claymore to shield myself. An arrow shattered against the flat of the blade, and Red Wine clapped. Another two—no, three were coming. I spun, clipping two and dodging the other as I dropped to a knee. The third came from a completely different position. *There's more than one attacker, but why is she clapping?* Annoyed, I scanned the woods, looking for movement or light. Another arrow caught my focus, and I blocked. Squatting, I killed the fire in the lantern at my feet. *That had to be a signal to start.* An arrow hit my shoulder but didn't travel through all the way. Cursing, I stood and dropped to the starting position again, giving her a bewildered expression. *This stance makes it flexible, but some forewarning would have been helpful!*

"I'm sorry. I told some friends to help tonight since my wrist is still in poor shape. Said Ashton was feeling rusty on his reflexes." She shrugged, chuckling. "And I might have told the gang they get a gold coin for every arrow that hits."

Another arrow whizzed past as I leaned out of the way. "You've got to be kidding me."

A flurry of arrows erupted from multiple directions. I swung, one clipping my shoulder; another lodged through my shin. I reset the stance. *There's not enough time to pull them all out.* Adrenaline kicked in, and I roared with frustration. I could hear them, smell them from where I stood in the small clearing. From so far away, I could hear their breathing and hearts beating. My body itched in a way I'd imagine a wolf would wanting to give chase to unaware deer. Without warning, I surprised myself as I launched forward to go on the offense.

Ale. We met, I know his scent and he's... I shifted my direction, confident that I ran in line with trees in a way he couldn't see me. Taking a hard left, I slid in the mud around the trunk of a large pine. An arrow skimmed my cheek and ripped a notch into my ear. I had managed to grab his bow in the moment, sending it flying before he could register what attacked him. With a squeeze of my fist, the bow snapped into two pieces.

"D-Dante, don't..." Ale shrieked. "Don't kill me!"

"Why would I kill you?" I jerked the quiver from him and tossed it into the trees. "No more of these. They hurt."

"R-right," he agreed, the smell of fear wafting from him. "I thought a damn bear or cougar had pounced me." He sunk to

78

the ground, rubbing his chest. "You were in the clearing and then… gone. I thought maybe I could hear you and guess but… you moved so damn fast for a man built like an ox."

The throng of a released bow vibrated in my ears. I caught an arrow midair. *Mead? She's been with Ale. That makes this easier…* I ran back through the clearing and paused, getting my bearings once more. *If this was the initial aim…* Red Wine took a sip from her canteen as if unaware of the battles unfolding in the forest around her. The wind shifted, and I blocked two more arrows with my claymore. *Sweat, footsteps, fear.* Between trees, I saw movement, and I launched toward it. I could tell from the broken sticks I was closing in fast. *Tree sap to my right.* I swung. *Shit, the tree…*

I blinked at the blade slicing through, my muscles burning with excitement. A yelp came from overhead, her footing failing her as the pine buckled and began to fall. She let the arrow fly, and it cut open my thigh. I abandoned the claymore and shouldered the falling trunk. The tree twisted and shook her down in the other direction from where it fell, keeping her from harm's way. Panting, puffs of steam rolled from my lips as I stared at where she lay, shocked. My legs shook, the adrenaline waning, and I sank to the ground. *I feel like an animal.* Wincing, I pulled the arrow from my back. *When did she hit me with that? When I went for Ale?* The wound closed faster than expected as I came to my senses.

"That's never happened to me before," announced the assassin lying flat on her back.

"Which part?" Glancing at the tree, the cut through the elder pine sent a shudder through me. *All those years on the farm I tried to do that with nothing but my hands being jarred until numb. I even tried over winter, but… what changed? What did Red Wine shake loose last night? And should I be scared to follow Ashton's footsteps beyond this?*

"I've never had someone cut the tree out from under me." She sat up, picking me apart. "How did you find me so fast, Prince Ashton?"

Prince Ashton? Shit, that's right. That's my name now, isn't it? Clearing my throat, I decided to speak normally. *Not like anyone in this century ever heard him talk.* "You ever seen a Willow hound trail game?"

"Y-yeah?" She crossed her arms. "But I'm no deer. And we've never met, so as a bloodeater from that distance, there's no way..."

"Oh, I could smell that sweat you broke out in when I caught Ale." She flinched, and I smirked. "And thanks to you two having some fun before coming this way, I could smell him on you."

She fell back, groaning. "I can't believe you could... don't you tell a soul!"

I laughed, but it was short-lived when I heard John's voice calling me. "Dante!"

"When a priest calls your name like that, you can't exactly disobey," I muttered, rising to my feet. "Granted, felling a tree shook everyone, I imagine. I meant to shake the trunk, not cut it down. My apologies... Mead?" I guessed.

She jumped to her feet, excited as she confirmed, "That's me. Your personal rogue and archer extraordinaire." Bowing deeply, she was even tinier than Red Wine in stature, light on her feet considering how fast and far she had climbed the tree. "You owe me three."

"Three?" We were walking back, and I bellowed, "We're fine! Coming your way!"

"Three gold," she demanded, flicking her fingers as she skipped up next to me. "For the three arrow strikes that landed and stuck. I think Ale only got one, but I don't think Red Wine will even count that one." She tapped my ear. "Still blood there I see."

"Here's six," I scoffed, digging them out of a pocket. "And five more coins for a new bow."

"New bow?" She took the gold, curious now.

"For Ale. I broke it in the heat of the moment. Thank you for allowing me to... warm up." A chill rolled over me. *John should be busting through right about...*

"Dante!" John stumbled to a stop, almost slamming into me. "What the hell happened?" He picked me apart, confused as he spoke slower. "I thought... with all the blood..." He wiped my shoulder, then the ear. "You're healed?"

Blood. Oh, how I want his blood and the warmth it brings me...

CHAPTER 11

The Priest's Barrière de Force

Mead had disappeared, leaving John and me standing in the dark staring at one another as if it were the first time all over again. Snow began to fall. The hushed tapping all around muted our hearts beating in a futile race against one another. *Blood.* My fangs itched. The terrible thought boiled up, and I covered my mouth to hide the monstrous canines I had grown weary of in the mirror. John's hand glided over me, chasing blood stains, and finding them hiding nothing or hints of how they appeared. With each discovery, his brow knitted further. I endured this confusing mixture of want made of *lust and hunger* as I indulged in the heat of his hands against my body.

At last, his blue gaze snaked back to mine and flinched. Guilt had to be written loudly in my expression. *Damn you for reading me like a book, John.* They dropped to where my hand covered my mouth. I didn't shake, I didn't recoil, and I couldn't bring myself to run away. *I'm tired of running away from this, even now that I want it more than ever.* He heaved a hard sigh, looking around before looking back to me.

"Are they all gone? Far away enough for us..." He struggled to find the words.

"They can't smell or hear us from here," I offered, hand muffling my voice, and averted my gaze.

"In that case, let's get this over with." Looking back, John tugged the white collar free and began unbuttoning his coat and shirt. "You're starving, right?"

My heart sank. "John... I can't..." *You foolish man, what is it have you been discussing with Red Wine?*

"Be fast. It's cold." His shirt opened, pulling it to expose a shoulder, his chest and neck glowing in the moonlight. "I'm not a fan of the cold these days."

"John, I'll be fine." Turning away from him, my blood rushed at the sight. *It wasn't like this back in the bathhouse. Has my training really changed me in only two nights?* "You saw I healed. I don't need... that."

"Don't think I haven't noticed," his voice cut through me.

I tensed. *That tone. He's pissed. No, it's the same way he spoke to me at the boulder. He's hurt.* Inhaling, every part of me turned to face him. *I can't afford to repeat the silence from that time.* I dropped my hands. He failed to hide the wince but recovered faster than expected. John swallowed, unmoving pulling his shirt open farther to reclaim his standing. As I rubbed my tongue against a fang, my shoulders shuddered at the urge to dig my canines into him. Still, *I better look him in the eye.*

"Noticed what?" Anger seeped forward, and I marched up on him, planting a palm on the tree he leaned against. "The fangs? Rapid healing? Maybe I'm faster? Or the fact I'm—"

"Hungry and haven't eaten anything." His words slammed into me, *something I hadn't noticed.* "I haven't seen you eat anything for..." Shaking his head in thought, he looked up searching for exactly how long. "That night between us over a month ago?"

Every nerve tightened. "I... didn't notice..." Knots twisted in my gut, searching back. *When did I lose the need to eat? I get exhausted, I get thirsty, then there's the moments of...* "John. I..."

He laughed, cupping my face with his hands. "You're hopeless, my love. This whole time you didn't even notice, did you?"

My lips closed tight with contempt, shame filling me. "I was trying to avoid it... avoid you..."

He forced my lip up, fascinated by the fangs. "You always had a set, but tonight, they seem... longer and unwilling to retreat."

Pushing his hand away, I let my eyes fall to his neck. "As tempting as this spot..." I caressed the skin with my fingers, the pulse pounding and calling to me. "It'll be an obvious place if they choose to check."

"And where do you prefer to eat from, *Barrière de Force?*" The title brought my gaze back to his eyes. "I did this to you, and I will pay the price."

The guilt in his voice was one I shared in my own as I confessed, "I didn't want this to be the price." In the distance, a wolf howled, long and sorrowful. "I feel like an animal who craves... you." I licked the salty tang of John's neck, temptation rattling through me. "And only you."

"I know..." breathed John, his heart beating like the drumming of a bird's wings. "And I'm a greedy bastard and love the idea of it."

Another lick and the excitement washed away the last bit of fear that he had been fighting back. *Never have I tasted something so intoxicating as you.*

He pulled me closer into him, his body shivering against my own and gruffed, "Honestly, I'd get too jealous and might kill a man if you did this with anyone other than me."

"Priest shouldn't kill people." I smirked, letting my hand wander into his open shirt.

"Well, I've always heard that it's wise to choose a *Barrière de Force* who is willing to put their life in harm's way for you." The scent of his arousal hit me, and I licked his neck again to goad it on. *So hungry.* "But what I didn't anticipate is I'd be still paying for it with my blood."

"I would die for you," I whispered in his ear. "But may you forgive me for the sins I commit."

My will broke. Fangs dug into his shoulder and regret slammed into me. *Fuck, he'll be sore, but it's at least not as obvious as his actual neck.* The way his skin popped as the fangs pushed through excited me. A rush of sweet heat filled me. I pinned him between me and the tree, and he moaned. *Pleasure and pain.* It only provoked me to keep drinking, my own heart beating to catch up to his. I drew it slow, fighting the urges to take greedier gulps. When I thought to pull away, he pulled me back, his shivering ceasing against the heat of my body. Another sip and I released at last.

Compared to the other night, he feels so fragile like this… Breaking our embrace, I searched his face. Part of me wished he would see me as the monster, but instead, he kissed me. Deepening it, he reminded me we had only made decisions for the sake of one another. *We're in this together, for better or worse.* The kiss ended, everything at my core settling for the first time since the first night I had been like an animal to him. He reached up to his shoulder, and I scowled.

"Don't make that face," he demanded. "The kiss works for most cases, right?"

I blinked, "Y-yeah."

"Look, Red Wine pointed out that I'd have to keep you going during the training. Granted, I didn't think you'd hold up this long or heal that fast." Swallowing, holding his shoulder still, John pushed me away. "But don't ever avoid me if you're feeling… hungry? Need me? Whatever that look you give me from across the room that makes me feel like a filet."

"Is it that bad?" I gaped.

"Dammit, the shoulder is a terrible place," he flustered. "We need to find a gentler place. I don't think my neck or…" His face flushed. "Didn't you bite me on the thigh once?"

"The thigh?" A chuckle escaped me as I approached, buttoning up his shirt. "Is that a request, my priest? Or were we having filthy thoughts about our prince again?"

John's eyes darted away, scrambling to check his pockets, and he produced the white collar. "I'm the priest. I confess nothing."

"Let's get back before they think we came out here to…" The heat in my cheeks rose as a mischievous expression crossed his face. "John, you didn't…"

"Wanted to give you no interruptions to eat so…" He shrugged before pulling on his coat. "Come on. Let's get some sleep."

Snorting only made streams of steam to roll from my nose like a tea kettle whistling. I grabbed up the claymore and followed him, grabbing his sleeve on occasion to redirect him. By the time we were back in camp, I had to throw some more logs on the fire. Red Wine sat awake and on duty. She frowned as the fire grew larger, and I nodded toward the shivering knight and princess. *She's a lot like me, forgets we can handle colder temperatures. Granted, she might be worried we will draw attention, but Landon would need more time to heal. With the news travelling fast about Ashton being back, I wonder what kind of chaos will be unfolding everywhere.*

John unrolled his bedroll and motioned for me to share. Red Wine tilted her head, the mask hiding the expression I imagined consisted of a smirk and raised eyebrows. I pulled on my own shirt and coat first, and she giggled as I relented. Laying outstretched on my back, John backed into me and in minutes passed out.

"How much did you eat?" She removed the mask at last, addressing me as she gave John a pitiful expression.

"Not enough for that," I reassured. "The man falls asleep anywhere, even sitting upright on the wagon." I nodded to Basque who flicked an ear in reply.

"Such children at heart, the both of you." She slid the mask back on. "So, is it true?"

"What is true?" I tensed at the obscureness of the question.

"That you two are indeed lovers." She leaned forward on her knees, speaking with a cautious tone. "And you've lost the need to eat anything except for…" Her chin pointed to John.

"It seems to be that way," I admitted, my chest stinging with the weight of the fact. "I hadn't noticed, but he had."

"I take it back."

"Take what back?" I pressed.

"You're more like Ashton than I realized," she agonized. "But what will you do when you outlive him?"

"Bury him under the cherry tree next to the man you loved, I suppose," I whispered, and she tensed. "He told me stories about you, but... I'm sorry."

"He fucking hated cherries," she scoffed, trying not to laugh.

"I know." And I remembered why I had done it.

The old man's words rattled me in a new understanding. *I only keep the cherry preserves for her. One day, she'll come back and want some more. I may not be here to see it, but I never want her to think I ever forgot what we had. John's like that. He doesn't move on. Too damn stubborn and maybe it's my fault or just in the blood, but... he won't let go, Dante. I'm warning you now in hopes you don't push him away like she did to me. That'll break someone's will if you shove too hard and never confess...*

"You liked them. He kept the preserves and made them fresh though he hated the damn things." She inhaled swiftly. "Not even when he struggled in the end did he forget you. Spoke about you more in that last year I had with him."

"You shouldn't talk about matters you weren't part of." She stood and began to march off. "You take watch."

Salty blood. That's why you got the mask. You cry and break when you are at your strongest. Let it flow. Let the red wine flow like blood...

A Mutual Understanding

Crossing the brackish waters had been miserable. The horses were shivering and the fire large as we worked fast to dry them. It had taken hours to get the large equines to stop shivering from their swim through the crossing with the boat. Red Wine had disappeared the moment she crossed, but her ability to scout ahead was invaluable. Biscuit had fussed, but her shivering would bring the tiny horse back to the warmth of the fire. As the sun fell, we managed to get all the gear across, the boat having to make a few crossings to move all the saddles and bodies. Regardless, I left to train in the woods once everyone had settled. She had appeared, watching as I held the stance for some time.

Pulling herself from the tree, she seemed more serious than the night before. "You need to learn the other stances. I expect you to practice them relentlessly."

"Of course," I muttered. "Are you kicking it into me, or am I mimicking you this first round?"

"Mimicking."

She only used a longsword she had taken from Valiente. *Wonder if she bothered to ask him?* Facing me, she dropped into the first familiar stance. I followed, hellbent on being her mirror. She went slowly, waiting for me to adjust my footing as we moved into the second stance. This one pushed me forward and tall, the blade thrusting forward. The next one was a wide slash and ending in a reflection of the first stance. After that was a sidestep, changing into a more defensive stance. Each new position seemed to fall back to the first stance. She sped up and began circling me like she had done the first night. She'd lunge with the longsword, and I'd block it.

"I'm trying to fix your stance," she insisted after the third block.

"Is it really that bad if I can still react and block?" I reset and narrowed my eyes at her.

"You can't keep it up and learn those moves without being in the right posture." She seemed miffed, and I smirked.

"Try to land a hit before sunup." I lifted an eyebrow at her, and she gave me a smug expression. "I'm betting that he taught you that, but his style is too reliant on fluid motion, and this works best for me."

"Bullshit," she sneered.

Red Wine launched a flurry of stabbing strikes. I pulled into the fourth stance, and the longsword went sailing. She held her wrist, her eyes glowing with rage. *Shit, she still hasn't healed.* I thunked the claymore into the ground and grabbed her arm. She allowed me to unbuckle it to expose the purple and red wrist still broken, healing horribly slowly. *Why won't she feed?*

"I know. I know what you're thinking but..." Swallowing, she shook her head, excuses flying from her lips. "I was born a bloo-deater. You're born daemonis, but I was different and..."

"You've been too afraid to feed." I couldn't judge her. *It terrifies me to think of John as lover and food.* "Is there a reason for the fear besides the unknown?"

"Unknown?" A huff escaped her. "I wish that was the case, but I said I've never met someone like me. Didn't say I didn't know how this works. There was someone on the Old Continent, and well, after one feeding, he lost all self-awareness."

"What about indirect blood?" *Perhaps Viceroy Falco at least taught me one interesting ability between daemonis and blood-eaters all have the ability for.*

"What do you mean?" She tried to retrieve her arm, but I refused her.

"It's probably the only thing Falco taught me that has any good use." I pulled her dagger and broke the flesh.

"Hey!" she hissed. "Are you mad?"

"Wait for it." I popped my thumb with my fang and ran my blood across her open wound.

"N-no..." she panicked, kicking, and pulling.

I let go, and she stumbled back. Glaring at her arm, she froze. Rubbing my thumb, I saw the cut was gone, and I waited to see if my speculation was correct. She held up her arm, bumping her fist. At last, she turned and punched a tree to assess the fortitude of her own flesh and bones.

"What was that?" Red Wine closed the gap and shoved my chest, and I threw up my hands. "What would possess you to think that was a solution for healing?"

"Look, Falco had some... questionable ways to express his love." She grimaced. "He enjoyed tearing me up in the heat of passion and slowly healing my wounds in this way. Once, he told me a story of how the daemonis always have a way to heal one another, and on the battlefield, it works in a pinch, but with the Madness, the art was abandoned."

She stared at her healed arm, amazed. "All these years, I never knew..."

"Glad I could teach you something for a change." I pulled the claymore from the ground and returned to my stance. "Besides, I broke it. It's my responsibility to make it right."

"I wonder if he knew about this, but the Madness..." She slipped the gauntlet on, buckling it. "I suppose now I can keep training you—just more efficiently now."

She closed the gap too fast, and a boot smashed into my face. *This hit!* My feet broke from the ground, and I slammed into the tree. The wind pressed out of me, yet I still managed to fall onto one knee with the help of the claymore. She stood at the ready with the longsword. Taking a deep breath, I rose to my feet. Falling into stance, it was my turn to charge forward. *Up until now I've been taking defense. Time to see what this does as offense.* Red Wine seemed faster, the swords lighting sparks in the night air. The clanging rung in my ears like metal wind chimes. *She wasn't this strong before. Is it my blood? Or was she sick and injured from... Winter's Perch? Frank ran her out so...*

We broke away, both panting. "Tell me—this whole time, you've been injured."

Steam rolled out from under the mask. "You only just realized that?"

"I take it Frank was to blame."

She ran hard to my left and kicked off a tree. The claymore blocked, my feet sliding in the mud and ice. I managed to switch my footing. She gasped, retreating. The swing had far more power, the force of wind it cast breaking snow from branches and making her stumble. A heat rose in my body, and I gave chase. She dipped and swung low. I launched to the air, spinning down on my descent to gouging the ground where she had been a moment before. *I have enough power and strength to close the gap in what I lack in agility. Even leap to the air despite my size and the weight of the weapon... was that your secret Ashton? Pure power in every move you took? Or is there something she doesn't even realize about what we are?* Launching forward, I wasn't going to give her time to think about outmaneuvering me anymore. *I need her in defensive measures to make her create an opening...*

The clack and scrape of daggers hit my ears, and I slid to a stop. The claymore rose before me as throwing knives hit against the blade. Gritting my fangs, I knew she was getting desperate. I cut to her left when she shifted to accommodate my mimicking her side attack, and I dashed behind the pine. *Her heart fluttered; she's waning. If this was a real enemy, I at least know I can cut through the tree for a surprise attack but for her...*

Needing to pivot, I gripped the trunk to help redirect my weight and shot back out the other side I had vanished from.

She caught me in her peripheral. *That flutter again. It's like doves taking flight...* Another low swing with her sword. Jamming the claymore deep in the ground, I blocked, jarring her arms. Abandoning my weapon, my hand swallowed her face. Her grip on the sword failing, I swept a leg behind her feet to ensure no footing would remain. A dagger aimed to swipe. *Too predictable. I heard her grip it.* My other fist closed on the wrist, *not too hard,* and I slammed her to the ground with enough force to make her mask fly off and squeeze the air from her lungs.

Blinking, she locked eyes with me. "What was that?"

"You said I needed to learn to abandon the claymore in battle," I offered, letting her go.

"Not that." Rolling to her feet, she began retracing the phases of the sparring grounds as if tracking our battle like small game. "You see this?"

I followed her pointing, retracing my moves. There were indentations from where I stepped. On a few trunks, slash marks that I hadn't physically placed there. She gripped my hand, pulling me behind the tree and planting my palm over— *claw marks.* I jerked it back, chasing my steps, remembering how it all felt.

"I just—I could..." The power of each step, each strike unnerving. "I've never seen anything like this."

"I have, though not to this caliber, Dante." I met her gaze as she took it all end. "I thought for a moment you were going to kill me, then I realized you were pulling your moves after the first strike that..." she pointed to the slashes in the trees, "left the marks from the sheer force of the swing. That's double the blade length. Wait, when did you feed last?"

Swallowing, I hesitated before admitting, "Well, that depends on your definition of feed."

"Stop being so childish." Lifting the longsword, I widened my eyes at the cracks and gouges. "When did you last truly feed? Wasn't it last night? Other times you've just been flirting with stolen sips... through your kisses, no?"

"How much do you know?" I fretted.

"Only what I have learned watching you two." She smiled to see me ruffled over the idea.

"Last night. It's only the third feeding ever." I looked over the claymore, not a dent or scratch. "Preveran blacksmithing is incredible."

"Three," she exasperated. "That can't be right."

"Last night. Once during our stay in the castle, a month ago—"

"A month ago? Dante, that can't be right. A bloodeater is lucky to go three days or longer, and you were turned at the start of winter."

"I've been trying my damnest to resist," I spat, insulted. "I love that man. He's everything I ever wanted to be and couldn't even be brave to do on my own. Not my fucking food."

Grabbing my shoulders, she shook me. "You're not normal, Dante. Frank can't last this long but Ashton... after he lost his source, he went centuries without. I don't know why or what makes your bloodline so special, but this is not par the course for a bloodeater. This isn't a change brought on by The Fanged Lady or the Madness."

"I know..." I muttered and sank to the ground. "I've been trying to find answers in the books for it. There's nothing there. I was hoping in The Church's Library I would have something old enough with hints of what is happening to me. See if I could get my hands on archaic materials from the Old Continent or written by the founding mothers of Grandmere."

"Who have you told about this?" Kneeling, she gave me a look of pity. "Who the hell knows about this?"

"You. You're the only one who knows." I pained over the confession. *Something is wrong. Why am I still changing beyond what makes me a bloodeater? Can I even stop this?* "They just assume I feed on him constantly, but..."

"Keep it hidden. Though, maybe Fallen Arbor... no, that's out of the question, too risky. Perhaps the archives in Prevera? Maybe even The Court or the Old Ones might know something." She was thinking out loud for the first time. Her heart raced in my ears. *She's frightened by this, too.* "Frank might know. They told me stories of a time when Ashton had been a monster, angry and indestructible so he could protect all that he loved... claws and fangs like a lion." I gave her a baffled expression, and she shrugged. "They loved telling me fairytales about themselves and Ashton, though Ashton frowned over it. But Ashton had lost that part of him when the reason to be that way... John."

"What about John?" Fear rose in my core. "Don't tell me he's some special candy for bloodeaters."

"No, that's not it, but..." Touching the scar on her face, she pondered in silence for a long time before offering, "maybe it's the spiritual connection or something more ancient."

Snorting, I rose to my feet. "Now who's telling the fairytales? Just let me know if you find any hints of what's happening, and I'll take to the books when I get to the city."

Why does my life keep taking these turns? And why do they come back to comparing me to a big brother I never knew existed other than hushed whispers and sour rumors? Fairy tales, indeed.

CHAPTER 13

Welcome to Leifseid

I t took us almost two days through the Farmlis Woods to reach Leifseid in the south. The forest had proved hard to navigate, the trees so large we had to take the horses around them until they could squeeze between the giant red columns. Regardless, my training with Red Wine continued as we both struggled to understand what my limitations were. My strength seemed ungodly in ways that would break lesser weapons. I had shattered Valiente's spare longsword, and it unnerved the Lord Knight when he speculated about how it could have happened. *It shouldn't happen at all...*

"I still can't figure out..." started Valiente, anger rising in his voice as we rode down the beaten path Red Wine had found.

"Here he goes again. I'm so sorry." Princess Sonja covered her face.

"... first, how this one stole a weapon literally off of me."

Red Wine ignored his rant once more. He had tried discussing the matter earlier in the day, but everyone had feigned too busy packing up camp to hear him out.

"Second, explain to me how you shatter a blade made for the king's personal royal guard."

"Preveran steel is far more superior," I repeated as rehearsed.

95

"But there's not a mark on that wall you call a sword." Valiente riled further, his voice growing louder with his growing list of complaints. "And worse, she put it back on me, and I would have been none-the-wiser if I hadn't been vigilant and aimed to clean my blade."

"If you were so diligent, why didn't you notice the night it had the notches and cracks put into it?" I asked, smirking. "Roughly four nights ago, I think?"

"You stole it on more than one occasion!" He shifted in the saddle to glare back at me, and Colonel whinnied his complaint at the sudden weight shift.

"Besides, I thought you discovered it..." John had that sparkle in his eyes.

Oh, here we go. He can't resist a chance to unravel someone.

"...when Sonja asked what all that jingling sound was when we started out this morning," he finished.

"That's right. I thought I heard a loose coin purse somewhere," agreed Sonja, giggling. "You insisted it was just armor clinking about. Not coming from your sheath as I had pointed out."

"How was I supposed to know it was my damn sword!" roared Valiente.

"Shame on you for not trusting in Mother Superior's words," tsked John.

"You owe me a new sword." He pointed back at me, and Colonel nodded his head.

"I didn't say I wouldn't replace it when the opportunity arose." I laughed, riding past him. "Does Leifseid have trustworthy smiths? Did you want to pick one, or am I buying whatever I deem worthy?"

Valiente trotted to ride parallel to me. "I'll let you pick. Then I get to brag the Blood Prince gifted it to me."

"Really, Valiente. That's going to be your reason?" Sonja scowled. "Extortion is an unsightly trait for a knight."

"Extortion!" he gaped.

"Now, now, Mother Superior..." John put on his best priestly tone, and I couldn't contain the smile growing on my face. "We must pray for him to rise above his shortcomings."

Valiente narrowed his eyes at the chuckling clergymen. "I hope you both burn in hell for being imposters."

I leaned in. "If I recall, they did do the training and studies, did they not? How far you have fallen to wish harm over the clergymen you have sworn to protect, Lord Knight Valiente."

"Not another word from you." He shoved me away. "Just replace the damn thing."

We made it around the bend, and there sat a wagon full of logs. The old man stood on the road, scratching his head with a frown for the wheel that had broken loose. His workhorse seemed just as old and worn out as he was, still hooked to the shaft of the wagon. John stopped and hopped off his horse without hesitation. The smile on his face was enough to make me pull on my reins. *This is the side of John I've been missing out on all this time. That desire to help any stranger, including a runaway prince sitting on a boulder in the dead of winter.* Basque's muscles twitched and he danced, excited to see a loaded wagon. Patting the side of his neck, I decided to join the conversation.

"Look Father, I don't think anyone can help me unless we unload the wagon. The great red pines here weigh a lot more than those shrubs you call trees in Captiva City." The tone of the old logger brought a smile to my face as nostalgia rolled through me. "My horse was struggling, and he didn't steer enough in time. It's my fault I overloaded it. Though I'd appreciate a ride into town to get help."

Squatting, I was pleased to see the wheel was intact. "Boxing slipped out?"

"Y-yeah." He seemed startled by my sudden appearance. "You're quiet for as big as you are, boy. Wait, isn't that a Guild mask?" He paled. "Look, I don't want any trouble..."

"Relax," John's cheerful tone and a firm grip on the logger's shoulder made him wince. "He's my personal guard, sir. Simply let us get you back up. We'll take you and the wagon into town. How about that?"

"I hate to spoil this for you, Father, but you do know they're traditionally all daemons. Your bodyguard." He knocked John's hand off his shoulder, insulted by my presence.

Ignoring the comment, I kept true to my aim and asked, "Do you have the boxing?"

"I always carry spares," he scoffed, insulted by the question. "What do you take me for? A yearling axe cutter?"

"No sir, just never know if you're out or lost them somewhere." I stood looking at the overloaded wagon and tuckered out horse. "I'll tell you what: my horse needs to burn off some energy." The old man glances at Basque where he danced and curled his lips at his own horse in anticipation. "Can he pull the load the rest of the way and give the old gelding a chance to recover?"

"Yeah, sure, soon as the wheel is on..." Rolling his eyes, the sarcasm in his voice did him no justice. "I suppose you have a means to solve that one, too. You gonna pray to the almighty spirits and saints to show up and fix it themselves, Father? Raise this wagon up with the biggest load of red pines, wet from spring?"

John smiled, snatching the boxing from him. "I'll put the wheel on myself." He shed his coat and collar and handed them to Mother Superior Sonja. "Hold these for me." Spinning back, he rolled up his sleeves and lifted the wheel up. "Da-Ashton, you sure about this?"

Inhaling deep, I took one more thorough look of the wagon's axles. "Well, it seems he got lucky thanks to the soft mud. Just a simple boxing slip. Axles are in good order." Standing, I gripped under the edge of the wagon and pulled just enough to make the load groan. "Unlatch the gelding, just in case the load shifts."

The old man scrambled over to the task, Valiente sliding off his own horse to assist. Basque had pranced close behind, nudging the knight to hook him up and snorting the gelding out of the way. I whistled and the horse went back into attention. *It seems we are both itching to burn off some energy. This is impossibly heavy, but I can't help but feel...*

"I can lift it for a short time if I put my legs and back into it." Looking over the load, I could see a spot on the side that would give John enough room for his task. "But I can't lift too high, or the load might roll and that would need a few more hands."

"Right." John avoided meeting my gaze and gave no rebuttal. "Everyone, step back."

Crouching, I leaned low against the wagon. It took a few tries to get my feet to find a place where they wouldn't slip in the mud. My arms strained behind me, fingers gripping the edge. I met John's gaze, and he wiggled the wheel as close as he could. The boxing hung from his mouth. He had found a wooden mallet and had it in hand as he turned the spokes to line up with the wedge. At last, I waited for his signal. He froze and, in a flash, a nod of his head was all I needed.

With a roar, I clenched my eyes tight and focused on the wagon's weight and my body. My feet threatened to slide until the wagon began to tilt behind me. A log shifted, and the muscles in my arms screamed with a fiery burn. I could hear the gasps of the onlookers but had no time to focus on who muttered what. Instead, my ears strained. The *scuff* signaled the wheel was slid into place and the *skid* of the boxing wedged at the joint was followed by tapping. Frantic, John broke in a sweat. *He's worried.* The mallet beat the boxing into place, fast and steady, matching the beat of my heart as adrenaline raced through me. My back ached, but the use of my muscles and stinging in my thighs and shins were a warm welcome from the training. *I miss this sort of simple labor... I miss us being simple...*

John backed away, speaking in a hushed manner so I could only hear, "Now, Dante, but slow, or the wheel will break from that height."

I opened my eyes. Cursing under my breath, I had lifted too high, but by some luck hadn't rolled the load off. *Dammit, this should have hurt more...* When the wagon settled down, I ignored the paling faces of the old man and my companions. Only Red Wine seemed unmoved, her heartbeat unchanged among the fluttering birds that pounded around us. Basque was more than willing to let me hook him to the shaft. He was almost too big for the buckles, tight and pulling on the last hole in the line.

John climbed on the wagon, grabbing up the reins as he commanded me, "Push in the back. Let's not make him lame for being eager to help."

I nodded. *Was that about Basque or me? He doesn't want to look at their faces either. We can't be doing things like this moving forward. It gives us away, but... could we really resist doing what makes us who we are? They would have tried to move logs with pulleys, but with limbs wet and iced up in places, someone could have gotten hurt or killed fixing this by normal means.*

With a grunt, I shouldered the wagon to make it pop up. Basque snorted and jerked the wagon the rest of the way onto the hard-packed road. The old man paled but didn't hesitate when John patted the seat and offered the reins back. The wagon trotted ahead with Red Wine and Princess Sonja close behind as I brushed mud from my hands and legs. Valiente lingered, his stare burning into me until at last, I sighed, offering to break the racing thoughts invading his mind.

"Go on: say it." I didn't look at him.

"Don't you think that's a little dangerous?" he grumbled as if to avoid any eavesdropping. "Lifting a wagon solo like that?"

"I know. I don't think a bloodeater could lift that much weight." I glanced to where the wagon had been stuck. "It was careless to not act like I needed the help."

"It's more than that." He circled Colonel in front of me, and his sharp stare hit me. "You're not alone on this path, Dante. Don't think you have to carry it all on your shoulders alone."

I winced, the words aiming for something deeper. "And yet, I find myself caught in the tangled web someone else left behind so long ago that half this continent doesn't remember why it was weaved in the first place."

Valiente rolled his eyes, speaking more sternly. "Look, just remember you're not fucking alone in this mission to go after Fallen Arbor." He pulled Colonel's reins, and I paced beside the old war horse. "And don't forget you owe me a sword."

100

"This again." I couldn't help but smirk, appreciative in the tactful change in conversation. "So, is this your mission or the King's?"

"Mine." He shuffled in the saddle, swallowing before confessing, "I have reason to believe Sonja's father might have made a deal with them. Or at the least is aiming to have her killed."

I frowned, the tension in my body made me roll my shoulder. "Does she know?"

"No."

"I see, and why did you think letting her come to Glensdale was an excellent idea, knowing where her father's allies and enemies lie?" My curiosity piqued. *How dangerous of a gamble did you make to visit John?* "Ah, it was safer to head north. We were cornered. Granted, they didn't know I knew they were waiting to ambush us."

"Fallen Arbor?" *Something isn't adding up.*

"The Berserk Brigade." He shot me a look that spoke volumes of his disdain. "They may be part of the King's army, but they are a pack of murderers under the direct orders of Fallen Arbor."

"But you're a Lord Knight—no, higher than that. Fifteen knots make you a Guardian of the Royal Family."

Valiente spun the horse around and stopped me in my steps. "I am, but the King made it clear in a recent law that the Berserk Brigade was higher than my station."

My stomach twisted, mind pulling the information together. "And so, crossing south, they could take her into their so-called protective custody by law or by force."

"I'm not a one-man army, Dante." The muscles in his cheek tensed. "Neither are you, but together, we just might have a chance if they plan on coming between us and Captiva City."

Before I could reply, he had Colonel trotting off and into the bustling village. John lingered by the sawmill, the old man shoving gold his way. Red Wine had disappeared once more, but Sonja squeezed closer to John and smiled when Valiente rode toward them. Basque was still hooked to the wagon, and the pings from a nearby forge redirected my aim. *Valiente is going* to need a weapon, but maybe... Following the sound, I ignored the suspicious glares from the villagers. Unlike before becoming a bloodeater, I could hear every whisper. They knew I was daemonis, but they feared having two assassins passing through.

Or at least, they pray we're just passing through and will be gone by morning. I wonder, is this a skill all bloodeaters have or if mine is deeper, more sensitive? Then, there's those whispers of wonder if we're the ones they came looking for...

CHAPTER 14

Bounty for Two Heads

I followed the bend to the south side of the town, the smells of ash and sweat invading my nostrils. Slowing, I realized Red Wine was speaking to two blacksmiths by the glowing furnace. On the opposite side, an assortment of premade goods spread across several tables, making it easier for me to feign disinterest in whatever matters she had with them. Looking over the items, I saw everything here was of lesser quality than I hoped to see in a renowned town so close to the battlefield. I tried to eavesdrop on Red Wine's conversation from where I stood, but she shot me a glance, and I turned away. *Not sure what I was expecting out of a Master Assassin. Of course, she can read me like a book at this rate.*

"Good day, Assassin," a woman snorted, wiping her hands on her apron from where she had been sharpening a blade. "You here to trade or need repairs like your friend there?"

"I need to buy a few things." I approached the table she stood behind, still unimpressed with the quality of the daggers on the table. *These look like yearling blacksmith goods. Where's the work that matches the two muscled brutes?* "I've got the gold, but I need something that can take more than one hit on the battlefield."

She scoffed. "This is it. All we got thanks to the war; we can't make weapons fast enough to keep up with the demands no matter if they're daemon or human. Gold spends the same."

Crossing my arms, I narrowed my eyes at her. "Look, I may be passing through, but these scream first-year smithing. Looking at your boys over there, even on a shit day they can make stronger, straighter blades. My ferrier back home could do better than this." Her face flushed, her gaze shooting away in guilt. "So, where do you keep the good stuff? Again, I mean it when I said I've got the gold for it. I need a longsword, a few daggers, maybe some armguards depending on what the quality is on those leftovers. Hell, if you have chainmail of some kind, I'll take that too. I'm not aiming to wipe out your stores."

Her eyes shot back up, squinting in thought before she whispered, "You really with the Guild? You don't talk or walk like 'em."

"Yeah, call me a new recruit under her." I nodded to Red Wine. "We're here escorting the clergymen as my first contract." I tilted my head the other way toward John, Sonja, and Valiente still talking with the old logger." These items are for my companions, to be honest. I've been hired to get them across the battlefield alive, but they've got cracked swords or no armaments at all. No offense—I don't think anyone wants a dead priest or mother superior on their hands, and neither do I."

"Ah, so you're the bodyguard for the clergymen, huh?" She sounded baffled. "Since when does The Church hire The Guild for protection?"

"Since Viceroy Falco tried to kill one of them and had the audacity to put a bounty on both their heads," I answered flatly.

"Shit." Her eyes grew wide, and after a moment, she whistled and exchanged nods with one of the blacksmiths. "Follow me to the shop across the way. Our best work is under lock and key. As you can imagine, thieves are plenty these days."

"The quick fingers that come through this place so close to the frontlines can't be good for any business. Desperate men do desperate sins." I shot one more look back to Red Wine, and she locked eyes with me.

104

She tapped her mask with two fingers and pulled it down the cheek like a tear before crossing her thumb across the cheek of it. *What the hell was that? A signal?* The woman was still chatting, her voice and demeanor coming off as nervous. *Shit... she didn't teach me anything about signals nor how to read them. Did she forget?* The lock slid, and she motioned for me to go forward. I reached out and held the door well above her own hand.

"Ladies first," I offered, tension building as my mind tried to figure out what on earth Red Wine's signal could have meant.

"Now we're going to be a gentleman all of a sudden," she ridiculed, entering before me. "So, you need a longsword?"

"That's right." I shut the door behind me, and she motioned for me to slide the lock. "I owe a knight one after breaking his."

"My, you're a ruffian, you are." She travelled through the home, the floors creaking under foot until we came to a sitting room by a fireplace.

A wave of nostalgia hit me, the smell of fresh broken earth underfoot told me volumes of what they were doing just below the floor. *They've been digging to make room for hiding goods.* I halted and watched her push against a chair but fail to move it. At last, she glared at me and waved her hands at the chair. I furrowed my brow. It all felt... *off.*

"Are you just going to let an old woman throw out her back?" she fussed.

"I was wondering if I was supposed to stay by the front door?" I offered, gripping the chair with one hand. "Where shall I move it to, madame?"

"Like I'll leave you there to let a friend or two in. No thank you, Mr. Assassin. I'm only going this far because The Guild has always paid and paid well for any of our wares in the past." She pointed beside a chamber pot in the corner. "There, now make qui–" Her words halted as I lifted the old red pine chair single-handed and gently placed it where she had mentioned. "Well, I ain't seen that kind of strength from anyone since the Berserkers came through."

"Ah, the Berserk Brigade has been here?" I lifted a brow, watching as she threw back the rug and started to displace floor panels. *We might be facing them. I wonder...* "Was that recently?"

"Yes, said they were lookin' for some folks who might be crossing this way." She locked eyes with me as she diligently kept working the panels free. *Her heart fluttered. They must have been here for us.* "In fact, they'd crossed paths with them in Tavern Way, and when they didn't meet at the border crossing south of there, they thought they might end up here any day now."

I licked a hidden fang, Red Wine's hand signal coming back in mind. *Two fingers, two blacksmiths. She was signaling she had them, would keep them. So, the thumb, moving back under the left eye, not across the cheek. Red was saying watch my back. I got it. She knows a lot of details in a very short amount of time... so the question now: is this a trap or desperation? I can forgive the latter, hell, even understand it. I wonder how much I can get out of her before she gets the courage up to pull a weapon on me.*

"You wouldn't know anything about all that, would you, Mr. Assassin?" Reaching into the hole, she unlocked a large chest. "I mean, that was only a week ago it seems when they showed up and trashed this place."

"I didn't think such esteemed men of The Tower would be after the Rabid Dog's bounty on clergymen of The Church." The quandary made her pause as if she hadn't thought the connection strange until I'd brought it to the table. "So, they weren't civil when they came?"

"Like a pack of wild dogs," she growled, pulling out several swords. "Don't move. Not until I'm done here."

Raising my hands, I took a step back to reassure her I would do as she asked. "Is that the reason these were hidden?"

Nodding her head, she continued her story, her voice dropping to a whisper, "They took the boy who made those weapons out there. He was the old logger's grandson, and now the poor old man has no one left. No idea if the boy's even alive or thrown into the training camp." Her face reddened, her heart racing in my ears. "He wasn't even old enough for them to be drafting into

The Tower's army. Poor thing still had a good two summers to go before his time to fight would be here."

"What was his name? Perhaps the knight I'm travelling with can do something about it." I watched as she pulled chainmail, greaves, and more daggers from the dark pool before her.

"You're a fool, Mr. Assassin. The King himself says their word is law." Breaking her stare from the stash, she gave me a grave expression. "Horrible to see murderers and rapists get their hands on power so great. They say they had their way with the tavern owner's wife and daughter. No telling what unspoken sins they committed before they left that haven't been brought to light. Two of our biggest lumberjacks tried to put them in line. Bless their souls. They're six feet in the ground for trying."

"I'm sorry..." I whispered. *It seems Valiente was right. The Berserk Brigade needs to be dealt with, and they will be coming between us and Captiva City.* "Will they be coming back for a second round?"

She winced at my words, sweat sparkling across her brow. "They..." She swallowed, reaching into the hole and freezing as she gripped something. "Can you help me?"

So, they plan on coming back here. These people are terrified. Her face stayed locked downward, her heart racing fast and hard. "Of course."

I didn't move just yet, glancing at the wares she had piled on the floor. *If she aimed to sell these to me, she would have spread them out or told me about each one. Instead, she's been focused on talking, making sure I am who the Berserkers had wanted, so I imagine they need us to earn protection. It's a trap, but one laid in desperation to feed a lurking predator just beyond their town borders. Can I really blame them?*

At last, I took a step forward and she tensed, hissing, "Are you always so damn slow?"

Silently, I approached and knelt. Now I could see how she trembled, the fear in her eyes and the smell of it starting to waft through the increased sweat building across her entire being. Her heart drummed as if trying to escape her chest. The shaking hands came out empty and gripped the apron in a weak attempt to make them still. She wouldn't meet my gaze. Glancing down, my eyes were sharp, and I could see there was an assortment of small daggers and a few rapiers left in the old iron box. *Nothing here needs me to be lifted. The chainmail was heavier.*

"You need my head to make them stop, right? Stabbing me won't kill me. I'm more monster than daemon. Sadly, it won't bring the boy back or undo the damage done."

Tears were falling, hands clutching tighter as her bottom lip trembled. *These people are so terribly desperate...*

"The old logger was stuck. I got him back here with his whole load in one piece. That's the kind of people we are, that I am. No harm or ill-will comes from us unless first thrust upon us. I was mucking stalls in Tavern Way when I was ambushed. That's who they are, criminals willing to play dirty without concern for the innocent lives around them."

She closed her eyes, the rivulets of salty tears falling faster.

"You help me now with the weapons and armor, and I'll kill every last one of them. The Berserk Brigade will become the enemy of Ashton, and they will pay in blood for what they've done and aim to do." Her eyes met mine, and she inhaled swiftly. "I'm a monster in my own right, one that will gladly devour the rest."

At last, her voice croaked, "We can't afford The Guild. They stripped most of us of our gold."

"I didn't ask for gold. I'm offering a trade my life for theirs. Besides, I still have gold for weapons, and some extra for any information you're willing to give me about the men who came here looking for me and my companions." She searched my mask, and I pulled it off, wanting her to see the resolve written on my face. "I don't show my face to anyone. This is the only faith I can offer that I will do everything I can to punish them, but as a friend reminded me, I can't do this alone. I need your skills and equipment if I'm to succeed."

Her eyes looked to the chair a moment before she turned to the pile of weapons she had pulled out. "Since when do Assassins have such silver tongues?" she spat.

Sighing, I smirked. "Well, diplomacy is a must when you consider my upbringing."

"So, they weren't joking when they said there's a Blood Prince posing as an assassin." She wiped her tears, but more replaced them as the tension eased and her beating heart slowed. "A prince … offering his life for a destitute village." A laugh escaped her. "Seems like the saints sent us a miracle."

"More like a Blood Prince training in the ways of The Guild," I offered.

"Ridiculous. How can a country take a risk like that on their prince?" She inhaled deeply and looked to the ceiling. "Most of us have a hard time sending our kids to the army, and I hear children are rare among daemonis."

Placing my mask back on, I chuckled. "They spoil me where I come from. But in times like these, I can't be soft. I can't stand by and do nothing. I'm in the right circumstances to do something, make a change not only for my people, but for the whole of Grandmere. We've dealt with the Rabid Dog and the cursed blade The Fanged Lady. Now we aim to sort out the corruption and the Berserk Brigade. It seems to be a good start to make a very loud statement that the people will not stand for this abuse anymore."

"But you're only one person," she derided.

"With resources like you to help, a Royal Knight and clergymen as allies, a Prince of my own country, and better yet, working for The Guild … I am more than one person. I think this makes me qualified to make changes happen where others have failed." I patted her hand, startling her, but the tension melted as she grabbed my hand tightly.

"This country needs someone to revive it. If that's your aim—to end a war with no end in sight—I can support that." Letting go, she turned and crawled toward the fireplace.

She reached up into the chimney, and I realized I hadn't smelled ashes or any of the usual indications a fire had burned there in some time. As cold as it had been, there should have been warm coals at best, but nothing but some half-burnt logs and ash laid inside the hearth. With a grunt, she pulled out a blade and handed it to me. *This was the quality of craftsmanship I was looking for, maybe a notch above that.* I stood, checking the blade's straightness, the grip and balance making both Valiente's swords seem like training swords in comparison.

"Perfect," I muttered.

"It's the best one Caleb has smithed to date. We hid it when they came in like bulls, but they took the rest of the high-end wares. I'm sorry." She began spreading out the items, shifting into a seller's mindset at last.

"Don't apologize." I set the sword to the side and knelt before the items. "I need daggers that are strong enough to deflect a sword or warhammer. Some chainmail that will at least keep an arrow shallow for the clergymen."

"R-right." Reaching back down, she pulled out several items before finding what she wanted. "These three are all I have in Preveran steel."

"Really? Is there that big of difference in steel here versus the Perines mountains?"

"It took twice the heat to melt those bars. They cost us a fortune, but it was a gift for my husband. He aimed to make a sword with the three bars but in the end settled for ornate daggers." Glancing through the chainmail vests and shirts, she sighed. "Well, I can't vouch for this one or these. This one is heavy and will stop an arrow from afar, and this vest should keep them shallow."

I rolled the chainmail between my fingers, grunting at the weight of the shirt. "I suppose the priest and mother superior will do fine. I imagine only the Berserk Brigade will aim for them, and the most that will happen is a rogue arrow. Did they have any long-range attackers with them when they came?"

"No. Wait … yes, of sorts." Searching the air, she recalled the men in her mind. "One was a spearman. The rest had larger blades, two-handed weapons seemed to be their specialty, but they can take a hit too. Built like bulls, every single one."

"A spearman?" *Shit, chainmail won't stop a hard toss from one of those. I'll have to make sure I find him and…* "Throwing axes or daggers? I'll need a few of those."

She laughed, leaning down to pull some out. "Have you even used one before?"

"N-no," I confessed. "But it seems I'll need to learn before I leave here."

Shaking her head, she handed me a heavy tomahawk. "Look, you've got strong arms like our Jacks here in town. Tonight, at the tavern, the boys will be throwing tomahawks at targets for drinks. They'll teach you all they know. I'll put in a good word for you."

Nodding, I looked over the weapon before sliding it through my belt. "You think this will do the job?"

"With your strength, if thrown well, this has the weight to break the spear at worse if he blocks. She'll cut through the air just as fast as knives and daggers, but you're aiming to disable him more than pierce. A pierced soldier can still attack, whereas a broken arm or weapon cannot."

"Point taken." Looking at the selection, there was one item I was missing. "No armguards?"

"Is it for you?" She began putting back the other items.

"Yeah, I've got a nasty habit of using my forearms like shields." I rolled up my sleeves to show off the slashes. "Any chances we can make some?"

She hissed at the thought. "You're too reckless. I'll talk to the boys. They should be able to smith something up once I measure your arms. Do you want a manica instead and armor a single arm from shoulder to hand?"

I blinked, the thought never crossing my mind to acquire one. "Do you have the time? We can't stay for too long."

"We will make time for you and for your party. In fact, it will take less time than two armguards. Like you said, you can't face them alone. You need the right gear to take those devils down, and I can't help but believe you mean it." She finished putting away the remaining wares and locked the chest. "You're Blood Prince Ashton, right?"

"Yes." Despite the speed of my answer, it still rolled off my tongue like a strange concept. *I am Ashton. Dante is missing or back in hiding far as the world knows.*

"Strange," she muttered.

"How so?" I aided in covering the floor and moved the chair back.

"Well, the commander of the Berserk Brigade said they were after Prince Dante, not Ashton. That and the priest. You really think they are aiming for Falco's bounty?"

I laughed. "Falco's dead, and no one will be getting that bounty, but news travels slow."

"D-dead? The Rabid Dog is dead!" She dropped the chainmail she had picked up.

I was thankful she couldn't see the wicked smirk on my face. "It took a priest and a Prince posing as an assassin to get the job done. He was an enemy to even his own country."

"R-really?" She handed over the chainmail and daggers. "There's an extra dagger there to replace the shit-one there in your hilt. How on earth you can have one keen and one dull blade is beyond me. Clearly an assassin in training." The last of her nervousness had faded as she grabbed the longsword. "We will fashion a strong sheath for this one. Send the knight to be sized up."

"Oh, as promised." I untied the heavy coin purse at my side, the gold far more than what was being bought. "The payment for your information and wares."

She nearly dropped the heavy thing as it hit her open palms. "This is too much," she gasped, counting the coins and shaking her head. "I can't take all of this. Not after what I intended to do when I walked you in here."

"Then give me back the difference." I held out an open palm.

Walking over to a small table, she emptied the coin purse. I watched, intrigued as she divided it in half, something I hadn't expected to happen, and slid it back into the coin purse. Holding her breath, she dropped the bag into my hand. She exhaled as if a great burden had been lifted.

These are good, fair folk much like Glensdale. They deserve peace of mind as much as my own city, and I will gladly do what I can to break a path open to allow that to unfold for them.

I bowed deeply and cooed, "Thank you, madame. The Guild takes your payment for the heads of the Berserk Brigade."

She paled, her voice trembling as she spoke, "You're something else."

They will fall for coming for me and daring to tread on the innocent to do so.

CHAPTER 15

Shattered Silence

As we walked out of the house, Red Wine was shouting and arguing over the price for repairs. The blacksmith's wife and I looked to one another, baffled at the foreign language she cursed in as she pointed a finger hard into the bigger man's chest. The woman brushed past me in a rush, the other blacksmith confused by our presence. *They were expecting to keep Red Wine in place while she tried to take me down. I wonder what language that is?*

"Caleb! Harrison!" Her voice jolted them to attention, Red Wine tilting her head at me. "All is well! These good folks have gold and already helped the old logger get home today."

"But Bessie..." Caleb started, but his eyes fell to the long-sword, and he frowned deeply. "Are you sure? You're putting us all in danger if you do this, my love."

"It's okay." I marched up and turned to Red Wine, slapping my coin purse in her hands. "She's paid for The Guild to take down the Berserk Brigade," I announced, earning a pinch from Red Wine.

"This is your fucking coin purse, Half-pint," Red Wine drawled. "I want to know how you convinced her to not only

114

hire us but give you the best damn sword I've ever seen come out of this shop."

Leaning into her, I purred, "With a sharp tongue and my good looks."

"Dog shit." Palming my face, she shoved me away and turned back to the three merchants. "So, are you doing the repairs or not?"

"We are." Bessie held her chin high. "Give us two days, and we'll have you and your party fit to do battle." She turned to the other man, barking orders, "You need to measure this man for a manica." Turning to her husband, her tirade continued, "And take this longsword and find the knight. He'll need a proper sheath for your precious star-blade."

The look he gave the blade could make anyone's heart ache. "Y-yes. I see."

"Left or right arm?" Harrison had produced paper and charcoal as he turned to me. "I recommend you use the weaker arm for the manica since it'll serve like a shield. If it takes a beating, it can still guard."

Red Wine chuckled at the question. *Shit, I don't know the right answer, but the old man said never let them know I'm really left-handed so...* "Left arm."

"You take the old Farmer's advice to heart. I never agreed with that, but..." She leaned in, whispering too low for anyone but me to hear. "Ashton was right-handed, ambidextrous honestly, but remember that as you keep yourself from using that arm. Manica might help with that."

Now she tells me. I held out my arm, and he used his hand to measure various places of my chest, shoulder, and arm. When he finished, I pulled the dull dagger from my side and left it on their table to do with it what they will: *trash, sell, or recycle.* Now I had two keen daggers, a tomahawk, and a claymore still on Basque. By the time I crossed the village and entered the tavern, Valiente was being measured by Caleb and the innkeeper was handing keys to John.

"Will that sword suit you?" I asked, meeting Valiente's eyes as he smirked.

"I didn't expect you to pry the blacksmith's favorite from his hands like this."

"Me neither," grumbled Caleb as he finished writing measurements and left.

Valiente continued, "I should kiss you for this."

John cut in between us, shoving the knight back a step. "I'd advise you keep your lips to yourself."

"Oh? Is that a threat?" Valiente settled back onto his stool and took another sip of his mead. "Didn't take you as a jealous one, Father John."

"I heard you got knuckles to the face for stealing one from my priest." Chuckling, I slid a coin across to the bartender. "You have ale here?"

"Aye. We serve all we can between the battlefield and our jacks." The old man had an eyepatch, scars saying he had served his time on the battlefield and managed to survive long enough to retire. "You want the house special or dark ale from Captiva City?"

"House special." Shrugging, I turned to face John. "You joining?"

"No, I'm going to see Sonja to her room." He eyed us both for a moment. "Will either of you be escorting us for our safety?" John met my gaze, and I held my breath.

I'm not ready to be alone with you just yet. My ale slid to me, and I feigned distraction.

"I'll do it." Red Wine marched in, soft footed as a cat and making us all jolt. "We have much to discuss, Father." She hooked John's arm and disappeared.

Exhaling, I took another gulp of the bitter ale, thoughts replaying the conversation with Bessie. The bartender had a permanent scowl on his face. As I took in the man, I could see the bruises on his neck from large fingers, the limp that made me wonder if an old injury or new one was to blame, and the red and purple peeking under the eyepatch. He reached for a glass, his aim off and knocking it to the ground in defeat. It shattered into a thousand pieces, and the tavern cut into a silence so deep I flinched. He stared at the shards, every set of eyes waiting to see what he'd do next.

Unnerved, I stood, setting my mug down loudly, moving the eyes all to me. "I'll clean it up."

He gave me a baffled look. "W-what?"

"You just lost that eye, right?" As I grabbed the broom leaning on the wall by the innkeeper, I circled back to slide behind the counter. "I got this. Can't have my bartender slicing up his hands. Go pour me another ale."

His lips drew tight as he stumbled back to let me do the work. Closer, without the haze of the ale to dull my sense of smell, I could tell the wound was fresh. I caught the tinge of infection along with the rattle in his breath; *Fuck, they even broke a rib. They'll pay. These are innocent lives caught in my crossfire, and I will take responsibility for this. These people won't be the last caught up in this...* Whispers rumbled through the patrons, all eyes on me still. Swallowing, the bartender turned to pour another ale and placed it next to my first.

"Thank you," he muttered.

"Don't thank me," I growled, tossing the shards in a bucket of more glass. *It wasn't the first one today it seems.* "They came looking for me, and you paid the price."

Fingers gripped my shoulder tight, digging hard into my flesh as he hissed in my ear, "The Commander did this to me and worse to my girls. You gut him, you hear me ?"

"You have my word, even if I have to do it with my bare hands."

I see the smiths have already spread the word on what we intend to do when we leave here. Let's hope others are as for-giving. But does John know what has happened here yet? He's as bullheaded as I am on something like this.

I sat back down, finished the first ale, and pulled the second closer. *Wish alcohol still worked to numb my mind...* I guzzled it, bitter at the fact I was beyond a bloodeater and couldn't seem to build any kind of buzz. Valiente's gaze burned at me, the knight furrowing his brow. The bartender poured a third ale, and I stared at my reflection, glad to hide all the emotions on my face behind the mask I wore. *Without this shield, I would be vulnerable to the world.*

"If you keep this up, you'll shatter like that glass." Valiente's words snapped me out of my thoughts. "It's an age of war. No one man is responsible for the tragedies we face day in and day out."

"I suppose this means they'll be waiting for us when we head south?" Dodging his words, I focused on what would be coming soon enough no matter how anyone felt. "What all will we need?"

"It seems you were able to secure weapons and armor, so that's a start." Valiente took a few gulps of mead and exhaled, looking at the grim-faced locals. "They hit this place hard."

"Yeah. They did." Tapping my thumb on the bar top, I followed his path.

"We need rest, too. And until then, it seems Red Wine and I have informants that should be getting back to us by morning. From there, we can try to prepare, but I must be honest, Da-Ashton," Valiente cleared his throat and stood, tossing a few coins on the table, "the commander of the Berserk Brigade is a beast, barely human if you consider the rap sheet of crimes and sins he's committed that I know of. You might be stronger, but he has experience and murderous intent on his side. You need to think long and hard how much of yourself you are willing to destroy to cut a path for real change to happen in Grandmere. Or at least, to protect *him.*"

He shot a dangerous look down at me, and I snorted. "I've already made my choice, Valiente. I can't change Grandmere overnight, but I can at least aim to disassemble Fallen Arbor."

"You do realize they own the entire Old Continent, right?" He scoffed, scratching the side of his jaw. "You're declaring war against an empire."

Arching a brow, I smirked. "But here in Grandmere, they are operating in secret. The question here is why—when you consider they are indeed an empire."

Valiente nodded. "I suppose there is something odd about that."

"They need something first, and I aim to get to it before they can." I finished the third ale and signaled for another.

"What do you think it is they want so badly?" He leaned over my shoulder, lowering his voice as he spoke in my ear. "You think it's Ashton himself keeping them in the shadows all this time?"

"That, and I have a feeling that soul weapons or the magic of curses like The Fanged Lady factor somehow. I don't recall any history or legends on bloodeaters or the plague in relation to the Old Continent. How about you?"

Whistling, he began walking away. "You're both deep thinkers, but I see why you ended up in love with one another." Chuckling, he waved farewell. "See you tomorrow!"

I can't make heads or tails of him. If I didn't know better, he was still crushing on John and starting to fall for me with the way his heart was pattering.

CHAPTER 16

King of Jacks

I had lost count of the drinks and abandoned my mask, tucking it into my belt. The air still had a hint of wintry bite at night, and the lumberjacks began to pour into the tavern. Sweat and freshly chopped red pine filled the air. Before long, the thud of tomahawks made me wander outside. Around the corner, laughter and shouts echoed through the forest. A large man with unkempt long hair and beard stepped up. Chugging his beer, he slung the tomahawk without a glance, and it hit the red center of the target. They had sliced a tree like a loaf of bread, a stack nearby to replace targets as they broke apart to become the wood for nearby campfires. Another wave of shouts and the faces glowing in the orange firelight looked primitive. These men seemed to be tapping into some ancient calling, generations spent laboring in the pines only to fuel the civil war in a never-ending cycle.

It's become a tradition in Leifseid: a supply chain for the war.

Inhaling deeply, I braved a seat behind the throwing-brutes so I could watch them. The first man had thrown his one-handed, not even staring at the target. The next several squared off their stance, two hands close together on the bottom part of the handle. Chest facing the target, they drew arms and weapon overhead, throwing with all their weight, much like chopping wood. These hit hard, a loud thud and the target stand would rock slightly back. Again, the first man stepped up, the rotation starting over once more.

It was then I noticed the three smaller tomahawks in one man's hands much like the one on my hip. Someone offered me an ale, and I took it without complaint. The brute locked eyes with me, tossing the three weapons as they grouped on the red mark without a glance once more. A snort escaped me, and he began a rolling fit of chuckling at my reaction. His stance was more relaxed, relying on the swing of his arm and trusting his body. There was no squaring off his footing but rather a side stance, and it hit me. *Peripheral.* He was relying on the movements, and though his target was stationary this time, this would serve effectively in battle. *He's a knight or fighter of some kind. Or at least was at some point.* Another swig of ale, and I watched as someone retrieved his tomahawks as he marched up to me.

"Assassin, do you not want to join us?" His voice purred as he arched an eyebrow at me. "The name's Jack, king of the Jacks. And you are?"

"I see. Call me... Half-pint." Sucking on my cheek, gauging the stares, I confessed, "I'd love to join, but I've never thrown an axe besides to split wood on the block."

"Well, that's the first lesson, Half-pint." He grinned, motioning for me to stand. "And how can you say you don't throw with such a nice tomahawk at your side?"

Stretching, I cracked my neck one way then the next. "I never said I didn't want to learn to throw. Figured obtaining the weapon would help when the opportunity presented itself."

"Well, then we shall call this an opportunity!" He spun around as if showboating for the audience, arms thrown up to encourage the roar of laughter and slapping of thighs. "Never know until you make that first throw, hmm? Mr. Half-pint?"

"True." He stepped back and motioned for me to step up to the crude line cut by a boot in the ground. "Any pointers for a first-timer?"

"Do you need it? You've been watching with such a serious gaze all night." Taking a sip from a fresh ale, the foam dripping off the heavy stein, Jack added, "I think you have an idea how to start already."

I took a deep breath, and the men's laughter shifted to a low babbling of voices like a creek. Pulling the tomahawk free from my belt, I tossed it from one hand to the other in thought. These didn't feel like the well-balanced throwing knives I had once played with in the Old Farmer's den on snow-heavy days. The head of the weapon was heavy as well as the end of the handle. It begged to lead and stretch across the span, though it reminded me how I used to toss horseshoes with the stablemen in Glensdale. I squared my stance and chest with the target, gauging the distance. Looking to the weapon, I finally exhaled.

This is meant for one-handed throws, so I'll have to take the other stance. Unlike the other lumberjacks, Jack's axes were smaller and nothing like the wood splitters the others had thrown.

Twisting, I lined the side of my body with the target and rolled my shoulder. *I'm going to throw like shit because it's my right arm, but...* Doing my best to mirror Jack's throwing, I brought the tomahawk high, letting my elbow lock and used the rotation of my shoulder. I slung it forward, and it landed in the dirt to the right of the target. The lumberjacks shouted and cackled as I marched up and retrieved it.

"You did alright, first-timer," gruffed Jack. "Point your toe at the target this time. After that, you need to learn how much power to put into it to keep her flying. Arm swing will do if you can keep it locked and swinging straight. Try again, Half-pint!"

Resetting at the line, I pointed my right toe to the target. *This reminds me of how Ashton's starting stance works. I wonder.* Squatting slightly, ignoring the whispers and chuckles at my awkward adjustments to the stance compared to all who had thrown before me, I relaxed my body more. Inhaling deeply, I held it. Slinging my arm, I gave it more power than before.

Thud! The tomahawk hit the side of the tavern just above the target.

"Shit," I muttered. *So close on my second throw. Too much power.*

"Well, look at that, boys!" Jack threw out his arms once more, addressing the watching eyes. "Who wants to put a coin down that he hits center next?"

"Horseshit," spat an old veteran. "I'll put a coin down he doesn't!"

"Aye!" Another man stood, raising his glass high. "He'll hit the dirt or the tavern again before the target as soft as his knees are!"

"How much ale has he had?" chortled a woman sitting in a man's lap. "He can't even stand up right."

A few more shouts and the coins were stacking up, easily ten to one odds that I wouldn't hit the target at all. Jack spun back to me as I stopped at the line once more. Pumping my fist, I flustered. *This would be easier with my left, but Ashton was right-handed.* Jack's heavy hand patted my shoulder. The bitter stench of ale on his breath as he came nose-to-nose with me. Locking gazes, there was a coy look in his eyes.

"You hit the target in the red, and I'll let you take the winnings," he offered.

"Heh, you sure you want to make that kind of bet?" I arched an eyebrow, smirking.

"What those drunk old men don't see is you knew what stance was right for the weapon on the first try." I froze, his words sounding too sober for as much as he had downed all night. "The second try, you tried to relax into a more knowing stance, yes?" My silence was more than enough to goad him on. "So, this time, show them what it means to be in The Guild."

"If I hit red, you keep the coins, and we sit in private for a talk," I demanded, chills rolling over me as he released his grip.

"You'd have to split the target in two for that honor." Jack spun, shielding his expression as he whistled. "Fresh target for this round!"

Snorting, I turned to the line. *I don't know who the hell he is, but something tells me he might provide insight on the brigade or even Fallen Arbor.* Again, I pointed my toe and this time stood tall. *Even when not looking, he stood tall but relaxed.* Stretching my arm out, I followed the invisible path of where my foot pointed until I stared the target down the length of my arm and axe. *That's right. He always did this pose, though fleeting thanks to his experience, I imagine.* Calming my nerves, I let the tension melt away like I did when settling into my training stance. In a quick, fluid motion I slung the tomahawk.

Thud-crack!

The target broke into halves, and the spectators leapt to their feet. A cacophony of whistles and shouts filled the air as they surrounded me in a rush. Slaps and pats, hand shaking, and praise waved out of them. *Where's Jack?* Over the crowd of heads, I saw him leaning on a tree at the edge of the dark forest. *Some place private. Let's do this.* Grabbing the coin bag, I handed it to the youth who had been running the targets all night, and he gave me back my tomahawk.

"Buy all these men a round and something for yourself!"

I didn't wait for a reply. The lumberjacks followed the boy like dogs to scraps as I cut between the rushing bodies. By the time I got to the trees, Jack had finished. His prints sank heavily in the mud, and his scent lingered in the air. I took a deep breath, listening close as I swiveled my head to the right. *He's leading me pretty far out, but I don't sense anyone else out here. I don't think it's an ambush.* Shaking the shudder from my shoulders, I pulled my mask back on. *Time to be serious.* My steps marched through the trees, the tomahawk in my hand as I found him leaning on a tree, lighting a rolled cigarette.

"Be honest." Deeper voiced now, he glanced at me with a cautious expression. "You're the guy the Berserk Brigade came looking for, aren't you?"

"I don't know of any other assassins travelling with clergymen."

He snorted and continued, slow and calculating, "I suppose you got me there. You seemed to have won over the villagers before I made it back from the mill. That's no easy feat after what they did to these folks."

"I wish we had gotten here sooner," I whispered.

"With the state of the gear and tired from travelling..." He looked me up and down, taking a slow draw of his cigarette before releasing the smoke. "...you would have made matters worse."

Crossing my arms, the tomahawk's blade hooked in my fingers, I challenged him, "If they took out the two strongest jacks, where were you?"

He shook his head, eyes darting up to express his anger. "Tricked. The Berserk Brigade didn't want to chance me being here when they hit. Otherwise, we would have had some fighting chance or tact with my help. Had me looking for a lost boy who'd broken his legs..." The hard pause and tension made me uneasy. "Don't repeat this, but the old logger's grandson isn't coming home. Buried the pitiful thing in an unmarked grave. There wasn't much to bring back. Fucking monsters left him to... to a pack of Flesheaters."

"I thought the Madness was dissipating?" Every nerve in my body was on high, tightening in my joints until they ached. "What is the status on the battlefront?"

"Look, Half-pint." Another long drag and he looked me dead in the eyes, this time with a glazed look. "Since the Berserk Brigade showed on this side, the Madness has flared up and regained its hold. Rumors say they have some way of causing it, like the Rabid Dog, but I don't know..."

A soul weapon. It can't be... but if Fallen Arbor is supporting them... "Tell me more about their commander," I demanded.

"He's the biggest with a nasty burn down half his face to the point his lips won't close all the way on one side and drool drips from his chin. Has a bull ring, and hell, every one of them are carrying blunt force weapons or large blades. Dasa is his name. No one knows much about him besides that the head knight of the Royal Guard brought him down and ended his spree of terrorizing the women of Captiva City. A few years later, the King declared a new ruling body and much to our horror, Dasa was named commander of the Berserk Brigade." One more drag and the cigarette was spent. He snuffed the nub under his boot. "At first, folks hoped they'd stay on the battlefield, but when a fight between them and the Royal Guards unfolded, we lost faith in who was in charge of The Tower. Who makes their word law knowing they'd have their way with his own daughter if left alone with Princess Sonja? The king aims to kill her because he'd rather see her dead before letting a woman sit on his throne. Back when the queen passed away, many suspected foul play, and I think he was to blame there, too."

Snorting, I soaked in the information before prodding further, "And what of the Princess?"

Shaking his head, he muttered curses under his breath. "Servants whisper that she's been missing since the start of winter. We can't figure out why no bounty or search party or something hasn't been issued. Shitbag dad of the year, that king of ours. The House is looking like a safer nation to align with more and more each year."

"Maybe he fears bringing it to light that she's not safe in the castle or even city walls." I shrugged, shoving the tomahawk in my belt. "It can't be safe to let The House know she's outside running amuck."

He shook his head, grunting, "Nah, he's always sounded the trumpets at first sign of anything he wanted back. No one's seen the King in some time, not even the princess herself. Only that shady Bishop Marquis seems to have seen him as of late."

A chill snaked up my spine, and I lowered my voice, "Then you think someone has taken his place in secret?"

"Let me ask you, Assassin. Have you heard of *L'Arbre Tombe?*"

"And if I have?" Narrowing my eyes, I wondered how deeply rooted Landon's reach lay just south of The House's territory. *Is the King of Jacks an operative, too?*

"Don't oppose them. They'll take everyone you love and hold dear from you." He turned and began to march away. "I won't be back before you leave, so take care and hope you live to see tomorrow."

Shit. Things are worse than I thought. Valiente and the princess haven't told us about the real dilemma in Captiva City, and until they do, I'm not leaving here without knowing.

CHAPTER 17

Sleepless Passion

By the time I made my way back into the tavern, the crowd of lumberjacks had dissipated and the bar was dark. Lanterns had been snuffed out, the inn keeper and bartender gone, and a man snored in a chair in a far corner. *Some security this place has.* A single figure sat at the bar in the darkness, and I pulled up a stool beside them, my senses telling me it was Red Wine.

"Did you get any answers?" Red Wine let her hood drop, placing her mask on the counter.

"More questions, I think." Folding my arms, I leaned forward and rested my chin on them. "I'm sure you already knew the Berserk Brigade slammed this place looking for us."

"I did, but I'm going to be honest, I haven't faced these men before." Pulling out a flask, she took a swig and closed it with haste. "I must say you surprised me today."

"I seem to have a talent of surprising folks." I snorted.

"You took a turned-upside-down-town into a support effort. Ashton wasn't so quick-witted or sharp-tongued as..." She paused a moment and corrected her aim. "No. Let me try again. You are both sharp-tongued, but how you use it is quite different, more beneficial for the whole."

"I suppose this is where you reprimand me and correct me to match my brother." I drew in a slow, deep breath and blew it out my nose.

"No. This I like about you, Half-pint." She propped her elbow on the table, picking me apart with her eyes. "Ashton cut people with his words. Don't get me wrong—you both are very intimidating when you speak, but he spoke to goad them into action for better or worse. Meanwhile, you got us out of a trap I hadn't completely figured out how to soothe over. So don't lose this gift. It suits you."

I grunted. "Did you just compliment me for being … me?"

"Perhaps. What else did you pry from the King of Jacks? He hasn't been an informant for me since…" her voice faltered and she frowned, speaking tenderly, "since I failed to get here in time to stop Landon's entourage from slaughtering his family."

"Ah, so that's what that was about." Puffing out my cheeks, I thought back and realized I had failed to ask one vital question. "Tell me what you know about soul weapons."

Her eyes shot away, her thoughts souring her face. "I only know what … what Warlord Sebastian told me about his own."

"You mentioned him before. He smuggled you out of the Old Continent."

"I hate how much you remember after only hearing something once," she spat, sitting up straight. "Look, the Ogre Clan was the first to make a soul weapon. It's taken Fallen Arbor a long time to replicate what they do, but they are inconsistent with the result."

"What is an Ogre?"

"Ah, that race that's stronger than a daemon or bloodeater." Her cheek twitched. "Sebastian has a great sword that carries the souls of all his clan's former warlords."

I sat up, the idea of it alarming. "More than one soul?"

"Yes." She smiled and tapped her fingers on the counter. "You see, they had many clans but only one remains. Ogre warlords have soul weapons. With the clans broken, they began to dissolve as Fallen Arbor took over, but Warlord Sebastian l'Ifrit is something… different." Her voice softened, and she gave a sigh. Shaking her head, she abandoned the memories that had disrupted her. "The Fanged Lady was a willing participant, and so were Sebastian's people. A soul weapon is only made from a living person who sacrifices their life willingly to become a weapon incarnate. Granted, it's more complicated, and Fallen Arbor can force people with dark magic. What shape and power they take on can change dependent on the person and conditions of the creation."

"How so?" *This whole time … she had the answers I wanted, but still…*

"Well, they often fall into three categories: cursed, blessed, then whatever Sebastian has. Self-aware? I mean, they all have some awareness of who they were, but he would carry on talks with the damn thing and covered it when we…" She spun away, stretching as she stood. "Enough of that. I don't know much else."

"Well, is it too farfetched to think a soul weapon is to blame for the Madness?" I stood, hot on her heels as she aimed for the staircase.

"A cursed blade created from someone's malice, like the Fanged Lady, was put out of commission, and the curse lifted, didn't it?" She raced up the stairs, whimpering as I stayed close enough to slip past and block the door. "Why? I'm tired, and you seem to be hellbent on being a sleepless brute."

"I think the Berserk Brigade has a soul weapon. That's the information I got from King of Jacks." She flinched and met my gaze before I forced her mask over her face. "You left this while running away from me. We'll finish this talk later."

Without another word, I marched to the end of the hall and came to a halt. *Shit, I don't know which room is which.* Rubbing my neck, I looked at the identical doors in desperation, hoping one of them could hint where I should go. *I'll see if the innkeeper's book has…* When I turned around, Red Wine stood in my way, arms crossed.

"Oh, I thought we were finished." I blinked.

"We were until I saw you standing here like a buffoon," she spat, annoyance riding in her tone. "Don't tell me you can't tell which room *he's* in."

My face flushed, and I shot my eyes from hers. "I forgot to ask anyone which rooms were ours."

"Let me rephrase this." She was being curt with me, angry even. "You're Ashton. He always knew where I was even when I didn't want to be found. Something tells me you're capable of doing the same thing, seeing how you hunted down my informants a week ago."

I bit my lip and swallowed. *She's right. I'm not even trying to use those skills now, and I need to be always using them considering our situation.* "I ... see."

She motioned her hand to the rows of doors. "So, Mr. Ashton. Which room?"

"Is this a test?" I scowled.

"You're going to be going through a battlefield," she shifted and spoke in a hiss, reprimanding me like a child, "and if we live through that, Captiva City is full of enemies I assure you it'll be easier to hear and smell long before you can see them. Falco's reach still lingers even there, but worse, you're taking a higher risk now that you've laid injury to Landon. He won't let that go."

Grimacing, I looked back down the hall one way then the other. I closed my eyes, shoulders slumped in defeat, and inhaled. So many scents invaded, something I had been purposefully numbing and blocking with the ales. Heartbeats surfaced from all directions, and the anxiety tightened in my chest. *At night, when there's no sounds to focus on, this gets a little much even for...* A chill snaked up my spine, and I turned on my heel and marched to the door she had lunged for.

"So, were the three of us sharing a room?" I lowered my brow.

"No, my room is next to the knight and nun." Red Wine smirked and walked through a door and slammed it.

Shit. This is overwhelming to keep going. Gripping the doorknob, I paused, inhaling John's scent and focusing on his heartbeat. *He's asleep. Good.* Pushing through, I was silent. John was hunched over the tiny table, his shirt and jacket tossed across the only bed in the room, and I scoffed. *Such a child.* Shedding my coat, pulling off weapons, and kicking off boots, I did my best not to let the weight of my items clunk against the wooden floor. Drawing the lock, I turned to the bed and pulled his items off, halting a moment as I stared at the jacket. *I hope I never have to see his blood across this cloth again.* Shaking the past from my head, I hung them on a coatrack and turned to the sleeping man at the table.

"...don't leave me, Dante..." John mumbled in his sleep. "...I promise never to leave you ever again..."

A smile crept over my face, running a hand over my forehead to move loose strands from my eyes. "You're hopeless."

It took some finesse to work his dead weight from the desk gently enough not to wake him. Hooking an arm under his knees, I lifted him with a grunt and marched him to the bed. Once satisfied he wouldn't roll off, I drew up the blanket and paused. His face twisted and frowned in his dreaming state. A golden strand hooked into the corner of his mouth. Gliding a finger across his cheek to pull it free, I gazed at his lips as my heart went racing against my will.

Such a lovely creature I've fallen for... Leaning in, I kissed him softly and pulled away, embarrassed and body flushed with want.

A hand gripped my forearm, pulling me off balance. Our lips pressed more firmly, opening to one another so our tongues could seek out one another. Chills rattled through me. The taste of his blood filled my senses, goading me to suckle his tongue, and he moaned in response. His fingers drew fire as they slid under my loosened blouse and climbed up my torso. I pulled myself onto the bed, straddling his torso as his hands explored my body until they pulled me down into him. We were drowning in one another's desire. Breaking the kiss, I searched the sleepy gaze, panting with provocative passion.

"You're late." His voice was husky.

"Not my fault you chose to wait at the desk and not in the bed," I retorted.

John's hands began the descent back down my stomach and gripped the front of my pants. "I want you."

I scoffed. "You already have me."

He gave a disapproving expression. "You're pushing yourself so hard, but you're not a one-man army."

I held my breath.

"I can fight." His fingers worked slowly, unbuckling the belt and unfastening my pants with well-paced diligence. "You have a knight and master assassin, too."

Closing my eyes, I groaned as the heat of his hands gripped the hardened prize.

"Dante, I mean it." John stroked slowly, his other hand rubbing up across my torso. "We chose this path together, to be lovers even. Do not try to walk it alone."

"John, I can't put—" My breath caught as he shoved me back, my shoulder blades pressed hard against the wall where the bed met it.

He towered over me, and my arousal made me moan at the sight of him. "If you ever leave me, I will hunt you to the ends of the continent and the next if that's what it takes."

"Is that a threat?" I huffed as my eyes lingered on his lips.

He licked them and cracked a smirk. "It's a promise. If we are to ever become separated, may we find one another under the cherry tree."

With that, he leaned down, the heat of his mouth taking in my hardened length, goading me to tilt my hips. His tongue hot and silken wiggled under my shaft as he sucked. Another moan waved through me, and hungry for him, I reached down to keep him there between my thighs. This time he moaned and took me deeper, the back of his throat tight as I panted. I rocked in and out of the wet warmth he offered, and it wasn't long before I grunted in release. He sucked long and hard, swallowing and flicking his tongue. My body flushed with my orgasm as he rocked back, his blue eyes bright even in the darkness.

"Feel better?" He darted his eyes away, clearly blushing as he pulled away.

Grabbing his arm, I pulled him back to the bed. "Yes but..." Rubbing my hand across the bulge in his pants, he moaned. "I aim to return the favor, my priest."

"Don't call me that, prince," he spat.

"Have I told you how much I love that angry look on your face?" I chuckled, mirroring the slow agony of unfastening his pants as he had done mine.

"Why must you bring the worst out in me?" Another flushing of cheeks and he looked away.

Gripping his hardened length, he grunted and looked back to me with frustration. Pressing my lips against his, we kissed deeply as I began stroking him. Breaking it, I wasted no time to take him deep into my mouth. He folded over, and I did not stop my pleasurable assault, tongue rubbing and deep throating him with hungry want. He rose to his knees, rocking his hip to fuck my mouth as our moans grew. At last, his body tensed, and I pulled him deeper into me, sucking hard as he released with satisfying groans. I swallowed the sweet-salty offering before pulling away.

John fell back onto the bed, covering his face with an arm. "I was only aiming to please you tonight."

"What makes you think I only enjoy getting off?" I laughed, standing to tuck myself away and steal the cup of water he had left half-filled.

"It was intended to be a reward," he mumbled, almost sounding ashamed of the idea.

Snorting, I turned back, furrowing my brow as I cooed, "You by my side is reward enough, John."

"Dante, you're both my shield and sword, my *Barrière de Force,* and I feel helpless but to watch how you're breaking yourself for me, for—"

"As you said before, we chose this together," I corrected, setting the cup down with a hard clank. "There will be a time where I will need you to be my sword and shield. And honestly, I loathe

the idea of it, but you've proven more than capable of doing that simply with nothing more than ink to paper."

Shoving him farther onto the tiny bed, I laid next to him, kissing his shoulder still scarred from my bite. A great weight of guilt crept forward as I inhaled his scent and threw an arm over him to hold him close. I'm not sure when or how, but I drifted to sleep the moment my eyes closed.

CHAPTER 18

Hunt for the Informants

I woke to an empty bed and room. Blinking, it became very alarming that I had been exhausted this whole time, though not in the sense I had known it. The release of physical frustrations made it easier to breathe, and the blood-filled kiss still lingered on my tongue. It at least quelled the thirst I had ignored. *I was worried using my skills make this grow, but it seems I need to acknowledge it's more dangerous to go without. John has accepted it. I should too.* Glancing at the window, I saw it was brighter outside than I wanted to see.

"I slept for far too long. Shit."

Making haste, I dressed and rushed down to the tavern. John and Sonja were eating breakfast at a table when I approached. They offered for me to sit, but I shook my head and looked all around. My mask hiding my disapproval, I didn't see the knight or the assassin anywhere.

"Where are they?" I demanded, cutting their laughter.

"I assume meeting with informants," offered Sonja. "They said to seek you out if we needed someone."

"I see," I huffed and turned to them. "Stay in the tavern until I return."

Turning and heading for the door posthaste, John called out, "Where are you going?"

"To practice a skill I keep denying myself. It shouldn't take long." I waved him off, feeling his eyes burning at my back as I marched out the door.

I groaned, seeing the sun at high noon. *Seems I do need rest just the same. Even if I can go without, I shouldn't push myself unnecessarily.* Taking a deep breath, I could pick apart their scents, both going in different directions. *Shit, which one should I follow first?* Another sniff, and I chose the weaker scent. *Red Wine. She's been gone longer which means she should be with her informant already. Valiente only left a few moments before I came down the steps.*

Swallowing, I realized she had gone in the direction the lumberjacks had traveled, back the way we had entered. Weaving past some of the townsfolk, I headed out of town. *I trust John to hold his ground if something happens.* Her scent cut through two marked red pines, and I slowed down. Here there weren't many people. Listening, I tried to pick up on anything and flustered as a breeze sent the trees scraping all around. Another deep inhale, and I found the trail fresh and stronger, leading into the darkness in the trees up ahead.

Looking to the ground, I saw she had been able to leave very little trail. As her smell grew, I could smell another one, their paths merging down a game trail. *Another woman? This one is human.* Voices hit my ears, and I froze, my head swiveling to a small cave under an uprooted fallen red pine. *There. But how should I approach?* Steeling myself, I aimed to approach slowly and silently. Cursing under my breath, for the first time, I was not thankful for being built like an ox.

Squatting low, I could hear them where I ducked behind a tree.

"So, no more information about Ashton, then?" It was Red Wine's voice.

"Besides the fact they are putting more effort into capturing him after rumors about he's back, no. It seems strangely inconsistent." The woman sounded older, her voice crackling with age.

"As for the informant, it seems he's alive but unable to move information out of The Church."

"As I feared." Red Wine paused a moment before offering, "I'll be going to him directly once we cross the battlefield tomorrow."

"Tomorrow?" guffawed the woman. "Do you know who is waiting on the front lines for you? I thought you were going via Tavern Way."

Red Wine sighed before retorting, "We were. But Landon showed up."

"My gods, then Landon is overseeing the hunt this time?" The scent of fear made me shuffle. "Is he after you again?"

"No, he was aiming for Prince Dante."

"And? Did he take the poor child?"

Red Wine chuckled. "He's built like a bull. I don't think anyone can simply take him. Dante put up a good fight, landed a hit on Landon."

There was silence.

"I know! There's very few who are alive who can make a claim like that," reassured Red Wine.

"Where is he now?" her informant's voice dropped to a whisper.

"Safe and in hiding."

"Ah, but I don't understand one thing," started the informant. "Why ask about Ashton if he's travelling with you?"

"Well, he seems to not remember much about the time that has passed. I suspect he was mortally wounded and somehow recovered," offered Red Wine. "All he knows is Fallen Arbor is to blame, and he will see them driven from Grandmere. Rather miffed about his little brother being a target. Now that's some news you can pass on at will."

The old woman chuckled. "I see. It's good to hear he's back. We were nearing peace when he was pushing back on these men of shadows and forbidden magic."

"Anything you can tell me about the battlefield?" Red Wine redirected the conversation. "What can you tell me about the Berserkers and the current state of things?"

"Both sides had retreated when folks started recovering from the plague. They say it was a sign from the gods that the fighting must stop." She sounded proud at the idea as she continued, "But the King sent the horrid Berserk Brigade, and they've been slaughtering friend and foe alike. They run about the field like rapid animals, hungry for blood. Since they showed, the Madness has come back, and those inflicted are coming down with it faster and more aggressively. If you ask me, Fallen Arbor has given them some sort of dark weapon or magic of sorts. Men cursing men with the plague is awful."

"How many are in the brigade?" she demanded.

"The Commander Dasa leads them, but he started as a murderer. These men are no strangers to killing and torturing the innocents, and it carries well into the battlefield. The only man to defeat him in battle is Knight Valiente but..." her words wavered.

"But?" Red Wine's voice pitched, and I imagined her infamous brow.

"Rumors in the capital say he's kidnapped the Princess," she whispered low as if the mice and insects may spread news of it. "Not one of us townsfolk believe a word of the rumors since they started it."

"They as in Fallen Arbor?" Red Wine sounded intrigued.

"No, actually the brigade," she clarified before continuing her task. "Dasa's second in command is First General Kayman. He was a sailor but was arrested when he punched a man's face in and killed him. Massive man, fights with weighted gloves and chains. Spearman Mythe is a wiry man, usually hangs back and rushes in to finish a kill with a spiked club. Other times, he takes pleasure plucking folks from their horses tossing his spears."

"I see. So, they do have some long-range skill in their numbers." Red Wine seemed to pause a moment as if to absorb it all. "Anyone else on the brigade with long range?"

"Hmm, perhaps the new recruit?" she offered. "Flintlock Betty is what they call her. Who knows what a Flintlock is?"

"Shit. They've brought over weapons from the Old Continent. This is getting dangerous. So, we have four to take down?"

"Well, five if you count Gallagher. But he's all brawn and no brain," she scoffed, and the sound of coins tinged in the air. "This is far too much. I barely had anything to offer this time."

"Consider it reimbursement for the travel and incentive to spread the word Ashton is coming for Fallen Arbor," announced Red Wine.

"Music to my ears, Madame Assassin. May the blood flow like wine."

Hiding behind the tree, I watched the old woman hobble off. Her cataract eyes made me marvel she could navigate the roots and forest floor at all, let alone travel from the city to here. It wasn't long before Red Wine marched out and paused at the tree. I stepped out, knowing full well her senses could be as sharp as my own.

"So, you made it in time to hear." She crossed her arms, fingers rolling.

"Indeed. So, what's a flintlock?" She began to walk, and I followed obediently.

"A hand cannon that stings like hell. It's as sharp as an arrow but can get lost in the flesh easy. Worse, it has a longer range than any archer can manage. A bullet from one can bring on infection fast, so I don't advise getting hit with them." She paused and spun back to address me, "Did the Knight go meet with his informant?"

"Yes, I was thinking of trying to track him down next—"

Red Wine hooked her arm around my own, sounding rather chipper about the idea, "Let's go crash the party, shall we!"

"I'm starting to feel this was the aim for my training today." Rolling my eyes, we worked our way back into town.

"Indeed. It took me a while to realize what you were doing drinking so much." She pulled her arm away and cracked her neck. "Then I realized that you've been in isolated places since your training started, and you've grown more powerful. How bad is it?"

Part of me wanted to remain silent, but after a brief pause, I confessed, "Head splitting. I can smell a thousand flavors of sweat in this place, and if I don't focus on one heartbeat, I feel like I am buried under a stampede of a hundred horses. It's almost nauseating." Halting, I took a left turn and slid between two buildings, and she followed. "If I have a target, like this, it's easier to drown out the rest."

"So, the ale was more for numbing the nose at the very least, then." The alley took a turn, and I stopped, turning to her. "Why'd you stop?"

"How did Ashton handle this?" I locked eyes with her. "I mean, he was stronger than this, right?"

"He was." Her voice softened, her stare falling to the ground. "He once told me that he had to face his own madness every day. I never really understood that, but perhaps what you are going through is what he implied."

I weighed her body language for a moment. "Sorry, I should stop asking about him."

"It's okay. I think there's only one other being that can truly tell you anything about him, but Frank isn't willing." At last, she shrugged and pushed me forward. "Now, the knight and his informant. Sniff them out, would you?"

Turning my attention to the trail I followed, I found it weaved through the buildings until we found ourselves exiting them on the far side of town. In the trees ahead was a run-down mill, and we took caution as the scent of Valiente and another person made me slow. As we approached, we started to hear voices. Squatting, we managed to crawl close enough for us to hear.

"They say you kidnapped her." The informant was a young boy, possibly a squire.

"I did not," scoffed Valiente, pacing in the relic of a lumbermill. "Any idea who created that rumor?"

"The king himself," declared the boy. "But none of us in the Royal Guard believe it."

"I suppose my reputation still stands?"

"That, and the fact that instead of us, he gave more power to that pack of murderers he calls the Berserk Brigade." The boy spat at the ground, scowling. "Look, where did you go all winter? They didn't even spot you all season in Tavern Way."

"You wouldn't believe me if I told you." Clearing his throat, Valiente's voice lowered, "We were being cornered by the Fallen Arbor, so I went north."

"North?" The boy gulped. "There's nothing but The House's territory... you didn't!"

"I had no choice. She was dressed as a mother superior and Father John had a church in Glensdale. It was my only chance at safety." He halted, his voice shaking as he continued his story, "But I think someone informed Falco who we were. I suspect he and Bishop Marquis are involved in those conspirators somehow. If it weren't for John and Dante ... we'd both be dead."

"Dante? As in the Blood Prince of The House Dante?"

"Why must you repeat things back at me like a sailor's parrot, boy?" hissed Valiente. "Now tell me, what did they find when they went to her room that night?"

"It was as you said, sir. They found not one but two assassins in waiting. They both had brands on them from Fallen Arbor." He paused, and when Valiente motioned for him to continue, he relented, "But when we showed the King, he didn't believe us. He said they were decoys for the kidnapping. The entire squad was outraged and that's ... that's when he called those criminals in and had the town criers make it known they were a step above our stations. Something wicked has twisted King Regius' mind. To abandon and endanger Sonja so..."

"I hate to tell you, Jimmy, but the King has had no love for his daughter," confessed Valiente.

"It can't be true. The whole city loves her. She's charitable and wise and—"

"Not the male heir he wanted," interjected Valiente. "He'd die before letting her ascend that throne. It's deplorable."

Red Wine smacked my shoulder, whispering low, "That's what I've been wondering about. It seems Fallen Arbor has finally gained power over The Tower. We're fucked if we can't pry it back into at least Princess Sonja's hands."

142

"We still need to go to Captiva City, regardless." I searched my thoughts and added, "Do you think they've even got control of The Church?"

"Some. Not all. But we're losing, Half-pint. We're going to need to convince The Court to break free of the mountains somehow. Lucky for us, I've sent someone to start that process for us." She started to crawl away.

"Where are you going now?" I hissed.

"Spook them. Do what you do best and block them in with that wall you call a body." She scrambled off.

Shit. I worked my way in silence to where I had sensed they entered and exited the wreck of a building. Hiding behind a piece of wall barely big enough to cover me, I waited. It wasn't long before I heard someone land hard on the ground. Metal met metal, and I stepped into the exit. The boy slammed into me, bouncing off and landing on the ground with a hard yelp. I offered my hand, and his eyes grew wide.

"T-t-the Guild!" he shrieked.

"You two are assholes," scoffed Valiente, pulling his blade away from Red Wine's own. "They're companions."

"C-c-companions?" stuttered the boy, who finally took my hand, and I yanked him to his feet. "But they're from The House!"

"Technically, we are our own thing," Red Wine corrected.

"But I'm of The House and wish to make peace. Princess Sonja makes it hard to say no." I chuckled.

"Is ... is what he says true?" marveled the boy.

"Yeah." Valiente rubbed his neck and nodded. "Yes, it's true. It seems both sides are being played the fool and pitched against one another. Falco is dead, and a peace treaty is being considered..." Sheathing his sword, he met my gaze and with a dangerous tone added, "...if King Regius will allow it."

"Him and Bishop Marquis," added the boy.

"Bishop Marquis?" I squatted to be eye-level with him. "Tell me what's he been up to."

"Well, he's become an advisor to King Regius."

My blood ran cold, and I shot a glare to Red Wine, angry as I spoke, "Did you know?"

"There were rumors, but now that I know, I'll send word." Turning to Valiente, she crossed her arms and tapped a foot in impatience, scolding him like a child, "What other information would you like to share? At the rate we're going, we're a pack of fugitives forcing our way back into the city."

"I didn't expect things to change this much over winter." He gave the boy a few hearty pats and handed him a pouch of gold. "Thank you, Jimmy. I would wait until we start crossing the battlefield and give you safe passage as a distraction. They're after us anyhow. Now go."

Stepping to the side, I let the boy run off. "So, does this mean Fallen Arbor has both The Tower and The Church in their grasp?"

"Afraid so," declared Red Wine. "So, the question is, do we bother to go to Captiva City at all?"

Valiente tapped his lips, his eyes searching for answers. "As much as I dread the idea, Princess Sonja needs to be returned. She can't aid us on the run, but with my trusted guardsmen, we should be able to regain some control if..." He met my eyes, his expression grave. "...you and I manage to take down the Berserk Brigade."

"Agreed. Seeing as Ashton is after Fallen Arbor..." She sashayed over and placed a heavy hand on my shoulder. *Shocked she's not on her tippy toes.* "...taking down the Berserk Brigade will tell Landon we're coming. As for Bishop Marquis, he's a target of The Guild, so any assistance from your inside connections would warrant we owe you one."

"Can your people also watch over Sonja?" Valiente furrowed his brow in worry. "And I might be needing passage out of the city after all of this."

"Ah, agreed. We can promise you safe passage and a spy among the maids can assist us." Red Wine nodded her head.

"One of the maids is a spy?" gaped Valiente, dragging a hand over his face in disbelief. "Which one?"

"Does it matter?" Red Wine shrugged, snickering. "They told us you were honorable and an open book at that. I have to say, the reports of you have made you an especially important player to keep active and alive."

"You make it sound as if you could've assassinated me on more than one occasion!" The anger in his face made it flush red.

She pulled on my shoulder, whispering, "I don't know why he thinks we hadn't thought of the idea considering where he falls in the caste system."

Sighing, I cleared my throat to set the conversation forward once more. "So, John and I are going to be headed for The Church and aiming to be in the Catacomb Library. Any chance we might be able to sneak ourselves in there without news spreading we are there? I want enough time to see if I can't find more about soul weapons."

"What makes you think The Church has answers on that?" Red Wine tilted her head in alarm.

"Books John brought back trying to research answers about the Fanged Lady."

"Soul weapons … like the Fanged Lady? There's more than one of those damned things?" Now Valiente seemed alarmed. "You can't be serious? Why would anyone make more of those things?"

"Power. Greed … give me a reason that isn't the same drive to send men to kill or wage war here in Grandmere or on the Old Continent." Valiente pursed his lips, a shudder shaking his shoulders at my words. "Exactly. The question here is why does The Church hide the books, or is it because at one point Fallen Arbor was using it as a headquarters and had to abandon them there? In fact, Red Wine, do they have a headquarters?"

"Now that you mention it, we suspected the docks in Captiva City, but considering we can't get a solid line of information in, you have a point. They must be using this as a control point…" She pulled out a map, placing it on an old table in a plume of dust. "Look. Their ships have been seen in both the Red Wave Bay and Amethyst Harbor. Considering they have more advanced equipment, I bet they can navigate the Hidden Swells on the east side of the continent."

"What makes you so sure?" Valiente leaned in, marveling over the details on the maps and reading the various notes.

"How else could Bishop Marquis not only slip past The Guild, but beat us here with time to take over?"

My stomach twisted. *Shit! She's right.*

"Look here, northeast of Glensdale." She tapped the map. "There's an old broken fort here, maybe even a castle. We call it *Abandonner l'Espoir or Abandon Hope*. Not one informant has found a way in or out, nor signs of anyone being there. There's a great plateau and hard cliff to the sea where it stands. Perhaps, this whole time, we missed the fact there's an entrance by ship. The place is barren besides a singular black tree said to pre-date the first settlers. In fact, the whole place gives me dark magic vibes."

"If they have a stronghold that large, then we'll need Glensdale to tighten the eastern borders," I concluded, heart racing with the anxiety to see danger so close to home.

"I spoke to Ruth and your father before we left. The Guild is assisting, but The House isn't strong enough alone. If Princess Sonja can sway The Tower that would weaken a resource, but ... she'll need time to untangle the politics." Red Wine then tapped the map to the north, a village on the edge of the Perines Mountains. "Frank the Immortal is here in Winter's Perch and won't be going anywhere for a while. I think you might have a chance to sway them to join our cause, Dante."

"Why me? Don't tell me it's because I look like my brother..."

She chuckled, nodding her head. "Precisely, I mean, it swayed me. Now, if they cave, they might lead us into Prevera, and if we can convince The Court with enough evidence of Fallen Arbor's current whereabouts, they will take up arms." She glanced up and the skeptical expressions brought an exasperated sigh from her. "I'm not joking. You're both too young to know this, but they turned on the other two for conspiring with the Old Continent. Later, they only waged battles against Falco Vendecci's battalion until they lost. To this day, we believe Landon and his witch were involved."

"Witch?" Valiente hissed, nudging her with an elbow. "And now who is the one withholding information!"

"There's only rumors," she countered, elbowing him back until he knocked into me.

"Let's not squabble like children," I drawled, rubbing my forehead. "Regardless, we will get what information we can here, for as long as we are *safe* and double back to Glensdale."

"Agreed." Valiente glanced at Red Wine. "And you, Assassin?"

"Depends on the situation." Again, she tapped the map on a peninsula to the west of Captiva City. "If we get separated, I think Terahime is a better option. They'd expect you to go to Glensdale, and you may put the city in danger. From there, we can charter a ship and sail north through the Frigid Waves. Depending on the ice, we can either backtrack along Willow Waters and come into Winter's Perch from the west side of it."

"W-wait. Isn't that the Moaning Forest of Wayward Souls? Isn't that an old battlefield and dumping ground for those with the Madness?" Valiente stood tall, crossing his arms. "You can't expect us to navigate that mess, do you?"

Red Wine chuckled, rolling up her map. "Look, that's been a good century or so ago. Don't tell me you now take children's ghost stories as fact, knight?"

"I don't." Valiente puffed out his cheeks, and we all followed her out of the old mill. "But that's rather risky."

She halted, and we both nearly slammed into her. "Look, the Berserk Brigade are peons to Landon. I'm the only one who has ever had to fight an official pack of Fallen Arbor operatives. You don't know how forgiving this plan will be. I'm willing to bet all of us will be wounded and in need of healing if shit goes badly in Captiva City. And I promise, it's going to be hell when that moment hits."

She marched off, and we kept on her heels, the silence between us heavy. *I hate this. Spending my entire life studying the history, and not one damn book had any of this darkness in it. Is this the dark past of Grandmere you wanted me to be free of, Father? I now see why. Nothing good will come of what we will put in motion ... our lives are forfeited to waging war and running to live to see tomorrow. I'm sorry...*

CHAPTER 19

Sacrifices and Saviors

Walking into the tavern, John and Sonja were still carrying on their conversation at the table where I left them. Red Wine and Valiente had headed for the blacksmith, and I was sent to retrieve the clergymen. *I feel like a hunting hound today.* I paused at the threshold, John's eyes locked on mine, and I flinched. *Is he angry with how long I took? Or did something happen while I was gone?* He knitted his brow and stood.

"I take it we've run short of time to relax," he offered, assisting Sonja to her feet. "It seems we are to make our final preparations, Mother Superior. Are we crossing tonight?"

"N-no. Early morning in hopes the fog will cover us." *Ah, he's fretting over the fact we can't stay here any longer.*

"I see." Sonja nodded her head. "So, where are we going? What do you need us to do?"

I motioned for them to follow me, and we marched down the street to the blacksmith's shop. Three knocks and Bessie opened the door to the shop across the way. She stepped to the side, closing and locking it behind me. We followed her back to the room I had been in before. This time, the fire was warm and welcoming, the chest of weapons pulled out into the open and chairs arranged for everyone to be able to sit. *This is what I expected to see the first time.*

"Now, Father, you're first." She motioned for Sonja and me to sit. "Forgive me, but I need to size you up, and the coat needs to go to make sure this does its job."

"Yes, ma'am." John winked at me, and I shot my gaze away, thankful for the mask.

As John pulled the coat off, he began to unbutton the shirt as well, and Bessie fussed, "Unless you plan on wearing this against the skin—"

"I am. I aim to hide the fact I have it on at all." He pulled the blouse free, his muscles glowing in the firelight.

The mark of The Church made Sonja and Bessie both gasp.

John frowned. "Is there something the matter?"

"J-john," stuttered Sonja, who stood in alarm. "Who did that to you?"

He smirked, a baffled expression on his face. "Don't all the priests get one, Mother Superior?"

"Y-yes, but not this one." She closed the gap between them, daring to touch the scarred lines. "Who put this mark on you?"

"Bishop Marquis," my voice cut across the room, sour as I spoke, "and I was the one who held him down for it. So, tell me, Mother Superior Sonja, what isn't right about his mark? Is it not the mark of an ordained priest?"

"It's not." Her answer knocked the color from John's face, and every muscle in my body tensed. "This is the mark of a saint. Priests only get a small branding here, at best, the size of my hand between the shoulders but this ... no one has been ordained a saint for over a century. I don't understand..."

"It was meant to kill me." John mustered a smile, warranting a sigh from me. "He had covered it in poison and ... I'm here now, and that's all that matters."

"John, this isn't right. He shouldn't have had access to that artifact—" Her voice was a shriek.

"Don't expect me to call you Saint John or Saint Thompson," I blurted, following his lead to break the tension.

150

Sonja blinked, her eyes bouncing between us as John started to laugh. "R-right. Please don't. It's awkward enough when you call me Father John." John's face flushed, and he turned back to Bessie. "I'm ready to be fitted, madame."

"I'm so sorry... I didn't know..." Sonja sat down, lost in her thoughts as she clutched the cross on her necklace. "I didn't realize how far the corruption had grown. Now as I return, I'll have to make some of the hardest decisions as..." Choking her next words, she looked to me in desperation.

"It's too deep to bleed out now that Fallen Arbor is involved. The flesh must be cut at this stage of the infection," I warned, and she nodded.

"I see." She bit her lip, eyes watery with the wave of emotions her thoughts brought.

"And I'm afraid it's rather a grim ordeal to go through, even after cutting down one like Falco." I watched as Bessie measured John, his whisperings making her laugh and steal glances at me. "But it's vital to get you back there, Mother Superior. You might be able to shift the tide before it's a complete loss."

"You think so?" I could barely hear her mumbled words. "But I'm just the..." She became aware of the extra entity and corrected her course. "...a *nun*. Not exactly the next *bishop*, by any means."

"Honey, you ain't foolin' anyone." I smiled at Bessie's interjection. *How much information did the brigade leave behind?* "We're all aware you're our beloved Princess Sonja."

"Um!" Sonja's eyes bulged as John and I chuckled.

"And you can tell King Regius he can shove his brigade where the sun doesn't shine." She pinched John and wagged a finger at me. "He needs to take a lesson from this man, here. In order to run The Tower proper, he's someone I'd gladly call King."

A chill snaked up my spine as the word *King* stabbed into me. "My father is a very capable man who is more than happy to end this Civil War."

"We would gladly receive you as the King if peace is your aim, Blood Prince," she scoffed, shoving John's arm up and out of her way.

"I was wondering why everyone in town was minding their manners and keeping distance from us." I met Bessie's gaze, and she gave a knowing nod. "It seems you were all aware that you had more than one royal playing dress up among you." Drumming my fingers on the chair's arm, I couldn't shake how the title of *King* haunted me.

"I must say you've made some good allies already, your majesty." She finished marking a few things on a scrap paper and handed it with the chainmail shirt to John. "Now, as much as I enjoyed the tour, Father, I'd appreciate you dressing yourself proper before leaving my house or old Gerta across the way is bound to see her chosen lord and savior sooner and not later!"

"If I must," teased John, dropping the items on my lap.

"Now, your majesty," Bessie chirped in Princess Sonja's direction, "let's get you into proper gear in hopes getting you home safely. I have far more female wares than male, sorry Father." Bessie gave a worried expression as John's blouse blanketed the marking. "May you find that ill-intended mark a blessing at the end of this path the Fates weave for you."

"If you knew what dark thoughts linger..." He paused, catching my gaze, and frowned. "I suppose who doesn't anymore." He tried sliding the white collar in place, but it caught on his shirt. "Da—Ashton." His face flushed as he failed to pull it loose, tangling it further. "Help me with this."

Standing, I narrowed my eyes at him, and he rolled his in reply. Lifting his chin, I released the collar that had caught the top button. With a flick of a finger, it slid loose, and he pushed it back into place. Pulling on his jacket, his body shielded me from the girls, and he whispered too low for them to hear.

"Should we even trust these people?"

He was working the coat's buttons from bottom to top when I pressed my hand against his torso, blocking his efforts. "You skipped a button," I gruffed.

"Oh?"

Playfully, I began unbuttoning the jacket then the blouse.

"Now you're teasing me." His face flushed, his torso tensing as my knuckles raked his skin. "And you fuss at me for flirting with danger," he hissed.

"You made the first move when you took your shirt off and forced me to watch her rub you down," I cooed, licking a fang. "This is simply my reply. Taking a stake in what is mine." I slid a hand up and under, fingers gliding to his collarbone before retreating to button the shirt closed with haste. "All these people have left is trust." I patted his chest with a fanged grin.

John swallowed, his eyes piercing me. "I want..." He covered his mouth and spun away. "Excuse me, I need to splash my face. Do you have..."

"Yes, down that hall and in the kitchen. You'll find a bowl and a pitcher of fresh water, dear." Bessie was knelt behind Sonja who faced the fireplace. "Now, I hope you're not feeling sick knowing you leave for the battlefield tomorrow, Father?"

"N-no ma'am. Just a little ... flushed from the, er, fire," called John.

"I know some good herbs for sleep if you need'em tonight," offered Bessie, marking a new paper and working around Sonja. "We'll be able to finish these adjustments tonight."

Grunting, I muttered curses to myself. *What the hell is wrong with me?* My restless muscles brought me to my feet. *Maybe a real fight might do me some good. It's not that I haven't cut a man down on the battlefield, but this will be the first time I believe in the cause.* Pacing the floor, I stretched my arms, trying to outrun the aching building at my core. *Is this what a caged animal feels like?*

"There's a chest on the floor by the front door. That one's for you." Bessie's voice brought me back from my thoughts. "If you've never worn a manica, I'll show you, and them, how to buckle one on. Eventually you'll get the hang of it and strap it on yourself."

"Th-thank you." The tiny chest had some weight to it as I sat it on the chair and pulled it open.

The leather was dark and gleamed with oil. As I pulled it from the chest to marvel over the scaled length of plated leatherwork, it sent chills through me. She motioned for me to come closer and began showing me the buckling pattern I would need to memorize. The chest piece would cover half my upper torso; a pauldron for the shoulder had magnificent ornamental features of raging horse. *Hmph, fitting considering Basque.* From there, the paneling down the length of the arm gave me the impression of the scales of reptiles I'd seen pictures of that were said to swim the shores of Terahime. It ended with a leather gauntlet designed to be as every bit of flexible as a rider's or archer's glove.

Bessie tugged at my jacket, and I began to pull it off, eager to know more about this new bit of armor. "What's the best way to wear this?"

"The style is an old one. Back in the time of the champions, they'd wear it bare-chested in the fights. We added length to the buckles, so you could strap it on top of the shirt and that leather vest there." Pulling at a strap, she managed to loose the last. "Impractical to wear it bare if you ask me. Just ignorant. No one's immortal, and you're not there to unnerve a single opponent. Now, slip your hand in the glove first—make sure we got the measurements right," insisted Bessie.

I did so, the leather worked with oil until it had softened to be battle ready immediately. "It's tight, but exactly how I would prefer it. This thing's heavy." She rested the pauldron on my shoulder, and I grunted, "Very heavy."

"We didn't bother to check the weight, seeing how you lifted the wagon the other day."

I sighed. *Consequences, Dante. Every action has a consequence that can ripple on endlessly. I can hear the Old Farmer howling and making a mockery of me from his grave.*

"Straighten your back, would ya? Princess, come give me a hand. He's too big around for my arms to get around him proper. Chest belt like a barrel, he is!"

John coughed, calling my eyes to him as he chuckled at the situation of being sandwiched and manhandled by two tiny women. "My, the quandary this is, Half-pint."

"Shut your mouth, Father," I spat, grunting as Bessie pulled the first buckle tight across my chest, the leather pressing into my back and upper ribs. "Am I not allowed to breathe?" I marveled at her strength.

"Stop your crying," she shushed, tightening it one more notch, and another grunt escaped. "Unless you want blisters in places that'll startle the ladies."

"The ladies, you say," I drawled, smirking under my mask at the disapproving face John made. "You keep scowling like that, and someone might think you dislike my new armor, Father."

"The armor is the least of my concerns." His face flushed, but he didn't dare look away from me. "It suits you, strangely enough. It reminds me exactly how broad-chested and strong-armed you are. Normally it's when you work the fields when I'm bitterly reminded how much stronger you are overall."

I opened my mouth but clamped it shut, holding in the words I wished to utter: *Is that the only time you feel how strong I am?*

John's face grew red as if some part of him could hear my thought. "Anyhow, I see we start with the glove, then the pauldron. Strap the chest and work down the length of the arm?"

Bessie pinched the tender flesh under my arm, and I raised it in alarm. "That's right, Father John. But the buckles can't cross the muscles here and here. You'll cut circulation or worse, hinder his movements. You want it tight, unmoving." She cinched one buckle and the next, securing the manica to my upper arm. "Now, Prince, because you have armor here doesn't mean you should use it on par to a normal shield. This is to minimize the damage and allow time to counter. It's not designed to prevent the inevitable but redirect blows at best."

"R-right."

She started buckling the lower part of my arm. "Flex. Bump your fist." Bessie watched my forearm, twisting it one way then the other. "This needs to be adjusted. You're built like a farmer;

the muscles are drawn farther into your wrist than a fighter."
Bessie froze, glaring up and meeting my gaze as she whispered,
"But I thought you were the Blood Prince?"

"I am." Snorting, I whispered back, amused. "But ask any
in Glensdale about their princes, and you'll discover we're not
afraid to get our hands dirty."

"Is that so?" Adjusting the buckles into a more comfortable
spot, I flexed to test her work. "Good, that's better, is it not?
Father, can you come tug on this?"

"I, uh, pardon?" John blinked, gaping. "Tug... on...what?"

Chuckling, Bessie pulled him over. "Grab hold and jerk him
good, a few times."

"Yeah, John. Jerk me," I replied flatly.

"I don't want to hear a word from you," hissed John, tugging
the armor hard to bring me closer, and his face reddened. "Not.
One. Word." Another jerk of the armor, and he pushed me back.
"It's attached to him like everything else he owns."

"Good! Now as the boys say, just keep it as well kept and oiled
as your willy, and you'll be in good shape!" She howled at her
own dirty joke as I began to choke and sputter.

Catching my breath, I grabbed my coat, avoiding John's
sheepish grin. "Well, off to do some training with the tomahawk.
Father, you'll find Valiente and Red Wine across the way."

Before they could say otherwise, I slipped out the door.
*Dammit. I can't keep it together around him anymore. Old Farmer,
you're to blame for this fire... It's not fair, the way the cards
are playing out. This path we follow seems hellbent on keeping
us together, yet we risk one another's lives chasing after what
we desire.*

CHAPTER 20

Last Day of Training

Avoiding the entire crew, I headed back to the old lumber mill. The new manica was heavy, and the last thing I wanted was to go into the battlefield without adjusting to the damned thing. Buckles and straps squeezed into me, and I muttered curses under my breath.

How such a small woman could tighten anything like this is beyond me. She must've worn corsets in her youth. Dammit, I can't breathe. Pumping my fist, I saw the leather glove moved well. I rolled my shoulder then my whole arm to gauge my new range of motion. Much to my relief, very little had been lost. *She knew what to recommend after all. I'll have to call on her in the future for things like this.*

Grabbing the tomahawk from my belt, I threw it at a chosen mark. I frowned, the results deplorable, and I tried again. By the time I stopped missing the mark, I had abandoned my jacket and mask, sweat dripping down my temple as I slung my braid behind me. Now I aimed for speed, running from place to place as I threw it with hard *thuds* against the wooden bones of the mill. Dust plumes and debris floated down through the holes in the roof. Panting, I had lost count of the passing minutes. *Or has it been hours?*

Still unsatisfied with my new skill, I started to play with not looking. The weight of my armor was long forgotten as the sun cast long shadows on my tiny game of catch.

Throw-Thud-Retrieve.

Throw-Thud-Retrieve.

Throw-CLANK!

Breathless, I glared at Red Wine and smirked.

"Not bad." Slung over her shoulder was my claymore in a new sheath. "We've run out of time, but I'm glad you wasted no time to train. Now for you to wield this like your brother." Dropping it to the ground, she walked over to lean on an old log. "But you'll have to go easy on your training partners this evening."

I scowled, leaning on my knees, swallowing to rasp, "And what team am I facing after exhausting myself so?"

"First off, me." Valiente came marching in, armored in a way I hadn't seen since the night he came in bloodied and desperate. "But I imagine the others will dive in just to get the feel of their armor and movements. At this point, we're all feeling rusty and need a good warmup if—no, when—we face the Brigade."

"I don't like this." I stood, inhaling deeply to slow my beating heart. "I've already tuckered myself out and..." John and Sonja came through the threshold. "...we both know I'm not going to know my own strength."

Red Wine crossed her arms, the armor polished and oiled for the first time since we left Glensdale. "Precisely why this lesson needs to be learned. We all need our muscles to act quickly. If you are all too sore in the morning, we can leave later or hold off another day. That's all I can offer."

"What's the matter, Dante?" John smirked as he shed his jacket and began rolling up his sleeves. "Afraid you can't keep up with us all? Red Wine tells us you've become quite the bat-tleworthy trainee."

"Has she?" I pulled the tomahawk from the mark and slid it in my belt. "Which weapon am I using?"

"Your hands." Her voice hit hard and sharp.

"Am I to catch blades with my palms?" I scoffed.

158

She shrugged, declaring, "Something like that. You need to learn to dodge now as well as adjust to the manica. It'll help you push a strike off aim, but please remember it's not a shield ... and neither are your forearms."

"So, you want me to dodge now." I started to take off my weapons when she made a clicking sound.

"No-no," she warned, wagging a finger at me. "You're going to dodge with full regalia. Time to start carrying that Claymore like it's your third leg."

"I already have one of those..." I muttered with a smirk.

"I swear, you two deserve one another." She picked up the claymore and tossed it at me. "Stop being so childish."

I grunted. "Who? Me and John?"

John rubbed the back of his neck and confessed, "I might have said something similar on my way here..."

"You two are just overgrown children far as I'm concerned." Huffing, Red Wine circled the group, shoving John and Sonja forward before passing Valiente. "And he's just as guilty for it. I need to know if anyone here has any fight in them or at least experience and training I can take advantage of and rely upon."

"I don't think my soldiers get this chatty before a battle." Valiente snorted, unsheathing his sword. "Trust me, I've already faced two of the brigade members and put them behind bars."

"Before or after their indoctrination with Fallen Arbor?" She paused, a glow showing in her eyes.

"Well, before." Valiente shrugged.

"Expect them to be monsters in comparison." She pointed a dagger at me as I buckled the last piece of the claymore halter across my chest. "Imagine them all to be his level but with more experience."

I frowned, adding my rebuttal, "I've seen a battlefield before."

"Yes, and nearly took an arrow to the head. I was there. The Guild clipped it." Without warning, she came in low and fast, her petite build adding to how far down she could sprint.

Using the manica, I barely redirected the first strike and leaned back in time for the blade to scrape across the mask. "Shit!"

John and Valiente both charged at me. A broadsword came swinging down from above. Seeing the middle piercing stab of the rapier, I twisted. The manica clinked as the broadsword rode it down to the ground. Behind me, the rapier scudded against the claymore's sheath. *A wall of a sword can double as a shield I suppose!*

"Good. Use everything you can," encouraged Red Wine.

Footsteps came rushing up behind me as John and Valiente backstepped to reset their offense. A heel landed hard, shoving the claymore between my shoulder blades, the wind leaving me, and I stumbled forward. Valiente swung and I sidestepped to avoid John, barely blocking a swing of a dagger from Sonja as I deflected it off the manica. A hard kick hit across the back of my knees. Growling, I failed to fight the urge to land buckle. As my weight came down, Valiente went for a downward piercing strike. Swinging my arm, I knocked the blade from his hands and jolted to my feet.

Valiente made a muffled yelp, leaping back as I closed the gap. He pulled a small blade and swung wide. I caught his wrist and yanked him between me and Red Wine's rear assault. She jerked to stop her punch, huffing as she retreated. Sonja and John came at me from both sides, so I threw Valiente to John, his feet leaving the ground, and they landed in a heap. Sonja, also wielding a rapier, came at me with a flurry of strikes.

Her style is fast and pushes the opponent back. Unlike John's strikes meant to pierce, these are meant to cut again and again and bleed the opponent out.

Frustrated, seeing Red Wine dipping a hand to her side, I decided to press forward. Stretching my arm out with the manica, I motioned in a circle, disrupting the flow of her strikes and turning her wrist to the side. Rushing forward, I hooked an arm around her lower torso. "I'm sorry for this," I gritted and managed to land her gently to the dirt.

Spinning, I now had three opponents ready for me. Red Wine, Valiente, and John rushed forward. A throwing dagger glanced against my mask. Valiente swung downward in the same place as the dagger, but I hadn't flinched, palming the broadsword off course. The swing slammed across Red Wine's armguard, and they lost balance trying to retreat. While Valiente fell onto her, John came at me with a determined expression.

"Stay still," he barked with a smirk.

"I only can use my hands," I countered, jumping back to dodge a wide swing. "I thought this was a lesson in dodging."

"And striking." He lunged forward with a piercing strike again.

I redirected it with my manica, stepping forward. "Got you!"

"Try again." John's heel kicked the side of my knee, and with another step forward, he landed a knee to my gut.

I wheezed as I retreated, holding my stomach. Sonja was back on her feet, brushing dirt off as she joined his side, nodding as they dropped into offensive poses. Raising my arms, I widened my stance, my knee aching from so many hits.

I get it. I'm a big guy, and our knees are shit.

They lunged forward, wide swings from both sides, one high and one low. *Shit, I can't dodge...*

Without thinking, I threw my arm with the manica into the crossing swings. Circling like I had before, the redirect made them lock into one another. Leaning my shoulder into it, the pauldron forced the blades toward them, and they pulled away. As I ran past, I dropped low and kicked Valiente's legs out from under him as Red Wine scrambled to avoid him a second time.

"Fuck!" he shouted. "Son of a..."

Red Wine chuckled, coming to her feet. "Okay, okay, that's enough. You can dodge just fine apparently. It's so hard with you tossing us into one another but a great tactic."

We all stood, exchanging glares at one another, the daylight dimming with warm hues among the trunks of towering red pines. I inhaled deeply, holding it to slow the pounding in my chest, and at last, exhaled.

I can't believe it I can move like this with all the added weight and already tired. This wasn't a lesson of dodging but one for me to realize how strong I have become.

Sweat dripped from everyone's chin, all but Red Wine who seemed the only one not winded from the explosion of energy.

"You're a monster." Valiente sheathed his sword and looked Sonja over. "I can't believe you shoved the Princess to the ground like that."

Sonja cupped her cheek and confessed, "Actually he did it alarmingly fast and gently ... even apologized."

John gave me a skeptical glare, fussing, "Yet you throw the knight into the assassin like scraps to the dogs."

Shrugging at his comment, I inspected the marks on the manica, pleased to see they weren't deep nor anything I couldn't buff out like on a saddle. "I like this thing."

"Exactly what made you ask for it?" Red Wine picked up her throwing knife.

"It was the blacksmith's wife's idea." I shifted the claymore, the weight on my left knee throbbing still. "Did everyone aim for the same knee on purpose?"

They looked at one another before all eyes fell on Red Wine.

"Well, did it work? I told them to aim for it before getting within earshot." She crossed her arms. "How's that knee feeling?"

"Like shit," I scoffed.

John grabbed his jacket, sheathing his rapier. "It's late. Let's eat, bathe, and steel ourselves for tomorrow's troubles. May the Fates that have brought us to these crossroads see us safe to our ordained stations. Sobeit."

"Save your prayers for those who deserve them." Red Wine sounded bitter as she marched out of the old mill.

John looked to me, and I threw out my arms. "I have no idea. There's a lot I haven't pieced together about her."

"I see." He smiled to himself for a moment and looked to Princess Sonja. "Well, I'll see you in the morning, Mother Superior?"

"Y-yes." She looked to Valiente, and he gave a knowing nod. "We need to do some planning, and we'll see you all at dawn."

John nodded, and I followed obediently. Marching back into Leifseid, I had fallen back into the bodyguard assassin. No one

162

looked my way. The only words exchanged were those with John as he stopped and gave grace to those asking and prayers for many who greeted him. Occasionally I'd earn a side glance or a knowing nod, but in the end, I was the thing that followed the priest like a haunting shadow.

Is it wrong that I wish secretly that this could be our life? To simply follow him, watch him be the priest he always aimed to be and bring smiles and hope to the people he encounters.

CHAPTER 21

Confessions

"Two for a bath." The innkeeper looked at John and me. "You two look like you went rolling in the mud with the pigs." He pinched his nose, pushing back half the fee. "It's on me since you might die tomorrow."

John swiped the money and marched off without a word. I followed hot on his heels, and we both disappeared behind the locked door. Unlike the bathhouse in Tavern Way, this one was well organized, everything marked and clean. There were fresh clothes offered, cloth to dry with, and the tub was filled with clean water with a fire to keep the water warm. John leaned on the tub, staring down into the water as if hoping his reflection would say something.

"What's wrong?" My voice came out as a whisper, some part of me afraid to know.

"Were you always that monstrous?" John grimaced, staring at my reflection in the water. "Never mind that. I suppose you were always the stronger one. I didn't mean..."

Placing a hand on his shoulder, he turned, and I kissed him. Pulling back, I at last whispered, "I will become whatever I must in order to protect what I love."

164

John pulled me into him, his kiss deepening. Tongues rubbing against one another, the sweet flavor of his blood filled my senses. Moaning, I sucked on his tongue, hungry for him in every manner physically possible.

I want him. To devour. To love. To have always. This is all I will ever want in this life is to be in his arms ... to hold him in my own.

Pulling away, I searched those blue gems that had jolted me the first time they ever met my own eyes. *The Fates have brought us together. The gods have sanctioned this—they must have. If I am to love and protect him, then ... Sobeit.*

"What thoughts I wonder lay just behind those maroon eyes of yours," he muttered.

Twisting away from him, I started to unbuckle my gear. "Does it matter?" The claymore *thunked* to the floor, my jacket on top as I began pulling at the buckles on my arm. "What if I made silent vows to follow you to the ends of this world?" The manica fell heavily as the last buckle came loose across my chest. "Would you stop me?"

"No," John whispered, unbuttoning his own blouse, pulling his belt free.

Our gazes were locked as we undressed before one another. "And if I was willing to forsake my birthright, what would you say then?"

"I'd prefer to follow you on that path than the lies I've been fed for ten years," he confessed, John's body free of clothes as he leaned back against the tub.

"Ah, so you'd throw away your life's dream to become a prince's consort?" The last of my leather gear and weapons hit the floor, the vibrations of it loud under my bare feet.

"What if I confess..." He paused, searching my face a moment before continuing, "...that the day I left, I had changed my mind already?"

"I thought I hid my feelings from you," I admitted, fingers working nimbly to unbutton the last stitch of clothes on my torso.

"I didn't care if you felt the same," John said sternly. "I wanted to protect you. Find some answer to the Madness, the Fanged

Lady, and even how to defeat Falco. The only place I knew that might have it was The Church."

At last, my shirt and pants joined the heap at my feet. "Then tell me," I started, closing the gap between us until John was pinned between the tub and me. "Tell me what it is that you wish in life, so that I can be the driving force to make it happen," I demanded.

"To be the Prince's Priest."

John kissed me as if it was the first time all over again.

It was slow, intimate, and made my heart race like nothing had ever done. To feel his flesh under my own, the rise and fall of the branding on his back under my hands only added to the longing I could never shake. That old ache in my heart and soul swelled, and I acted on it. Kissing and licking at his neck, and much to my horror ... my fangs sank into his neck.

So hungry.

John moaned, his fingers gripping the hair on my head and holding me there, encouraging me to not stop. *I want to devour him.* My blood rushed and I latched on harder, earning a grunt.

"Don't stop..." he rasped.

I swallowed deep long gulps. *He tastes so sweet.* My body was on fire. Feeding on John wasn't enough. *I want more of him. I want all of him.* Releasing my bite, I licked at the wound I had made. Kissing it, I continued to suckle my way across his collarbone, down his chest, before running my tongue back to the open flesh. John slid away from me, the sound of the water slapping against the tub bringing me back from the feral state. Gripping my wrist, he pulled me in, the water spilling over the edge as we sank into the steaming liquid.

I couldn't break my gaze on the blood rising from the open wound, trickling down his chest. Licking a fang, I was back to sucking on the sweet red ambrosia that poured from him. Gliding my hand down the center of John's body, I pushed my thigh between his legs. A grunt escaped John as I wrapped my fingers firm around his hardened length. He tilted his hip, moaning,

166

and I lost the fight with my desire; fangs dove back into the open wound, the hunger and lust for his body overwhelming.

The taste of him, the feel of him, the way he smells and moans and ... so sweet on the tongue no matter where I choose to taste him. I can't stop. I won't stop... He won't let me this time...

Another moan escaped him. "Dante..." His fingers pressed hard into the muscles of my back. "I'm yours," he reassured me, and I broke away, alarmed.

My back connected with the far side of the tub, water pushed upward, slapping across the ground and a shelf. "That's enough," I panted, rubbing the blood from my chin. "I've taken more than enough..." Twisting, I reached for a small towel and inched closer to press down on the fang marks. "I'm—"

"I'm sorry." His hand covered my own as John brushed hair from my forehead. "You ran away to avoid this fate, and here we are right where you didn't want to be on my behalf. It's not fair what I did to you."

"I can't run away for my legacy forever. At least, it was done in a way that I chose for it and not forced upon me." I raised the towel and winced, pressing back down with eyes shut tight. "Next time pull me off if I get aggressive." Scowling, my heart raced with the rising anxiety. "I lose myself every time, more and more. This can't be safe."

John pulled my forehead against his own, grinning as I opened my eyes. "We decided to travel this path together. Never forget that ... so stop running ahead without me. Unlike Ashton, we're doing this together, and I don't mean just the two of us by ourselves either."

Peeking under the bloodied towel, I was relieved to see the bleeding had stopped. "That's going to be impossible to hide..." Sighing, I rung the blood from the towel. "What if they search you for..."

"I think that will be the least of our concerns. We'll have to try to get to the church library in secret. Perhaps there's a way through the catacombs themselves." John pushed the towel away when I tried to place it back over the bite. "We'll blame that on Falco if needed."

It pained me to think of it, but I couldn't find any words to refuse the concept.

"Stop fretting over me, my prince." He exhaled and leaned back into the tub, throwing his head back, eyes shut. "Let us enjoy the last peaceful evening we'll get for a while, no?"

I couldn't break my stare from the wound. *Falco used to leave those same marks on me...* Shaking the thoughts from my head, I began scrubbing myself, unwilling to break from the guilt. Without warning, John's foot smacked the center of my chest.

"Stop glaring at it."

My face flushed, and I shoved his foot off. "I wasn't," I lied, pulling myself up and out of the tub. "Shit, I need to clean some of this. Everything I wear is some sort of halter or armor." Hands on hips, I stood dripping over the heap of equipment. "Do we have any mink oil and scrub in the..." Looking over my shoulder, John had one eye open staring at me with a sheepish grin. "You're the worst priest ever."

"Saint," he corrected. "So, I'll have to do some research on what this marking means. Wonder if Bishop Montgomery knows anything."

"Last I recalled, Saints were martyrs to the Church's cause." Snorting, I began unraveling my braid. "And you're very much alive, so that makes you quite the anomaly for a Saint."

"By the heavens and hells that keep us here." He sank down into the tub, submerging completely before popping back up with a splash. "Why did I never ask about the branding other than insisting on you holding me down for the thing?"

Shaking my hair loose, I came over to the tub and dunked my head into the water, scrubbing before coming up to meet him nose to nose. "Some part of me suspects that your mind was lusting after things no priest is allowed to have."

John's cheeks turned red, and I pulled away before he could reach for me. "You tease, Dante."

"Do I?" I smirked, leaving the guilt behind and letting the tension fade. "If you behave, I'll redo your braid upstairs." Drying my hair in the towel, I crouched over my gear and began cleaning various pieces.

"Did Grandpa really leave those scars on your body?" John hadn't asked me about it, and nostalgia rolled through me.

If he sees these, he's going to give me an earful and chase me to my grave. I smiled, the Old Farmer's words echoing in my mind. "He was stronger than any teacher I ever had growing up. But honestly, they would be gone if I had bothered to cover them with salve or shirt while tending to the fields."

John abandoned the tub, towering behind me as the water tapped against the floor. "These three are deep." His finger traced one over my right shoulder blade and sent goosebumps over my skin. "What happened there? They don't look like a sword cut."

"Wow, I forgot all about that." Blinking, memories came rushing back to the third summer spent on the farm. "There was a bear that got into the pigs. The old man was asleep that night, but I heard the commotion and thought I was big boy enough to handle it alone."

"A bear?" He walked away, and I could breathe again. "I don't remember ever coming across one before."

"Later, come to find out, there was a fire in the Moaning Forest of Wayward Souls to the west and drove a lot of animals to the farm. In fact, we had an abundance of game to make up for the loss, but the vermin were near impossible to keep out of the stores, cabin, and decimated the crops that year. Who knew rabbits could be so ravenous?"

John chuckled, drying off. "Yeah, I've had to climb in a burrow once for Grandpa. Still got a scar on my knuckle where one bit me."

We laughed, both hiding the mournful thoughts of how much we missed the farm, the old man, and more importantly, the life we were forced to abandon. Our days of dreaming about living out our pitiful lives on the land had been gone for some time.

The smell of freshly broken dirt, the squeak of the water pump, and thud of the hoe were nothing but distant memories. Blood, sweat, and tears now covered the faces all around.

"Sorry. I know it's not easy for you," I whispered, looking at the branded back of the youth who had become a hard-muscled man. "Not being there in time to see him off to the next life."

"That's why I left you there," he replied, grabbing up his shirt. "I've entrusted all things I hold dear to you … including my heart and life. It's exactly the same payment you've given me since that snow-laden day I found you. You gave me everything you had to offer, and I realized, I wanted to do the same the day I left."

"Why do we do this…" I flustered, brushing the dirt and mud off my gear, and I began dressing. "Constantly circling back to saying sorry, to reminiscing to what could have been, or worse, reminding one another how much we've given each other?"

He huffed, and after a long pause, answered, "Because we were too stubborn to say it all to begin with. Just making up for all that lost time, I suppose."

Freezing, I blinked a few times before agreeing, "I guess we have so many unspoken confessions of love, loss, and regrets."

"Something like that," he admitted. "Enough of this. We need to eat and sleep."

Always needing the last word, but it's just an easy way for me to go silent when I please to do so.

CHAPTER 22

Salvation Road

John tugged on the straps and buckles of my armor, tightening two by one notch and making me grunt. The priest's high-collared jacket hid the bandaged bitemark. *He should have stopped me...* If John was sore, he didn't dare let it be known in movement or make a sound to reveal it. *Stubborn.* Downstairs, I left him to eat breakfast with Sonja as I prepped the horses with Red Wine and Valiente. No one said a word to one another, nor did the locals seem their cheerful selves. None of us wanted to point out the problem already presenting itself as the first light hit Leifseid. *Where the hell did the fog go?*

Basque took the carrot I offered and stood still for my preparations. I had spent the last of my own gold on armor for him, though it had needed adjusting due to his size. As for the supplies, we packed lighter and sparingly. If we could break into a full gallop from here to Captiva City, it would take half a day to get to the gates. Unfortunately, we were going to have to take Salvation Road, and rumors had come in that the Berserk Brigade had setup a checkpoint no one could come near without being killed or wounded. Worse, the Madness had increased on the main road to the point attacks were on the rise.

Leather and sweat filled my nostrils. Everyone had fretted over their gear last night and even this morning to a point of near obsession. *Did any of us sleep at all besides the assassin? Does she even sleep?* Red Wine's body language didn't hold any signs of stiffness from the sobering realization we were riding into an active warzone. In fact, she hummed and seemed light on her feet. *She was a champion for a time, right? Or did I make that assumption?*

"Are we still going through with this without the cover of fog?" I couldn't ignore the unspoken concern among us any longer.

"Well, we can't wait any longer," she declared, checking Biscuit's saddle straps. "With fog, I don't think we would have gotten much farther. On a clear morning such as this, both sides have lost the chance of a pre-emptive strike, but we'll have to square off evenly. Don't worry, Half-pint. My goal is simply to get both of your princesses to safety. Speaking of which..."

John and Sonja walked out of the tavern, weapons haltered, chainmail clinking as they pulled up into their saddles. Both Jasmine and Elegance snorted and shuffled under the weight of their riders, sensing the tension and knowing what the armored horses meant. Colonel and Basque seemed excited with the additional armaments across their heads and chest for added protection. *I'll have to put him through warhorse training after all this.* Red Wine spun Biscuit in a tight circle, the horse ready to take off running in the thrilling atmosphere.

"And should we keep in mind who needs to square off with who?" I asked, shifting the claymore at my back.

"First, let's ride out. We have time to discuss this on our way there." Red Wine slapped her legs, and the tiny horse jolted forward.

Everyone fell in line with Red Wine in front, the clergymen in a second row, and Valiente and me side-by-side in the back. We looked like a tiny legion or calvary unit at best. The sounds of falling trees and the lumber mill soon faded, and we found ourselves alone on the road as the trunks became smaller and more spread out. I pushed Basque to go around everyone and match Biscuit's canter.

"So, as we were discussing?" Red Wine glanced over at me, tilting her masked face. "You said we'd be squaring off with them?"

"We know we have two long-range attackers to be mindful of when we engage with them. One I'm certain is a Fallen Arbor agent, and I will deal with her personally. The others I will leave to you and the knight," she declared. "But I advise you take down the spearman above the others."

"You can't be serious?" Valiente roared, pushing between John and Sonja. Elegance and Jasmine nipped at Colonel who snorted in reply. "It took everything I had to take down Dasa when I faced him!"

"Ah, so, you take on the commander and leave the rest to Dante." She snickered.

"That's three against one." I swallowed, my shoulders visibly shuddering. "Do you really think I'm capable of doing that?"

"As Dante, I have no idea." She shrugged and at last looked me in the eyes. "But Ashton ... that's another matter. I've seen him and Warlord Sebastian level a hundred Fallen Arbor soldiers and mages to cut a path for others to walk safely through." Her head turned away fast, her words breaking off sharply for a moment before she added, "Today you will have to decide if you really plan on going through with being your brother and if you even have the killing intent needed to pull it off. He never hesitated, and neither should you. Show no mercy."

"Are you mad?" Valiente hissed. "You expect him to take on three solo? These aren't just normal soldiers! These men enjoy killing people, and what about getting John and Sonja into the city? Are you going to use us as a distraction?"

"Yes, and I'll get the clergymen into the safety of the walls and through the battlefield." Clearing her throat, she spoke more sternly. "Remember, with the temptation of capturing Ashton, they may disregard the Princess and Father altogether. If you get shot by the flintlock, don't let it phase you, Dante. Flinching once in battle can have dire consequences. It's going to burn like hell, but I can't promise I'll find Flintlock Betty in time."

"I still don't know what to think of that idea." Mumbling, I looked back to John who lowered his brow.

"I'll be waiting for you," John reassured.

"In fact, we'll meet by the main sewer grate in the canals to the east of the cathedral." Red Wine brought Biscuit to stop, spinning to glare at everyone. "There will not be another option for a meeting place with all that I know is unfolding. It's not ideal, but it will give us a way to sneak you all into your aimed destinations. I've worked hard to make these arrangements. It's not up for debate. Do I make myself clear?"

"Why there?" Sonja shifted in her saddle, knitting her brow.

"Because from there, I have members of The Guild waiting so we can sneak you and the knight into the castle, and we'll be cutting through the catacombs to get to my informant and drop these two into the library. We can't let Bishop Marquis know we have made it to the city now that he's pulling King Regius' strings. He's made no effort to hide he's working under Fallen Arbor either." Red Wine twisted, pointing at Valiente. "You need to gather as much information before letting the bishop know she's back inside the castle. The maids will need to swear secrecy for her safety until we can move these two back out from under the Church. If this goes bad, blood will spilled in places you both might regret."

"Are you threatening us?" Valiente's expression darkened. "And how long has The Guild been able to sneak into the castles?"

"When we decided it was worth the risk to protect potential allies," she hissed. "Now promise that once you are back in her room you stay by her side until we regain ground from Fallen Arbor. Give us until fall at the least."

"Fall!" Valiente's frown deepened. "I don't think we have that sort of time with how fast they took over during the winter!"

"You have a good point..." Red Wine shifted in her saddle, hands tightening on the reins. "You think we can manage two months before we get discovered then?"

"We'll make an effort. It should give me time to sort out who will align with Sonja and who is aligned with the bishop." Valiente let Colonel fall back behind, and I joined.

"That should work." John at last joined the conversation. "If we can get in via the catacombs, does that mean we can escape from there as well?"

"Yes, but there's more than one tunnel. I only know one route, but rumors say the network spans beyond Captiva City and halfway to Terahime. You can get lost in there for days if you don't die trying to find a way out." Pulling on her reins, she started down the road once more, and we followed. "I'd only make that attempt if it were the only choice left, Father."

"Understood." John cleared his throat. "So, not to be a bother, why the canals? Can't we wait in a tavern or someplace more discreet?"

"I can't promise anyone's safety within the city walls. Neither can Princess Sonja at this point." The fact was cold and bitter leaving her lips. "Captiva City has become enemy territory, and we're losing informants left and right. Peace may not be possible for some time."

"I will make this treaty happen." Sonja straightened her posture. "My father has gone too far, and it seems I now hold the favor with the people of our land more than I realized. Change will happen upon my return."

"Good." Red Wine didn't bother to look back as we exited the forest into a clearing. "The Guild will support you as long as this will be your aim. You have us at your disposal, a first since the war started."

We all slowed to a stop. The clearing was on a hill overlooking the battlefield, and the wind brought a foul stench upon it.

Death. Decay. Despair.

In the distance, the city could be seen like a mirage between the pillars of smoke. Bodies were burning in huge piles, the road cutting between the mounds of flesh, and flames twisting until there was nothing but dirt and red flags at the halfway point. *The Berserk Brigade.* They were too far off to see what they looked like other than a single tent. By some twist of fate, we would be crossing during a time of rest, seeing no active battalions squaring off. *Or perhaps the Brigade has snuffed the will to fight out of the rest.* Both sides seemed to have retreated to their opposing stations.

The Civil War had waged for over a century, and at some point, Salvation Road had been deemed safe through a treaty on both sides. It was better for business to trade and be able to gather supplies and keep the war in designated zones. *Perhaps the age of Champions encouraged this practice. It was nothing more than a never-ending pissing contest where lives were thrown at one another.* On occasion Falco or some new human general would incite a "hard-push" to reclaim the line or a town on the outskirts. Leifseid was just deep enough in the woods to not bother with, but other places had become havens of trade, mercenary headquarters, and a place for all the cutthroats to settle in.

We've forgotten the reason for the war. I snorted in our silence, hearing my father's words in my head. *We stack and burn the dead, but to what end? Sure, we don't like how bloodeaters make the Madness either, but did it really start with them? No, it didn't. I was there to see how it all came about. If you ask me, everyone has lost the passion and the reason behind why we put on the armor and swing our blades anymore. Bloodeaters are no longer slaves, so why are we even still in a war over it? I can't remember the last human king who even knew the initial incident that started this wildfire. Someone needs to just make it stop and give us new hope for all and not the greed of one.*

The mask did very little to spare me from the decay and rot that filled the air. Generations of blood had spilled on the land under us until it changed the landscape permanently. The ground was stained black and red, the stench of it iron and sour. Archers called the Faceless were tasked with guarding the road and shot any who seemed to suffer from the plague. These were devout men and women from both sides who wore no sign of their faction and lived on Salvation Road. *They abandoned their*

176

former lives to simply serve a purpose for the whole. Wearing all black, their faces covered in the traditional cone-shaped mask that gave them a birdlike look, they were a harrowing presence, neither foe nor friend. Wide brimmed hats blocked the sun overhead, and they burned incense to combat the smell of rotting flesh. They never spoke, nor were others allowed to speak to them.

You ever seen the Faceless? I took in their presence with curiosity, remembering what Lord Knight Paul had told me one night during a hard blizzard. *I spoke to one once. Well, he'd gotten himself overwhelmed, and I rescued the man. They wear thick leather armor to spare them from most bites by flesheaters, but...* He had taken a long drag of his pipe, letting the smoke fall from his lips slow as he stared aimless into the fireplace. *Be kind to them. And if you ever need aid, you tell them the Old Owl sent you. There's something secretive about them, but they do have a community, though I think it's their way of building a faction that chooses no sides. What gets me is how much of their equipment was Preveran steel. If you ask me, they might be agents of The Court to keep some form of Sanctuary in place between The House and The Tower. Then there's the priests...*

Priests alongside knights serving as white flag barriers were aiding survivors scattered all over the battlefield in the distance. These men prayed for the dead, adding them to piles or setting them to flame in hopes of ridding the battlefield of the rancid corpses. Some of these victims had fallen in battle, but today, most were flesheaters who had met their end or close to it. Sobs and cries seem to float in and out of the air, making one wonder if they came from the piles or somewhere beyond. Smoke and dust filled the air like a polluted fog and limited the range of sight at times and stung my eyes. The most vexing were the newly awoken, those who had come back from The Madness.

The Fanged Lady's hold is still fading, and for the first time since the creation of bloodeaters, the victims of the Madness are waking from their nightmares, but...

A man sobbed among a pile of ravaged bodies drenched in blood, screaming, "I didn't mean to eat them! I couldn't stop! Oh, Divine Father, I couldn't stop!"

I swallowed, my chest ached with the memories of my own brush with the Madness. *So hungry. I still feel it creep forward like last night...* The ghostly whispers encouraging me to eat the things I love, devour what I care for the most made my stomach twist. *I'm not alone with these thoughts, and some have followed through with those demands.* Families, friends, or brothers and sisters in arms had all heard them, felt them, succumbed to them for over a century now. Guilt crashed down on me. My title, *Second Blood Prince of The House, the last-standing Crowned Prince of Bloodeaters*, struck a chord against my soul that left me feeling at fault for the destruction surrounding us as we traveled down the hardpacked dirt and cobblestone road.

I don't know if breaking the curse is only adding to the damage at this rate. Would it be best to not ever awake from that nightmare of the Madness' possession and its hunger for flesh? Will any of them ever forget the taste of loved ones on their tongue? Will it always be that desire to taste something so...?

I stared at John's backside and swallowed. As much as I wanted to feel nauseated about the moments feeding on him, there had been an elation like no other. Dropping my gaze, I tightened my grip on the reins. Each time had been more pleasurable, more satisfying than the last. It was addicting...

"Eyes forward." Valiente's voice jolted me from my thoughts.

"Sorry, I..." I couldn't think of what to say. *What am I doing losing my focus to self-loathing?*

"It's hard to watch from the city gates. I've grown numb to it, though the Awoken are miraculous despite their despair." A long sigh left him before he continued, "Look, we fight together when this goes down. We're allies from this day forward, no?"

"R-right." I nodded, unsure where he was going with this. "In this battle and those to come."

"I can push Dasa back, but we watch each other's backs in this fight," he instructed. "And more importantly, he most likely knows my weakness is the princess and yours is the priest. Mythe will take pleasure in aiming for one or both if they try to ride hard and fast to the gates."

"You think so?" I held my breath. *This could get dangerous.*

"I'm certain. Watch Spearman Mythe. If anyone will make a move to take out John or Sonja, it's definitely him. He can take a man off a horse as far as any arrow can reach." He unsheathed his sword, grumbling, "The Faceless are missing here, so be ready to cut down flesheaters."

Weapons unsheathed as we slowed the horses. We pulled tighter together. Here, the bodies had not been set to flame. At last, we crossed a pile with a dead Faceless and the first of a red flag bearing the emblem of the Berserk Brigade: *a wolf and lion rearing up against one another.* The buzz of flies muted the world all around and even the moans of the dying in the piles that overshadowed the road. Buzzards and vermin fought over guts, bickering over one another, and chasing each other with entrails dragged behind them.

"Rrrrrrgggggghhhhh..." A woman, skin and bones, her clothes rotting off her, stumbled in our way.

Red Wine came to a stop, plenty of space between us and her. The woman swiveled her head, half her face missing, though the foam dripping from her agape mouth. *She's in the end stage of the Madness... Her body is breaking down.* Another groan escaped her, her left arm twisted and rotting. She tried to lunge forward, but her leg snapped, bone cutting up through the flesh. The horses sidled and snorted, though their training kept them from taking off with the riders who pulled on the reins to steady them.

Valiente rode around us, his sword swung with practiced motion to split her skull, and she fell back motionless. "Nothing we can do for one that far gone. Keep an eye out and don't hesitate. My reports say they get more prominent closer to the brigade."

"Same." Red Wine trotted closer, looking at the victim. "I don't even think this one was a soldier. They've been busy for a while out here it seems."

"I'll kill them." Valiente circled back into position, and we pushed forward.

At first, there was only the occasional rotting flesheater, but with each passing mark, they grew in number. Swords swung with accurate reprieve for the victims who lunged at us. They'd been horribly maimed in most cases, so even if they woke from this nightmare, they would die from the injuries. The red flags of the Berserk Brigade had taken the place of where the Faceless would have stood. Signs of armor and masks, arrows with raven feather flights dotted the area. *They tried to fight, but...* By the time the brigade's camp was in view, we had all cut down countless flesheaters, leaving a wake of bodies. Blood splattered across the horses; red painted the once silvery hue of our blades. Each of us felt the weight of the grim terms of those who suffered from the Madness, arms aching with our efforts.

Why are they more prominent so close to their camp yet not encroaching this close to the yurt? Which of them is wielding a soul weapon? And how in the hell do we break the spell it holds over its victims?

CHAPTER 23

Berserk Brigade

We paused before the encampment as Commander Dasa stepped out of the yurt, red flags snapping in the wind and a row of spears lining either side like a spiked wall. Despite the clearing all around with towers of smoke, not one flesheater shambled across the open space. Dasa gripped a giant cleaver as thick as a claymore but a third of the length. He was thicker muscled than me though shorter, coming easily to my shoulders. Much to my surprise, he was bald and grey-bearded despite the muscled body that spoke of years of battle experience. Red paint covered his bare torso, spiked wrists guards added to his intimidating aura. He was smoking something pungently sweet and herby, pulling a drag before dropping it to the ground and smashing it under his boot. Scars ripped across his skin, old and fresh overlapping one another like embroidered threads of red and purple.

"Well, if it ain't the honorable Ex-Royal Guard Captain Valiente." Laughter rolled from him like thunder. "I've been looking forward to crossing blades with you again. I bet it put quite the knot in your knickers to hear the king gave us authority over you, and seeing how you fled, I guess we're enemies today."

"Careful." Red Wine's voice caught my ears. "That herb he's smoking is Monkshood. It will dim a daemonis' senses. Foolish to snuff it out so soon."

I grunted. *I know why he did. He doesn't think we can beat them, plus his opponent won't be me anyhow.*

Nodding, I pulled off my horse along with Valiente. Unsheathing our weapons, we built a wall between Dasa and the clergymen on anxious horses. Weapons drawn, the rest of us paused on top of their saddles as the horses' hooves stomped close behind me, vibrating underfoot, ready to fight or flee. Basque nudged my back, but I ignored him. Red Wine circled and cut between John and Sonja, whispering something to them, but my beating heart and senses were on Dasa and the other men yet to leave the yurt.

I need to make sure they all focus on me. "Clear the way, or I'll remove you personally," My voice didn't feel like my own as I barked the warning so all could hear.

The rest of the men came out, two more brutes the size of their commander and a scrawny spear thrower, *Mythe. He's already eyeing John and Sonja.* Looking over the opponents before me, they were all laughing at the idea of facing off with just two of us. One brute with orange hair and a braided beard wielded a set of one-handed battleaxes with black paint across his chest and face. Leather breeches with scuffs and cuts gave him the image of a brawler who'd seen his fair share of professional fighting rings.

The other brute was the most armored next to Mythe. He wielded a thick chain, rusted, and twice his height in length filled with heavily dented links the size of my hand. Much like Dasa, this man had spiked wrists guards and similar markings painted on his armor. He wore a metal headband with foreign symbols and a large belt and buckle with similar writing. His clothes reminded me of the monks from the Old Continent from my studies, though gauntlets and armguards and weapons weren't anything like what I had seen in my history books.

Are these two from the Old Continent? Dasa and the chain-wielder?

"You can't be serious," cackled the orange-haired axe man. "You're threatening us? Who the fuck do you think you are?" He threw out his arms, circling in his laughter. "What could one bloodeater hope to do to us!"

"Careful, Gallagher," Mythe warned. "Rumors say that's the First Crowned Blood Prince and Grand Champion Ashton."

"Bullshit." Gallagher spat at my feet, casting a dangerous glare. "Prove it."

The excitement I sensed in him seemed to feed my own, blood rushing in my veins to fight. "I don't have to prove shit to you." I sheathed my claymore, and Valiente gave me a bewildered look. "Fucking come meet your death if you need proof, pumpkin."

Laughter erupted from Gallagher, this time singular and loud as cannon fire. Gallagher started to march away, one well-paced step in front of another, muscles growing tenser each time across his back. His bicep twitched with anticipation of his next move; his torso twisted. All his muscles drew tight. With a flick of his wrist and swipe of his arm, he tossed an axe at me.

Snorting, I didn't flinch. I had watched him step into it like the King of Jacks had shown me. One swipe of my arm, and the axe deflected off the manica with ease.

Gallagher came rushing at me like a raging bull. Spit slinging from his screaming lips, he swung with all his weight. I caught his wrist. My palm slammed into his elbow, bending it backward. A crack hit my ears, and his eyes grew wide. His scream shifted from rage to alarm. The other axe fell as he stumbled back, clutching the broken limb. Snarling, he pulled a small blade from his belt and took a defensive stance.

I gave him no reprieve.

No mercy.

Ashton shows no one mercy, and I will do the same.

My muscles taut, I reacted faster than I could think. The dagger left my sheath with speed. Gallagher's shout halted. His mouth clamped shut, muffling his cry of pain as his eyes rolled back into his sockets. The weight of his body swayed, and fresh blood dribbled from the corner of his mouth. *I feel nothing for someone like this. Nothing at all.* Yanking my dagger back out of his chest, I backstepped into my starting point, slinging blood from the blade before sheathing it. Much to my surprise, he at last slumped to his knees and fell forward, face in the mud.

"Useless," the man with chains spat on Gallagher and kicked the body over. "Why did we bother to put up with this one for so long?"

"He served his purpose, Kayman," reassured Dasa. "Fodder to see whether we had the predator or the prey. It seems we are facing Ashton, which changes how we handle this."

His glare fell on me, but Valiente stepped in the way. "I have unfinished business with you, Dasa."

"Indeed, we do." He glared back at Mythe and Kayman. "Remember, Landon wants the bloodeater alive. Let's see how rusty the Grand Champ is these days."

"No worries, Commander." Kayman craned his neck one way then the other to crack it. "He'll be alive, but very broken." He started swinging the heavy chains about, the weight of them slamming downward, cutting the ground with a thud.

Unsheathing the claymore, I dropped into my starting stance. *If I can take hits by the Guild and Red Wine, how much worse can this really be?*

"What the fuck is that?" Mythe began giggling, slapping Kayman in the shoulder. "No one told me he was bringing a table into battle."

"Every time..." muttered Valiente. "You know this is going to be a constant. No one uses those archaic things anymore."

I didn't move. I didn't reply. Instead, I waited. *Don't let them see you react,* the Old Farmer had repeated in every session. *Don't show pain. That's just a reminder you're still among the living. No rest, no emotions, not until you're the last thing standing.*

"I think he's waiting for you to come at him, Kayman," Mythe scoffed. "What balls this guy has!"

A loud clank of metal filled the air; Dasa and Valiente locked swords. Mythe reached back and threw a small spear, and I twisted the claymore to block. Kayman was faster with his own attack. I placed the claymore down into the ground by my side. The handle jarred my hands as the heavy chains slammed into it. *This brings back to the first time I hit the hoe to frozen ground. Shit!* The overlapping slack swung around the blade and bashed into my right shoulder blade. Grunting as the injury burned, I held my breath as the sharpness twinged when I pulled the claymore up as the chain pulled away.

Dammit! I think he broke something! I can't take direct hits, or I'll definitely be at a disadvantage.

I reset my stance like I had done in my beating from Red Wine. Mythe paced back and forth, his gaze jumping between all of us as he licked his lips. Chains came whipping down hard and heavy. Using the broadside of the claymore, I swung up to keep the slack from whipping around again. The power behind the hits again jarred the handle. Nostalgia crept in, and every muscle tightened in preparation of the sensations and struggles that would soon follow.

This is what I've been trained to face!

The Old Farmer's words screamed into every fiber of my being: *If you hit a shield hard enough, it'll jar you like that. Get a worthy opponent and lock blades, it'll jar you again. That mud is your enemy, and you're John's shield. Don't let me see you drop that hoe again until it breaks.*

The chains retreated, clanking against the blade. My hands and fingers ached from how tightly I gripped the handle. The jarring made them numb, made my joints scream, and my muscles threatened to let go. Gritting my fangs, I launched forward and swung wide and low. Kayman leapt back. Mythe tossed another spear to counter. I caught the glint in my peripheral and shoved back a step. It thudded in the mud, and I stomped on the handle, breaking it, and pushed forward again. Mythe spit at his feet, pulling another spear from the prepared row and paced like an animal as he watched me.

A roar came from Valiente. Furious swings of his sword kept pace with the hard blows of Dasa's cleaver. Already, the knight panted trying to keep out of range of the short blade. A few red gashes painted Dasa's arms and shoulder. A dented line in Valiente's pauldron showed he'd already taken a dangerous blow once. Sweat trickled down his temple, and his braid had begun to fray. The whistling of chains spinning in the air brought me back to my opponents.

Kayman let one side slip, and it shot out like a whip. *Shit! It's too long...* My attempt to avoid being raked by the offending strand failed. I managed to strike the claymore into the ground, stepping away to let the manica take some of the blow. *Dammit, this hurts!* Roaring, the chain circled me until the last piece hit me square in the chest. The air left me, muscles and joints bashed in a way that made everything burn, broken and bruised. My reactions seemed involuntary, like a feral animal being caught in a net or snare. Kayman yanked on the chain, and it tightened around me. I pushed back, refusing to let the gaps between the claymore and my raised arm to close.

"You're like taking down a bull," growled Kayman, yanking again, and I lost some space. "Mythe, give me a hand."

"Gladly," he replied, shoving the spear back into the ground, grabbing a hold of the chain. "Say when."

"When!"

They both pulled, and the muscles in my arm betrayed me, and I lost a few more inches. My foot and other arm were still stretched out, braced only by the claymore that tilted from the pressure of my weight being pulled into it. I rolled, my back taking the pressure of the chain now, both feet against where my blade was rooted into the ground. The shriek of horses and thudding hooves made me realize Red Wine and the clergymen had taken off.

Good, the spearman is distracted and too busy to attack. John will be safe...

"The clergymen. I can," Mythe started.

"Don't you let go of this chain, or we'll be at a loss, Mythe," warned Kayman. "Now pull!"

Another yank and I grunted, my arms buckling under the constant pressure, sore from being jarred and slammed by the chain. I still had some wiggle room, hilt in my face, rendering the claymore useless for anything but a shield. The chains creaked, the jagged rust-covered links cutting into the skin of my back and shoulders.

At least John will make it to the city...

"One more..." Kayman instructed.

"No, they'll be out of my range!" Mythe rebelled.

"Dammit Mythe, Betty will have them." The chain loosened, though still digging deeper into me as it slid across the muscles. "Let her shoot them..."

"That's my prize! I want the price for that priest!"

Mythe let go, and I pushed the chain off enough to fall and leap back out of the tightening circle. *Know when to abandon the claymore,* Red Wine's advice rang true as the chains tightened and knotted on the blade. Turning, I pulled the tomahawk from my side. Kayman lost his balance, chains taut and tangled with the abandoned weapon. Mythe took aim. *John!* Foot pointed, arm stretching back. *POW!* Fire ripped through my back, blood splattering out of my stomach. I didn't stop my swing. I did not flinch.

Ashton never fell once.

The tomahawk had left my hand.

Kayman paled, wide eyed as I kept running toward them. The world slowed before me, though the pain became what I knew.

First lesson. You hold the stance.

Mythe's arm started forward. The tomahawk hit his forearm but didn't halt. Arm and spear fell to the ground while he finished the cancelled throw.

It cut clean and fast. Always put power in the throw if you can, hit the target and aim to split it.

I locked eyes with Kayman, and he let go of the chain and readied spiked brass knuckles. I raised my chin, posture tall and forcing his eyes to look up at me on the approach.

Your enemies are below you.

Something truly monstrous woke in me. *Fallen Arbor wants me—no...* The blade clanked and skidded across armguards as he blocked, feet sliding across the dirt from the impact. *They want Ashton.* He ducked and weaved my next strikes, the scent of fear spilling from him. *Instead, they got something far more dangerous.* A spiked fist swung for the open wound in my torso. *Let him land it.* Grunting, blood rolled on my tongue, and I swallowed it back down. *Unlike me, he won't be breathing when I break him.* I swung the other dagger out, slicing his shoulder and the bridge of his nose. *They're shooting from behind... That was a grave mistake, giving what I value safe passage.*

POW! Once more, something grazed my shoulder.

"Shit!" Kayman muttered curses in a foreign language as blood dripped down his face and off his chin. "Do you not feel the hot lead, bloodeater?"

"Still waiting for you to come and break me," I growled, the anger rising at my core as I swung my dagger at Kayman.

Leaping back, Kayman's back straightened, blonde strands of hair sticking to his face. I had run him into the row of spears. Lunging forward, I swiped, but he managed to duck low. I lobbed off several handles. He spun, swinging a leg across the ground. I slid my stance to be wider.

I will not fall.

Kayman's leg connected against my shin. With a roar, I stabbed downward, nipping his thigh as he rolled away and jerked to his feet. Spinning around, I now backed him up against the claymore. He bounced forward, blocking another slash from me against the armguard, slashing my left forearm with the spikes of a punch. We made this exchange two or three times before at last I grew annoyed.

I scissored my daggers with a double swipe, pushing him back. Kayman dodged to one side and caught the right dagger with a downward punch. Dropping it, I stepped forward again, continuing to drive him into the pile of chains he had abandoned before. *POW!* Something slammed into my mask. Flinching, eyes

188

shut tight, something hot embedded into it, shattering it. The sharp sound rattled me, ears ringing. I abandoned it, flailing to throw the shards off and away.

Shit! I dropped my dagger! Stumbling back, I left myself open. *Dammit! No time to*—Kayman punched in a flurry of strikes. Spikes bashed into my gut and chest, starting with the open gunshot wound, working their way up.

My eyes locked with Kayman's own; his pupils dilated. His body was at its limit as pain drove adrenaline through his veins. Being this up close to me, we both became very aware I was in another weight class. The way his body jerked, he found himself failing to fight. Another punch thrust forward, and I caught it with my right hand. A spike tore through my palm and protruded out the back of my hand. My grip did not falter as I heard one, then two more bones crack in his fist. Jerking back his hand, he held it into his torso. Backstepping, he locked heels with the chains, and flight took hold of him.

A roar escaped Dasa who landed a kick into Valiente. The broadsword slid across his inner thigh, but the brute's eyes were on me. Valiente thudded on the ground in sync with Kayman's own loss of balance and twisted onto the chains. Dasa left a trail of bright red on the blackened ground as he rushed me. *The claymore!* It unfolded so fast. Reaching out, my left hand yanked the claymore free from the ground. Dropping down, I spun away and back around, building inertia in the one-handed swing. Dasa slid to a stop, blocking with the cleaver. *It's too weak to hold*—

With a clank and ping, the cleaver broke. An ethereal scream escaped it. The claymore did not lose momentum though. Flesh split as the edge ripped through his torso until I hit the knowing scrape of his hipbone and pulled the blade to me.

He crumbled to the ground as I stood panting. I didn't know any more if the red painting me was Dasa's blood or my own. A curtain had sprayed forth and worse, shards of the cleaver had bitten into the berserker, none hitting the ground as if it had bitten its owner. Kayman wailed, rushing to the lifeless head of his commander. I couldn't hear his sobs. My heart pounded loud and fast, the blood rushing in my veins rendering my hearing useless. Dazed, I glanced up at Valiente who paled. His lip busted as he threw himself back onto the grass, gasping for air. *He was starting to lose the fight until he—*

"Why did he come to protect you?" My senses snapped into place, and I drove the claymore into the ground.

Kayman slid his fingers over Dasa's eyelids, forcing them closed. "Because we were both exiled from the Old Continent. Granted, his was for sins and mine was being bred from a sinner."

I inhaled deeply, the smell of blood thick as I picked apart which metallic aroma belonged to which body. "You're his son."

Kayman locked eyes with me. "I am. You win, Ashton. Take my life. Because if you don't, Fallen Arbor will finish me for you."

The sun bright overhead cast my shadow across him. He looked pitiful with blood beginning to crust on his face. *No mercy.* Scoffing, I walked past him. *That's where my brother and I don't align. I know when to give mercy.*

CHAPTER 24

The Faceless

Marching past Dasa's half-torn body, I searched the horizon between the camp and castle. We were still a long way off, and luckily, the rest would be within the city gates before dark. Standing over Valiente, I offered a hand, and after much contemplating, he at last reached out. Locking grips, I pulled him to his feet with ease, and we took in one another's state. He had a bruise developing over his left brow and cheek, lip busted, armor dented and cleaved open with slight cuts on the right side.

"By the fates ... how in the hell are you standing?" Valiente muttered, circling me. "How much of this is your own blood, you fool?"

"I..." The adrenaline was slowly leaving me, the burn of my broken shoulder blade coming back, the throbbing of cuts, wounds, and muscles used inappropriately all screaming. "A lot of it."

I watched as he circled back and cupped my cheeks, a toothy smile across his battered face. "You actually took down the whole fucking brigade on your own! I think I'm in love!"

Without warning, Valiente's lips pressed firm against my own and I froze. Heart skipping a beat, his lips parted to deepen the kiss, but my hand found the rope of his braid and pulled him off. Yelping, I shoved him back, and he gave me a baffled expression.

"Don't kiss me," I declared in disgust.

"Forgive me for feeling glad we're alive, your majesty!" Snorting, he rubbed the back of his head and turned his gaze to Kayman who had wondered over to Mythe. "What about him? Why didn't you finish him off? Isn't it dangerous to leave him alive?"

"About that..." I watched as Kayman sank to the ground, holding his head in despair. "I don't think it'll be safe to take him with us."

"No, Fallen Arbor will be looking for the last man standing in the Berserk Brigade. Grave news waits for him." Valiente whistled, and Colonel started to trot closer. "Let's get ... shit..."

"Basque is following him—" A shiver rolled over me as I looked beyond where the horses were left. "Is that flesheaters or ... the Faceless?"

"I don't know. Both maybe, but are there enough Faceless to make an army battalion?" He swallowed, turning to pluck his blade off the ground. "Get ready. I have no idea what's going to happen."

"I have a guess." A chill snaked up my spine. *This better not be another bullshit fairy tale, Old Farmer. I find myself facing them and not in the position to fight.* "Kayman!" I roared, grabbing my claymore and tossing his chains to him. "You need to tell me about your father's cleaver, now."

Kayman stared bitterly at the chains on the ground, just out of reach from where he sat. "A corrupted gift from Landon." He pulled himself up, furrowing his brow to see us backing up closer to the yurt. "It had a spell on it, some dark magic. Anyone who was cut and died came back as a flesheater. This wasn't like the Madness, but similar, one that would force the body to move as long as the heart and head were ... the Faceless." His gaze at last had swiveled to where we stared at the horizon with such intensity.

"I think it was a soul weapon. Destroying it will help, but the spell takes time to undo." Looking all around, I saw black cloaked figures were moving in on all sides. "I saw a few of them dead on the road. Who went on a rampage picking them off?"

"They weren't supposed to..." Kayman glared down at the passed out, pale Mythe. "Son of bitch. I suspect Mythe and Betty had a day of it."

"Well, hope you're not too attached to your buddy over there." Valiente shot an angry glare at Kayman. "The Faceless sort of serve as the law on the road. Though they believe in mercy, they show very little of it for those who dare break the peace on the road."

"Fuck Mythe. Fuck Fallen Arbor." Kayman spat on Mythe and readied his chains. "Don't get me wrong. I'm not completely on your side either."

I grunted, watching as the Faceless came closer. Archers downed the last flesheater between us and the unit that moved forward. Only one sat on a horse, their wide brim hat holding a bright red plume, and they wore a plague mask of white and gold.

The Cardinal, leader of the Faceless, he's the talker. You'll know'im when you see him, boy. He is the tallest, the only one with gold and a flair of red in his hat. You need to make a deal with them, you deal with him. But I warn you now, I think he's been walking this earth a long time. Not sure if he's human, daemonis, or something completely different.

"Put your weapons away." Recognizing the Cardinal, I sheathed the claymore and smacked their shoulders. "Drop them. Trust me. Then kneel."

They shot one another a glance and caved to my request. The Cardinal halted his unit and tilted his head as I dropped to one knee.

Valiente scoffed. "But he's not royalty."

"On your knee, Valiente," I growled, pain surging through my body to hold the position.

Kayman followed my posture, and as the unit started forward again, Valiente joined. They came close, and the Faceless spread out and began securing the yurt and assessing the bodies. The Cardinal dismounted and approached until he was at arm's reach from me. He squatted, and I met his goggled gaze.

Again, a tilt of his head as he took me in before the deep rasping voice whispered, "You are not Ashton." The statement came with a knowing tone. "So, who are you, imposter?"

"Dante, the little brother." This man held power and smelled nothing like anyone I had met. *You pegged it, old man. This man isn't a human or daemonis.* "I could never be my brother, not to those who knew him personally."

"What game do you play at, little falcon?" He glanced at the other men and laughed, adding, "And why do you travel with the nightingale and a crow? So strange."

The naming of birds was strange, but I answered in honest. "I am pretending to be Ashton to draw out Fallen Arbor. If my actions have caused—"

A loud scoff escaped him, and he flicked my forehead. The strength behind it stung. "Falcons can't be eagles, don't you know?"

Standing, he flicked a finger at two Faceless and pointed to Mythe. "We only want this man. The rest of you we will escort you to Captiva City. Any chances I can get the name of the Fallen Arbor woman?"

"Betty. That's all she ever gave us. She serves Landon if that's of any consolation." Kayman didn't hesitate to out his former companion. "I hold no allegiance to anyone."

"Ah, the crow caws." The Cardinal stood and started for his horse as they dragged Mythe over. "Landon shouldn't let his peons meddle in his elder's affairs. If any of you see him, tell him the Cardinal will not allow Fallen Arbor on the road anymore."

"Cardinal!" I rose to my feet, my heart racing. *This man is stupid strong ... but what the hell is he?* "Is it true you owe Lord Knight Paul a favor?"

"Ah, yes." There was a sense of amusement in his voice as he mounted his horse. "But I would imagine the old Owl has found death by now. His kind seem to find it quicker than he ever did though."

"Y-yes." Swallowing, I glanced back at Kayman and inhaled deeply. *What the hell am I thinking?* "Can you take in Kayman to serve the Faceless?" *But every fiber and instinct tells me this may help me out in a time of need.* My father's words slammed into me: *Dante, never pass an opportunity to protect those in a hopeless situation. Nurturing the weak will only gain you surprising strengths later when allies are hard to come by.*

"What?!" shouted Valiente and Kayman.

"You don't just ask something without discussing this!" Valiente threw out his arms, waving them in disbelief.

"I think I like that idea, to be honest." Kayman looked around and took in the Faceless, their numbers matching or surpassing any army. "They don't pick sides, just protect lives, right? Granted, I'm shit at archery."

The Cardinal trotted his horse closer, taking in the blood covered brute. "I like the idea of owning a crow. It's been a while since I nurtured one. I'll take him, but this isn't an exchange of favors, little falcon. Now tell me, Crow, you're from Balmueth or close to it, yes?"

"I-I am." Kayman shook his head, excitement in his voice as he added, "Does that mean you know the Old Continent?"

"It was once home." Another raspy chuckle and he motioned for Kayman to follow. "This place is too wet and green. I miss Balmueth, but alas, I found a new clan to lead here in Grandmere."

Kayman circled back as I rose to my feet, grabbing my hand and shook it. "Thank you."

I gave him a bewildered look. "We were just trying to kill one another."

"It never crossed my mind I had another option, another cause more in line with the teachings I once treasured." Kayman's eyes were filled with a sense of hope. "One day, I'll pay this forward, this act of mercy and salvation. I take back what I said. Perhaps I could support your cause if this is the way you treat your enemies."

Huffing, I waved at the Cardinal. "I don't know what you are, but something tells me our paths will cross again!"

"Yes, little falcon! I will find you when you outgrow the eagle's shadow." He whistled, and the Faceless began to retreat besides two archers. "Let my bluebirds escort you. I wish to see more of those fighting skills—reminds me when Ashton and I crossed blades, but that's for another time. May the Nameless Prophet grant blessings to the falcon and nightingale."

I turned to Basque, and he flipped an ear back as if to say, *you're a mess.* Everything hurt. Unbuckling the halter to the claymore, I strapped it to Basque with help from one of the Faceless. My shoulder blade had at last locked up, and I couldn't bear to lift my arm without sharp pain. Valiente removed the dented chest plate to reveal bruises from the impact. Grabbing the saddle, it took the last of my energy to get onto the saddle, and Basque bobbed his head. Colonel snorted, making him stop as he held steady for Valiente to mount. Without a word, the Faceless took the lead, and the horses followed. I leaned down onto the saddle, exhausted and weak.

"So, the leader is called the Cardinal?" Valiente broke the silence, waking me from the shallow rest I had slipped into.

"Yes," I confirmed.

"And you're little falcon?" he asked, furrowing his brow.

"Yes," I scoffed.

"And if Kayman was the crow, then that makes me the... nightingale?" he questioned.

"I suppose so. And my brother must be the eagle. The Old Farmer an owl... it's a fascinating system he has going there," I confessed, pondering further on it. "I know owls mean wisdom, but they can also forewarn death. Falcons are related to royalty but ... I don't know if that's part of the naming system."

"You're a clever one, little falcon." One of the archers snickered to herself.

"Wait, I thought they don't talk to anyone?" Valiente sounded offended over the disruption.

"Oh, we can," answered the other archer, his voice making it clear he was young under that mask. "But the Cardinal says only to other birds."

"Huh." Valiente straightened himself in the saddle and at last demanded, "Tell me what nightingale means."

The two archers giggled, and the girl replied, "The secret lover."

My face turned red, and I locked eyes with Valiente. "Don't you dare tell John."

"Nope!" He grinned. "But I have to admit, the name is fitting for me, no?"

"If it implies you like to sleep around and steal kisses, then yes." I turned my head the other way, trying to reclaim some rest once more.

"Oh, c'mon. Don't be that way," Valiente fussed as the archers laughed.

Who would have thought so much of what Lord Knight Paul told me would ring true? So many bittersweet memories, but they all serve a purpose. How many of these did he share with John too, I wonder? Or did he mean for me to take them and use them at my will? Did you see me today, old man? I almost cleaved a man in half today, just like you said I could do ... but I don't find this comforting. This was one small battle, and I may have served as his shield today, but when I see him, will I be able to keep my hunger at bay? Would he even stop me when he sees the mess I have become?

CHAPTER 25

Captiva City, Capitol City of The Tower

"**B**y the Divine Father, is he even alive?" guffawed a voice. I stirred from my rest to the smell of kerosene torches and the sight of the stonewalls outside Captiva City. Everything hurt as I grunted to sit up properly. The blood had dried, crusted and sticky across my entire body and invading my senses with a souring stench. The city guards paled, but Valiente called their attention back to him, and after muffled whispers, we were allowed to pass. I didn't realize the Faceless had left us in my slumber. Rubbing my torso, I found that the bleeding had stopped, even healed some, but an open wound lingered. *I should be healing faster.* Scoffing, I tried rolling my shoulder, but I had only regained some of the range and was still limited in how high I could raise my arm.

"You doing okay over there?" Valiente's voice was low as we rode side-by-side, tight through the narrow back alleys. "We could have gotten to the canal faster down the main street, but with you covered in blood … I thought maybe you'd like to take a moment to clean off."

"I'm alive." I swallowed, the dryness building in my throat made me far more uncomfortable. *So thirsty.* "Yes, I'd like a moment to clean off."

"Not much farther." Valiente hadn't even glanced my way, focused on leading us through the turns.

Valiente pulled Colonel to a stop, and Basque snorted and clacked a hoof on the cobblestones in an effort to complain. With a whistle, a back door opened, and a haughty woman came out, clothes loose and her breasts nearly hanging out of her shirt. I deadpanned Valiente as he got off his horse, greeting her with a kiss on each cheek. Looking down the alleyway one way then the next, it became very clear we were in the backstreets of the shops and docks. *You've got to be kidding me... We're at a Scarlett House.*

"Monica!" Valiente waved his hand to me, and I straightened my posture on the saddle. "My friend would like to wash the blood of his enemies off, but we are in a bit of a rush to our next destination."

"And here I thought you were swinging in to give me and the girls a fun time. Looks to me you both need a good scrubbing." She winked at me, licking her lips and groping a breast. "My, who is your new friend?"

"A mercenary I've commissioned to help me get through the battlefield." His tone shifted, grin falling into a stern expression. "As promised, and thanks to him, the Berserk Brigade is no more."

Her hands covered her mouth, eyes wide bouncing between us before hugging Valiente. "Thank the Knowing Mother! You did as you promised! My ladies and I are safe to wander the streets again!"

So thirsty and tired... I need to find John. Managing to dismount, body burning with my injuries, I interjected, "Forgive me, but I'm in a rush." *I need to know he's safe.*

"Ah! Yes, this way!" She threw the door open and shouted into the hallway. "We've got a request for a hot scrub, girls. Get these boys right as rain! The Brigade has fallen!"

I followed close on Valiente's heels as he travelled down the corridor, insisting on kissing every girl on each cheek as they came out of the doors on either side. Monica continued shouting and squealing in celebration of the news he had brought. It all was a mangled, blurred flurry of sounds and figures with the pain rolling through me. *I feel drunk ... or as if I'm stumbling through a dream of sorts.* The building smelled of sweat and *sex.* My face flushed as thoughts of John took hold of how *hungry* I was to be with him again. With each inhale, my fangs ached, and I ran my tongue over them each time as if to soothe the sensation. *Are they bigger?* A girl took me by the hand, my eyes averting away from her when they caught her shirtless torso and pink nipples. *Of all the places he could have taken me to... a brothel. I should have known coming from the Nightingale.*

Smells and touch distracted me, sending my eyes searching only to drop my gaze at the lewd scenes found all around. I could hear every panting body in the building it seemed. *I want blood...* The beating of hearts all around, some racing in the moment of a climax, thudded like a stampede. *So thirsty...* I struggled to chase the conversation unfolding between Valiente and Monica. *Is it because I'm injured? Or hungry?* The dryness in my throat grew to being more painful than the throbbing in the open wound in my gut and back. *I need John.* Taking a turn down a hall, I caught a glimpse of myself in a mirror and froze. *Or is this how things will be?* Chest aching, I was covered in black and red blood, shirt in tatters and flesh laid open or bruised. *I can't let him see me like this.* I was a broken monster. Tugging at my shirt, I didn't recognize myself anymore.

"What would John think of me?" My mind raced, lost in where I had ended up in the building. "I'm a monster."

"It's okay, sweetie. Let's get you cleaned up." Grabbing my hand again after a few tries, at last she tugged me through a door, shutting it behind us. "Strip down so I can start scrubbing, dear," she demanded as I took in the tight quarters of the one-man tub, the room narrow enough to stretch both arms out to touch the walls. "Not sure if I'll be able to get all the blood off with

200

wounds like those." Her voice carried a heavy accent I'd never heard before, but I was eager to wash my face as I stumbled to the tub. "You're a bloodeater, right?"

I stiffened and stuttered, "Y-yes." *Technically.*

"You need blood?" My heart skipped a beat at the serious tone in her voice.

"No," I began stripping down. *I need to get to John. That's all that matters.*

"But the wounds—" she started.

"I don't need it," I interrupted, yanking the buckles of the manica free as the armor fell to the floor. *This fucking thirst for John makes me so angry.*

"It's okay. We serve your kind here, and we're discreet," she reassured. "Consider us always available for—"

"I'm too thirsty," I blurted out, surprised at my confession. *Shit! Maybe if I...*

"Oh." She fell silent, grabbing what I shed onto the floor and began to scrub it in a bucket off to the side. "Perhaps after you calm in the tub, you'll want to give me a taste."

Hesitant, I stared at her frail neck with the smattering of scars from previous bloodeaters. *Perhaps I could try...* Shaking my head, I shed the last article of clothing and rushed to dump myself into the scolding hot water. Dunking my head under the surface, everything was muted.

I hate this. All the moaning and racing hearts had added to the thirst and want to feed. *I hate myself.*

Each time the thought of hunger and thirst rose, the answer landed the same. *John. It's all I crave, all I want, and all I live for.* Exploding to the surface, I gasped for air, sour for returning to the noise and scents against my will. *I need to feed...* My gaze fell on the girl who froze a moment before rushing back to her task.

John's words came back to me, and my heart fluttered. *But don't ever avoid me if you're feeling ... hungry? Need me? Whatever that look you give me from across the room that makes me feel like a filet.*

"You're a handsome one," she mumbled, stealing another glance at me with her eyes lingering. "We don't see bloodeaters of your station here ever."

I can't. Her scent doesn't arouse me to feed like... Splashing my face, I confessed, "I've never travelled this far south before. Only my companions have. I see you are all well-acquainted with Knight Valiente."

"Y-yes. He's a regular, but the only one who gave a rat's ass when some of the girls were murdered in the alley here." She brushed the boots free of their grime, but grabbing the shirt, she hesitated. "I don't think we can save this, love. I'll get you a fresh one. Would you like some new leather pants as well? We provide such wares for guests who stop here first after a hard day on the battlefield."

"Please." I was unknotting my braid. "If you could, I would like a hooded coat as well."

"Understandable. Hood, you say?" She sloshed a bucket of water and soap over the manica, brushing it before another slosh let the dirt break free. "In that case, short or long coat?"

I pondered a moment before answering, "Long. With lots of pockets if possible."

"Aye." She slung the manica on a chair, and at last, I found myself alone.

I realized there was a shelf of items above my head. Standing, I clamored through the vials in search of anything to use to numb my sense of smell. *Most of this is oils for...* I smirked to myself. *Of course it is. I'm taking a bath in a brothel.* Popping open the bottles of unlabeled scents, I was relieved when it began to flush out the smell of the brothel. Generously, I poured rosewater oil heavily into the hot water and grabbed a cloth hanging on the edge. Scrubbing furiously, I found a nugget of leftover lavender soap and worked every part of me over until all that remained was the one wound that just refused to close in my gut.

I suppose I look more alive and don't smell like the dead. Searching, I aimed to clean the wound fast and be ready to dress on the woman's return. *I can't stay here long. John needs me.* My eyes caught a rusted mirror leaning on the shelf, small but sufficient. I propped it on the tub edge beside the lantern, leaning into its reflection for a better angle of the wound in my stomach. It was nearly closed now, the cleaning aiding in the healing that had slowed in battle. *Need to remember bruises lighten with the help of hot water and herbs.* Turning and pulling my hair to slap it across my chest, I could see how the entrance wound still bled. Crimson mixed with water fell in slow streams as it ran over my hip and ass to disappear in the steaming water at my thighs. Something black seemed to be embedded in the open red and white of the flesh, keeping it from healing. *A chunk of metal?*

"I didn't expect so many scars considering..." The woman had entered, clothes in arms as she drew near, but I moved out of her outstretched hand. "Let's have a look. That mirror is shit; I can't even do my hair in it. Let me do what I do for all the other warriors here. You ain't the first to come in here still bleeding, sweetie." Her smile eased as she set the items down and reached for a box on the shelf. "See, we keep needle, thread, and salve on the shelf for this very reason."

"I..." I eyed her, my head swimming with exhaustion, and I caved. "I think there's something in the wound." Leaning on the shelf, I felt my muscles twitch and draw tight at her touch. "I can manage the pain," I offered, fearing my reaction would be misread. *Heh, only John has touched me ... and before him that was... Why in this moment does it become clear that my past is painted across me, and John's never asked me once of it? Yet, here in this brothel...*

"With these scars, I can see you're no stranger to that much in life. Are some of these bitemarks?"

I bit my lips as fingers dug into exposed flesh, dodging the question.

"It's a chunk of metal. Give me a minute."

The retreat of her prodding was short-lived as the familiar sensation of a blade cutting into my flesh pushed into the wound. My hand acted on its own accord. Her wrist gripped tight in my fingers. Adrenaline spiked once more as fight or flight itched to be chosen, whispering, *Fight.* She froze, glaring up at me. *When did I become an animal?* The fear on her face melted to an empty smile, one clearly done in practice for moments like this and elsewhere in the brothel.

"S-sorry," I muttered and let go, alarmed by my actions and looking away in shame. "I thought ... I'm still on the battlefield it seems."

Her voice was soft as she agreed, "I wasn't thinking either. Considering the scars, where you are ... I didn't think deeply on it, your majesty. Almost done, but you're a fast healer despite the damage and blood loss. I've got to cut it free..."

Wait, your majesty... Stabbing, sharp pain disrupted my panicked thoughts. The twisting and slicing made the wound open wider, letting me know how difficult the fragments were for even her tiny fingers. I heard three pieces clack against the wooden floor before she huffed. She rinsed the knife and her fingers in the tub water before grabbing a cloth. I winced in silence as she flushed out the wound, her heart racing in my ears. *I'm so stupid. I just rode into Captiva City with my braid to the wind. So much for discreetly entering the city.*

"The braid gave me away, didn't it?" *I don't know why, but I want to hear it.*

"It's hard not to notice a braid as long as yours or Valiente's." She reached past me, retrieving the lantern. "At first, I thought you were a guardian of the royal family like him," she confessed, checking the fresh scar on my shoulder. "But seeing that you were a bloodeater was a tad unusual." I shuddered as her had glided down my back as if searching for further signs of injuries. "Those top two knots so high on the crown of your skull had me miscounting until you dunked yourself into the water."

"So, there's a chance the guards didn't notice in the torch-light." Some relief came to me as her fingers pressed around the opening she had tended.

"Maybe. Is it true that you're the missing first blood prince, Ashton?" Leaning down, she seemed to be inspecting the wound closer now as she drew near.

204

"Yes. What of it?" *After meeting the Cardinal, I feel guilty for bearing my brother's name, but he didn't discourage the idea either. Perhaps he's curious to see how this plays out.*

"It seems you ruffle a lot of feathers in high up places," she mused before scoffing. "I don't think I got it all out, but it seems to be wanting to close now. Are you sure you don't need to feed to regain your health or speed this up, Prince Ashton?"

"No." Her hands glided back up across my shoulder blades and pressed on one. "Leave me. I should be fine."

"It's broken here, but the bruising looks to be displaced with the way the arm sits lower," she announced. "I thought it was bruised, but if you don't let me push it in place, it'll heal where that arm can't lift up properly." Her fingers traced rings from my shoulder, across the broken bone, and stopped by my spine. "These are General Kayman's chain marks, aren't they?"

"Yeah, I blocked but didn't account for it to whip around and slap me." Staring at the vials, I searched my thoughts before braving to ask, "Can you fix it? It seems Scarlett women have many talents that I didn't know about."

"Honey, this is a brothel." She laughed, pulling on my torso to make me stand straight, then held my shoulder as she lifted my arm slowly. "Wanda throws her shoulder out every time the bishop comes in for his session. Granted, we are held in high standing, on par with high class and shop owners because we offer a variety of services when it comes to those needing utmost discretion. If you're ever in need, find a Scarlett House."

"Which bishop?" I demanded, wincing as the arm gave resistance and wouldn't lift any further.

"Marquis." Without warning, she shoved and jerked in such a hard jolt a loud pop hit my ears; pain and relief made me feel breathless. "There we go! Monica would be proud to hear I manage to do it on the first go!"

"There's some soreness, but thank you." I froze, pumping my fist and dared to roll the shoulder. "I thought priests and bishops and all clergymen are sworn to celibacy?" Thoughts of John's face in the throes of passion flashed in my head, and I pressed, "And isn't it a death sentence for breaking one's celibacy?"

"Aye," she nodded. "They come through that back door like you did and down the hall more times than the soldiers if you ask me. Pay with deep pockets, they do. By the way, the name's Elaine."

"Thank you, Elaine." I grabbed up a vial of saddlewood and cinnamon perfume and a large canteen of oil. "Forgive me, I'm going to take these."

"Got someone you're aiming to impress tonight, I see. Now turn around, let me have a lookatcha." Elaine laughed, tugging me against my will to face her. "Boy, you're built strong and long, and I mean in all the right places." My face grew red as her eyes gobbled up my world before she was back to inspecting the other side of the wound. "Ah! Another piece. Hold still."

"Shit." The knife was back in her hand, cutting into the freshly healed bits until a metal chunk flicked out. "I'll have to avoid being shot in the future."

"Those are nasty things from the Old Continent. Been seeing more and more of 'em as of late." She scrubbed the wound and checked it twice before rinsing her fingers once again. "What's this one from?" She poked her fingers into the scar left behind by the Fanged Lady. I huffed.

"Ah, that's where my lover stabbed me to kill my ex." I smirked as her eyes shot up to meet my gaze. "It was a complicated situation."

"You still with them?" she marveled.

"Can't leave him if I wanted to." I shrugged.

Snorting, she patted my bare chest and walked away from me. "Well, I'll leave you to dress yourself. Don't judge me on the rush wash job on the armor. It'll take days of proper cleaning and scrubbing to get that out."

"It will do just fine, Elaine." As I stepped out of the tub, she began to fan herself. "You okay?"

"I shouldn't be lusting after a Blood Prince but..." She bit her lips, her eyes lingering between my thighs before she threw up

206

her arms and faced the door. "You ever want a woman, come find me! It'll be my pleasure!"

The door slammed, and I sighed. *I really should stop thinking about John and the perfume bottles in situations like this. But at least I feel a little less like a monster...*

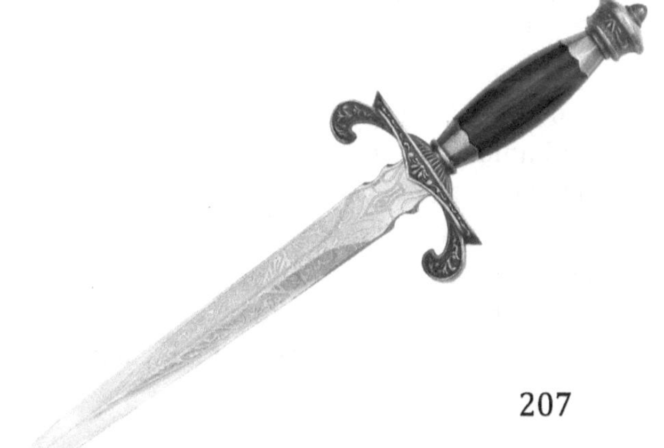

Chapter 26

Canals, Catacombs, & Castles

Basque snorted all around me, knocking the hood from my head as if displeased with my new look and smell. After a few chastising whispers from me, he took the sugar cubes and fell back to his normal apathetic state. The brothel girls had offered more than clothes and bath, handing us parcels of food and refilled our canteens. Captiva City was very much alive despite the half-moon being high overhead. Valiente twisted through the tight corridors of the back alleys until they grew so narrow, I fretted over Basque not fitting. The smell of salt in the air made my blood rush. *The Bay of Red Waves! How I've always wanted to see such a sight!*

We pulled out into the open, the shadowed figures of ships at the docks with glowing spots of torches and braziers. Despite the time of night, sailors and dockworkers were busy loading and unloading vessels farther down. Basque followed Colonel until we chased the canal to a stable. There a member of the Guild bowed and took in the horses. Glancing into the stables, I was relieved to see Elegance, Jasmine, and Biscuit all neighing to greet their travelling companions.

"They made it this far, then," I whispered to the assassin.

"Safe and sound, though you took far longer than we antici-pated. If they aren't at the entrance, we've made plans accord-ingly." The soft-spoken assassin bowed, "My name is Bourbon. Please follow me."

Without warning, he walked to the canal's edge and jumped. Valiente and I looked to one another, skeptical of the path our guide had chosen. I ventured to the edge, seeing the narrow walkway at water level, and motioned to Valiente. He gave a surly expression, joining my side to peek down.

"After you," I offered.

"You do know I have broken ribs, right?" he countered.

Nodding, I gave him a hard pat on the back, and he grunted in pain. "I've had that before becoming a bloodeater. The sooner we go, the sooner we can both rest."

Grunting, he eased down on his knees, groaning. "Give me a hand, would ya?"

Laughing, I used my good arm and helped ease him down until I eventually had to let go, so he could land at a shorter drop. Taking a glance all around, I saw the stables here were void of anyone unlike the singing that could be heard farther down on the docks or back where the front of the Scarlett House sat. Stepping off the ledge, I landed without an issue as Valiente coughed, wheezing and stumbling forward.

Bourbon waved, and we followed slowly toward the nev-er-ending sea. The closer we came to the bay, the louder the water slapped against the walls or waved over our feet. Here the pleasant saltwater twisted to the pungent smell of old bait and cast out filth, human and animal alike. I drew my arm over my face, missing the mask already as the wall began to curve. We went from nudged between narrow walls of a canal to a path against the open bay, and a torch glowed up ahead. Drawing closer, I saw a huge gate-filled archway blocked our path. Bourbon dug into a satchel and produced a ring of keys. After a few tries, he found one that allowed the gate to creak open. Standing off to the side, he let Valiente enter, and as I fol-lowed, he grabbed my arm.

"Ashton." He shoved the heavy ring of keys into my hand. "I was told to gift these to you."

"Keys to the canal?" I lifted a brow, unsure what I was being offered.

"Yes, but…" He glanced at Valiente who had stumbled out of earshot. "These are keys to Grandmere. We assassins have made copies of keys for centuries, and this ring holds all known locks, new and old. Please keep this with you at all times."

"Interesting." I pondered if this explained how Madame Plasket seemed to get around faster than I could run on foot and smirked. "Thank you."

"Now, let's see if they waited." Bourbon patted my shoulder, and I winced.

Grabbing the torch, Bourbon continued to lead us deep into the underbelly of Captiva City. Water dripped all around, the stones slippery, and the entire place reeked of shit and rot. A glow appeared after another disorientating turn in the bleak darkness past identical chambers and pathways. The torchlight seemed to be throwing my ability to see in the dark, my pupils competing on how to adjust. *I could have navigated the maze far better. Another aspect I haven't discovered, I imagine.* Voices whispered and bounced through the tunnels. Bourbon stopped, whistling softly before approaching.

John rushed into the opening, and my heart leapt. Pushing past Bourbon, we rushed one another. The heat of his body against my own and his scent brought a calm over me I had been craving. Breaking our embrace, John kissed me, and the hunger demanded more. *Thirsty.* I backed him against the wet damp walls, pulling the collar open to reveal the bitemarks from before. *So hungry…* Not satisfied with the trickling teases from suckling his tongue, I sank my fangs into him. *I need him. I want him.* I was vaguely aware of a grunt of discomfort, his fists balling their grip on my back and pulling me close. He at last croaked something, but…

Still so thirsty. Another muffled croak and I pinned him. *More…*

I bit down harder, and he grunted in discomfort once more.

I need more. I want all of it.

"Dante!" his voice echoed off the walls, ringing in my ears.

Retreating against the far wall, I covered my blood-soaked chin with my arm, panting. Bewildered, I watched as John sank to the ground, his expression hidden from me as Bourbon and Valiente rushed to help him. Red Wine appeared, a dagger at my throat.

What have I done?

"What the hell is wrong with you?" she growled.

I tried to move so I could see John, but her dagger bit into my flesh and I froze.

His heart ... but I...

"Answer me!" she roared.

"I was so..." Dread rattled through me, my soul breaking. "...thirsty."

Red Wine blinked, backstepping to let me sink down holding my head. She turned, rage riding on her voice. "Valiente, what the hell happened out there?"

"We survived," he uttered before coughing and wheezing, holding his side. "Dammit. I can't breathe with these ribs."

"The priest has passed out; the wound seems to have stopped bleeding, but we can't move from here for a while," Bourbon announced.

I was breaking.

Bloodeater.

Monster.

Red Wine landed a punch square on my cheek, jolting my head and breaking my stare from John's pale face and red painted neck. "Pull it together and tell me what happened."

The throbbing in my cheek brought me back, and I locked eyes with Red Wine. "I was... shot."

"Okay, but that doesn't explain losing it to feeding," she retorted, standing to kick me in the bad shoulder, and I grunted.

Shoving her foot off, I slowly gathered my wits. "I was shot three times, once through the gut, clipping the shoulder, and in the face. I took hits with the chain, broke my shoulder blade, and dislocated my shoulder completely at one point. Then I took a beating with spiked knuckles... I lost a lot of blood."

Red Wine covered her face a moment. "This was why I needed you to dodge."

"I did. I tried..." I watched helplessly as Valiente and Bourbon pulled John off the ground and stumbled to the dry room up ahead. "I lost myself... All I could think..."

"I can only imagine." She offered a hand to help me to my feet, and I stared at it. "Look, we stayed here in fear you were in bad shape. You looked fine, but considering..."

I looked up at her, and the trepidation on my face made her flinch, her mask hiding her expression. "I'm a fucking monster," I declared. "I'm going to be the one to kill him despite trying to save him at every turn."

"Stop it." She kicked my boot, and I at last surrendered my hand to her and rose to my feet. "Let's start with ... how are you feeling?"

Blinking, I rolled my injured arm and was met with no pain or resistance. "Healed there." Reaching behind and in front, I marveled, "My injuries... They're..."

"Right. So, remember, the more repairs needed, the hungrier you will get for him," she warned. "Now, go wash your face and take care of your stubborn priest. It's like watching a lamb raise a lion with you two. Fools."

"Is he..." I grabbed my canteen, rinsing John's blood from my face and arm. "Did I..."

We walked into the dry room, a fire burning as everyone turned to face me. Scowls painted their faces, and as I met their eyes, they averted their gazes. The weight of my guilt came crushing down as I looked to John. He was completely passed out. His heart pounded, shallow and slow. *Dammit.* Even his breathing seemed ragged and his complexion pale. His neck had been bandaged, red seeping through it, and the sweet aroma made my stomach turn. *How could I not stop? Was this really the injuries or some deeper desire I can't fight back anymore?*

Marching over to John, I sat and stared over him. "I'm so sorry."

I watched as his chest rose and fell slowly in his current state. Lying beside him, I rolled away, his body against my back as I stared at the stone wall. Sonja, Valiente, and Bourbon all had racing heartbeats. *I frighten them.*

"Why didn't you feed on Elaine?" Valiente's voice cut through my bitter thoughts.

"It doesn't work that way," I mumbled in my despair.

"You're a bloodeater. You just need any blood to heal," he concluded.

"Not him," interjected Red Wine. "You see, there's two kinds."

"Two?" Sonja had abandoned her Mother Superior disguise, wearing clothes fitting of an archer. "So, he's the other kind?"

"Y-yes," Red Wine seemed hesitant. "His kind can only feed on one donor."

"That's dumb," flustered Valiente. "What if they kill them or the donor dies?"

Rolling over, I watched as Red Wine removed her mask and replied, "Precisely why he's more dangerous. Even after his kind loses their source, the power they unlock is damn near godly."

They all glanced back to me, and I rolled away again to avoid the weight of their expressions. "It's a curse. I'm not like the others who lost some of the thirst when the Fanged Lady lost her hold. John and I, we made this choice together."

"You've got to control it, Dante," Valiente demanded.

Sitting up, I let my anger pour forth. "Don't you think I'm trying?" I gritted my fangs and snarled. "I've been to the depths of the Madness and back again! Worse, do you know what it's like being in love when your inner most thoughts are—"

John's hand reached up, gripping the back of my coat, and flung me down. "Enough."

"J-John," I marveled as he wrapped an arm around me, pressing himself into my back.

"I'm cold and tired," he mumbled, his voice weak and broken. "Keep me warm and stop bickering."

My chest swelled, cupping my hand over his, he clasped his fingers with my own. "John, I—"

"Enough." His head pressed hard between my shoulders, and he whispered so I could only hear, "I thought I lost you. You were so thirsty this time that it startled me, my prince. Don't make me bury my shield before I see you the King. Promise me."

With a deep breath, I whispered, "Promise."

I can't ever decide if I love or loathe the idea that with only a few words he can change how I feel about even myself in a blink of an eye. And since when was he so concerned with me reclaiming the throne? What do you know that you haven't told me about again, John?

Chapter 27

The Informant

Waking from my fitful dreams, sweat trickling down my temple, the last images of my sins faded from my eyes. The battle pounded through my entire body, and the itch of my fangs digging into John still haunted my soul. Reaching over, my hand gripped John's arm, and I exhaled. *He's still here ... and warm.* He rolled and furrowed his brow at me, but I didn't meet his gaze. I could smell the sweet aroma of the blood on his bandage, and the craving rolled up at my core. Anger and fear mangled in my heart, my body tensing against the sensation.

I'm in hell.

"Are you still hun—" he started, and I rushed to cover his mouth.

Searching his eyes, I scowled. "Don't ever utter those words to me ever again."

John pulled my hand off, snorting. "Look, I didn't sleep a wink the night before. It wasn't that you startled me. I was exhausted and passed out in relief. Everyone overreacted," he reassured.

Guffawing, I hissed, "Are you kidding me? I didn't hear you calling my name until I pulled off."

John gripped my coat and pulled me down into him, his lips tickling against my ear. "Tell me why I was still gripping you close to me before I passed out? I told you—I'm plenty strong to shove you off if it came down to that."

"John." I tried to sit up, but he yanked me down into him. "I took too much. We both know it."

"And what did I tell you that night? I'm a greedy bastard." His arms wrapped around me, and he kissed my neck tenderly before whispering, "I'm not afraid of what you are. Don't forget that. I did this to you, I made you into something you dreaded, and I will pay the price to keep you at my side."

He let go, and I pulled away to take in the stern expression with his longing eyes. "You keep reminding me." I paused as my heart raced against my will. "But some part of me fears that one day, I might end up being the reason you breathe your last breath."

John gave a crooked grin, cooing, "I promise when that day comes, my love, it will not be because you sent me to the grave." I grimaced and he tilted his head. "We both know we'd die for each other if it meant saving the other. So, let's just face the fact we're playing a dangerous roulette with both our lives. We're as guilty as the Devoted Sister and Sacrificial Daughter when it comes to the Fates."

Swallowing back the sorrow, the truth of his words stung. "I hate that you have a tongue more silver than my own."

Frustrated, I pulled to my feet, becoming very aware of the eyes and ears watching us. Casting my gaze across theirs, the only one who didn't avert her stare was Red Wine. She tilted her head, and I held my breath. *This situation is proving more dangerous than I anticipated. There was a level of fear in her voice when she pressed the dagger into me but...* I followed her out and down a long stretch of the sewers until the morning light peeked in through small gutters at our feet. *I feel like a dog with my tail between my legs, but rightfully so.*

"He seems in high spirits," she said, her voice deep and disconcerting. "So, tell me, Dante. Was that the first time?"

I leaned against the far wall; arms crossed, I stared down at my boots as light streamed across them. "It was."

"And he's willing to pull you in that close?" She seemed unsure, her prodding growing aggressive. "Does he remember?"

"Better than I do," I confessed, inhaling deeply and holding it a moment. "He didn't even try to shove me away. I pulled away first."

"He was passing out while calling your name, and you didn't stop," she argued.

"Then patronize the stubborn priest on why he didn't stop me," I barked in reply, my eyes striking hers. "We're not children. When he slid that blade across his tongue and offered his blood to me, we were both very aware of the danger." *We both chose this path.*

Pulling her mask off, she tossed back her hood and closed the gap. "I'm responsible for you!" she roared, a finger poking into my chest, and I tensed in silent rebellion. "Your father personally asked this favor of me! Do you have any idea how ashamed I am to even allow you to convince me to let you play pretend and now this?"

"Why did you agree to it?" I spat back. "Clearly no one thinks I can fucking do this!"

"Not at the rate you're throwing yourself in harm's way!" She smacked the heel of her hand into me, and I grunted. "Taking hits willingly isn't going to make you feel normal, Dante!"

"I KNOW THAT!" I reeled, throwing my arms out. "I'M NOT EVEN A BLOODEATER, NOW AM I?"

Her bottom lip protruded, and she sneered, "You don't even know your heritage, do you?"

"No, I don't. Everyone I cross paths with seems to know more about my family than I do." My arms were back to being crossed and I stood taller. *Chin up.* "But we both know that's not my fault, now, is it?"

Her gaze shot away, a hand half covering her face. "Dammit Germaine. Why must you strive to push them to live their own lives... First Ashton, then me, and now..."

"And who are you to let my father's first name fly from your lips so freely?" I spoke in a steady tone, straddling the line of command and reprimand.

Scoffing, she shoved me again. "You're an idiot. Don't make me say it."

"Say what?" John's voice jolted us. "Go on. I've been enjoying this bickering to be honest. I don't even poke and shove him that much."

"Children," she scoffed and stomped off.

"Dammit, John." My arms unfolded, and I leaned back against the wall. "I just want to hear her say it."

"Oh?" He arched a brow, leaning into me. "Now this sounds strangely familiar and stubborn." I rolled my eyes, and he chuckled, adding, "We better get going. Bourbon has left with Sonja and Valiente. They said to tell you they wish you well and thank you for helping get them this far."

"I imagine I startled them last night." I covered my face with a hand, but he slapped it away. "We're in the sewers, so try not to touch your face."

Gaping at him, I watched him march away, waving a hand for me to follow. The fire had been snuffed out besides a single torch. Red Wine's mask was back in place, and she simply started down a dark corridor I hadn't noticed from where we had entered. John snatched up the torch and we followed, silent and obedient. Not once did she bother to look at us. Soon the sewer and filth faded into a dry labyrinth of hallways. The torchlight cast deep shadows across the walls of the arched corridor, revealing bones laid into the masonry like mosaic tiles. *We've entered the ossuary.*

Passing through the many twists and turns, the smell of incense and marrow tickled at my nose. On occasion we'd pass inlays of full skeletons or even bones designed in elaborate wall-to-floor arrangements as if offering a place to pray for the dead. *We are so deep into this place. Who could ever find their way here to pray?* I slowed, curious to see an ossuary's catacombs in person after reading about them with so much wonder. Stumbling to a stop, I took in the most elaborate of all the prayer

218

totems. There among old incense pans and dried flowers was the skull of a daemonis. *Saddlewood, meadow sweet, and rosemary?* Leaning in, something sparkled in the eye socket. *A jewel, or is that a pommel? But why is a daemon here among the bones of all these humans?*

Sticking a finger into the eye socket, I touched the cold object. *Stone, gem, or metal?* I turned to ask John to bring the torch and found myself alone in the darkness. *Shit.* Turning back to the daemon skull, I pained over it. *There has to be a reason something is hiding here.* I pushed two fingers through the socket, and my heart skipped a beat. My fingertips grazed past the round pommel to rub against the starting of a leather-bound handle.

This is a pommel on a weapon of some kind, but why place it here in the catacomb walls under the church?

"You shouldn't poke at the dead," a deep voice mused.

Jerking back, I squinted my eyes down the corridor one way then the other. I could see clear and far, the faint glow of the torch still visible down a turn. *John's voice isn't that deep.* Inhaling, I couldn't smell anything but the lingering scent of John, Red Wine, and burning pitch of the torch. After a moment, I was back to glaring at the daemonis skull, wondering if I had imagined the voice.

"You're starting to lose it, Dante," I muttered.

There was silence. Looking to the shiny object in the skull's eye socket, a chill rattled me.

Could it be? I crouched to be eyelevel with the strange arrangement. There was something here, my instincts tight in my joints egging me to reach for the object hidden within the head of this misplaced ancestor. Goosebumps rolled over me, and I shuddered again. Glaring at the skull only gave it personality, the fanged grin growing high despite the lack of a bottom jaw.

What if I reach under? Again, I probed my fingers into the skull, four fingers cupping under the front teeth to reach up and... *Gems, metal, and leather ... it's a handle of a weapon for sure!*

"You know I was sleeping here until you started touching shit that's not yours. Someone needs to teach you a lesson," growled the voice, making me retreat and bash into the far wall.

"What the hell is wrong with you?" marveled Red Wine, pinching my arm.

"Did you hear that?" I looked all around until my eyes fell back to the daemonis skull. "I think it's talking to me."

Red Wine followed my gaze and snorted. "It's not the only daemon skull here," she announced. "Are you unwell?"

"No," I snarled. "There's someone else here. And there's something in that skull."

She leaned down, removing her mask for a better look. "Huh. So, there is. Good eye, little Traibon. What would your father think to know the crowned blood prince has turned to grave robbing?" she jeered, pushing at my arm. "We're halfway there. Stay close, or you'll get lost. There're more tunnels leading to dead ends and endless twists in these parts."

As she walked away, I glared menacingly at her. "I hate this."

"Hey. Blood Prince," the voice whispered back to life, the skull seeming to cackle at me. *"You can hear me, can't you? Does that mean you've taken the path of a true guardian?"*

"Guardian?" The information wasn't something anyone had said before. "What if I say yes?"

"I pity you," the voice twisted and spoke with resentment. *"You're a fool as I was when I was alive. But I can't lie—I am happy to see she's still among the living."*

My heart skipped a beat, a revelation surfacing. "Wait, who are you? How do you know her?"

Silence.

"Dante! Move it." Red Wine's voice echoed, and the smile faded from the skull.

Reluctantly, I abandoned the curious object. *I will find it again. The daemon prayer totem with the pommel. There's got to be a soul weapon hidden there, but who or what was he?*

I caught up to John who pushed me in front, the two sandwiching me between them like a willful child who aimed to

220

wander off. Every time I began to whisper about the skull, I was shushed until finally I gave up. Hours of twists and turns made me think we had zig-zagged in a large circle. Everywhere I looked, not once did I see another daemon skull or an arrangement as large as the one that had whispered to me.

Light glowed up ahead, and John placed the torch in an empty holder on the wall. "Bishop Montgomery tends to these. We aren't far from the library."

"Isn't he the one that you worked with in the last few years here?" Some part of me was excited to see where he had spent his last years at the Church.

He nodded, but Red Wine's glare made it clear to keep our tongues still.

Following the line of torches, we found a stairwell leading to a large room. The wrought iron gate was left open, though the oak door had been shut. Red Wine knocked twice. After a long pause, she knocked five more times and walked away. John and she sat in chairs, making themselves at home. Flipping back my hood, I began dusting off the cobwebs I had collected in my moment of alarm, flicking a piece of bone from my shoulder.

The oak door swung open, and an old monk froze, locking eyes with me. "By the Fates, it's Ashton."

Blinking, I shot a gaze at John and Red Wine before I confirmed, "I am."

Tears built in his eyes, and he sank to his knees. "Please forgive me. I was only a child then."

Red Wine rose to her feet, cutting in between us. "He has lost his memories, my precious informant, and you sound as if you may know why?"

"Forgive me, Master Assassin." He groveled at her feet.

"What is the meaning of this, Bishop Montgomery?" John paled.

"Father John, I confess before you and the Fates and pray to free myself of this lifelong guilt." The monk sobbed, his elderly voice breaking and struggling to pour forth the words. "Prince Ashton had me sneak him into the library. He was looking for something—or someone." He gasped, trying to catch his breath, and wailed, "But I didn't know who they were! They said he had come to harm The Church! Fallen Arbor had been a rumor! I did what you asked," he pleaded, hands shaking as he reached for me. "The books, I hid them just as you hid me in the crate that fateful day. They needed virgin blood, had arranged for me to be the sacrifice, and instead the young woman... My god, you foamed at the mouth over it like a caged animal." His words picked up speed in the rushed panic of recalling his childhood trauma. "How could you be angry at that? They were aiming to kill you, had pierced you with cursed iron until they pinned you on the holy sarcophagus of Saint Raphael! Blasphemous! You cried the Saint's name, cursing your life, his life, and..."

He shook, folding to the ground and praying in hushed murmurs as if preparing for the next portion. Red Wine held her hand to me, palm on my chest to stay quiet, to stay back. She trembled, hearing the story that would change all that she had sought and fought for. John leaned on his thighs, brow low as he glared at his mentor with concern.

"I was only a child," he muttered, gasping to take a deep breath. "You never once looked my way. I lived but what unfolded was ... Dark magic. Twisted and harrowing. The dark ones certainly had their time with trying to rip your soul from your body. You raged for hours until at last, you fell silent. I peeked ... watching in that moment of eerie calm on your face. That resolve that I've never seen on the face of any clergyman in this lifetime. Flesh crumbled to ash until all that remain was a weapon. The dark priests reached for it, but the white-haired bloodeater came down on them with vengeance. But you're here!" He wobbled to his feet and motioned with hopeful eyes. "You have been returned to flesh! She found a way!" Red Wine's palm fisted and gripped the chest guard of my manica. "You must go after them, my prince." The old monk was back to the ground, kneeling in allegiance. "They have covered Grandmere in darkness in your absence. It cannot go on much further," he begged, muttering more prayers to the Saints and the Fates.

"Tell me, Bishop." Red Wine's voice seethed with rage. "Why have you never spoken a word of this?"

"She said not a word until she found a way." He motioned to me. "He is back among the living. I am freed from protecting this place." Turning to John, he marveled, "To imagine my pupil would be here and bring me the answer to my prayers. You are worthy of being a Saint, Father John."

John looked away, shoulders tensing. "I wouldn't declare that so easily, Bishop Montgomery."

"So, Frank knew," hissed Red Wine. "They knew and swore secrecy, but why?" Letting me go, she gripped Bishop Montgomery's arm. "Come with me, monk. We have much to discuss."

"John, the books!" The monk called out, "Give Prince Ashton the books."

John rose to his feet. "You mean the ones I took three days of lashes for finding?"

I thought those scars were from sword practice. Have we both kept secrets?

"Forgive me, Father, please. Both of you, forgive this tortured old man..."

Red Wine shoved him through the door.

John and I looked to one another, inhaling and holding it until we released our breath together. I followed him as we traveled through storerooms, a small kitchen and fire, rooms void of personal effects and occupants until at last we climbed another stairwell. This one put us in a cathedral-sized room with no outside lights or windows to be found. Large chandeliers hung throughout, reflecting the light of the blazing braziers of oil under them. It was warm and stifling, unlike the chill in the catacombs and sewers. All around us were shelves of books lined floor to ceiling, ladders scattered about, and bookshelves protruding out like fingers. Tables with ink and parchment lined the center, only disrupted by the occasional glass case or brazier, and went on farther than I could even make out.

"Takes one's breath away, doesn't it?" John grabbed me by the wrist and tugged me along as I gawked at the ornamental work of bones, wood, and books of old. "I thought you'd love to see this place. It puts your library to shame, but I didn't want to tell you that."

"John, what was it that you found to get lashes for?" The place held so many artifacts of faith, some behind glass, some books with chains and locks, while others lay abandoned on tables where someone had left them after study.

"You will see." He didn't look back at me once, pacing through the pillars of tomes at a steady rate. "I told you. It was here that I knew I could find answers, but I needed your help to get to them."

What the hell happened to you, Ashton? How are we all so connected to the last place you were ever seen alive?

CHAPTER 28

Saint Raphael de'Traibon-Thompson

By the time John brought us to a stop, we had left the books behind us. A door hidden behind a swinging bookshelf led us to a spiraling stairwell. There we stood in a tiny square room with a white marble sarcophagus as if we had left the dust of books and catacombs behind and entered a mausoleum worthy of a king. Stunning lions and statuesque champions fighting one another lined the outer edge of the center piece. The room was lit with candles all around, and something tinged the air here, making the hairs on my arms stand on end. *Blood and ... is this what magic smells like? Sulfur and metallic to the point of tasting it on inhale?*

John walked up to the sarcophagus and glared down at the name chiseled into its lid. Black stains filled the imperfect cracks and crannies of the lid. *Ashton's blood.* I inhaled deeply, and chills rolled over me. *It damn near smells like my own and a lot like Red Wine's. The smell of a Traibon born daemon, but this name etched into it.*

"Saint Raphael de'Traibon-Thompson." The words came out of my mouth strange. "I've never heard of this saint." A shiver shook my shoulders, and my mouth ran dry.

"Neither had I until I volunteered in the catacombs." He motioned to the candles. "There's magic here. No one comes to light these. They stay lit, and the wax never drips. Bishop Montgomery made the mistake in not noticing I was on the ground reaching for a fallen book when I saw him sneak into here. And naturally, I had to see this place for myself."

"Why didn't you tell me about this place?" Part of me was angry. *Always keeping me in the dark, and so many secrets, I can't fathom what else he keeps from me.*

"It was one of those things I'd have to show you to believe." He ran a hand over the name. "Don't you find it strange it's both our last names on this coffin? How could I even make something such as this believable in a world void of magic?"

"We're going to have to either corner my father about this or go to the one person who knew Ashton the best." I squatted, marveling over the scene of champions fighting in marble.

"Didn't Red Wine know him?" John traced each letter of *Thompson* with his finger.

"Not exactly." Squinting, I realized all the figures had fangs and only one didn't have a braid yet carried a claymore. *Ashton.* "Frank the Immortal. They know. They must know. Maybe like the monk, seeing me might jolt their memory."

"But that's clear on the other side of Grandmere," snorted John. "Winter's Perch. I read that the snow and ice never cease there nor in the Preveran Mountains."

"What choice do we have?" I stood again, daring to come closer. "So, these books ... where are they?"

"Ah." He flicked his eyebrows and rammed a shoulder into the lid, scooting it a few inches. "In here," he grunted.

I patted his shoulder, signaling for him to move. Bracing myself, I shoved, and the lid slid. The scraping of it filled the air until it revealed blue silken cloth lining the inside with splotches of black stains and the stale scent of blood wafting up. *And I*

226

thought I bled out on the battlefield, but this is ... so much. Inside, books lay scattered and piled. Scanning from one end to the next, I realized there were no signs of an actual body ever being laid to rest inside the sarcophagus. Reaching in, I began glancing at the titles or opening blank covers to discover journals regarding dark rituals, daemons, the Old Continent, and...

"I know this handwriting," I muttered, wide eyed as I flipped to the beginning of the book. "This is ... this is my father's writing, but centuries old."

John leaned over, peeking. "But why is his diary in a dead Saint's coffin?"

"I don't know." Shaking my head, I began gathering the books up. "We'll start with these and see what we find."

"Agreed. We'll keep them in here." He emptied my arms, reprimanding me, "But let's keep the lid on it for now."

Looking back to the sarcophagus, I reached over and pulled the lid back in place. The muscles in my arms stung to pull on the weight of it, but it was best for it to remain safe. By the time we settled on a table in a far corner, we could hear Red Wine and Bishop Montgomery whispering to one another. They came around the last bookshelf, finding John hunched over a book next to a few stacks while I had leaned against a shelf, idling flipping pages as I scanned them with morbid fascination.

"Did you find everything you were looking for, Prince Ashton?" Bishop Montgomery smiled, a great weight had lifted from him both emotionally and physically.

"I suppose I have." I flipped through my father's journal, passing entries filled with chores of farming and discussions with Lord Traibon over the disputes among other nobility. *This is around the time they made champions mandatory for winning land and more.* "There's much here I didn't realize came from my father." I flipped the book around, and Red Wine marched over to retrieve it. "How much do I not know, Red Wine?"

"I swear, King Traibon is a foolish man. He's got tighter lips than any assassin I've ever known, spies included." She flipped through the journal until she found something that piqued her interest. "Ha. Here, this is where the discussion of *you* having to join in the Champion Wars."

Arching a brow, I mused, "I wasn't looking for an action-adventure story." Glancing at it, I saw the retelling seemed to be my father's self-reflections of assuming the role for the sake of both families. *The nobles being Traibon, the daemons being Thompson?* "Ah, John." I broke him from his own book and flashed the page. "Here, it seems Traibon was the nobility line Raphael came from and here," I slid my finger to the adjacent page, "Thompson was my father's actual last name. At some point we swapped, so that means..." Pulling the claymore out of its sheath, I twisted it to face Red Wine and the Bishop. "This family seal, the one Lord Knight Paul Thompson has on all his armor and weapons, it's the same as the Traibon-Thompson seal from long ago, isn't it? The same one in the tomb."

"Not quite, but eerily similar to the one my father had on his weapons, yes," Red Wine confessed, plucking up another book and glancing over the pages. "There's so much of our forgotten history here. Why hide such vital resources here of all places?"

"And books on dark magic too." John flipped around the book he had been engrossed in reading and flashed it to everyone. "Look at the diagrams. All of these seem to call for blood and tying souls to other people and even objects. This one seems like the notes of an acolyte trying to figure out how to recreate something he noted at the start." John flipped through the pages until he found a sketch of a peculiar sword. "This weapon houses many souls. Only one of its kind."

Crossing her arms, Red Wine tapped her fingers a moment, staring at it. "I've seen this sword. I know it well, in fact."

"You have?" Bishop Montgomery seemed amazed of all the otherworldly items seeming to manifest themselves. "But isn't that written in the Old Tongue?"

"It is." Red Wine glared at John, her words articulating each syllable of the strange language. *"Skaz mir, kwie vast vy chilis fu elate au Spatrom Lazyke?"*

"I read ... a lot." John closed the book and leaned back in his chair, sucking on his cheek. "It's interesting to hear it spoken, the Old Tongue, but when you have three years of being confined to a bone-covered library, you find a way to read the impossible." He pointed to a few shelves, snorting. "You can find many books in here that make an attempt at teaching it. I didn't bother to learn to speak it, but I can write, read, and translate loosely."

Sighing, Red Wine relaxed. "I didn't realize the Church invested in such works."

"Oh, they once had a thirst for that. At another moment, we were hunting certain tomes down, and they are found chained here." The Bishop stroked his beard, huffing out a breath. "Come, let me cook you all a meal. You may bring the books to your quarters."

"What? Really?" John seemed excited about the news.

Bishop Montgomery turned, chuckling, "I suppose you are no longer my pupil. You were always a clever one, Father John, but perhaps more so than I had initially realized."

We watched as the old monk left us behind, and I turned my attention to Red Wine. "Did you get your answers?"

"Some." She pulled up a chair and took off her mask, rubbing her eyes in frustration. "He hasn't gotten word out because the Church is on lockdown under Bishop Marquis' order by decree of King Regius."

"Shit." John glanced over to me, explaining, "It means no one can come in and out of the cathedral without written permission from the bishop in charge of the lockdown. In short, Marquis. Granted, no one travels down this way without explicit orders to study or locate old information, but in the three or so years I spent here..." he searched his thoughts and announced, "maybe half a dozen, if that. Most of the foot traffic was to supply the kitchen or deliver messages to Montgomery."

"We're going to have to see how much Princess Sonja, the Royal Guard, and a few Guild members can do to open communications again in the city and undo this mess." Red Wine looked up, her eyes bouncing over the books and library. "I hate books."

"Leave the books to us." I smirked, beginning to flip through the journal some more. "John and I will research what we can from what was hidden. Until then, how are you feeling? Weren't you searching for what had happened to Ashton once he chased Fallen Arbor to the Church?"

"I don't know what to think anymore." She inhaled deeply and huffed the air out in frustration. "Frank knew, but threw a tantrum when I asked. I would think I had the right to know or at least, let me help. The problem is, I don't think Frank is finding any answers in Winter's Perch so..." Pausing, her lips twisted. "I think he died here."

"I think so too," I whispered, meeting her eyes. "His blood is thick on that sarcophagus. It matches the monk's story. What I'm curious about is what happened with the weapon they made from his essence. Do you think Frank has it?"

"No. Frank's not that kind of fighter." She stood, putting a hand on her hip. "In fact, now I regret not doing some grave robbing. Perhaps there was something special behind those old bones, but then again, half a dozen nobles were buried with weapons down there in that maze."

"She's right. There's a ton down there, the easiest in the alcoves. Though, hiding a weapon among many would be smart if they needed to keep it safe until a solution was found. If one even existed." John closed a book and stood, grabbing up the stack. "Let's eat and rest, shall we?"

We followed John slowly and steadily back through the length of the library. Red Wine stared at her mask, her feisty demeanor lost in the wake of discovering Ashton was no more. John didn't even glance back, but my eyes burned into him. *Secrets.* He had come here to help me, but instead became so educated that he surpassed me in knowledge stretching outside of Grandmere to the point he could reply to a language I hadn't known existed. *I wonder...*

"John." He stopped and turned.

"Yes?" Arching a brow, he looked tired.

"12-knots," I replied.

He squinted, thinking hard for a moment before answering, "A Count."

Smiling, I corrected, "Lord Knight."

"Dammit." His face turned red, and he started marching away, faster than he had before.

"How could someone mess that up?" marveled Red Wine.

"I spent a year trying to help him learn the knots, and he still can't remember his grandfather was a Lord Knight." Some relief washed over me. "But yet, here all alone for all those years, he absorbed all he could in hopes of saving me from Falco and Grandmere from the Madness."

"Huh." She blinked. "What a peculiar duo you two make."

I suppose he's still the same John that left me behind all those years ago. Perhaps I shouldn't fret about the things he does and doesn't know and instead enjoy the idea he will always find some way to surprise me when I least expect it.

CHAPTER 29

Losing Patience

Red Wine had left by the time I woke from my rest. John dove the hardest into books written in the Old Tongue, often reading excerpts out loud to share with me on occasion. Overall, the collection had been a strange mixture of journals from my very own family, a few from the Saint himself, and the strange assortment of Dark Magic research bearing no name and always written in the foreign language. On occasion, we would get hints of how they would achieve making a soul weapon. These excerpts often involved lots of blood spilling, and there seemed to be conflicting information. One journal seemed to suggest that it was possible to attach a soul to a created weapon while another insisted that the body itself evolved into the weapon. Some of the notes even seemed frustrated at the idea that the individual must choose to be one and could not be forced into it or it created a weaker cursed variant. A few times, we found rambling side notes insisting it would be easier to acquire a blade from the Ogre clan but ... only sketches and case studies from afar would follow shortly after.

As for the journals, it was strange to read first-hand what my own father's life was like before his title of king. Teamed with Saint Raphael's own, it captured the political pressure that would eventually buckle and create the Grandmere we all knew best. Civil unrest had stewed far longer and in a deeper way than I'd realized in my own studies of our history growing up. The lords used champions to resolve disputes until they turned against the daemon. We had been equals who protected their households from harm's way. As the friction grew among the original founding Houses of Grandmere, daemons were being enslaved.

Lord Raphael was the last to be forced into this method of resolving disputes of all kinds, including land claims, in order to hold their ground. The strange idea was his silence in addressing what my father did record: *Ashton becoming the household champion instead of him.* I flipped open both books, watching as the Lord took months before coming back to write: *I may have protected what is ours, but at what cost? If I had known what these sins would have cost, I would have forced another path or perhaps claimed the throne to govern the fools who put this travesty into motion. But again, I would have lost what I cherished most down that path too.*

Despite it all, we read the secret books one by one, putting them back to the sarcophagus or leaving it in the stack we wanted to circle back to for more information. The days were beginning to blend, the outside world nowhere to be seen or felt in this underground sanctuary bearing no windows. There was no sense of when night or day passed beyond these walls of bones and books, no hourglass or measurement to keep track of such trifling matters. *I feel like we can spend eternity here indulging in one another's company.* I'd barely spoken to John other than sharing findings in the books we scoured. Each time we retired for the day, I was met with his frustrated glare as I refused to share the same quarters or even step through the threshold of his room. Worse, Bishop Montgomery would seek me out on occasion and want to chat about the past, though we had insisted I had no memory.

Why do I feel so damn guilty about avoiding intimacy with John and that I'm not Ashton at all?

"Prince Ashton, tell me, what was it like being the Grand Champion of Grandmere?" Bishop Montgomery mused, a cheeky grin on his face as he placed a fresh loaf of bread and pitcher of water at the table with John.

"I can't remember it, so I don't know how well I can answer that, Bishop." Hiding in a dark corner, I idly read the latest journal with intrigue. "It seems before I came here I had quite the adventure chasing Fallen Arbor."

"So I've heard." He filled three cups and sat staring at the books.

John met his gaze, smirking as he offered, "You are more than welcome to peek, Bishop Montgomery."

"I decline, Father John." A shudder shook him. "I've been involved in enough secrets."

"Well, I must confess," I mused as I shot a glance at John breaking the bread. "You kept the greatest secret of the century, no?"

A chuckle escaped him before the monk confessed, "Guilty. I'm curious though. Many of these seem like personal memoirs and journals. From whom, exactly?"

"Well, this one is..." I cleared my throat, nearly saying, *my brother's* and redirected, "...my own, apparently."

"Oh? Any memories worthwhile?" Montgomery's brow raised high as he sipped his water. "I do hope you recover your memories, Prince Ashton."

"No matter if I do or not, it does not change the course we have set ourselves on." Another stolen glance at John revealed the scar on his neck and winced.

"Any word from The Guild or Princess Sonja?" John pulled his collar up as if he could feel my eyes prying.

"None." The old monk took a piece of bread for himself and rose to his feet again. "It's been nice having company again in the library. Though, much to my surprise, you both barely say a word to one another."

John smirked, explaining, "We're just exhausted, Montgomery. It wasn't the easiest winter nor did our trip here give us much time to rest."

"Ah, I see." He bowed his head ever slightly, drawing a hand across his shoulders before dropping the arm palm up down the center of his body. "I hope the Fates reward you before your next battle. Forgive me, but I must tend to dinner and before that, rest. This body of mine isn't getting any younger."

The tension in my body left me as we were left alone once more. Page by page, I read my brother's words. He was short and curt when he wrote. There were very little signs of emotion in the words but more of a record of some kind. The words filled me like taking in an old ship's log, nothing more than an inventory of action taken between two points of his life. This one recalled his chase of Fallen Arbor to the Old Continent, something I had heard fleeting bits about through the Master Assassin.

"Another journal in the Old Tongue," John fussed, bitter and frustrated. "These are nothing but spell books for the dark arts filled with grotesque rituals."

"I wonder who they belonged to." My words fell from my lips in a detached tone as I engrossed myself in reading Ashton's journal. "We have a plethora of my father's own, filled with whining on par to how he still lectures me at times. In fact, they must be connected to the others here."

"Agreed. It must be someone connected to them." John searched the covers inside and out. "I see LLI written or etched in some of these. Perhaps its initials, but nothing else. You think they are stolen or even secret research from one of them?"

Snorting, I flipped the page, eyes chasing the lines of script. "There only seems to be my brother, my father, Lord Raphael, and one from a high noble, Preston Thompson. He seems rather sour about Raphael and Ashton, leaving their respective houses at the turn of the war and leaving him with no assets. What was it he had said? Ah, *'Incompetent lovesick fools who think keeping a distance will be enough to protect them from the reach of their enemies.'*"

"You think grandpa has something in the cabin that links Preston to me? Or even Raphael?" John flipped aimlessly through the pages, disinterested in the drawings and notes within.

Glancing up, I watched him furrow his brow to squint and read something. "You think you're really of that bloodline? I mean, after all that we've recovered in these books and compared to others in the library here, that would technically make you the rightful heir of Grandmere."

He laughed, muttering under his breath, "Not where I was going with that, Dante."

"Ashton," I corrected. "Speaking of which. He's been rather dull to read until this page."

"Oh?" John took a bite of bread, chewing it.

"Listen to this," I mused, pulling myself off the shelf to walk closer. *"How could he! How could she! I did not give them my blessing! One can't just marry into obscure diplomacy through marriage without the powers involved agreeing to ... and what would Grandmere and a clan in the Old Continent be able to do with this? And worse! To find them consummating the marriage when I barged into the Warlord's tent! By the Fates, what did I do to deserve this turn of events?"*

John choked on his bread, managing to croak, "Who is he referring to?"

"Oh, that's the fun part." I leaned closer, whispering the next bit, *"'I did not name her after the love of my life and good Saint Raphael for her to give the Traibon title to that fucking ogre!'"* I licked a fang, entertained as I went on. "He was rather miffed about this ordeal, but I suppose he was simply concerned."

Swallowing his food, John scoffed. "Sounds like he's about to kill someone. What makes you think it was more worry than anger, knowing the things we've encountered about your brother thus far?"

I raised a hand, silencing John as I continued my reading, *"'Does he love her? I never wanted her to be sworn into her status as crowned princess for the sake of politics and especially not like this! How am I to explain this to my father, Frank, hell, the whole*

236

of Grandmere when we return? Raphaëlle insists it was not against her will, but she should have known I would come for her! When I am finished with Fallen Arbor, I will address this diplomatically or by force with Sebastian. He may have kept her safe, even smuggled me into the country and brought me here but ... I never wanted her to be with a warlord. I never wanted her to end up with someone like me who would kill without regret. I am losing patience with her. As is the way of a parent, I suppose. What shall I ever do with this life you have left for me, my love?'"

"Raphaëlle?" John took a sip of water before standing to peek at the pages. "Who is that?"

I made a dubious expression. "I don't think you'd believe me if I told you. She's been travelling with us the whole way." John took the book from me, but I backed up to make distance when the scent of his sweat sent a chill across me. "I am pretty sure our..."

John came closer to give chase as I sank back into the dark corner. "You mean this is the Master Assassin? Red Wine is..." My back hit the bookshelf, and he pinned me, whispering in a husky tone, "Why are you running away from me, Dante? Tell me now," he demanded, staring at my lips.

"I don't trust..." I started, taking in his scent before confessing, "...myself."

"That's not for you to decide." His thumb rubbed my bottom lip. "Did I ever tell you ... I'm losing my patience waiting for you? You have no idea how badly I've wanted to be with you these few weeks, do you?"

"You've made it known in heated glares on more than one occasion." I gripped his wrist and pushed his hand off my face. "John, I can't ... not after—"

He rolled his hand, now gripping my wrist in counter. "I want to feel your touch..." Willingly, I let him lead my hand to the bulge awaiting me under his pants. "I've already told you, I'm not afraid of you ... I love you, my prince, my assassin, my love."

"John," I breathed, cursing the bookshelf and books pushing into me from three sides. "I don't know if I can keep myself in check. You know that. Look what happened—"

"Then let me decide how far we go," he purred.

John's lips were like fire as he suckled on my neck. I moaned, groping him, and he grunted, tilting to press himself hard into my palm. His fingers made quick work of my shirt's buttons then my pants—and I cursed his name for it. *It's so blasted hot in this place I stopped wearing my armor. He makes me feel so ... vulnerable.* Teasing, his fingers glided across my torso, my breath catching at the wave of arousal he invoked. The way now open, he licked and sucked across my collarbone and down my chest. He shoved my arms out of his way, and I braced them on either bookshelf, my knees weak with thoughts of what would follow.

"John..." I panted, but he paid me no heed.

I watched him as he descended my torso, tugging my pants open to reveal my own throbbing bulge, my body on fire. His fingers wrapped around me, a firm thumb stroking the underbelly making me moan. The bookshelves creaked and cracked under my weight and pressure. *I will not dare to let go... I will not make a move in fear...* The silken heat of his tongue rolled over the tip before he took all of me between his lips. Goosebumps cascaded across my entire body as he started slowly. Blue eyes shot a glance upward, and I throbbed in reply. It was enough to goad him to pick up pace.

"Shit, it's been too long..." My words were stolen from me as I teetered on the edge of an orgasm too soon. "...Slow down," I huffed. "I don't want to come so soon," I confessed.

He pulled slowly off with a pop of his lips and grinned. "And here I thought you wanted to be quick as to not be caught."

I shot my eyes away, heat rising in my cheeks. "No one ever comes here, you said that yourself, and Montgomery sleeps like the dead on the far end so..."

John snickered, undoing his own pants. "So, we agree on that much."

As he took me back into his mouth, my fangs ached, and my heart raced. Engrossed in the building pleasure, he worked slower all the while stroking himself. I throbbed, and he moaned until he pushed me deep inside. Tilting my hip, the back of his throat sent shivers of bliss through me. A hand snaked up across my torso, and I gripped the shelves harder, fighting the urge to grind deeper across the wiggling tongue. I took a deep breath, John's lustful desire and pleasure seeming to fill the air. The saliva in my mouth built as if anticipating a meal.

"We need to stop," I exhaled.

Again, the agonizingly slow retreat and release of his lips. "I already told you..." He rose to his feet, hands gliding over me and sending a shudder through me. "...I get to decide when we stop."

"You don't understand." I looked away, too afraid to let go of the shelves. "I want you in so many ways it's impossible to pick apart the hunger from the..." John's tongue lit my skin on fire as he licked up to me ear. "J-john..." His pulse throbbed in my ears like pounding drums, turning my head only gave John more access to suckle my earlobe. "You should keep your distance."

"I'd ask, but I promised not to say those words," he whispered. "So, tell me, my assassin, what other things do you thirst for from me other than what flows in my vein?"

Again, one of his hands were back to stroking my hardened length, and I moaned. "Three years I sat in here amongst these shelves imagining a moment like this between us, Dante. What of you? Did you ever ... think of me?"

I inhaled swiftly, arms aching as I refused to let go, blood rushing when John pressed his body against mine as his lips tickled at my ear. "I tried so hard to convince myself it wasn't love ... that I was there on that farm waiting for you because..."

"We knew what it was between us when I showed you the scythe." He snorted, his breath washing over my neck, making me shiver. "The way you stuttered, and both our hearts raced in that moment—I knew and so did you. We had plenty of chances to do the lesson, but avoided it because it meant we'd have to be too close to one another..."

I broke my hold, arms rushing in to lock lips with him. Now he found himself pinned between me and a shelf, my tongue diving into the folds that had brought me to such a state. He moaned, cock pressing into me as I suckled his tongue. The sweet flavor of him, of his blood, of his lust with the heat of his body and racing pulse. It broke down the wall I had tried so hard to put back in place. *Damn you... You knew before I was willing to even accept it...*

"I want to tell you to turn around so that I can break you..." John whispered before kissing me once more, pressing something into my hand.

"What's this—when did you?"

"You took it from the brothel, right?" He had stolen the flask of oil from my quarters. "You can't tell me you weren't thinking about it..."

Licking a fang, I turned him around and licked across his shoulder. "I take pleasure in this." My hand rolled over his ass, and my cock pressed between his cheeks. "This is the way I prefer to take you but will gladly submit to how you see fit, my priest."

John reached up, gripping the bookshelf. "Don't you dare deny me this moment, Dante."

"I won't," I huffed over his shoulder, oil slick across my cock and hand, fingers teasing him as his pants began to slide down.

John shifted and my finger slipped inside, my cock throbbing. "Stop going so fucking slow," he demanded.

"Yes, my priest," I purred into his ear as two fingers slipped inside. "But be patient. I haven't taken you, and you've grown so tight again."

John grunted, his body shuddering as I stroked in and out of him, stretching him. "I like this better," he confessed. "Though I might want to take you again later."

"I am yours," I whispered, my hand retreating, slick with oil as I glided over his hip to stroke him. "I'll teach you all the dark secrets of passion if you wish." The tip of my cock slid inside him, and his heart fluttered in my ears. "Only you may ever take me

240

in such a way," I promised, rolling my thumb over the dripping tip of his cock as I pushed deeper inside him. "Don't you dare come so soon, not until I have a taste."

"D-Dante." He began panting as I started grinding slow against him.

I throbbed in the heat of his body, thrusting ever faster as I held onto his own hardened length. His hand cupped mine, encouraging as I stroked him in rhythm of my fucking, and I followed suit. Every muscle tensed as I sucked at his neck, thoughts of feeding replaced with the needed to release and lay claim to the man I loved with every part of my being.

Is this how I can overcome the thirst?

Pleasure shot through me, pounding hard and fast with the shelf creaking from our efforts. Every muscle tightened as I pressed firm against him, sliding deep one last time, and I released. His cock jumped in my palm at the sensation, and I slowed the stroking. It was a slow return to grinding, just enough to keep him panting, moaning, his heart fluttering when I slid slightly faster at times. His hand gripped mine tighter over his cock as he leaned back into me.

"Please..." he breathed, "...so close."

I broke away from him, my hand firm on his wrist as I marched him to the table. Pushing him on top, the cups spilled and rolled to the floor as I tugged his pants full off.

"D-Dante!" John inhaled swiftly as I pulled his cock deep into my mouth.

Fangs teasingly touched the hardened flesh that throbbed between my hungry lips. I sucked, bobbing fast and taking him deeper with each swallow. More items fell to the floor as he struggled to sit up until at last he gripped the back of my head. He grinded in sync with me, and when the muscles in his thighs tensed, his cock stiffened and released. I swallowed yet didn't slow my task. Another round of swift breaths, and he bucked and folded onto me as he came a second time.

"Dammit," he hissed. "That's too much. I can't keep going like you..."

"I'm not done," I announced, rising to my feet and shoving him onto his back against the books.

"The books—"

"Fuck them. They don't have answers to the questions I'm wanting." Hooking an arm with a knee, I parted him so I could push back inside.

I towered over him, and once I found my stride, I leaned into him, locking eyes, nose-to-nose. The smell of him was intoxicating, and all the flavors of what he could offer like the sweetest of wines drove my desire. I braced on the table, thrusting hard into him, watching how his face flushed deeper until I came once more. As I throbbed and pulsed inside him, he pulled me down and kissed me deeply. Breaking it, I began burning a trail of kisses and suckled down his body, salty sweet filling my senses until I licked at his cock once more.

"No more," he flustered. "You win. I'm satisfied."

"I am not." I began kissing and sucking, the vein in his inner thigh teasing me as it pulsed. "May I have a taste?"

"There of all places?" He propped up, musing over it before rubbing the scar on his neck. "Only if you promise to be gentle."

I sank my fangs in, the flesh here less resilient, parting gently. His cock jolted, and I began stroking it, feeling how aroused my drinking made him as I drew long gulps. A moan escaped him, his blood hot and sweet as it slid over my tongue and down my throat. Another jolt drew my attention away, satisfied with the little I had taken before pulling his length back between my lips. I took barely three or four deep sucks before he released a third time, cursing me for ruining him in such a way. Swallowing, wiping my face on my sleeve, I threw his pants at him.

"This is your fault." I hid my grin under my arm, heart racing, body and urges satisfied. *Perhaps Red Wine is right. This hunger is more in-tune with injuries after all.*

John scrambled to pull his pants on, disregarding fastening them to rush to pick up the fallen items. "I will need to bathe now before dinner. I feel like a whore."

242

"It was your idea to use the oil," I countered, buttoning my shirt and putting myself back into order.

"You're the one who smuggled it into a church," he scoffed, a twinkle in his eyes. "Don't take too long. Bishop Montgomery is a short napper and will be serving dinner soon enough. Then afterward, come by my—"

"No. You got what you wanted," I mused as his face flushed. "Besides, we're too loud to be in close quarters next to a monk's room."

John twisted away, hiding his expression from me. I chuckled, reaching for Ashton's diary. *I suppose we both have a knack for goading one another's emotions to a frustrating peak. And now, to see how this one ends. This page says he was heading here, and that means he had the diary on him the day he was ambushed. So, did Frank hide these before abandoning this place? Why not burn them?*

CHAPTER 30

The Town Criers
Have Spoken

John snorted at me from where he read a book, feet propped on the table. I came out in full armor, something I had done on occasion to train. We had been stale and cooped up away from civilization for a few months by this point. To say I didn't miss the burning of my muscles for training on a daily basis was an understatement. Little communication had reached us or even news of Bishop Montgomery visiting The Church. No signs of the Guild, no word of Fallen Arbor, and nothing from the Royal Guard and Valiente. The only news had reported that the search for the Princess was called off, notice of Falco's death at last reaching this far, and the fall of the Berserk Brigade was creating a mixture of alarm and relief in many of the ranks of priests and monks who came down to gossip to Father Montgomery.

"This again," drawled John, flipping a page.

"Yes, this again," I scoffed. "Come on. Get off your ass and spar with me."

Puffing out his cheeks, he slid a falcon feather between the pages. "Do I have to dress up, too?"

"Yes," I demanded. "We don't know when Fallen Arbor might decide to make a move." I furrowed my brow as he stretched and yawned in annoyance. "And it's not like I can spar Bishop Montgomery or the other priests, now can I?"

John laughed, dropping the book on the table. "Fine. I'll be nice and put on the full regalia … if," he shot me a side glance and smirk, "you move tables out of the way, so we can have a real sparring session."

"Deal." I winked, starting to shove the table with one hand between two shelves.

By the time John came out chatting alongside Bishop Montgomery, I had moved several tables and shifted braziers to open the center of the library for us to train. It revealed a ring mosaic with the symbol of the Fates, something unheard of this far south and certainly in a Church that put the Divine Father above all else. Looking at it, it looked fitting as a fighting ring. John paused, grimacing to see it, adding to his disdain to train. With a sigh, he began rolling up his sleeves, cursing my name under his breath. Bishop Montgomery pulled up a chair, a twinkle in his eyes.

"I must say, I didn't realize how studious you are to keep in shape, Prince Ashton." The old monk grinned wide. "And the idea Father John can even keep up! My word!"

John scoffed. "I think Ashton intends to put me through my paces today. He's been going easy for weeks, Bishop."

"Really?" he marveled with excitement. "I do enjoy watching. I once dreamed of being a knight, but alas, I had a higher calling."

"Come on, John." I twirled the heavy wooden sword in my hand. "It's only sparring sticks."

"No offense. You can break bones with your strength," John jeered, circling the center of the space with me.

"Must you always roll up your sleeves?" I teased, stepping forward to strike, and he blocked.

"Sleeves are too stifling to do swordplay with," John answered. "Must you fight with the claymore strapped to your back?"

A few strikes exchanged between us before I pushed him out of the circle's edge. "It's to your advantage. A means of slowing me down."

John's face flushed, and his lips twisted. He stepped back in with a swing and came at me with a flurry of stabs. I dodged and blocked until managing to drop down and swing out a leg. He leapt back, air huffing from his nostrils. Sliding forward, I gave a wide upswing. He aimed to block, and I jarred the sword from his hand, sending it skidding to Bishop Montgomery's feet. The old man clapped his hands gleefully, and John gave him a sour expression.

"Exactly whose side are you on?" John hissed.

"It's amazing how big and agile he can be!" Bishop Montgomery beamed.

John twisted away from the bishop and locked eyes with me. "Oh, so very agile in and out of battle."

"Keep up with those compliments, and I might have to kiss you, Father John." The red in his face rose, and he lipped his complaint for me to quit. "Exactly what are the parameters of being a priest? What shall thou not doeth?"

John came at me, swinging hard and heavy. The knocking of the wooden blades cracked loudly through the library, and the skulls of the ossuary watched with wide gazes. Sweat trickled down John's temple, yet I hadn't even begun to feel exhaustion or the exertion of my blocks and swings. I let one swing smack my shoulder, twisting my arm to catch his wris,t and lurched him forward.

"I've never thought to ask," I added.

John broke from me, biting his lip in contempt.

"Well, Prince Ashton," Bishop Montgomery cleared his throat, answering with a serious tone and glare, "a priest has many restrictions and expectations. First off, they either lead a church or congregation; if not, they are sent to work Salvation Road and the battlefields. They have sworn abstinence, to keep body and soul cleansed of temptations of the flesh. More so, they are to follow their bishop's orders without question and protect the church and those who serve it with their lives. Even though they may carry a sword for protection, they are not to give a killing blow. Ever."

My heart skipped a beat, frowning as John jerked out of my grip. Rage-filled swings jarred the wood in my grip, and I tensed. The look in those blue eyes were filled with worry and anger. *He would have never answered me on this. We both knew he had sinned when he...*

"As far as their promise to fight back the Madness," Bishop Montgomery continued as our blows clacked like thunder, "they promise to never allow a bloodeater to feed on them, to never support making new ones, and more importantly, never to serve The House."

I broke my gaze to meet Bishop Montgomery's expression. John's wooden blade hit across my knuckles, and the sword fell to the floor. John gripped the front of my armor, but I didn't budge. He whispered pleas, but I ignored his words as I pulled the truth from the bishop.

"But I am of the House," I pressed, seeing the dangerous look in the old man's eyes.

"Yes, but you aim to bring this to an end, so you cause much conflict among the clergymen. We are divided on you and your brother as of late. You are of the House, but you follow a path to end the Madness like ourselves." A grim expression filled his face.

"And the crime for breaking any of these rules of faith?" I demanded.

"Death," the bishop answered.

John landed a punch across my cheek, his own wooden blade bouncing onto the floor at our feet. Gripping the front of his coat, I twisted and pinned him against the shelves behind me. Both our hearts were racing. *You fool! What have you done?*

"Don't say it," he hissed, veins pulsing at his temple with rage.

"You fucking broke every damn rule they gave you, John." I hissed too low for the words to reach the bishop.

"I did it for you," he murmured, his rage slipping into despair.

Footsteps echoed from the hallway, and I broke away. Bishop Montgomery rose to his feet, and Knight Valiente pushed through the gate. He paused, eyes bouncing between John and me, a deep scowl across his face. Looking over his shoulder, he dismissed the priest and knight who had followed him and shut the gate.

"What is the purpose of this?" The alarm in the bishop's voice made my stomach twist.

"Easy, Bishop." Valiente came closer, motioning for us to calm down. "Bishop Marquis has the whole city in an uproar this morning. I'm here to help."

"I despise that man." Crossing my arms, I arched a brow at Valiente. "But that doesn't explain why you bulldozed your way into the library against code and tradition."

"You're right." Valiente rubbed the back of his neck, shooting a glance at Bishop Montgomery. "I'm here to take you into custody. You're being called before the King's council to question you on Father John's character and whereabouts."

Bishop Montgomery guffawed. "You can't be serious!"

"I am, Bishop. It was either the Royal Guard or those ruffians he claims serves the King." Valiente locked his eyes on John. "Marquis claims to have evidence that not only did you deliver the killing blow to Viceroy Falco, but you worked as an assassin on behalf of the House, therefore breaking your priestly vows."

"What evidence do you think he has?" I demanded.

"No idea. Sonja and I have been fighting against conspirators since we got back within the castle walls. Without the Guild's help, she and I would be dead from the three assassination attempts. I think it's been a way to keep us off his heels long enough to get news to the town criers this morning to put a search out on John. Fallen Arbor is trying to draw Dante and Ashton to the surface according to my resources. So, the criers are all informing the people of Father John's crimes and the bounty on his head along with both blood princes."

"He can't do this!" riled Bishop Montgomery, throwing out his arms. "Father John has done so much for this church! How could Marquis turn on you before even confronting you on these accusations? He was your sponsor and responsible for you ascending to your title!"

"Because he's already tried to kill me more than once." John's words made us all shuffle uncomfortably. "He conspired with Falco to deliver priests to Glensdale to satisfy his perversion for eating them and then, there's the other matter, isn't there?"

Valiente turned to Bishop Montgomery, his tone deep and stern. "Indeed. Forgive me for questioning you, Bishop, but aren't you the one in charge of guarding the Iron of the Saints?"

Bishop Montgomery shot us a baffled expression. "I am too low of rank. That honor goes to the Headmaster of the Church, Hamilton. Why?"

John began to shuffle off his coat, scowling. "Would you recognize its mark if you saw it on the flesh?"

"Of course, I would." The old monk began to tremble, fear rising in his whole being. "Now that I think on it, no one has spoken or seen Hamilton besides Marquis..."

"Exactly. Neither Sonja or I nor the Guild have been able to reach him for months," Valiente added, glancing back to the entrance to make sure no prying eyes peeked over the threshold. "Do this in the shelves, John. If it becomes public knowledge, it may work in his favor."

"Yes, please do." I grabbed his coat and shoved John between the shelves, up against the table. "Hurry, chainmail and shirt too."

"What is the meaning of this?" Bishop Montgomery followed, leaning on a shelf as his balance wavered under the weight of his distress. "Why do you need me to check now?"

"I didn't realize it until Princess Sonja saw it." John gave a broken-hearted expression. "Didn't think to question Bishop Marquis or ask you for more detailed information on the iron cross used in the Rite of Priesthood that I would bear."

"Child, why would you need to question your bishop?" He gaped.

John pulled the shirt off and spun, leaning against the table. The horror filling Montgomery's face only made my own guilt rise in not realizing Marquis would be so bold to go so far. He stumbled forward, muttering prayers under his breath. Bony fingers traced the scar, the branding a magnificent pearly white and raised lines cut through the tanned skin of his back. It was both breathtakingly gorgeous and harrowing. After taking it all in, Montgomery gripped John's shoulders and rested his head at the cross-section of the flourished symbol.

"I am so sorry, Father John," he uttered at last. "This mark was never intended to be worn by the living."

"So I've been told." John inhaled deeply, holding in the rage written in his eyes.

"The fact it does not stray shows the amount of resolve you have for the path you've chosen, child." Tears were falling down the cracks of the old man's cheeks. "Pack your things. You cannot be found, or surely Marquis will use this against you. I will dare to add fuel to this fire with these next words and pray to the Fates that they bless you on the path you have been given in life." Sniffling, he stepped back so John could turn and face him. "A saint does not have to follow the path of a priest nor adhere to the vows. You are only ordained as a priest with the proper mark upon your back. May this give you the freedom to protect yourself when the Church has at last failed to protect their own. Marquis has broken his vows with these acts, and I will do what I can to turn the tide and make them question his rash moves to take action to kill another priest and place a bounty on his fellow clergymen."

Blinking, some glimmer of hope hit me from his words. "In short, John didn't break his vows because *Marquis didn't make him a priest.*"

"If you don't mind, I will relay that information." Valiente seemed to feel the weight lifted from me and gave a slight smirk and huff. "But I'll buy you time. You think you can slip out of the cathedral through the catacombs?"

"I don't know if I could navigate the catacombs. John, do you think we can slip through the church instead?" Turning, I saw he was pulling his chainmail vest and clothes back on.

"Yes, I think we may be able to slip past not long after Valiente takes Montgomery. They can serve as a distraction." Slipping on his coat, he turned to the table. "But what of the books? With Bishop Montgomery gone, no one will be here to guard the library, and I can't help but feel this is intentional."

"By the Fates," gasped Montgomery. "You are right. Last time this happened, Prince Ashton, you were…"

"Burn them," I answered, looking through the stacks. "We'll take the important ones, but the rest … burn them."

"Dante, you—!" John covered his mouth, my name slipping from his lips.

Silence fell over everyone, and I scowled. "John…" Unwilling to meet the old monk's gaze, I paid no heed to my name. "I'm serious. Grab the ones on soul weapons, but the rest are about a past that holds no weight on the present or future. We've read them all at least twice or more between the two of us. They can't help us anymore, but they may provide fuel for Fallen Arbor." Grabbing a few of my father's journals, I tossed them into the brazier. "Most of these are my own father's mutterings and would only support the evidence that you or even Montgomery conspired with the House. I think this might be his aim. Fallen Arbor must know what they abandoned in here, and they intend to utilize it."

"Grab your things—" Valiente's words were cut short as Bishop Montgomery gripped my arm, eyes wide with wonder.

"You look so much like him," he whispered, but I still couldn't bear to look at the broken expression wrecking his face. "But you took pity on me, didn't you, Prince Dante?"

Swallowing, I spoke with sincerity, "I did. You've carried your guilt for too long. Thank you for your help, Bishop. You've been kind to me these few months despite it all."

He let go and stood a little taller. "Thank you, Prince Dante. You never shied away from conversation and lent a hand without ever being asked. It's hard to imagine you are royalty with such a drive for demanding work."

I met his face, the resolve in his expression making my chest ache. "You and my brother sacrificed much. It's a faith in oneself, and may the Fates bless you."

"I don't need their blessings. My failure was your brother, but now I have a chance to do right by you," he offered, drawing his hand from shoulder to shoulder and bowing as his hand opened in the center, palm up in a Hail of the Fates.

Snorting, I turned away and shoved two of Ashton's journals into my coat. "Let's hope we live to see it through." John grabbed one of Saint Raphael's journals, aiming to toss it in the brazier, but I caught his wrist. "Keep those. It may prove helpful. That and the other one from the noble who was blood related. Call it an instinctual notion. Seeing that we have complicated things involving the Saint's Mark, this may provide a link to you like we spoke on before."

"I don't like this plan of yours. Besides, that's a lot of books to add to the weight of gear," John grumbled, dividing the stack. "These are the three that have useful information. The other ten or so here are just accountings and recollections of affairs on the property that no longer stands and align only with your father's own ramblings."

"Fine, the three stay, the rest to the fire, which then leaves..." I grabbed up the three and shoved them in my satchel, "how many in the Old Tongue?"

"All seven. I still don't understand them at all and can't tell you which are useful." He shoved them to the side and tossed more of the Saint's journals into the flames, a dark smoke rising from the brazier sending flakes of ash fluttering into the air. "And who will carry those? They may be small journals but..."

"I'll carry it all if I have to." I scooped the remaining books into my arms and tossed them into the brazier. "Now, pack your things. Grab some food. We may have to hide out before moving too far out of the city."

"Yes, please hurry or the Marquis' men will be taking you instead of the Royal Guard," insisted Valiente, following John and Montgomery. "I'll stand post at the library entrance."

I turned my attention to moving the library back in order in a weak attempt to hide our presence. There wasn't much I could do about the disturbed dust, so I aimed to make it look as if a failed attempt to keep up with it all. Grabbing a stack of books on modern fauna and flora of Grandmere, I marched to the hidden room and tossed them into the sarcophagus. Assuming the Fallen Arbor or Marquis' henchmen wouldn't bother to question the contents, I pulled the lid tight and paused. Palms flat on the cold marble slab, I glared bitterly at the Saint's name and the black bloodstains that made the letters louder. Ashton's blood seemed thicker in the air with the weight of events unfolding upstairs. A shudder shook me to think he may very well have died there on that white marble coffin of his lover.

Is this the fate waiting for me in the end? No, John and I will not follow in their footsteps. We walk our own path. The past needs to stay in the past. It's our choice to forge a future of our choosing just like Ashton tried to do later in his life. I can't say we'll do much better or not fail as he did, but it's worth fighting for, isn't it, Old Farmer?

"Living is fighting for not only your survival, boy, but the survival of the things you love most in this wretched world. Show me how much fight you're willing to give it. Show me how much blood you will shed to carve your way to live as you see fit."

Every nerve tightened as I recalled the Lord Knight's words. He had beaten me without mercy but brought me to my feet with those very words and proved that I could always find the will to rise to my feet, no matter how battered my body might be. *Did you see that battle that day on Salvation Road? Hope you cackled and puffed on your pipe with pride wherever you may be beyond the land of the living.*

Spinning on my heel, I marched for the stairs, but a harsh gust stopped me, blowing through the room. The candles blew out, and a chill spiraled up my spine. Peering through the darkness, I saw nothing, but deep down, it seemed as if some spirit agreed with my resolve, perhaps the old man, the Saint, or even Ashton himself sending a sign from the great beyond. *This magic has served its purpose, I suppose.* Shaking it off, I marched upstairs where Valiente argued with another person at the threshold.

CHAPTER 31

Hallowed Grounds

"You tell that Marquis Dog the Royal Guard already has the bishop in custody! The old man deserves a moment to gather his things," roared Valiente, his voice bouncing off the ossuary walls. "Does Marquis show no respect for his fellow priest?"

"Sir, we'll do what we can to hold them back, but they're threatening to take action and draw swords against us," stuttered the younger knight. "They seem to not care for the fact no blood is to spill on hallowed grounds such as these."

"Damn it all." Valiente turned to me, hands on hips. "You might have to fight your way out of here. I'm sorry. Marquis has the King's blessing, and Sonja is gaining favor with the council to overthrow him as we speak. Until she can make that happen, we have all this shit to deal with."

"We appreciate the support." Shuffling closer to where he stood just out of view of the hallway, we both stared at the doorway where John and Montgomery had disappeared. "Glad to hear you both are alive."

"Barely," he grunted before whispering, "About that kiss—you know it wasn't meant to be..."

I held up my hand, silencing him. "Not a word," I warned. "Any news of Fallen Arbor?"

"Well, we discovered Marquis has aided in corrupting the king and church," he offered. "Never did I think I would live to see the day I needed to rely on the Guild and the House for aid. Sonja has pitched the treaty and the resources your father and Ruth have sent in good faith have helped until this mess."

"So, Marquis is trying to use the House as a means to cover up his involvement with Falco?" Adjusting the satchel, I groaned at the added weight from the books. "Figures."

"I don't see what evidence he has though. And then the matter of John—"

"Argh!" The man standing in the threshold fell down the stairs, sprawling across the floor with his throat gushing and sliced open.

"Shit!" Valiente pulled his blade and laid a back against the wall to obscure anyone coming into the library from seeing him. "Check on John. Something's not right."

Pulling a dagger from my coat, I rushed across the span. An arrow whizzed past me, confirming suspicions they were lying in wait for us. Sliding to a stop, I saw John squared off with a henchman farther down the hall. The attire matched that of the masked men back from the stables in Tavern Way, and my heart skipped a beat. John roared, Montgomery quivering in the corner behind him clutching his bag. The masked man was agile, but not fast enough for John's flurry of strikes.

A flash of silver and blue set me at ease. John had managed to get to his rapier in time and lashed out. Blood blossomed in the air, reassuring me that John's strikes were doing damage. The man stumbled back, and I launched forward. Before he knew what had happened, my dagger slid across his throat and dropped him at my feet. John spat on him before turning back to Montgomery, offering a hand. The old man shook his head, grabbing it, and they went running forward. I spun and followed behind them. They halted at the archway, faces paling at the scene I could not see yet as I closed the gap.

It's a full-on attack! Valiente!

Pow! Black powder burnt at my nostrils. John shouted out and fell to his knees as he gripped his side. Rage filled me. Turning, I saw a woman was reloading her flintlock. A wicked grin crossed her face as she glared at me. As I marched toward her, everything in my being boiled with vengeful desire.

"Don't ya want to check on'im?" she roused.

I gritted my fangs, heart pounding fast and hard in my ears. "Flintlock Betty. The Cardinal is looking for you." I pointed a blade at her, and she paled. "I think I'll deliver you personally to that monster."

"The hell you are. Should have come at me faster, boy-o!" The muzzle rose with flame and smoke exploding into a plume.

Pow! The ball was so clear in my sight that I leaned my head, the bullet clipping my left ear. Eyes wide, Betty slung the rifle across her back and pulled out her dagger. I rushed her, slamming her against the wall as our blades sparked from the connection. She squealed, pulling another blade from her belt, forcing me to leap back to dodge. I came swinging as her, and she ducked under it and into the kitchen. Grabbing a bowl of bread, she threw it at me, retreating posthaste. I let it bounce off my chest, seething with each step.

"Landon sends his regards." She lit something and tossed it, pungent smoke filling the room.

Shit, I know this smell. It's that damn herb again, but will it really bother me anymore? Inhaling deeply, I dared to take the chance. A hint of gunpowder and sweat called my attention, and I closed the gap. Swinging in a wild attempt to land a strike, I manage to draw blood. She yelped, and the scrape of stone against stone encouraged me to chase the scent of blood. The smoke opened for a moment. Blood ran down her face where my blade barely scraped across a brow, skimming across the bridge of her nose, slicing her cheek. She kicked something, and the stone door swung into me, shoving me to the floor before sealing and locking.

Scrambling to my feet, I slammed my shoulder and weight into it, but nothing budged. Coughing, I could tell the smoke was fading but still starting to take its toll on my strength. I shoved the tables and anything heavy against the hidden passage before running back into the hallway. Relief washed over me to see John back on his feet, but the smell of his blood in the air sent goosebumps over me.

"Let me see," I demanded, and he pushed me off.

"Help Valiente and his men," he commanded. "Did you find where they came in at?"

"Y-yes."

Valiente ran another henchman through, but he and a Guild assassin were surrounded as they poured in.

"I blocked it. Stay here and protect the bishop." I dropped the satchel and claymore at their feet. "Wait for me."

Pulling the other dagger, I ran fast and hard. The henchman closest turned in alarm, catching me in his peripheral. He swung instead of blocking, and I grunted in reply. Pushing off the strike with one blade, my other dove in and out of his chest, piercing his heart. This earned a moment of distraction in the man next to him, and the assassin took the opening. Hopping over him, I blocked the strike intended for the assassin. The henchman yelped, unaware of where I came from, my swing slicing his throat. Kicking him into the remaining two gave Valiente a chance to strike.

An arrow stung my shoulder. Grabbing the tomahawk at my side, I reacted with precision, and the blade lodged between the archer's eyes. He buckled and fell forward before joining the poor knight they had killed earlier. Pulling the arrow out, I hissed with the pain. A chill snaked up my spine, the excitement and satisfaction of exerting so much energy. *Or is it the satisfaction of delivering a killing blow?* Walking off the thought, I retrieved my tomahawk and glared up the long stairwell for any more intruders.

"Any more?" I asked, glancing back to Valiente and the Assassin.

"Not yet." I recognized the voice as the assassin who had given me the keys months ago. "Master sent me here to watch over this one." Bourbon threw a thumb at Valiente, then pointed at me. "And tell you the plan still stands. Whatever that cryptic shit means."

"Thank you, I think." Valiente leaned on his knees. "I wasn't expecting for a fight on hallowed grounds."

"They came through a secret passage and jumped John." I turned, marching to where John leaned on the wall, squinting in pain. "Can you lead us out of the catacombs, Bourbon?"

"No can do, big guy." He was picking the pockets of the henchmen, taking items and money as he went. "Orders are to watch Valiente. 23, 43, 77. Take all left to leave. Take all right to rosary."

"What?" I turned, confused by his riddle.

"The turns." He paused to read a note found on one of the dead men. "Oh, this is a fun note. Ah, back to directions. So, remember 23, 43, and 77. Turn left at 2, turn left at 3, as in opening or door-ways. Doesn't matter. You still got those keys, yes?"

"I see, and yes, what about them?" I watched as he finished cleaning out the contents on the last body.

"77 ends in a locked path. Only keys can pass. Be sure to close the gates to cover your escape," he instructed, standing to check the hall. "Hurry. They won't take long to send more down. I can hear sword strikes still."

"R-right." I twisted away, gathering my things at John's feet. "How bad is it?"

"Stings." John pulled himself off the wall and sheathed his rapier. "I'll live. Bleeding has stopped. Burned like fire, though my back felt worse by comparison."

"Indeed," I snorted. "She hit me three times on Salvation Road with those."

"No wonder you were..." He redirected his words, "Bishop, we leave you in the care of Valiente and our assassin friend."

"But you're hurt, both of you." His eyes bounced between the red painting my right arm and the blood soaking John's jacket and partially down his pants.

"Par the course." John managed a sheepish grin.

He marched away without a word, and I followed obediently. As we slipped through the heavy oak door, we heard shouts echoing down into the library. We slipped back into the dusty corridors of the catacombs. John reached for a torch, and I grabbed his arm. As I shook my head, he abandoned it, and I took the lead.

At least they didn't sneak into the library via the catacombs. I wonder if that's because the Guild keeps them from using them. I repeated the numbers in my mind over and over again: *23, 43, 77.* It felt as if we were spiraling in circles and just twisting deeper into the underbelly of Captiva City.

John gripped the back of my shirt and pulled on the claymore's halter. "I need a moment."

Glaring down the catacombs, I heard and smelled no signs of any other living thing other than the rats and insects scurrying all around. John leaned on the wall, panting in the wake of his pain. I could smell the blood coming from him, and for once, it didn't incite a need to feed. *Is it because I've been satisfied for some time?* He held the spot and coughed, grunting in annoyance.

"Let me see," I offered.

"How? I can barely make you out and you're in front of me," he fussed.

Pulling his hand away, I squatted and pulled up on the shirt and jacket. The bullet had ripped through the chainmail with ease but at least managed to enter and exit his body. The entry had come through his back and out the front of his torso. Reaching in my satchel, I was glad I managed to pack in preparation for us leaving one day. *Granted, I never imagined we'd be swinging our blades inside the damn church.* I wrapped it tight to help with the bleeding. It wanted to stop, but moving so quickly to escape had continuously goaded it to bleed. Tying it off, I pulled his clothes back in place.

"Shocked you didn't lick my wound clean," he teased.

Leaning into his ear, I countered, "I still can if that pleases you." His heart fluttered in my ears, and I snorted, "My arm aches, but it's already healing. It'll do us no good for you to lose any more than you have."

With a deep breath, he pushed me back and steeled himself again. "Let's get to safety."

"Agreed." I reviewed the numbers and picked up where we left off.

Three openings down, I took a left, and after a few paces was met with familiar smells: *saddlewood, meadow sweet, and rosemary.* "There's something I want to check on before we leave here."

"If it means I can sit for a spell, I won't argue," grunted John.

Two corridors farther, I took a right instead of the left, following the smell. "Sit here to mark the corridor. I shouldn't be long."

John slid down to the ground, eyes closed and his breathing heavy with pain. "Sitting is nice."

Inhaling deeply, I followed the scent, weaving in and out of turns until, at last, I stood before the item I sought. The grand prayer totem stood before me with its fanged skull. My heart raced, and I swallowed, curious if all those months ago had been some fever dream. *No, otherwise I wouldn't have found it so easily. Please let it still be here in the wall.* Squatting, I peered through the eye socket and saw the bejeweled pommel still in place.

"Anyone home?" I flicked the skull on the forehead.

"You're a rude fuck," it scoffed. *"So, what has brought you back to my resting place once again, little Traibon?"*

"I don't know who or what you are, but there's a weapon in the wall here," I proclaimed.

"You already have a weapon, do you not?"

"I do. A claymore that's chipped and cracking after some chains slammed into it. Preveran steel can only take so many hits." My mind raced. *How can I convince this spirit to give up his weapon? If we get ambushed at the exit, I can't depend on the claymore I have not to break.* There was silence, long and agonizing as I played the weeks through my head. *We thought we would see someone that could take it to a smith or—*

"*A claymore?*" It sounded intrigued.

"We're being chased by Fallen Arbor and—"

"*Pull the blade,*" demanded the voice, a chill rising in the air all around. "*I was made for cutting down Fallen Arbor, my sworn enemy, and if you wish it, I will aid you down that path to destroy them.*"

I reached for the skull but retreated, every muscle tense and heart racing. "And what does that mean? What if I decide later to not continue to hunt them down?"

"*Then you lay me to rest back in these catacombs. It's not like I can pass on after what they did to me.*" Something blue glowed, the jewel on the pommel pulsing to life with an eerie light. "*Now pull me out! For you, I will spill blood to protect what you love! Is that not someone special to you who bleeds in these halls as you argue with the dead, little Traibon?*"

The words spurred me into action. Yanking the skull out of the way, I gripped the hilt. I pulled, muscles stinging as it slid slightly in my hand as it locked against the stones and bones catching the rain guard. As I grunted, my wound ached and seeped.

"*Fucking pull, you weakling!*" My skull rattled with the voice now, the handle on fire with the rage it projected, and I gripped it tighter.

Power pulsed through me, and I placed a foot on the wall. Another hard yank and the hilt knocked once more until the wall broke. A claymore came loose, and I stumbled back into the hall where I leaned on the wall wide-eyed at the iridescent blue tone of the blade. I could see myself reflected in the blade, and something hauntingly familiar made me shudder. Ancient runes much like The Fanged Lady came to life and a seal of the House of Traibon that matched those of the white sarcophagus made my stomach flutter.

Was this a blade of someone from the start of the Civil War?

I bounced it from one hand to the next, the balanced lightweight blade seeming unnatural. Again, I pulled the wide side of the blade close, the glow pulsing as if staring back with the same level of curiosity. *Is this a soul weapon?* Another pulse and the runes flashed again in reply. *Indeed, it must be, but what kind? Blessed or could it be...*

"*By the fates, you could pass as me, little Brother.*" A snort escaped it, and a shudder shook me to realize the voice came from the blade itself. "*Now, let us be on our way. Where is this person bleeding with the scent of Raphael? I am curious to see them.*"

Little brother? This means ... I'm actually holding... I slid to the ground, shaking as I took in the blade and its voice before at last muttering my suspicion, "A-Ashton."

"*I used to be Ashton,*" it replied with a sour tone. "*Now I'll be the blade to snuff out Fallen Arbor. On your feet. It seems you need to toughen up if this brings you to your knees.*"

"You're a soul weapon," I declared, standing slowly.

"*What of it, little Brother?*"

So, what the monk had seen so long ago was a complete and willing transition. Had it smelled Frank coming down the hall? And why did Frank not give chase to Fallen Arbor with Ashton in hand?

Chapter 32

Keys to the Kingdom

P ale and shaken, I followed John's scent back to the cross-section. He'd fallen asleep, and I gently leaned the soul weapon on the opposite wall. Sliding down, I sat next to him, listening to his arduous breathing and taking in the sweet aroma of his blood. Glaring at the claymore, goosebumps flowed over me, and I folded my brow. I hadn't said much else the moment it all hit me. *My brother, Ashton Traibon, is a soul weapon. Not any but a sentient one at that.*

"Staring is rude."

The heat in my cheeks sent my head swiveling to John. I leaned over, peeking at the bandage. My scowl deepened to see it already red-soaked. Covering my face, I leaned back against the wall, muttering curses under my breath. I couldn't get a single thought to finish its course before another took hold. Emotions conflicted with one another at every second. All I knew was my lover was hurt, my brother a soul weapon, and Fallen Arbor would surely be waiting for me outside of Captiva City.

"What's the matter with you?" Ashton's voice made me flinch, and I dropped my hands to glare at the sword across from me.

263

"Trying to make a decision but I can't seem to still my mind long enough to figure out which is more important to me," I confessed.

"Clearly his injury has unnerved you, has it not?" Looking to John, I hated that he looked so pale, and a cold sweat painted his forehead. *"Just carry him out."*

"Then how am I to carry you?" I drawled.

"I'm a fucking sword, little Traibon," Ashton growled. *"You clearly have a sheath worthy of carrying two claymores on your back, fool."*

I couldn't hide the expression on my face and murmured, "But that feels ... wrong."

"By the Fates, get to your damn feet, shove my ass in the fucking sheath, pick him up, and get him some place where he can heal!" Ashton's voice rattled in my skull, sending my heart racing and eyes bouncing.

Jerking to my feet, I hissed, "Fine. We'll do this your way!"

"Do what ... my way?" John stirred from his sleep, gripping my leg. "I'm sorry. I lost too much..."

"I'm going to carry you out," I announced.

John coughed, grunting as he pushed back to his feet. "You can't be serious. What if they catch up?"

"Then I hope he's prepared for you to drop him on the ground," mused Ashton.

"They aren't giving chase through the catacombs." I took a deep breath, steeling myself before revealing what I'd concluded. "Which means they are waiting at the exit for us."

John's eyes were drawn to the glowing claymore. "Where was that?"

"Hidden in the walls. I noticed something on our way in, and well, you're looking at a hidden soul weapon with—"

"You are not to speak of who I am unless I wish it so." A chill snaked up my spine at the threatening tone that vibrated through every fiber of my body.

"—unknown powers," I redirected.

"Wow, it's beautiful. Nothing like *L'Dame d'Croc.*" He reached for it, and I gripped his wrist. "What's wrong?"

"He can touch me..." I shot a disapproving glare at the blade and shook my head, lipping *no.*

"There's strange magic, and I can't say what this one is capable of doing." Cheeks red, a sense of jealousy rose in me, and I grabbed up *Ashton.*

"I won't bite. Just wanna get a sense of who he is... Come on, let him touch me."

"I don't think it can do much to hold it," rebuttaled John. "Nothing ever happened with the Fanged—"

"We can discuss it later." My words were curt.

Pushing past, I continued down our path to the exit. Both Ashton and John fussed at me, their words mangling and muting in and out of my head. Ashton at last gave up when I slid him beside the other claymore. They both went silent as I pulled the buckling tighter on the halter and reached to scoop up John. He shoved me away, twisting to head down the corridor toward a gate. Moving slowly, John grunted on occasion and held the bandages tight against the wound.

"You can carry me when I pass out," he announced, annoyed with me.

Sighing, I slid past him, digging the keyring from my satchel. I beat him to the gate, starting to try the keys one by one. *I wonder if the same key that works here will work for the next gate.* There had to be a good thirty or forty keys of all shapes and sizes. I could hear John shuffling closer. One after another, they failed, either too small, too large, or not turning at all. Joh reached me, a rattle in his breathing, and I dropped the ring at my feet.

"Son of a..." I muttered as I scooped them up, staring at the fray. "Shit, which one was I on?"

"You know you can ask me if I know, right?" Ashton snickered in the back of my head. *"It's a bronze key."*

"There's still a good twelve of those on here," I mumbled.

"Well, it should be long because of the type of lock. And thicker, since it's an outdoor gate," he offered.

Raising my eyebrows and cocking my head, I picked out two that met that description. "Huh, so one of these should do it?"

John came closer, leaning to view the keys. "What makes you think it's one of those two?"

"Uh, intuition?" I offered, trying the first with no luck. "Then that leaves this one..." The second slid a little deeper into the lock, and with ease, it twisted, and the gate squeaked open. "Wow, I'm impressed."

"I used to be in charge of the keys," drawled Ashton. *"Hated it, so I gave them to Father, and I see he gave them to you."*

Locking the gate behind us, I laughed. "Good thing the Assassin's Guild gave these to me."

"What the hell was he thinking!" Ashton's voice rattled through me again, and I stumbled and caught the wall. *"Shit!"* His voice seemed panicked as I held my face.

"Dante, what's the matter?" John leaned on the wall.

"I didn't realize I had..." Ashton spoke more softly, a whisper now, *"...that I could throw your balance and impact you physically. I'll be more careful."*

"It's the sword," I confessed. "It's why I didn't let you touch it. I'm not ... used to it."

"Leave the cursed thing. It's not worth your life." Some color rose in John's pale face.

He's angry I would take yet another risk. "I will not abandon it." My tone made John visibly jolt. "It's more important than you realize."

"So be it." John turned, shuffling through the open gate and closing it behind him. "But I will toss it to the bottom of Sullen Lake if it does you harm."

"I see why you're in love with him." Ashton was back to his playful tone. *"Makes me jealous. Wish Raphael had that much sass... Wait a minute ... is he a fucking priest?"*

"Slow down, Saint John," I mused, smiling at myself and the entirety of the situation.

"Don't you dare start that. It's as bad as you calling me Father John." He couldn't hide the smirk on his face as we made a turn.

266

"Ha! We Traibons always want what we shouldn't have" Ashton seemed pleased, almost content with being able to reconnect with the living before falling horribly quiet.

We halted; another gate glowed with daylight just in reach. Beyond it, a green meadow speckled with white, yellow, and pink flowers fluttered in the sea breeze. *We made it, but...* John leaned against the wall and watched as I marched toward the gate. Slipping the keyring out, I shot a glance at John before turning the key. The gate creaked open. *Huh, got it on the first try.* Slipping through it, I closed it and held the keys to him. Huffing, John took them and grimaced as he locked the gate. We stood glaring at one another with the wrought iron between us. I leaned forward, and he mirrored the motion as our forehead managed to touch in the gaps. Silence fell, our heartbeats throbbing ever faster in the anxiety chomping at the bit of what would come next.

Why is it so hard for us to protect one another? "Stay here." I turned away, every nerve strung tighter with each step and inch gained between us.

"I can't get far without you," John's voice sounded defeated. "I'm sorry I'm not strong enough to help you this time."

Snorting, I exhaled in thought before replying, "We both know I will always be your shield, and I now have the means to be a proper sword, too." Pulling Ashton from the sheath, the blade buzzed with power. "I know they must be there just out of view. Every part of me screams with it. I can smell them, hear them even."

"Don't you dare be reckless." I could feel his eyes shift to the blade. "Are you sure you want to use that here and now?"

"Oh, I'm very sure of that."

He half-laughed and added, "Does it have a proper name yet?"

"Don't you dare use my name, brother," warned Ashton.

Pausing, I smirked and looked to John. "I'll call it *La Serra de l'Aigle ... The Eagle's Talon.*"

"I like it." John huffed, his eyes sad as they shifted to the meadow behind me. "May you strike them down swiftly."

"Remind me to tell you about this eagle meeting a cardinal and almost losing the battle," Ashton scoffed, *"but something tells me you've met him already."*

I took a deep breath. Beyond the smells of the catacombs and ocean breeze, I could smell the sweat of men and women who'd sat in the sun in anticipation of my arrival. Closing my eyes, I listened to the breaths, the heartbeats, and finding only one of them calm. *These are seasoned fighters. They don't fear me … yet.* I flexed my muscles, the shoulder healed from before, though still marked. Looking down to Ashton, goosebumps rolled over me, all the events flooding forward like priming the pump to draw from a well of fighting prowess.

"There's something I need to tell you," I whispered down to Ashton, gripping his hilt tight as my heart fluttered. *It's only right to tell him what it is that I've been doing under his name.*

"Don't tell me you've never been in a fight." The blade shuddered.

"No. It's just—I've been pretending to be *you* these last few months," I confessed.

Laughter rolled from him, and the blade glowed brighter. *"And what makes you think you can fill my shoes, little brother?"*

Snorting, I cooed in reply, "Let me show you what I've learned about being you, and you are more than welcome to correct me if I don't do your namesake justice."

Stepping out from the tunnel, I was blinded by the sunlight for a moment. My eyes adjusted, and the four Fallen Arbor soldiers stood before me like black strokes harsh against a canvas of pastels. Again, they all wore the same masks and tripoint hats I'd seen the henchmen in Tavern Way sport. I took the standstill as a moment for us to gauge one another. One had no weapons, but the familiar smell of sulfur made me wonder if she would prove the more dangerous opponent. My eyes lingered on her until she stepped back behind her colleagues. The pair of rogues in the middle had dual daggers, and the one on the far right carried a large shield and broadsword.

So, they have range, offense, and defense—not a bad grouping. They planned to face me, but how much do they know about my fight with the Berserk Brigade?

CHAPTER 33

The Rise of Ashton

Dropping down into a starting stance, my body seemed excited to return to this pose, the flutter in my heart adding to the building thrill. Ashton weighed nothing compared to the claymore I had trained on and used against the Berserk Brigade. I shuffled my stance, nervous of the weight difference and the heat emanating into my palms as if the claymore exhaled with my own breath.

"Interesting. Seems you've been taught a thing or two about how I fight. More importantly, you've done well to convince Fallen Arbor you might be the real deal seeing they met you at the exit with so many." Ashton's hilt hummed as if the power soaked into me. *"Fix your footing."* My foot shifted as if some unseen foot had kicked it. *"Lower the stance."* Again, the invisible force pushed on my shoulders, and I let it correct me. *"There. You're ready now."*

A familiar burning in my leg muscles made me grunt, and a force pushed my elbow higher before I whispered, "Stop. Let me fight."

The male rogue in the center charged forward, the mask and hat hiding his expression well. I raised my chin, wide eyed as he came inching closer. Every muscle tensed, waiting to see which way he would come at me. Despite their calm exteriors, their hearts of my enemies sounded like a stampede of horses, adding to the rush washing over me. *I'm the only calm one now.* He came close, and when I still did not flinch or give hint of movement, he startled and leapt back. *Nothing in his body said he aimed to attack just yet. He must be a master of counterstrikes.* Only a few steps off, he left the ground broken. I hadn't moved to block or attack, and when we connected gazes, he lost his nerve.

A roar escaped the shield-carrying soldier, and he came in with a strike, shield held tight into himself to block his torso. I spun, swinging Ashton easily with uncanny speed, arms stretching, muscles alive. I hit the shield with as much inertia as possible as I came back to meet my opponent. The blow clunked loud, the shield denting, the sword dropped in the seconds before he was slung across the field. He bounced a few times, and his companion closest to me sidled back.

The exhale left me, and on the inhale, I reset my starting stance. Again, the initial attacker sidled back to whisper to his counterpart as she swallowed, heart thudding in my ears as her cold sweat competed with the ocean's salt in the wind. The sulfur-scented woman rushed the soldier, her hood falling back to expose a sigil etched into the back of her shaven head before she yanked it back up. Without even dropping my eyes to the soldier, I could hear how he gasped for air.

If you can't cut them down, boy, the Old Farmer's voice filled me and a sense of pride followed as I remembered his words like a whisper, *then be sure to knock the wind from them.*

The crunch of grass breaking, and the scent of freshly broken dirt made my body tighten. I launched for the rogues, both a few steps into their attack. My own speed was alarming as I closed in on them, and the man faltered, sliding to a stop. The woman did not, despite the fluttering of her heart. She stepped into my path, thrusting her daggers together to stab me in the stomach. I twisted using my momentum and planted my heel hard into the soft ground. Ashton did not slow as he ripped through her. I turned and came from behind, her eyes wide as her body cleaved apart, dead before it all finished falling to the ground at my feet. Blood rained down on me, hot and thick.

Surreal, lost to the adrenaline, I heard my father's words, and they struck a new chord: *You are a Prince, and you may take anything you desire, and not one soul can stop you.*

Raising my chin and gaze, I glared at the other rogue and reset my stance once more. Horror filled his face and he turned, running from battle. Shifting, the knight was stumbling to his feet, and the weaponless woman reeking of sulfur stood between us. She chanted in the old tongue, eyes on me. Scarred fingers and arms flashed in the sunlight and the smell grew stronger.

"Is ... is this magic?" I muttered to Ashton as I stood my ground.

"There's nothing magical about it," Ashton growled as the heat of his rage seemed to seep into my own being. *"She's a failed soul weapon. It happens with humans, where the blessing or curse awakens, but they come out scarred. Humans can't be soul weapons. On the Old Continent they call them the Fractured Ones."*

Sparks began to flicker in her open palms until torch-sized balls came to life, and the smell of burning flesh engulfed my senses.

"Not many humans live or remain intact after awakening their powers." Ashton's words were a mixture of pity and disgust. *"And those who do make it out? Their magic eats at them every time they use it... Beware, her flames are hotter than a raging fire in a blacksmith's forge."*

The Fractured One came marching toward me. My eyes landed on the balls of fire in her hands, the flesh bubbling and boiling as it stung at my nose. My eyes watered, and my heart raced at the very concept of all the scars. Her hood slipped off once more, the sun shedding light on her shaven head and the countless scars splotched across her face and skull. One ear was missing completely, melted to a point of nonexistence. I cringed, gritting my fangs.

"What do I do with her?" I growled through clenched jaws.

"You put her out of her misery, Dante," replied Ashton firmly.

Some enemies will beg you to take their life. The summer storm sky flashed and boomed, rattling the jars that night as the Old Farmer started gnawing on his pipe. *Then, you'll find an enemy with that look in their eyes, the look that begs to end it for them since they no longer have the strength to resist or die on their own. If you ever see one, just do the humane thing, Prince. Make it so they can rest six feet down after you cross paths.*

Inhaling the bitter stench, I launched forward. A screech escaped her, pain and rage engulfing one another as tears fell down her face. She tossed a flame at me, and I sidestepped and flinched as the heat stung at my flesh, evaporating the sweat and baking the blood on my skin. Her heart skipped a beat, and she stumbled, dropping the other flame. The ball exploded, catching her and the knight on fire, and they screamed, a harrowing howl of pain as their flesh melted.

"Dante, now!" Ashton's shout worked as an invisible shove.

Risking the flames, I swung fast and true, racing through the fiery chaos. The screams had ceased as I slowed and turned. Heads fell to the fire as their bodies slumped and folded. I watched as the meadow of pastel flowers became scarred with a second ring of black ash and a smattering of red. The flames died off, the heart beats no more except one racing in the short distance.

I will gladly give mercy.

John stood in the shadow of the tunnel exit. Our gazes met, and he dropped the keys and slid to the ground. I resisted the urge to race to him. He paled, shaking and distraught. I stood at the center of what I had done, covered in the blood of my enemies. At last, I looked to Ashton, the blade clean despite the cuts made. Scowling, I hated it. *I wanted to be his sword and shield so badly, but was this really what I intended? Neither of us wanted this to be the path taken.*

"Well done, little brother—"

I slid Ashton into the sheath, muffling his praise.

"Don't praise me," my harsh whisper sent a shiver through him. "Taking a life should never be praised."

I will always show mercy.

Marching to John, I offered a hand down to him. He hesitated, searching my face before grabbing hold. Plucking the keyring from the ground, I shoved it into the satchel. Turning, I squatted on the ground and offered my back to John.

"You can't be serious," scoffed John.

"I am. We don't have time before the rogue comes back with more," I countered. "Now hop on."

Grunting, he wrapped his arms around my neck, and I grabbed his legs before standing up. John hissed, the gunshot wound still seeping, the smell of his blood and the pattering of his heart telling me how much he fought against his reaction. Without any hesitation, I headed south, following the cliffs of the coastline.

If I keep going this way, eventually I should find Terahime.

"I'm sorry, Dante." John's words made me tense as he nuzzled closer into my ear. "You tried so hard to escape this, and I thrusted you into it."

"The line was drawn long before us." My words felt empty even to me despite the attempt to accept the fight had started long before our meeting. "We're just trying to survive."

"No, we're pushing back." His arms tightened around me. "We're in over our heads."

"We've always been in over our heads." I shifted, pulling him back onto me better.

"Don't lose yourself." His words made my heart leap, and I stumbled to a stop. "Promise me, Dante."

I clenched my jaw tight, brow folding. *Is that even fair to ask of me this far into losing myself?*

John began pushing and twisting, forcing me to let him back onto the ground. The gulls screeched in the setting sun, the ocean roaring loud as the wind kicked up. A storm in the distance flashed with strings of lightning too far to hear the rumbles of thunder. Behind me, I felt John's eyes digging into me. I didn't want to face him; I couldn't face him. *I'm such a monster now that I can't even reply to him. How can I promise something I've already lost?*

A hand gripped my wrist, and I found myself being tugged down a seaside path to the rocky beach. John pulled me to a pool of water caught in the sandbars until I knelt in the wet sand, dumbfounded. John stripped off his jacket and tossed the priestly collar to the wind, as if a declaration of renouncing his priesthood. Taking the knife from his waist, he began shredding his jacket into rags and strips of cloth. Before I knew it, he washed the blood from my body, scrubbing it from my face. I sat silent and obedient, watching him with desperation that I couldn't put into words or action. By the time he finished, the tide had started to rise and the moon high above made the breaking waves glow. The storm vanished, and a calm cloudless sky filled with stars had taken over.

Satisfied he had completed his duty, John dropped the rags and cupped my face. "I promise to help you find yourself again."

I inhaled swiftly, the words striking me at my core. *He knows ... that I can't make the promise because ... I'm never going to be able to go back to being simply Dante. No, I'm the Blood Prince, I'm a bloodeater, I'm a monster who devours life... I can't make that promise.*

The heat of his lips pressed firmly against mine. It was hungry and impulsive as he parted his lips to deepen it. I followed, wanting this aching in my chest and soul to stop. Wrapping my arms around him, I let myself fall back into the sand, pulling John with me. His blood was sweet, his warmth welcoming, and his desire needed. A wave rushed up on us, breaking the moment as we scrambled to our feet and backed away. I turned away from him, ashamed and lost.

"Dante, I love you now and always." He spun me at the pathway and kissed me once more. "I didn't want to ever see you so broken."

"It can't be helped." My fingertips pulled strands of his golden hair from his eyes. "I'd happily destroy myself for you."

"Don't say it like that." He dropped his gaze and shoved my hand away. "Let's keep moving. We've rested long enough that I can walk for a while."

I covered my mouth, mumbling to myself, "What am I to do with this?"

"You cherish it." Ashton's voice made me shiver, remembering we weren't fully alone again. *"And you continue to protect it at all costs."*

I chased after John, and we walked in silence, following the coastline and chasing the hints of torchlight and the lighthouse in the distance.

Can I really find myself again after all I've done and bring down Fallen Arbor? And exactly how far will I go to protect him above all else?

CHAPTER 34

Terahime

Much to my relief, there were no gates surrounding the seaside town of Terahime. It was much larger than Taverns Way or even Liefseid in both size and population. A woman dropped her baskets coming out of her door as the sun rose to signal morning. At this point, I had John's arm slung over my shoulders, and he teetered on the verge of passing out from pain and exhaustion. She rushed us to the apothecary, and they cleared a table to inspect his state and wound. I stepped back, helpless and dirty. The old man pulled bottles and began mixing items in two various bowls.

The woman left us, and the old man turned to me, stern in tone, "Lock the door and turn the sign."

I did so and returned posthaste. "What can I do to help?"

"Grind these until it's a mash of sorts." He shoved a bowl and pestle at me. "The crow said you'd be coming yesterday, and one would be injured. He's a mess. Already fighting an infection and you both smell like death."

"We had to go through the catacombs and sewers," I offered, and his face grimaced at the news.

"In that case, I'll have you grab the two jars way up on the shelf. A dash of both in the bowl. He'll need something strong,

277

considering the elements the wound was exposed to." He turned and shoved John, forcing him to sit up, still in a half-daze. "Come on, boy. Shed this shirt."

"N-no." John gripped the buttons stopping the apothecary. "Only he can."

I blinked, marveling, "That's never happened before."

John motioned me closer, leaning heavily on my shoulder to slur, "I can't let anyone see this mark since it's not of a priest."

And with that, he passed out onto me. *Shit!*

"Ah, we can finally—" I gripped the old man's arm and pushed the bowl and pestle into his hands to block his reach for John.

"I've got him. It's a long story, but he wishes no one to see the scars he bears." *The half lie will have to suffice.* "I take instruction well, but I'll need a safe place for us to sleep."

He grinned, turning to the worktable. "I'm Henry, and you can stay in the basement room. I offer sanctuary to all The Guild, and I was told you two would need a safe place. Now, if you push on that shelf, you'll uncover the steps, and I'll bring the supplies to you."

"Thank you." I hoisted John up in my arms and navigated through the shelves.

John shivered, and his body burned with a rising fever despite how pale he had become. I put my shoulder into the shelf, and it scudded and swung open. The steps spiraled once, and below I found a table, chairs, and two beds. Peeling the wet clothes from his body, I rolled him on his side to inspect the wound. I covered my nose, the smell of infection making my stomach twist. Steps creaked upstairs, and I pulled the covers up to hide his branding.

Henry had a bucket filled with supplies and another with steaming water. "Look, you need to scrub him clean, and after that, use the black stuff for in and around the wound. The green one he needs to drink a tablespoon of, and this herb is meant to cover the open wound when you wrap it. Can you do that much for it, boy?"

278

"Why does every old man I run into call me boy?" I muttered, taking the buckets from him.

"You've got a pretty face and haven't learned to stay out of trouble yet." He chuckled, turning back for the stairs. "Rest up. You'll be waiting for your companions for a while. Captiva City is in a complete lockdown. No one in and no one out by cree of the council."

"I imagine so." I soaked the cloth in the hot water. "The royal guard was engaged in a skirmish in the church when we escaped, which I imagine caused—"

Henry turned, confused. "You don't know?"

"Know what?" A chill snaked up my spine.

"King Regius is dead, and Bishop Marquis has gone missing. He's under suspicion for murdering the King, though who knows since both had Guild contracts out for their heads." My expression said volumes, and he sighed, offering, "Look, take care of him, and I'll have the inn pull you a bath next door. Sounds like a lot more chaos went down in Captiva City than we know about. Best to let it settle and sort itself out. Nothing you can do about it anyhow in the state you're in."

Henry hummed to himself as he climbed the stairs and left me there in the lantern's flickering light. I cursed under my breath, the heavy breathing and slow heartbeats of John reminding me I had more important matters to fret over. Pulling the covers back off, I went to work cleaning and scrubbing. John winced and hissed as I went but drifted in and out of his haze. Next was the jar of black salve. It smelled of tar and stung my eyes. The first dab woke John, and he gripped my wrist, locking eyes with me, and I smirked.

"We should really stop taking turns at putting our fingers into one another's wounds like this." I flicked my eyebrows high, and he sighed.

"Make it quick. I'm exhausted." He laid back into position, releasing me. "This stuff is as bad as the last salve you painted me with. In smell and bite."

"Well, it doesn't get any better." John grunted as I dabbed a second portion onto the open wound. "This apothecary has brought you something to drink for the fever."

Reaching into the bucket, I handed him the bottle of liquid syrup, and he raised it to the light. "I don't like the looks of it. Why is it so green?"

"I can only assume because most herbs are green." I pulled him to me and dabbed salve on the other side of his torso. "A tablespoon. That's all you need for now."

John grunted, muscles tightening as the salve met open flesh. "Dammit, that stings like fire." He opened the bottle and gagged. "How can anyone drink something so rancid?"

"It's either you drink or continue to fight the chills," I offered.

John fell silent, glaring at me. I didn't meet his eyes. Instead, I focused on his wound, circling back to add salve in places it was missing or seemed to have absorbed into the wound already. Capping the jar, I reached for the herbs and bandages. John sat up, heart fluttering. I began the tedious task of wrapping his torso, my breath sending goosebumps across his skin at being so close to his body.

John, this isn't the time to feel this way...

John's forehead connected with mine before I could pull away. "I don't think I'll ever get used to the idea you can pick up on how my body feels before I do."

Searching the air, I mustered the best response I could. "I still can't read your thoughts, and that's far more dangerous."

He kissed my forehead and pulled away. "I suppose we both are in the dark about one another's inner workings." He cracked open the jar, and we both jolted back to cover our noses. "This is..."

"...more putrid than the sewers." Our eyes met, stinging. "Drink up?" I offered.

John scowled, staring at the green ooze. "Please tell me I have a chaser for this."

Looking around, I spotted a bottle of whiskey on the table. Opening it, I confirmed indeed the bottle hadn't expired. "Whiskey?"

Closing one eye, John took a gulp and swapped bottles. He chased the syrup with hard long gulps of whiskey before shoving the bottle to me. John's disapproving expression behind the forearm over his mouth only goaded me to take a few long draws of whiskey. The liquor was enough to numb the instincts screaming inside me wanting to take our playful banter to the next level. John flopped back onto the bed, and I pulled the cover up to his shoulder as he turned to face the wall. Pulling away from his side, I left the supply bucket just under the bed and turned the lamp low. Lugging the water bucket now stained red with blood back upstairs, I found Henry waiting patiently for me.

"You don't have to close the store on our behalf. He'll sleep for a solid day at this rate." I lifted the bucket. "What do I do with this?"

"I'll open in a moment," he gruffed, pulling glasses on to scribble something in his book. "Splash it on the cobblestones and take the rags and bucket to the bathhouse next door. Tilda will know what to do with it and you."

"R-right." I started for the door and stopped. "Thank you for your help. Let me know what I owe you."

He waved a hand, not breaking from his scribbling. "You've managed to get this far, Blood Prince. If you aim to end this war and push back the Madness, none of us will get in your way."

I pushed out the door, heart racing. *Dammit, does everyone know who I am? How the hell am I going to travel without leaving a trace at this rate?*

"Will he be okay?" Ashton's voice was soft, nothing but a whisper.

I sloshed the dirty water across the street and looked for the bathhouse signs before whispering, "He'll live. He's too stubborn to die."

"I don't think I've ever seen love like the kind you share with one another." Ashton paused a moment as I pushed through the

Tainted Lady Inn's doorway. *"I've felt that way for someone but never seemed to receive the affection in return without some stipulations and sense of duty interfering."*

I looked around the bustling place. Sailors and merchants gambled and drank. Plenty of scarlet women and men led them to booths with curtains. The ale and liquor mingled with the scent of lust and roasted meat. On the large hearth, some strange creature was turned over the fire by one attendant while another scooped stew from below it where the dripping and meat fell to add to the mixture. It was lively for so early in the day, reminding me of a daylight variant of the lumberjack's gathering in Liefseid. I caught sight of the inn's bathhouse and room signage and started for the counter.

"Oh! You're from the apothecary!" A petite woman seemed to appear out of thin air, hooking her arm in mine and guiding me to the back of the inn. "We'll get you good and scrubbed down, sir!"

"R-right. I can do it myself—"

"Not here! In Terahime, it is tradition to provide bathing services. Just call me Tilda, sir." She led me into a large room with many tubs steaming with fresh water. "Henry paid for a private session. Normally we are packed, but it's early enough we should be left to ourselves."

"Um, I really don't think—" I tried once more.

"Here, here. Let's start to undo these pesky buckles." Her fingers were quicker than my refusal, my belt and manica loose before I could grasp my surroundings. "So heavy!"

Gripping her wrist, I stopped her at the claymore halter's first buckle. "This stays close to me, and you are not to touch him."

"Him?" She tilted her head, arching a brow.

"It," I corrected as my cheeks reddened.

"You're hilarious," giggled Ashton.

I propped Ashton against the tub and ignored his commentary. "I assure you I can do this myself—"

In an instant, Tilda had the buttons of my shirt fileted open with practiced expertise, and she pulled the armor from me. "My, you're a big boy. Don't you worry, I'm the best the inn has to offer."

"Look, I'm not looking for a Scarlet Woman," I blurted.

"Oh, but she's offering," Ashton announced.

Tilda pulled on my pants, pulling the belt free. "Well, they didn't pay me for that, but..." Her eyes drank me in, dropping my pants to the floor before giving me a sheepish grin. "...I might offer that for free."

Flustered, I pulled my shirt off, boots kicked off and was in the tub faster than she could chase me. "Thank you, but I'm fine." I worked fast to unlace my braid, fearing she'd notice the sixteen knots. "I'd like some privacy—"

"Here she comes!" he warned.

Snow-white arms were swift with soapy rags as she reached in over my shoulders and scrubbed the dirt and blood from my chest. Her breasts pressed against the back of my neck, and I became very aware of how thin the fabric was, more so now that it began to grow wet from her sloshing. Her scrubbing ventured farther and farther down until I gripped her arms to stop her descent.

"What's a matter? Never been scrubbed down by a woman before?" Her voice was husky in my ear. "I don't bite... much."

"Don't let her lie. They all bite," warned Ashton.

Closing my eyes, I searched my panicked thoughts before at last confessing, "I'm sorry, but I prefer male companions."

"Never stopped me." She licked at my ear, and I sloshed to the other side of the tub, out of reach. "Ugh, no fun." She tossed the rag in the water and crossed her arms. "Fine, but don't take too long. I have other customers to tend to."

With that she left, and I could breathe again. "First the brothel, now this one."

"I have to admit, you're built like me in more than one-way, little brother. You could have endless pleasure at your disposal with—"

"Hush. I've had enough of your patronizing commentary." I dunked my head underwater, scrubbing my hair free of blood and dirt. Bursting up, I searched the shelf for some soap and whispered, "So who was it that you chained yourself to? You only fed on one person too, right?"

"We can just leave him here and keep going." Ashton changed topics.

"Never." I dipped into the water to retrieve the cloth, coming back up. "I promised the Lord Knight Paul I would be John's sword and shield."

"Paul Thompson?" Ashton seemed intrigued.

"Yes. He taught me to use the claymore. Raphaëlle taught me to be you." Grabbing a bottle of rose oil, I dumped it into the water. "So, that leads me to what I've been wondering... She is indeed your daughter, correct?"

"She is." Ashton seemed to be relaxed, settling into the conversation. *"And Paul Thompson and your John are Lord Raphael's bloodline."*

"John suspected as much after reading through the books in his sarcophagus. I take it you didn't put those there since your blood covered it." Sniffing the various bars of soap, I found one with rose and saddlewood and began soaping myself down.

"Well, to make a long story short," for a sword he seemed to do plenty of huffing, *"I served to protect the Traibon family, but when civil war was inevitable, we swapped names, and they went into hiding. As the heir to The House, I married Francesca Vendecci."*

"Falco's long lost older sister?" I scrubbed myself clean of all my filth, physical and emotional. "But didn't she die in battle?"

"The hell she did," scoffed Ashton. *"Look, we both agreed to it because we wanted freedom and were the last standing champions before the war. But when she conceived a child, it changed the course of everything for both of us. We were obligated to sire a child and well ... Raphaëlle became a target, and before I knew it, I had to chase her kidnappers to the Old Continent. Then there's Sebastian ... that bastard."*

I smirked recalling the journal. "So, that makes her the rightful ruler of Grandmere, or does that mean John is?"

284

Ashton fell silent for a long while before daring to reply, *"If you want to be technical about it, you and John would be rightful heirs of Grandmere. As for Raphaëlle, she's now the rightful Virago of the Ifrit Clan in the Old Continent. If that dirty old warlord can overthrow Fallen Arbor, they'd be the ruler of all the people there."*

Pondering on the information, I dunked into the water to rinse the soap before coming up for air again. "So, our family owns the world?"

"Well, huh. Now that you say that... It didn't start that way, nor did we aim for it." Ashton started and stopped a few more times before at last confessing, *"I don't think we intended it to unfold that way. Every choice has been made to protect family or our homes. Perhaps this is just the Fate's plan all along..."*

"Fates..." I snorted, climbing out of the tub, and circled around, searching the room. "Shit."

"What's the matter now?"

"She left me with no clothes or towels."

"Where was this Tilda when I had a body to reward her with?" Ashton chuckled before adding, *"The bold woman is the best in bed, no?"*

Scoffing, I admitted, "I've never been with a woman, brother. Nor have I ever had the desire for it. Wasn't born that way."

"Ah, I swing both ways! Both are a good time," he roared enthusiastically.

"Yet you loved Saint Raphael the most," I pressed.

Silence fell and the bathhouse door opened to the gawking eyes of Tilda. "Oh my. Let me get you some fresh clothes and towels. How careless of me." She stood there for a long time until I turned away, though I could feel her hungry eyes lapping up my backside just as happily. "Oh, what was I supposed to do... Ah, yes. Clothes for the god of flesh in my bathhouse."

"She'd be worth a try."

"No more from you," I hissed.

Now, what will all this old-world information mean? Does our heritage still hold value in present day? And what good will two kings be to a broken continent?

Chapter 35

The Apothecary Shop

I came back to the apothecary with all my gear in my arms, and my satchel full of supplies to clean it all. He glanced up from his bowls and bottles at his workbench and nodded. The open sign was back, and he had customers asking him questions. I slipped between the shelves to the back and disappeared without notice. John snored from his bed, a cold sweat painting his body as the fever tried to break.

Whatever that green goop was, it seems to work well.

Spreading out my gear across the other bed, I pulled up a chair and got to work. I had spent many days helping clean tack at the stables, and this was no different. The low lighting didn't bother me, my eyes piercing the darkness with ease. I sat in silence, focused on the mundane task at hand. The sounds of footsteps, heartbeats, and breaths came and went in the shop above us. Not once did the old man whisper and lead on of our presence. Many of his customers seemed to be recovering for a cold of sorts, but one stood out among them all.

Henry spoke gently and for the first time since that morning, left his chair to tend to her. "Miss Gail, you could have asked for me to come to you."

Her voice was broken and rasped, "Thanks to you, I'm feeling better and needed out of the inn for a change."

"How are you recovering? I imagine you need more medicine for the headaches," offered Henry, returning to his chair with a screech as it slid.

"Yes," she cleared her throat, trying her best to speak louder. "To imagine I would wake from the Madness. It's a miracle, Henry."

Freezing, I listened deeper, curious now.

"Indeed." He was mixing something, the sound of bottles and things shuffling around. "Give me a moment to prepare something for you, Miss Gail."

"Thank you." I could hear her footsteps as she wondered through the shop. "Any news as to why we are waking up?"

Henry sighed, and after a moment at last asked, "Would you believe me if I told you the Blood Prince broke the curse?"

Gail's steps stopped and replied, "Why would The House want it broken? Was it now their way of pushing for victory?"

"No." Henry spoke sternly as the sound of scrapping and mixing filled the air. "It was just as impactful on them as it had been on us. An unforeseen side effect of using magic, I hear."

"Oh?" She came closer to the old apothecary, intrigue riding on her broken voice. "So, how did the Blood Prince do it?"

Henry paused from his mixing, his voice lowering, "The Blood Prince and his lover were said to destroy the Fanged Lady, the magical weapon that made bloodeaters."

"Why would he do that?" she croaked. "Is that not treason against The House?"

"There's no bounty on his head coming from Glensdale," he countered. "And now they say the First Crowned Blood Prince is back."

"I remember my grandmother telling stories of him. Prince Ashton, yes?" A jar slid across the table. "Oh, thank you, Henry."

"I've said too much, Miss Gail. Please know we are hoping to see you find a new life despite your nightmares." Henry's heart fluttered. "Don't cry, dear."

"I'm sorry. I ... I didn't mean... Let me go." And with that, she was out the door.

"You destroyed the Fanged Lady?" Ashton's voice brought me back to the room where my ears were filled with John's heavy breathing and steady heartbeat.

"Technically that was John," I whispered, oiling the last few panels of the manica.

"Falco's got to be hunting you both down for that one," guffawed Ashton.

"He's dead." Dropping the manica onto the bed, I grabbed the last item to clean—*Ashton.* "That too was John's doing."

"What kind of priest is he?" he fussed.

"He's a saint, or at least the marking on his back declares him one." I first started to polish the hilt, surprised how resistant to grime and dirt he had stayed, unlike the rest of my gear and myself. "It's a long story, brother."

"Perhaps you can tell it to me some other time," he offered. *"I don't need to be cleaned. Get some rest, and I will let you know if someone comes. Pull you out of bed if I have to."*

Staring at my reflection in the blade, I probed, "About that. It was as if I could feel hands and feet correcting me. Does that only happen in connection to me or...?"

"Honestly, I couldn't do that or talk to Francesca in the fleeting time she wielded me. There's something about you unlocking our Ancestral heritage that connects us in a way I've only seen Sebastian have with his blade. If you meet that dirty old man, ask him. Surely an ogre would know more about what is happening to me ... to us." Clearing his throat, he changed topics yet again. *"He's shivering rather hard. Perhaps he needs another blanket."*

Snorting, I tilted him on the table, imagining it gave him a better view of the room and stairs. Sitting on John's bed, I could tell his heartbeat raced, and he pulled the cover tight around him in his restless slumber. I let myself lay beside him, my back to his as I stared at Ashton. *What a mess I find myself in the middle of.* John shifted, rolling over to nuzzle hard into my back as he threw the covers over me. His arms wrapped around me and pulled me tightly into him. A sigh escaped me as his shivering slowed, and his heart settled.

Perhaps we are good for one another. I don't think we could have gotten this far without one another's strength. If Captiva City is in panic, then it'll be a while before everyone will be able to make it here. We're stuck until they do, but that's to our advantage. John will need to recover, and I will welcome the chance for calm while I train with Ashton. The fight will be difficult if I must face more skilled Fractured Ones. We will need the help of The Court at the very least, but will they even consider an alliance with The House after driving them to the mountains so long ago? Perhaps Falco's death may serve as a token of good faith...

"I love you, Dante," John muttered in his sleep. "I promise to find you again."

My chest ached with his words, whispering a reply, "Long as I love you, John, I know who I am at any given moment and will find home in your arms."

Holding his arms there, I let sleep take me for the first time since we left the library.

TO BE CONTINUED...

About the Author

Valerie Willis is the Chief Operating Officer for 4 Horsemen Publications, Inc., an expert digital typesetter, and a fantasy romance author based out of Central Florida. When writing, she loves crafting novels with elements inspired by mythology, legends, folklore, fairy tales, and history. As COO, she oversees the design of all books including covers, typesets, and author branding where she pulls in creative print design while making versatile eBooks.

You can find her hosting workshops or attending as a guest speaker at many events (MegaCon, DragonCon, OCLS Writers Conference, Florida Writers Conference, SavvyAuthors, Women in Publishing Summit, etc.). She's been on panels with best-selling authors from Peter David to Delilah Dawson sharing her expertise in writing, research, worldbuilding, character development, book design, reader immersion, and more. You can also find her co-hosting on the Drinking with Authors Podcast speaking with Jonathan Maberry, Heather Graham, Charles Gannon, and many more on their own journeys as an author! Or talking about the spooky stuff over on Eerie Travels with topics such as big foots, mermaids, and even Bloody Mary!

Her award-winning dark fantasy paranormal romance, *The Cedric Series*, is a blend of genres that appeals to a wide range of readers who describe it as "dramatic, lustful, and fantasy fulfilling." The motto here is: "No immortal is beyond the ailments of man" that includes powerful creatures, demons, witches, and deities! Many of the monsters are derived from Medieval Bestiaries adding a fun flavor of new yet deeply-rooted assortment such as Coin Iotair, Shag Foal, Cynocephali, and more.

Like many authors, her writing journey started in grade school and carried her through high school. Many who grew up with her talk often of the traveling binders that were often kept safe in their lockers. This was the precursor to the now complete young adult dark urban fantasy of the *Tattooed Angels Trilogy* starting with *Rebirth.* This alternative historic piece about immortals and a failed reincarnation Hotan covers a wide variety of life lessons such as whether to follow your own lifepath or the one chosen for you, breaking toxic traditions, and the obligations of cleaning up our family's mistakes and destruction. Inspired by her own life tribulations, it has been the beacon to keep her moving toward the world of books and writing even now.

For readers of fantasy MM romance, check out her pen name V.C. Willis with the Traibon Family Saga starting with books *The Prince's Priest* and *The Priest's Assassin.* If you are looking for steamy paranormal erotica, chase down Urban Legends and modern retellings of fairy tales with Honey Cummings. Many have found themselves laughing out loud and fanning themselves while reading *Sleeping with Sasquatch* and *Wanton Woman in White.*

In 2021, she left her day job to join 4 Horsemen Publications, Inc. full time to bring over a decade of typesetting skills and industry knowledge to the table. Nothing is more rewarding for her than making fellow author's dreams come to life in physical format so they may share them with readers. Designing and writing books has been a longtime passion since childhood of hers and she continues to inspire and encourage authors around the world whenever possible, indulging whenever she can to chat about the books folks are reading and writing.

WRITING AS VALERIE WILLIS

Cedric: The Demonic Knight
Romasanta: Father of Werewolves
The Oracle: Keeper of the Gaea's Gate
Artemis: Eye of Gaea
King Incubus: A New Reign
Queen Succubus: Holder of the Crown

Val's House of Musings: A Mixed Genre
Short Story Collection

Rebirth
Judgment
Death

Writer's Bane: Research 101
Writer's Bane: Formatting

ANTHOLOGIES & COLLECTIONS

A World of Their Own
Work of Hearts Magazine Release
*How I Met My Other: True
Stories, True Love*
*It Was Always You: A Thrill of the
Heart Anthology*

*Demonic Wildlife: A Fantastically
Funny Adventure*
Demonic Household: See Owner's Manual
Demonic Carnival: First Ticket's Free

The Hunted—Thrill of the Hunt 3
Urban Legends Reimagined—Thrill of the Hunt 4
Buried Alive—Thrill of the Hunt 5

PUBLIC DOMAIN REMAKES

Bulfinch's Mythology with Illustrations
Book of Werewolves
The Fairy Faith of Celtic Countries

WRITING AS HONEY CUMMINGS

Sleeping with Sasquatch
Cuddling with Chupacabra
Naked with New Jersey Devil
The Erotic Cryptid Collection

Laying with the Lady in Blue
Wanton Woman in White
Beating it with Bloody Mary
The Erotic Ghosts Collection

Beau and Professor Bestialora
The Goat's Gruff
Goldie and Her Three Beards
Pied Piper's Pipe
Princess Pea's Bed
Pinocchio and the Blow Up Doll
Jack's Beanstalk
Pulling Rapunzel's Hair
The Urban Erotica Fairy Tale Collection

Curses & Crushes: KU short story

Queen's Incubus: YONDER webnovel

Book Club
Discussion Questions

1. Dante seems alienated or even sheltered from his own family's past. Do you think this was intentional on his father's part? Or do you think Dante leaving when he did prevented the prince from discovering more?

2. Ashton's legend seems to precede him and shadow Dante's journey in this book. Do you think this is a typical big brother syndrome since the story is told from Dante's point of view? Or do you think Ashton has impacted the world greatly before Dante's first real attempt to leave Glensdale?

3. There are a few bathhouse scenes throughout the novel, each with their own intent and experiences. Do you think the author did this intentionally? Does this help the reader see a transition in character development for Dante? What about John?

4. Red Wine's real identity was very hushed. Do you think this is due to her past with Fallen Arbor and Ashton? Or part of her new role as the Master Assassin for the Guild?

5. Dante is learning to fight again, though this time more like
    Ashton. Do you think if he had not disguised himself as
    Ashton that events would have unfolded the same way?

6. There were far more connections with the Church and
    Fallen Arbor than Dante expected. Do you think John sus-
    pected something during his time there? Do you think Fallen
    Arbor would have been able to achieve their goals without
    the Church?

7. Princess Sonja's return was a mixed bag. Returning her to
    Captiva City didn't mean her safety either, and she seemed
    to know this. Do you think it is vital for Grandemere's future
    for her to have returned so soon?

8. Dante lost himself more than once. His cravings for John
    become stronger and more dangerous when he's been hor-
    ribly injured. Do you think he can control himself in the
    future? Is it possible that it's more about his mental state
    than his actual carnal cravings for blood?

9. John confesses it all. When we think no more vows could be
    broken down, we get a wonderful raw exchange in the library.
    Do you believe his confession? How do you feel about his
    choices? Did he really want to be a priest at all? Or do you
    believe his was more to be Grandemere's savior and hero?

10. The soul weapon has been found, its identity known. What is
    the significance of this, and how do you feel this will impact
    Dante as a person as he carries this weight moving forward?